The Star Woman

Laer Carroll

Summary: Karen Danburn has always known she was adopted. But on her 18th birthday she is told she was born on a planet orbiting a far star. She is given three gifts: a tiara, body suit, and car. Each has almost magical powers.

So begins The Star Woman. It chronicles the first few years when Karen learns how to use her powers, first as a Marine Ranger, then as a covert crime fighter and guardian of the helpless everywhere.

Disclaimer

All people, places, and events are fictional or used fictitiously. They exist in an imaginary alternate reality, and any resemblance to actual people and events is purely coincidental.

Credits

Other Books

by Laer Carroll

Elizabeth Bennet: Shapechanger

The Eons-Lost Orphan

The Orphan in Near Space

Voyages of the Orphan

The Once-Dead Girl

The Twice-Dead Boy

The Thrice-Dead Girl

The Super Olympian: Bloodhound

The Super Olympian: Mystic Warrior

Sea Monster's Revenge

Shapechanger's Birth

Shapechanger's Progress

Shapechanger's Destiny
(forthcoming)

For my son:

Nick

father, provider, concerned citizen,
hobbyist, fun lover

of whom I'm prouder than I should be
as he is much more his own creation than mine

The Star Woman

Laer Carroll

Part 1 - Revelation

On the morning of July 1st, her eighteenth birthday, Karen Danburn was sitting outside the military recruiting center in the mall in the northern LA suburb of Riverview. She watched two men and one woman unlock the glass double doors and go inside. She waited for them to get settled in. Meanwhile she refreshed her memory of several items she'd bookmarked on her slate phone/computer.

After 15 minutes she put away her slate and entered the center. All three recruiters looked up from their desks. The two men returned their gaze to their computer screens.

The woman, a wiry Navy petty officer in a white uniform, rose and approached Karen.

"How may I help you, Miss?"

"I'm here to join the Marine Corps."

"Let's sit down. Would you like coffee, water, something else?"

"No, thank you."

"Let's discuss this, shall we?" The woman motioned toward the chair in front of her desk and went back around her desk to sit in her own chair. She smiled at Karen.

"I need to see some credentials and ask you some questions, then lay out your options."

Karen placed the manila folder she'd been carrying on the woman's desk. The woman opened it and began to read. Several times she looked up. The last time she said, "You are certainly qualified for just about any position in the military."

She half turned to the man whose desk was closest to hers so that the man could better hear her. He swiveled his chair to face Karen and his colleague.

"You've completed Junior ROTC with the highest marks in every category. You're the valedictorian at your high school and have what amounts to two years of college in your advanced courses. With the highest grades in all courses. And you're a multi-threat athlete: soccer, basketball, football.

"Football? How'd you manage that?"

"Our high school was required to accept females in the football program starting five years ago. There was a big court case."

The man closest to them, an Army staff sergeant in a dark blue dress uniform, said, "What position did you play?"

"Quarterback."

The third man got up from his chair and came over to stand on the other side of the Army recruiter's desk. He was in the lighter-blue Air Force uniform.

"You're Karen Danburn."

Karen nodded. The Air Force recruiter spoke to his co-workers. "She's the reason why Riverview High has won every game this last season."

He spoke to Karen. "Miss, you must have a dozen college recruiters after you."

"Yes."

The Navy woman said, "With your marks and your athletic history you could attend college for four years, take ROTC during that time, and go directly into any military service as a lieutenant."

"I know. But I also know what is best for me. The Marine Corps. And scout/sniper service."

The woman looked at her colleagues and back at Karen.

"Ms. Danburn, it's not our job to turn away qualified and motivated recruits. But it's also our duty to find the best fit for you and for the services we support. You're way over-qualified for that particular specialty."

Karen took a deep breath. She needed the self-discipline and outside structure the Marine Corps could give her to tame her forceful and sometimes violent nature. How could she get across her need without seeming deluded or a sociopath? She had worried about how to do that and had rehearsed several different ways to get across her need.

Well, here goes. She hoped she would not sound deranged. Or as desperate as she felt.

"It is exactly the best fit for me. And it might be the best for society in general.

"I have a strong need to excel. I have quick reflexes. I'm very strong and fast. But I also have a hair-trigger temper. It makes me worry I'll accidentally kill someone. Or several someones. I need to learn self-discipline, and control."

She took a deep breath, glanced at the Air Force recruiter. His gaze was open and sympathetic. Was it fake?

"In less than a second I could kill all three of you. Do you want that kind of person walking around outside of the military?"

The army man had been subtly shifting his chair backward and his body forward. Perhaps without realizing it he was readying to stand and fight.

"How would you do that?" he said.

Karen nodded at the desk before her. "There are at least four items on that desk which I could use for projectile weapons. I'd only have to lean over."

The Air Force man was nodding his head as he spoke to his colleagues. "I know it sounds as if she's exaggerating but I live here. My daughter goes to school here and is a cheerleader. So my wife and I go to all the games. I've never seen anyone run as fast or throw as well. ANYONE. Even pro athletes. Even Olympic athletes. Look, here's a web video some fan made of her in action."

As he'd spoken he'd taken his info slate off its clip on his belt and tapped a few virtual buttons on its surface. Now he handed it to the Army recruiter, who held it so the Navy recruiter could also watch the video playing on it.

Karen sat with her head down. She'd seen the video and knew what was in it: several very brief shots of her throwing the football and several more running with it when there was no one in a good position to receive it. Then the part which bothered her: her plowing through two defensive linebackers. The shot had been slowed down so that it prolonged the impact, making it look as if she was some unstoppable force meeting very movable objects, sending them flying. One had gone to the hospital.

The Army recruiter had a question.

"Miss Danburn, they had a four-to-one weight advantage over you. Why didn't you dodge around them? You're so quick on your feet they'd never have been able to react fast enough to stop you."

Karen kept looking at her hands. She felt again the sick sinking feeling she'd had in her belly when she turned from the other side of the football goal posts to look behind her. The two men had been lying on the turf, bodies and limbs twisted in unnatural ways. She still had nightmares about that moment. It was one of the reasons she was sure she needed this.

"I got impatient."

The Army sergeant spoke to the Navy petty officer.

"I don't see we have any choice." He moved his chair back into place and began to deal with some matters on his computer.

The Air Force man stood looking at Karen for long moments. "Good luck with your career, Ms. Danburn."

He grinned briefly. "God help your drill instructors."

That evening her parents threw Karen a birthday party. Her older brother and his wife and seven-year-old daughter had come up from San Diego to attend. After presents had been opened and her brother's family had left Karen returned from seeing them off to sit with her parents in the living room amid the opened presents.

Her mother, Marta, sighed and spoke to her husband.

"It's time."

Jonathan Danburn nodded.

"Dear, you know you are adopted. But we told you this when you were three, so maybe you've forgotten."

Karen smiled. "I haven't forgotten. Why bring it up now?"

Her mother said, "Because it's time to tell you about your real parents."

Karen sat forward a bit. "YOU are my real parents. You mean my birth parents."

Her mother's eyes glistened with tears. "We've always thought of ourselves that way. I'm happy you agree."

Her father said, "Brace yourself, dear. Your biological parents are from a star system very far away."

Karen believed her parents. They were too down-to-earth and honest to tell her nonsense or lie to her. The implications staggered her. Earth had had space travel for the last several decades, but only robots traveled beyond the moon. Earth certainly had no interstellar travel.

"Do you know why they gave me away? What this means for my future?"

"It means what you make of it. At 18 you are now an adult and can do whatever you want. But that future will include presents from your...birth parents. Wait just a moment, honey."

He went to the nearby hall closet and returned carrying three gift-wrapped packages. He dropped the smallest box into Karen's lap and returned to his seat, placing the two other packages on the glass-topped coffee table in front of the couch.

She looked at the box from several angles, but the outside gave no clue what was in it. The shiny blue paper and ribbons were lovely but ordinary for all that. She tore them off the white cardboard box inside. Inside the box was a narrow diamond tiara. In the center was a large blue faceted gem.

She looked up, confused. The jewels looked real. If they were, this must be worth thousands of dollars.

Her father said, "This is a device. It has three functions. It's a computer, communicator, and something like radar."

"When you wear it," her mother said, "all you have to do is think what you want and the computer will do it. Don't do that yet!" She spoke abruptly when Karen lifted the tiara to put it on.

"Wait till you have some time to explore its uses. When you first put it on it will brief you on how to operate it."

Her mother handed her the next box. It was wrapped in shiny green and about the size of a box for shirts or pants. Inside it was a garment, a somewhat strange one. It seemed to be a lacy white body suit with footies attached, very pajama-like.

"This is a spacesuit. It will protect you from many threats and support you for an indefinite time. Like the tiara it will brief you when you put it on. Take off everything before you do that."

Her father passed her the last box, a red one. Karen ripped off the wrapping to find something which looked like a brick-sized bar of creamy soap but made of a harder substance.

He smiled at her puzzlement.

"This is actually a vehicle, strange as that sounds. Come on. Let's show you."

The three got up and went through the hall to the door into the adjoining garage. It contained her father's dark red sports sedan but not her mother's SUV. In its usual place was emptiness.

"Tell it 'Imitate vehicle' and toss it into the empty space."

Karen did so. The ivory-like block arced into the center of the empty space but expanded into an exact copy of the sports car. It floated to rest onto the garage floor.

She turned to her parents in amazement.

"That is so incredible..."

They grinned at her and came forward for a three-way hug. Karen forgot herself and hugged them more strongly than she'd intended. Her mother squeaked and Karen broke away and apologized.

They gave her a kiss on both cheeks and left her to get acquainted with her new toy.

<>

It turned out to be her best toy ever.

Karen walked around the duplicate of her father's car, exact down to the slightest scratches. After a complete circuit it introduced itself as a silent voice inside her head.

It told her it was made mostly of force fields and powered by "unbending space," a process it said it could not explain but said was "effectively infinite." It could emulate any kind of mechanical vehicle so well that even an engineer could not tell the difference, even to the point of containing and seeming to burn gasoline.

It could fly anywhere in or beyond the solar system, with a top speed of a quarter of the speed of light. Further questioning revealed that it could create air and copies of food inside itself to support her life and those of any passengers.

And it and its contents could become invisible.

Karen shook her head at the revelations. Then spent a half-hour having her vehicle change such things as its skin color (to a deep blue), less showy wheel caps, and a soft grey interior. It had the same new-car smell that her father's car did.

After an hour Karen sat silently in the driver's seat of her car and turned over in her mind all she'd learned. For the first time that day of sometimes high excitement she felt tired, something she rarely did, having enormous energy reserves.

She got out, slammed the car door behind her, and went upstairs to bed.

<>

Then she found she could not sleep. The events of the day returned to her, buzzing around in her head in no order like a swarm of flies. Finally she sat up in the dark and swung her legs to one side to rest her feet on the floor.

In the subdued green and orange glows of her several electronic devices her eyes could dimly make out the tiara and spacesuit resting on her dressing table. She got up and went to the table, picked up the tiara, and placed it on her head.

A voice spoke inside her head similar to that of her car, though with a slightly feminine tone rather than the slightly masculine tone of her car. It briefed her on its capabilities.

It could communicate with any sort of earthly and many very advanced unearthly comm systems. It had a sensory system somewhat like radar but using "gravity occlusion." When she tried that out it produced a vivid image of her bedroom as if it were in broad daylight. It could see through walls if she wanted that, out to several dozen miles.

And it was a supercomputer far more capable than anything Earth had so far created. She fed it a few complex multivariate equations taken from her Advanced Placement Calculus class and got instant results. That just barely scratched the surface of its abilities. It told her it could handle problems billions of time as complex.

Could she use the communicator to browse the Web? Yes. How? She need only think clearly what she wanted; it would take practice to perfect this skill but Tiara insisted that she would find it easy.

Karen returned to her bed, lay back, closed her eyes, and asked Tiara to patch her into the internet. Instantly she seemed to be floating in space. The impression was so strong that only the pressure of her bed on her back and bottom kept her from panicking.

All around her was a swarm of balls of all colors. Each was a web page in cyberspace. Links from them to other pages showed up as nearly invisible lines creating a vast spider web that seemed chaotic at first. They stretched out to a seeming infinity, growing ever smaller until they disappeared in the distance.

It took her some time but eventually she learned to frame her desires so that she could "see" any web page anywhere in cyberspace--including encrypted ones. To the super-advanced computer in Tiara the encryption might as well not exist.

THAT was a little disconcerting. She'd have to be sure she never let on that she could read all those secrets. She could get into big trouble if she failed!

Tiara said it could make encrypted web pages semitransparent to cue her to avoid them unless she wanted the secret information.

Karen gave Tiara a command to do just that. Instantly the vision before her changed to reflect her desire.

Wow! So much was secret!

She could also hear and see audiovisual files. She relaxed while viewing some of her favorites and discovering new favorites, and drifted off to sleep.

Karen woke to birdsong and the distant barking of some dog. She focused on the dog for a moment and her view of the ceiling above her tilted and a view of her bedroom wall rushed toward her. She flinched from it but her viewpoint was already rushing through her neighborhood till it revealed the dog, a beautiful border collie sitting in the doorway of its doghouse in some neighbor's back yard.

She was still wearing Tiara, who (which?) was responding even to her vague and unspoken desires.

She reached up to take off Tiara. And found nothing on her head.

Yet in her mind was this silent waiting. Tiara was still with her.

Karen sat up in bed, stood, and walked quickly to her bathroom. The mirror showed nothing on her head.

"Tiara. Where are you?"

"I'm inside your brain where I can be most useful. It would be inefficient and socially awkward to remain visible."

"Come out! Now!"

"I cannot do that. I am now part of you."

Shit. What had she gotten herself into?

Further questioning of Tiara revealed that this was part of Tiara's design. All super-advanced tiaras were like this.

Tiara also reported that she (she?) would keep Karen's brain healthy. She almost sounded apologetic.

Karen ordered Tiara not to make any changes in her brain. The device asked if she would mind if Tiara sometimes suggested improvements. After a moment Karen said Yes. She could always say No, and almost certainly would. But she did not think her bioparents would have given her a harmful gift.

Though why she believed that she did not know. Was she being manipulated by Tiara?

She shrugged off the thought for later consideration. For now she wanted to get ready for the day and try out her fantastic new car.

<>

A toilette and breakfast later Karen said Goodbye to her parents as they left for work and returned to her bedroom. Seeing the spacesuit on her dresser reminded her of its almost magical qualities. She picked it up. The lacy white garment was very light.

She sat on her bedside, removed all her clothing, and examined the suit. It was open in the front from waist up. She pulled it onto her feet, first one leg, then the other.

The material was so light and thin she'd expected to have to inch it on like tight stockings. But as she slid her feet into the opening it began to expand and slide up her legs, just fast enough to make clothing herself easy but not to hurry her.

Standing, she pulled the top up, or tried to. The garment slid up her torso and chest on its own, again at an exactly convenient pace.

Long sleeved arms went on just as easily. And at the last minute the slit up the front closed itself over her chest and shoulders to form a collar. The lace was not peek-a-boo. It seemed functional.

The suit introduced itself with a silent voice inside her head. The tone was completely genderless, unlike that of Tiara and her vehicle. It told her that it would protect her from all sorts of threats.

She held up her naked hands. "Except here. And my head."

Even there. There was an invisible force field which covered every seemingly exposed body part. It stored air in a very compact form which would let her go for months and years, recycling the air as needed.

She could fly short distances. Experimentally she wished to rise upward.

Oops! Her head almost hit the ceiling before she wished to stop.

She hung in the air while her heart rate eased back to normal, then slowly returned to stand on the floor. Best to wait till she was in a bigger space before she experimented further.

Questioning revealed that if she urinated or defecated the suit would transmute the urine and feces into air. She could eat and drink ordinary stuff and the suit would allow it, transmuting poisons to air as well.

Karen looked down at the snowy material covering her arms and the rest of her. "Kind of plain, though."

Not so, Suit told her. Just wish what she wanted it to look like and it would adjust its force fields to copy the look. It could be solid colors, have stripes and checks, different textures and thicknesses, even pockets and a belt.

Even more, she could have it form gowns and cloaks and coats and foot wear, indeed any design, in an instant. The apparently bare parts would still be protected by an invisible skin.

Karen experimented with various looks, some silly and some practical. All were perfectly comfortable no matter what she did. They would come and go instantly. The only limits were those of her imagination.

Lastly, and more staggering to her, it could transmute the designs from air into real garments which she could hang in her closet. Suit (she named it) could copy anything down to the tiniest detail. She would never have to buy another stitch of clothing!

The only problem was, it would never come off. Its main function was to protect her and off it could not do that.

Karen sat down heavily on the side of her bed. As with Tiara she'd been too naïve about accepting a gift.

Damn!

She pondered her problem for several minutes.

Did this mean she could never again feel the touch of wind and water on her skin? It answered No. It could be immeasurably thin but still be armor against anything harmful.

"What if I want to have a baby? Are you going to block sperm?" Yes, but if she decided to have a baby she could command Suit to let sperm into her.

Karen wondered about what would happen when she gave birth but didn't ask about that. The event would be years in the future, if ever. Best to put off such considerations until later.

She would have to give more thought to how to use Tiara and Suit, especially any downsides. But for now she wanted to explore her near-magical vehicle. INCLUDING looking out for downsides!

<>

She used Suit to create light-sensitive sports sunglasses and a billed cap and put them on, running her shoulder-length blond hair into a pony tail out the back of the cap. Then she dressed in her favorite run-around outfit: blue tennies, dark red jeans, and a sleeveless blue tee shirt with the red T-in-a-heart for "I love Taylor Swift." Then she took up her wallet and house keys and exited the house, setting the alarm and locking the house behind her.

The remote clipped to her force-field car's sun visor opened the garage door as capably as if it were an ordinary remote. Her car started up smoothly when she pushed the Start button. The motor sounded exactly like that of an ordinary car. She backed out of the garage, triggered the garage door closed, and carefully backed into the street.

She drove through her neighborhood to the main street of Riverview City, turned onto it, and went north toward the city's center. The first mile and a half were lined on both sides by car dealerships.

She told her vehicle that she wanted it to answer to the name of the flying horse of legend, Pegasus.

"Can you scan the vehicles you pass and learn how to make copies of them? I may choose to change your shape some day."

"I am now doing that."

"Brief me on your other capabilities, ones you have not yet made me aware of."

Pegasus told her it had the same ability to shield itself from detection as Tiara and Suit. It was connected to her by using quantum entanglement, a communication medium not yet used by Earth scientists. Thus she could command it without regard to distance.

It could fly, as she already knew, but repeated that it did so by "bending space," a process it was unable to explain. And it used energy gotten by "unbending space," a similarly mysterious process. There were no practical limits on the energy it got that way.

"I'd like to go invisible and fly. We need to go someplace where we can't be seen before we try it."

"Several possibilities are nearby." It projected into her brain a street map of the area ahead of her with a red X on each spot. The nearest was an alley between a tall bank building and the solid rear side of a parking garage. She drove a quarter mile further north and made a right turn into the alley.

"Now!"

Her view of the alley did not show any suggestion that she and Pegasus had been made invisible, but the car lifted in a smooth arc up and out of the alley. The bright California day opened up before her and the city fell away below. To the north rose the San Gabriel Mountains. On top of the bigger eastern sections she saw several snowy peaks.

"Can we go higher without running into any aircraft?"

"That is any height. I detect and avoid everything in the air."

"Keep going up."

"I am staying below the speed of sound to avoid making sonic booms so that we remain undetectable."

"Good thinking."

"Thank you."

That was odd. Last night Pegasus had told her it was not a person or an AI and so did not have feelings. Yet it was acting as if it did.

She mentally shrugged. Apparently it was mimicking polite ways of speech. Not a surprise, she supposed. She had noticed that its silent speech to her was colloquial and had a standard accent.

Ah! That was it. It was imitating her, and she was reflexively polite.

Meanwhile Pegasus continued to rise. The sky was becoming a darker blue and the curve of the earth was becoming ever more obvious. She saw patterns of white cloud dotting the air below her.

It was quite beautiful. She wished the view out of the front of the car was not so restricted.

"Shall I change to a space vehicle configuration?"

"Without endangering us?"

"Of course."

"Do it."

Everything began changing. The seat below her became more padded and form fitting (though its color remained light grey), the steering wheel and dashboard disappeared, the windows lost their posts and expanded to a larger more rounded shape till the entire front of the vehicle became transparent. Her extended feet eclipsed the blue expanse below her. Looking up she could see the crescent moon above her.

"Could we go to the moon?"

"Anywhere in and beyond the solar system, but I would caution about visiting Saturn."

"Why?"

"It is englobed by a set of star gates maintained by a very advanced computer. I do not have the protocol in me to navigate the space and communicate with the computer. It might view us as a threat."

THAT was staggering information. She felt dizzy and could not breathe. But only for a few instants. It was no odder than the fact that she had been born hundreds of light years away into a super-advanced human civilization.

"I'll settle for Paris. Are there any problems going there?"

"It is 7:08 pm there. Sunset is at 9:47 pm and the weather is mildly cloudy. The temperature is 79 degrees and the humidity 51 percent. The flight will take 13 minutes. There will be approximately an hour and a half more of direct sunlight when we arrive."

"Sounds delightful. Can you find an outdoor cafe near the Eiffel Tower?"

"Of course."

"Let's go then."

A quarter of an hour passed easily when there was so much to see as the Earth turned below and behind them. The Midwest had clouds reaching into the stratosphere and spider webs of lightning within. The highest clouds were still many miles below Karen and Pegasus.

The mid-Atlantic had a white crescent of a cloud front sweeping down from Iceland and Greenland, extending hundreds of miles southward. Farther to the east Karen could see the advancing arc of night. Behind it was a web work of golden light as lights came on in eastern Europe.

Soon the coast came up below them and Pegasus arced down into the atmosphere. Their tremendous speed slowed quickly with no perceptible feeling of deceleration. Nor was there any hint of the hurricane force of air pushed asunder by the rounded body of the super-advanced spacecraft in which Karen rode.

Details of the green land came into view and then the spires and sprawl of Paris, cut through by the winding course of the Seine River. Long shadows pointed east away from the lowering sun.

Coming up to them was a tall hotel and a multi-level parking structure beside it. Karen paid more attention to the top of the structure than to their surroundings, so concerned was she to be sure no one was atop it. They alighted and the interior of the vehicle morphed back into that of her car.

"I can wait here in this form or follow you in my compact form."

"Stay here."

"Very well. Tiara can guide you to the café. When you get ready to return Tiara will guide you back if necessary."

"Thank you. I may wander a few hours after I snack."

"Remember that your suit can shield you from sight as well as danger. And I can come to you very quickly."

Karen thought for a moment about what she should wear rather than ball cap, tee, shorts, and tennies. She consulted the internet through Tiara to view everyday fashions now current in Paris. Karen chose a black silk armless blouse and a black leather skirt to mid-thigh. Her legs she covered with sheer black leggings, her feet black sandals with a modest heel.

Over it all she placed a grey cashmere jacket. To her surprise Suit formed a small purse of grey leather and a long strap without asking her and hung it over one shoulder.

Tiara suggested an updo of her hair. She surrendered to the super-scientific machine and felt her hair arranging itself. It first parted and then pulled back to each side to form a low pony tail. This then twisted around itself to form a loose bun at the back of her head.

She examined the back and sides of her head with Tiara's sensors. It felt funny seeing herself from different angles without turning her head. But what she saw satisfied her.

Lastly Tiara--prompted by her subconscious desires--tinted her lips with the illusion of a faint pink lipstick.

She got out of her car and closed the door. It shut with the quiet CHUNK of perfect fit.

On her way to the stairs down to ground level Karen detoured to the south side of the parking structure and leaned on the waist-high concrete parapet. Before her a block away across a busy street was the Seine River. A long white tour boat was passing along it. Across the river and to her left was the Eiffel Tower, rearing high into the sky.

The sun had not yet set but lights were coming on in the grey steelwork of the edifice.

Karen drank in the sight and the greenery of the park which extended to each side and several blocks south beyond the Tower. Hundreds of people strolled in the park.

Satisfied for the moment she plunged down the squared spiral of the stairs, emerging onto a walkway beside the structure's In and Out streets and a central shack containing a parking attendant. He cast an admiring eye at the beautiful woman leaving his protection.

Here at ground level she was in a gathering twilight though the sun was still up. Tiara guided her to a café with both an interior and a sidewalk dining area.

In her schoolgirl French she asked the black-and-white clad waiter at the entrance for a view of the Tower. He eyed her up and down and seated her at a table for two near a sidewalk protected from sidewalk traffic by a low open-framework fence. She guessed she presented an attractive and chic enough sight to those strolling nearby that she might troll in more customers.

The tall laminated menu gave her a large selection. She chose a Quiche Lorraine and a buttered croissant. Asked what wine she wanted she told him to choose something for her. He chose a Pinot blanc.

She stayed there an hour. Near the end of it she ordered a creamy chocolate pudding with a demitasse of Kahlúa as a coffee companion.

The waiter was taken with her, or at least thought she was a likely candidate for a good tip. In between services they chatted. He was a student at a nearby college of the American University of Paris studying film.

She paid with her credit card, adding a generous tip to the base cost. As she stood to leave the waiter said, "When you first came in I thought you were American. But now I'd swear you are Parisienne."

She smiled and thanked him.

As she walked back to her car, enjoying the falling twilight and the awakening glitter of the Tower, she wondered idly how she'd come to learn the young man's accent so quickly. Without prompting Tiara spoke.

"I was feeding hints to your brain's already high linguistic talent."

"I am concerned about that. Is it possible you will damage my

brain by such efforts?"

"No. That was once a possibility. But this is a practice which has been perfected for thousands of years."

"This learning of an accent was not something that took place in you?"

"No."

"I wonder if I might become so dependent on you that my mental faculties atrophied."

"Again, what was once a possibility is no longer a danger."

At the parking garage Karen paid more attention to how her body worked as she strode up the stairs. It seemed that her already excellent muscles were working better. Was that Tiara's influence? Or maybe Suit's?

In her car she let her outfit and hairdo revert to its appearance during the day. As the vehicle rose it returned to its spaceship shape. She was distracted by the sight of night falling over Paris. The sun had sunk below the horizon and the approaching night was blanketing the city. More and more lights were coming on, bringing a golden web of light alive within Paris.

Then she saw a sight she'd never expected to see. The sun was rising in the West.

<>

The next day she spent more time exploring her gifts. She learned so quickly that by the end of the day she was expert in their most basic functions.

Noticing that quickness, and remembering how adaptable she always had been, led her to consult Tiara.

"You are fully human. But you've had many centuries of genetic cleaning and very careful enhancements. That's why you never suffered any childhood illnesses. That's why you are so strong and quick and agile."

This led to the discovery that Tiara contained an encyclopedia. It had not only text but lots of visual and audio material. She snooped into the parts on alien cultures in the part of the galactic arm in which existed the Human Interstellar Confederation, the home society of her birth parents.

This led to a discussion of political philosophy common in the

Human Interstellar Confederation. It was somewhat conservative. Human nature was not considered perfect, but it was a highly successful result of evolution. Rather than change their bodies Confed humans used machines to enhance them and extend them.

"So are there no people with, I don't know, maybe, combinations of male and female sex organs?" She'd read about rare hermaphrodites being born, whose parents usually had them converted to a standard sex via surgery--an awful thought to her but understandable.

"Sex change is routine in the Confederation. Individuals take a pill containing nano-technological devices just before sleep. The next morning they awake changed. They can tailor the change to hybrid forms. This is not considered tampering with the basic human model."

She wondered what it would be like to be a man. The idea did not appeal to her. She was perfectly happy with the equipment she had. She'd lost her virginity a couple of years ago and, after the first few awkward and unsatisfying experiences, she'd come to enjoy sex.

Of course, she'd picked boys she'd known a while who were not total jerks. It seemed to her that many boys thought they were SUPPOSED to be jerks to be thought grown up!

Not that she slept around. This last year especially she'd avoided dating. She'd planned to join the Marine Corps soon and didn't want any unhappy partings.

Which was just as well now that she'd gotten the news about her birth parents and received their birthday gifts. She needed a lot of practice with them before she went to boot camp.

Part 2 - Recruit

Three weeks later Karen Danburn dropped down out of the sky in Hilton Head, South Carolina, a city on an island on the U. S. eastern seaboard. She landed atop the terminal of the small international airport there. At a command Pegasus unfolded its shields from around her and she became visible. He took up his usual invisible station a yard above her.

She approached the door in a closet-like box which housed the entrance to stairs downward. She tried the knob and found it unlocked from this side. She had guessed it would be.

Karen entered the stairs and came out onto the main concourse. It was moderately busy in the early evening. She asked a woman at one of the gates where the Marine-recruit waiting area was. Getting directions, she walked till she came to the waiting area set aside for recruits. About two dozen were there along with a Marine staff sergeant in camouflage utilities and boots and a flat-brimmed hat. She approached the sergeant and handed him her papers.

He examined them, examined her, said, "Sit over there. Be quiet."

Karen returned the papers to her blue-plastic folder, obeyed, closed her eyes, and used Tiara to examine the people around her, then the larger area, and watched the sergeant briefly.

For more than an hour she sat perfectly still, browsing the internet via Tiara. Her stillness began to bother the sergeant, so she opened her eyes, stood, approached him, and said, "May this recruit visit the head?"

He blinked. From her research she'd learned that this form of third-person reference was how recruits in training were supposed to refer to themselves, never as "I." Nevertheless, he gave permission.

Karen visited the restroom and spent several needless minutes in a stall, then returned to her seat. Thereafter, though she remained still, she occasionally opened her eyes, shifted her weight, and looked around, before becoming still again.

Such could not be said for the other recruits. There was a lot of fidgeting and attempts to talk or walk around which were met with reprimands. Every once in a while another late arrival showed up. Then no one for two hours, then one last hurrying man.

At midnight the sergeant barked an order to follow him. He walked out of the waiting area through a door onto the front of the airport. Waiting at the curb was a large yellow bus. The recruits boarded when their name was called. Karen sent Pegasus up about fifty feet with orders to feed her information about her surroundings.

Karen was halfway down the list. She found a window seat midway down the aisle, sat, and closed her eyes.

Silently overhead Pegasus followed the bus. Karen idly traced their generally westward passage through the small city from its viewpoint. The images she saw were a synthesis of infrared, intensified starlight, her "gravity radar," and photos taken by the Mapper military satellites. The scene was full-color and stereoscopic.

They passed over a couple of bridges which brought them to the mainland. This was like the island, flat, with a mix of trees and pastureland, though this was visible to those in the bus only dimly via the narrow corridor of the bus's headlights.

After twenty minutes or so they turned north, went a few miles, then turned east. Another twenty minutes brought them over a bridge and then over a long causeway over a river. They were now near Parris Island. The training center was another ten minutes or so away.

They entered a small city lit by street lights and those lights outside various buildings. A bit later they crossed under a sign reading WE MAKE MARINES.

A few blocks later the bus pulled up near a two-story red brick building. A sergeant wearing the traditional flat-brimmed hat of a drill sergeant bounded up into the bus.

"NOW! Listen up, sit up!" He let moments pass while everyone oriented on him. "Now! Out! Out! Out!"

The recruits rushed out of the bus to be directed to stand nearly back-to-belly-to-back on a set of yellow footsteps on the concrete.

"Now. Pay attention to these two articles from the Uniform Code of Military Justice. The law you will live under as long as you are in the Marines."

He glared at them.

"You will not strike another Marine. You may not run away from your unit. Either of those will earn you punishment."

Another long pause, then he pointed at a red-brick building and yelled at them to get inside, sit, be silent.

Karen was not bothered by the yelling. She'd read a lot about how

Marine training was done and knew what to expect: lots of techniques to break civilians down and remake them into soldiers who'd obey orders instantly and automatically. The yelling was the least of those techniques.

The doors of the building were open and two other sergeants stood on each side of the doors. The recruits nearly ran up short stairs and into a large classroom starkly lit with neon lights. Most of the floor was covered with metal desk chairs with attached desks. They hurriedly sat.

The sergeant followed them inside and took up station behind a lectern in front of and to one side of a huge flat screen. The screen lit. He pointed out several vocabulary words they would henceforth use. Not floor but deck. Not door but hatch. Not pants but trousers.

He had them write a number on their hands with a magic marker resting on the desk: 4044.

"This is your platoon. It is your address for the next 12 weeks. Use the pen in front of you to write it in the From: area on the envelope in front of you. Write the address of your home in the To: area. Then read the enclosed letter."

The letter was from the commander of the center. It said the recruit had arrived safely and could be written to at the From: address on the outside of the envelope. It said a few other things about the importance of the service they would render their country and of the training to make them ready for that task.

Next they were told to inventory their clothing by checking off and writing in blanks on a standard form lying on the desk. This included shirt and jacket (if any), pants, shoes, cell phone, info slate, jewelry or other such wearable items, wallet, drivers license, passport, cash, credit cards. Those would go into storage in the next room.

"One item you will be allowed to keep: a neck chain with a SMALL religious pendant such as Christian cross or Muslim crescent. But, if you can, put it in with 'jewelry' since it is easy to get lost during the vigorous training activities. And we will not allow searches for such lost items."

A long list of contraband items would go into the orange trash barrel on the entrance to the next room: drugs, sex protection, snacks, drinks, weapons, lighters, etc.

Then the recruits were sent two at a time into the next room. There they received clothing and foot wear after being measured by a 3D computer imager. They then were given one minute behind a privacy screen to change out of their clothing into the recruit clothing.

Karen managed it do it so quickly that she had time to blouse her pants leg bottoms into her auto-closing boots precisely as they should be. This was not quite as impressive as it might seem, since she had JRTOC training in high school and had been silently and invisibly shadowing recruit training at Parris Island for much of the three weeks between enlisting and now.

That done, they returned to the two people issuing clothing and placed everything on their inventory list into a box. It was then sealed and that fact witnessed by the two personnel and the two recruits, who signed their names to the inventory list which then was taped to the box of property. This was digitally scanned and the information transmitted to the Training Command database computers.

A duffel bag was then given to each recruit containing two blankets, three sets of underwear, and several other items which they'd need in the dozen weeks on Parris Island.

Lastly each recruit was sent through a room in which all their head and face hair was removed. Karen skipped this since she'd had Tiara remove all the hair on her head just hours ago. Thus she was sent to stand at the head of one of four lines on the floor with more yellow footprints.

In less than a minute another recruit was behind her, nearly pressed against her in his attempt to place his feet over the yellow images. By mistake he brushed against her back and whispered Sorry. She said nothing.

It was now almost 4:00 am. Karen felt sorry for the rest of the recruits. Most had been up for nearly twelve hours now and some of them were reeling a bit. She, with her superior physiology inherited from her Confederation parents, felt no fatigue at all.

They were given brief basic instruction in marching and went two blocks to their barracks.

Inside the large room were bunk beds arranged in four rows of ten beds, two rows on each side of a central walkway. Two white lines at the edge of the walkway made for a lane a yard wide. They were lined up toes to white line on each side of the lane, their duffle bags lying beside and behind them.

The sergeant walked up then down the aisle, eyeing the recruits. Periodically he shook his head in apparent disgust. Two other sergeants, not noticeably of lesser rank, one of them a woman, did their own inspection. These sergeants were focusing on clothing details and posture, stopping frequently to quietly correct problems.

Finishing his once-over the sergeant came to the center of the aisle and spoke. FORBES was the name sewn onto the right breast of his uniform.

"Sad. Sad. That the Marines have such sorry stuff to work with. But work we will. When you leave here you will either be a civilian or a deadly warrior able to be the cutting edge of any ground conflict.

"NOW. You'll stow your gear and learn to make beds. You are assigned bunks according to the alphabet. That--" He pointed toward the entrance to the long rectangular hall. Entering, they had passed a restroom and a large shower stall. "--is A. The other end is Z. When I tell you, take your duffel and find your bunk by examining the name taped atop the locker at the foot of your bunk.

"Open the locker. Remove the pillow and place it on your bunk. Put the contents of your duffel, and the duffel folded neatly, inside the locker. EXCEPT one blanket, one sheet, and one pillow case. Those you will put on the bunk. Then you will stand at the head of the bunk facing this center aisle. NOW!"

The room exploded into chaos. Karen waited a few seconds while the surrounding recruits ran away from her, then with one hand smoothly swung the heavy duffel up onto a shoulder and walked quickly but calmly to her bunk. The alphabetic bunk assignment made it easy to find. Her short delay meant that there were few people in her way.

At the bunk she followed the instructions. She was done before anyone else. Going to the head of the bunk she observed the recruits closest to her. She delayed a second to pick up a pillow beside one bunk, swat it to remove any dust, and drop it onto the bunk. Even so she was at the head of her bunk staring into space before anyone else.

One of the two satellite sergeants who were assisting Sergeant Forbes drifted by her, observing the other recruits. He quietly said, "JROTC?" without looking at her.

"Yes, sir."

"SIR, yes, sir." Bookending each answer with Sir was what the main sergeant had told them earlier.

"Sir, yes, sir."

Karen in her last two years of high school had taken Junior ROTC and attended a camp in the summer between. But her efficiency came naturally to her. Such as the delays which ended up speeding her overall actions. As did her urge to help others such as the recruit with the errant pillow.

Some of the recruits lagged behind the others. The longer the delay the more attention they received. The last recruit had a sergeant to left and right urging her on.

She looked harried but not flustered. She finished her tasks properly.

Karen made note of her. It would be interesting to see if the woman was naturally slow or thought too much when she worked.

She might also be a worthy companion in the chaos of a firefight.

"NOW," said Sergeant Forbes from the center of the long aisle. His voice was pitched loud enough so that even the most distant recruit could hear him.

"Pitiful. But maybe a microscopic bit better. A few of you show promise. But don't get cocky. Cocky gets you killed. We spit on cocky. We stomp on cocky.

"You will now learn to make bunks. We'll start from the A direction. The first four bunks on each side will learn first. Sergeants."

With that the two assisting sergeants stepped from their locations at the A end of the aisle to the beds indicated. The four recruits watched as each sergeant slowly showed how to cover the pillows with their cases, apply the bed sheet so that each of its four corners were neatly boxed with edges folded a certain way and tucked underneath the corners, and the blanket folded a certain way and placed at the foot of the bunk.

Then the bed sheets and blankets were pulled into crumpled piles and dropped onto the middle of the bed. The recruits were set to copying the assistant sergeants.

Karen's first try at making her bed when it came her turn to do so was nearly perfect. Nevertheless the sergeant crumpled the bed clothes and ordered her to do it again. And again. And again until all four bunks were done to a certain minimum.

Through it all she remained calm and moved quickly and efficiently. She'd known all recruits would be treated this way.

When the Z end of the room had finished Sergeant Forbes announced it was time for chow. He gave instructions on how they were to proceed. Soon the 40 women and men were marching erratically five blocks to a cafeteria. Here they were ushered through the two serving lines serving only recruits. There were no choices here, as there were for the other four lines for regular Marines and civilians.

Karen piled her plate high with eggs and sausage and toast and orange juice. Seated at a silent round table with other recruits she ate quickly but with great enjoyment. The food might be basic but it was cooked well.

Fifteen minutes only were allowed from the moment they sat down to the moment they stood up. Karen was not the only one to finish with minutes to spare. She memorized who her fellow efficient eaters were. The information might come in handy some day.

Next they were marched to a building and broken up into five groups by alphabet. Eight officer psychologists spoke to eight recruits at a time in as many private offices.

"Karen Danburn," said the greying forty-something year old man in grey-and-brown camouflage uniform with Captain's bars on his shoulders. "Sit and be comfortable. Slouch if that will make you feel better. We have 15 minutes to talk about anything whatsoever. Then 15 minutes about subjects essential to you and your possible career."

Karen smiled and sat relaxed but by no means sloppily, one leg crossed over the other.

"Say," she said. "What's with those Cardinals?" A glimmer of a smile showed on her perfect lips.

Captain Alexandriou (his name tag said) chuckled.

"Cocky?" he said.

"We spit on cocky. We stomp on cocky."

"Melodramatic, I admit. Also true."

"I know, Mario. I enjoy the silliness of the lines. But I also know the awful failures that can come from over-confidence."

"Interesting that you would assert that you are my equal despite the gulf in our ages and statuses."

"You are an excellent judge of character. I can read that on you, not by making assumptions about an experienced officer with a psychology degree. I too am an excellent judge."

He looked at her steadily for long seconds. She looked back. Tiara told her much about his mood and mental state. It also gave Karen an overview of his background summarized on the internet, including the most secure sites. To a computer from a super-advanced civilization there were no online secrets.

"So," he said, "how are you feeling about your experiences so far?"

"I feel perfectly fine. So far the drill instructors and the whole recruitment training process is working well."

"You don't feel stressed?"

"This is what I expected. And it would take a lot more than this to stress me."

"I see no signs of exhaustion."

"I can go for days without sleep. Then the usual sleep-deprivation psychoses begin to kick in."

He examined her dossier on his computer screen, more to give him time to think than for the information on it. She'd have bet he'd done a quick once-over of it before calling her into the room.

"Why did you want to go through the enlisted program rather than the officer channels? You'd have excelled in that program, too."

"At this time it's best for me to become a Marine scout/sniper. An enlisted specialty. I am supremely deadly and driven. Something in the civilian life along the same line would not be good for me or for our country. And that's true even more for any covert government programs which we might have. I want to be a protector, not an assassin."

He examined her thoughtfully for long moments, then said, "I agree and am so recommending."

He wrote a decisive few sentences on the terminal, then touched the Send prompt. Tiara reviewed the form and summarized the likely reception it would meet when it was called up by those who used such forms. Her conclusion matched Karen's intentions.

"I've enjoyed this chat. I wish all of them had such a happy conclusion."

"I'll do my best to help those around me with their problems, Dr. Alexandriou."

"I hope we meet again under less formal circumstances."

"I'm sure we will. Though it might be a few years in the future. You now are part of my...cohort."

<>

Karen had been released a few minutes earlier than most of the recruits. So there were three more groups of eight to go through the interview with the head doctors. Most of the 24 recruits looked at least a bit nervous.

"How'd it go in there, Danburn?" said one of the recruits seated near Karen. He spoke very quietly and they all covertly eyed the one sergeant who was overseeing them. He didn't seem to be paying much attention to them, however.

Karen guessed the "inattention" was a ruse but decided to act as if it was not. She answered in the same quiet tones.

"OK. They're Navy or Marines. So they're looking out for the service. But they were all doctors before they were officers. I THINK they're looking out for us, too."

He turned to the nearest recruit. "The Burn says it's OK."

"The BURN?" She already had a nickname? She knew it would happen. Everybody got a nickname in close groups like these, though she'd expected it to take days and weeks. Then she realized her mistake.

The recruits had been both deliberately and accidentally cut off from all their previous family and friends. And many of those had not been close or caring. So they watched the sergeants as closely as dogs watched their masters. To ensure they took care of them and didn't abuse them, much.

But they also watched those around them closely, too. For the next few weeks at least the other recruits were their family. They might even be family for years and decades to come.

So they'd noticed that Karen was calm, efficient, and helpful. They couldn't help but imprint on her.

Or come to hate her. That, too, went with being outstanding.

<>

The next few days were not that stressful. The yelling and rushing stayed the same but the confusion diminished. They could now all march, though still imperfectly. Terminology was beginning to sink in. They could salute, and knew who to salute and who not to. The daily routine was established. Sleeping and waking habits were becoming habit.

Agonizing to many were the physical tests: pull-ups, push-ups, running, crawling. Even those in mostly good physical condition found they had weak areas.

Karen stood out. No matter what was asked of her she could do, easily and accurately. Her reflex tests were off the charts. When she had to move fast her arms and legs were a blur. And she seemed to have eyes in the back of her head.

A big skinny boy, Anson, was a bit of a class clown. While some of them, including Karen, were waiting for several others to finish an exercise he threw a clod of dirt at her back.

She merely leaned to one side and it flew by her. Without turning she said, more as if she were curious than anything else, "Anson. Do you really want to get your ass kicked?"

"Marines don't hit Marines. You can't kick my ass."

"Oh, boy. You don't know that soon we're going to be learning hand-to-hand combat? And practicing on each other? I can practice real good on you, Funny Boy."

Which was how Anson became Funny Boy. He bore the name proudly. Every name The Burn gave made the recruits proud.

The best day was when they were issued their rifle. It was in perfect condition, new except for being test fired. In the next weeks it would be their constant companion until they were discharged or graduated. It and its successors would save their lives and those of their comrades and of those they were charged to protect. It stayed in a rack on each side of the barracks. It was part of them, and made them who they were.

They learned to call it their weapon by learning an immortal saying. "This is my weapon, this is my gun. This is for business, this is for fun."

One third of the recruits were women, who had become fully integrated into combat several years ago. They thought this mantra hilarious. At least when Karen amended the ending reference to a penis.

"This is my weapon, this is my gun. This is for business, this is just funny."

<>

On Monday the stress returned, intensified. They were marched to a different barracks right after chow, duffels over their shoulders and rifles held crossed in front of them. This barracks (they now saw) was the actual 4044 platoon building.

They were given just a few minutes to hurriedly rack their rifles, unpack their duffle into a new locker, and dress their bunks.

Then they were marched to a nearby drill field. Three officers, the highest the base commander, spoke to them of the high-minded ideals and tough realities of being a Marine.

The officers vacated the area and the recruits were attacked verbally by five sergeants: the primary drill instructor who wore a black belt over his camouflage uniform and his assistants who wore green belts over theirs. They were insulted to their faces from an inch away by the green belts, never with obscenities but with more scalding criticisms.

Karen got the most attention. At one time all four assistant drill sergeants stood around her haranguing her. At one time two of them were giving her contradictory instruction about how many pushups she should do.

She remained perfectly calm and did all that was required of her, doing both sets of pushups like a perfectly maintained machine. This time, due to the level of punishment, she called on Suit to aid her slightly to maintain this perfection.

Finally one of the sergeants issued a "dumb insolence" demerit, the first she'd ever been given, and the DIs abandoned her for another victim.

Karen finished the last of the pushups and rose smoothly to stand at parade rest in the ranks. She was only lightly sweating and breathing barely faster and more deeply than usual.

Sergeant Finley, the primary drill instructor who would take the 4044 the rest of the way through their training, ambled by. He stopped, looked her over.

"Did you deserve that dumb-insolence demerit?"

"Sir, this recruit must have, sir."

"No, I think not. But I can't erase it. Carry on, recruit."

"Sir, yes, sir."

Karen thought she knew what was happening. It was like those cop shows she'd seen, with one cop playing the bad cop and the other the good cop. The criminal would be so frightened of the bad cop he would open up to the protective good cop. Except in this case there were four bad cops and one fatherly good cop: the primary DI.

But she felt little fear. She had read much in the encyclopedia contained in Tiara about the history and nature of the Human Interstellar Confederacy. It had over many centuries cautiously improved the genes of the human race. When highly stressed her body did not spew massive doses of adrenaline into her body to protect itself with desperate measures. Instead it roused her to peak efficiency in some other ways. Ways which used only small amounts of adrenaline.

In the days to come Sergeant Finley and two of the four green-belted DIs from the first day fully in 4044 began a more methodical training schedule. There were short classroom lessons in the laws of the UCMJ, first aid, military organization, and so on. There were tests on each subject.

Karen of course passed each with perfect scores. As she did when tested in the field by screaming sergeants while she was marching, running, crawling under obstacles. She was given more dumb-insolence demerits despite her perfect answers.

Early in the third week they were marched to a drill field and instructed in the use of pugil sticks. These were plastic sticks two inches thick and about a yard long, the length of their rifle. On each end were tough foam rubber cylinders about four inches through and six long.

The instructions were in their use as simulated bayonets and rifles butts used as weapons. The recruits were dressed in padded clothing and helmets.

The first bouts were done on a wooden platform a foot off the ground and about a yard wide and six yards long. Three pairs of recruits preceded Karen.

Perhaps coincidentally, she was paired with the biggest and

toughest of all the recruits. They faced off about two yards apart.

She waited to see what Bear (a nickname she'd bestowed upon him) would do. He was hesitant to hit her, maybe because she was female, or respected by him, or possibly plain fear. By now The Burn was a known quantity to all the recruits.

The DI began shouting at him, urging him to kill her, kill her!

She nodded at him and he charged, swinging wildly. She easily deflected all his blows and backed up in a sliding foot motion which tested the surface behind and beneath her feet.

The sergeant was screaming at her to fight, pussy, fight! A derogatory term which would earn him a reprimand that night from his superior as sexist and not in the best traditions of the Corps.

After a half dozen buffets she began to strike back as well as deflect. Soon he was beginning to be pushed back, and back.

Just before he'd fall off the platform behind him she eased up and called out to him.

"Attack again. More science, more science!"

They began a bout in earnest, back and forth, her leading him to smarter and fiercer action.

The sergeant, Conley, yelled at them to break it off. At that Karen made a deflection with one end of the stick which flowed smoothly into a bayonet-like jab to the gut with the other end. Bear collapsed before her.

As he did so Karen reversed the stick and struck down on his head as with a rifle butt. She pulled her punch to merely stun him. If she'd used her full strength the blow would have killed him despite all his padding and that of the stick.

Sergeant Conley told a couple of recruits to get that "trash" off the platform. They hurriedly got up and dragged Bear away. The sergeant jumped on the platform and began to berate Karen for "playing" and lacking fighting spirit and so on. She listened calmly and apparently with great interest to him.

She was given another dumb-insolence demerit.

In the next week the pugil sticks were wielded again, this time from a narrow rope-and-plank bridge twenty feet above a stream of water. When it came Karen's turn she was set upon by two recruits on both front and back sides of her.

Again she "played" with them, teaching them more than the DIs could, by egging them on and quietly instructing them in the midst of furious activity. Screamed at to finish she did so with two whirling strikes too fast for human eyes to follow.

One recruit collapsed backward onto the bridge. The other reeled sideways and pitched over the waist-high rope parapet strung all along both sides of the swaying bridge.

He did not attempt to halt his fall, too stunned perhaps. Karen dropped her pugil stick and was at the parapet in time to grab one wrist, then the other, and haul him back up onto the platform.

She received a demerit for insufficient fierceness, two for interfering with training (she should have let her opponent fall into the water), and five for "losing her weapon."

Now in the fourth week of their training recruits were allowed Sunday mornings for chapel or other religious observance and afternoons for leisure activity.

As in the previous weekend Karen spent the afternoon after lunch studying and taking care of her gear: shining shoes, disassembling and re-assembling her rifle and practicing cleaning it. This was unnecessary because as yet the recruits had not been allowed to fire their rifles but it was good practice.

This time she had an audience. As she'd had the week before, but then only with three recruits. This time she had thirteen surrounding her bunk: one leaning on a support column, several on the edges of nearby bunks, and several more squatting or lying on the floor.

There was much good-natured bad-mouthing of each other and an occasional insulting remark about this DI or that.

Karen put a quick end to the last.

"Shut your mouth unless you have a real complaint. That you take to the chaplains or the admin corrections office. These 'clowns' are teaching you how to live through combat."

Funny Boy Anson had a serious comment for once.

"They don't seem to be teaching you much. You already know it all."

"It only looks like it. I went through Junior ROTC and read a lot about what we would be going through here. I'm ahead of the rest of you but I'm not fooled into thinking that I know it all. They have real experience I can't match."

"They just seem to yell at us a lot and hurry us too fast to do a good job."

"That's tame compared to what it's really going to be like in the middle of a firefight. All that yelling and hurrying is training us to overcome the stress and fog of war. You've heard that phrase? Think sometimes about being in a REAL firefight and how you'd do."

There were moments of quiet but soon the chatting started up again, about the upcoming pugil stick practice. And the day when they'd be able to fire their weapons.

In the fifth week they were introduced to the Marine Corps martial arts practices. Karen's years of aikido training both helped and hurt her here. It had given her skills at assessing opponents and defending against more than one of them, timing, and body control. But aikido was mostly a defensive art and the Marines were mostly about offensive measures. Nevertheless in that first week she worked up from tan through grey to the green belt level.

Pugil stick practice of bayonet and rifle butt techniques continued. By now Karen had become widely recognized as far ahead of everyone else. There was much speculation about how she'd do against opponents in other platoons.

The fifth Sunday Karen instituted a practice which continued through the last and twelfth week. By now her afternoon audience had approached the level of an audience with a monarch, with up to thirty people coming and going during the afternoon.

At 3:00 someone suggested they all go to the Base Exchange. Karen foresaw a problem with that.

"They let us in because we go at scattered times and don't make a big splash at any one time. If all two dozen of us invade at once they may limit our access."

Dennis Southey was a spindly but tough redhead who was always arguing points of regulations and laws, so was nicknamed Chaser for ambulance chaser. He began a long explanation of why this would be illegal. Karen cut him short.

"You're probably right, Chaser. But I'd rather not chance it. Suppose we march there and then go in five at a time?"

There followed much discussion of this suggestion and of ways to implement it. Finally they agreed that Karen would march them there in a formation of four abreast and the front four would go in first. The formation would be ordered by height, tallest first.

Karen agreed, but only if she could swap off her unit leader status with someone else whenever she wanted to, to whomever she wanted.

Thus almost two dozen platoon 4044 recruits assembled outside the barracks. Karen stood to one side, facing them, and said loudly enough for all to hear, "Platoon, FALL IN."

"PITIFUL," she yelled after a couple of minutes of much confusion. "Do you want everyone to laugh their asses off at us? Again, NOW, dress...RANKS."

Secretly Karen knew part of the fault was with her. She was relying on her memory but, good as it was, she'd had no training nor studied how to give the commands a unit leader did. Still, keeping things simple, and with much haranguing, the fragment of their platoon was soon in reasonably good order, the tallest in front, the shortest in back, height dropping off to the right.

She gave the command, "Platoon, forward...MARCH."

The result wasn't too bad. By now the recruits had developed the minimal habits they needed. But Karen wasn't satisfied. After a block she gave the command, "Platoon...HALT."

They did that well enough. Then she walked in among the ranks and gave instructions to two of the worse offenders.

She returned to the front of the group, by now augmented by a few more recruits. She spoke up so all could hear.

"Look, this is only going to work if you take this seriously. I know I'm not trained for this. But I'm willing to give it a try. But not if we look like clowns. We can't let Forty Forty-four down."

She looked them over. They seemed to be taking her words to heart.

"So, if you can't do this right, or don't want to try it, drop out now."

A couple of recruits did. Most straightened their spines and stared straight ahead.

She went to the side near the head of the unit, faced them, and again said, "Platoon, dress...RANKS. Platoon, forward...MARCH."

This time the recruits did a better job. She let them go till the end of the block, then gave them the command, "Right turn...MARCH."

She'd given the command just at the right time. The turn was done well, each rank turning right when they reached the correct point.

She had them turn left at the next block, march a block, turn right, and continue to the exchange. There she gave the command, "Platoon...HALT."

Then she said, "First rank...FALL OUT. Platoon, AT EASE."

By now it was mid-September. The heat and humidity had eased off but it was still not comfortable on a bright sun-shiny day. Nevertheless, the recruits stayed in ranks.

After ten minutes Karen said, "Platoon, atten-TION. Second rank, FALL OUT. Platoon...AT EASE."

This continued until the entire group who'd marched to the exchange had entered it. Karen followed the last recruit.

The incident did not go unnoticed. The next day Sergeant Finley called them into formation after mid-day chow.

While they all stood at attention he said, "Some of you thought it would be fun to march on your own to the BX yesterday. We are now going to spend two hours drilling the right way."

And so they did. At the end, all sweating except Karen, they were allowed ten minutes to "water up and piss out" before entering the class room for their first lesson in rappelling: sliding down a rope from a helicopter, cliff, or building top.

The sergeant stopped Karen from entering and spoke to her.

"I hear you played unit leader yesterday. For that we're going to have two hours of instruction Sunday after noon-day chow. So if you ever do it again, you'll do it right. Understood?"

"Sir, yes, sir."

"Now get in there and learn how not to kill yourself."

That week two recruits, unable to conquer their fear of heights, dropped out of 4044.

<>

Two other recruits showed up that Sunday afternoon and took instruction with Karen in drill leadership. Afterward half a dozen recruits marched to the BX under her leadership. By the time the platoon graduated nearly the entire platoon used an hour of their leisure time each Sunday taking part in this now-traditional march on the BX.

In Week Seven Platoon 4044 learned how to fire their rifles. But only dry firing with plastic dummy ammo inserted to protect the firing pins of the rifles as they were aimed and triggered. Much time was spent on short lectures and longer practice of each lesson in breath control and aiming and pulling the triggers.

Karen had already gone through this in the summer camp between her high school Junior and Senior years. But she kept silent about this experience and renewed her knowledge of the basics.

In Week Eight much of each day was spent on slow and timed firing practice. At the end of the week Karen earned the Rifle Expert badge, one of a very few recruits who did so that year.

Week Nine was obstacle courses, eleven different types in all. As the week progressed the obstacles became taller and taller. The recruits practiced in four-man fire teams, learning to make up for their weakest links and finish together.

Three more recruits dropped out of Platoon 4044.

Much of Week Ten was devoted to day-movement exercises. Their ears bombarded by simulated gunfire, the recruits went over walls and under barbed wire, again in fire teams.

One recruit dropped out.

Week Eleven was the culmination of all that training. There was a full week of review, and review, and review. Then over a long weekend the recruits underwent 64 hours of "The Crucible" while every test was applied to them several times over. They were allowed little food and sleep.

At the end of that time, the recruits were marched to the Emblem Ceremony. They were ordered to parade rest and the base commander spoke to them.

"Congratulations. We have treated you tough. You have proved you are tougher. You are Marines. You are among the best military forces in the world. In the years ahead you will have an impact far beyond your small size, in your communities, in your nation, in the world. I salute you."

He braced and saluted them. The ranks in perfect unison returned the salute.

Then their drill instructors presented their platoons with the

Marine Corps Emblem made up of an eagle and anchor over a globe. They were Marines.

Most of the recruits were promoted to E-1, Private. Seven became E-2s, Privates First Class. Karen was awarded Outstanding Recruit of the Year. She was also promoted to E-3, Lance Corporal, the only recruit so honored in every fiscal year of October to September.

<>

Each Marine was usually allowed a full day of recuperation. Thanksgiving was this Thursday, however. So on Tuesday and Wednesday the several platoons visited the "head doctors" for assignment.

Most new Marines were offered an assignment and there was little choice in the matter. They could either accept or leave the service. A very few did, often citing "extreme family emergencies." They were let go without penalty. The Marines did not want anyone to stay in who was not committed to service of their country.

Some Marines were offered two or three choices. Karen was offered none. Instead she was counseled first. So early Wednesday afternoon she met with Dr./Captain Mario Alexandriou.

They exchanged salutes. He shook her hand and gestured at the seat before his desk. She was in her dress uniform.

"Congratulations, Karen. I'm not surprised you made Outstanding Recruit."

"Thank you, sir. I feel honored."

"We've got a full hour if you need it. Please drop the military courtesies.

"First, how are you generally?"

"Excellent. Looking forward to seeing my family."

"Good. Now. I'm sure you know this but I'm obligated to state it. One of your choices is to leave the service with an honorable discharge. There are no penalties of any kind. We only want people who really want to be here, not because they were forced."

"I'm staying in."

"Glad to hear it. But hear out all the options before making a final decision.

"One is a full scholarship to a four-year college. You'd then go through Officer Candidate School. Or, if your college has ROTC and you participate, you could immediately become an officer on graduation.

"Another is the Naval Academy. From there you'd become an officer directly, no OCS. You'd have to be nominated by a member of Congress but that should be merely a formality for you."

"I intend to become a scout/sniper in the Marines. If there are no openings I'll leave the service and find a similar position in another military organization."

The doctor looked at her. He was clearly puzzled, even without Tiara's special diagnostic senses.

Karen did not perfectly understand her own firmness nor why this position was important enough to make a special effort to get it. She spoke slowly, thinking matters through.

"I do not disdain killing as so many civilians do. Nor am I persuaded by the Marine attitude that a fierce desire to kill is a virtue when it's focused on enemies. It is simply a necessity sometimes, when it's the only solution to a problem.

"I mean the ONLY solution. Not the easiest one. I'd rather avoid it, and take great effort to do so, even if it means giving up some important advantages otherwise."

She nodded. Her attitude was clear to her, perhaps for the first time. Maybe it wasn't clear to the doctor. But she felt no strong need to make him understand.

"The other part is that from the earliest I can remember I've known that I'm more capable at just about everything than other people. Physical, mental, social abilities, I'm superior in them all.

"Maybe not emotional. I'm not sure what 'superior' in that would be. Very healthy, I suppose, is the closest I can come to a definition of emotional superiority.

"I don't mean that I feel godlike, above other people. Something to be proud of. It's just a fact."

She focused her attention on the doctor. He seemed to understand. And not be making judgments pros or cons. But then that WAS his job. To understand, first. Making judgments must come later, if they did.

"The more I understood that, the more I felt that I should do more with my abilities than just please myself, or my family. Or friends. I should do as much for as many people as I can.

"I studied the jobs people do when they grow up. The military seemed worthy. As long its main job was protecting others. I know in other countries the military's main job is to make the generals and admirals rich. And our country isn't without those types. But on the whole we do more than pay lip service to Protect and Serve."

"Why not join a police force? That is their function as well."

"Scope. Even the federal police forces are limited to our country. The military's mission is global."

"Why the Marines? Why not one of the other forces?"

"Opportunity to make a difference. We're small compared to the others. What I do here will make more of a difference."

"And scout/sniper?"

"In the army those two specialties are separated. Their combination in Marine operations means I have a lot of independence."

"You are usually paired with someone when acting as sniper. One person spots, the other shoots."

"I would not like that. I need to work alone."

"Why?"

Karen considered whether to say "personal preference" or give the real reason. She chose truth. She told Tiara to monitor all the doctor's electronic communications, then expand that to ALL communications, and stifle any reports of what she was about to admit.

"I know many people are amazed at what I can do. I've even heard a few say I can't be human, I combine so many outstanding abilities. But my actual abilities go beyond what I've let everyone see."

"Interesting." Karen could see the doctor only believed she believed what she'd said. Not that she was truthful.

"I see you are skeptical. I don't blame you. But you know my claim to be outstanding IS true. The Corps has documented it.

"So, consider if I were paired with someone. I'd be held back to their level. I couldn't serve as well. Lives might be lost. Wars, even, might be lost."

Karen was silent as the doctor thought. The man took many long moments, then nodded.

"I'll so recommend. Let me see what positions are available."

The doctor pulled on a recess in the surface of his desk. This swung up a screen and keyboard and positioned it in front of him. He gestured at the screen and a 3D sensor read the gesture and the computer displayed something on the screen. He then placed his fingers on the keyboard and began to type. Occasionally he'd lift a hand, make another gesture, then type some more.

This continued for a couple of minutes. Karen sat, relaxed and using Tiara to follow what he was doing. So just as soon as the doctor knew something, so did Karen.

"I see three positions available that fit your criteria. Each requires you to go through the four-week Land Recon course, then the 12-week Scout Sniper course. The earliest school opening is two weeks away. The latest five. Here is where you'd likely be posted and other details."

He swung the screen around so she could read what he'd described. At the same time a silent printer on a nearby table began to print out the screen contents.

Karen pretended to study the screen contents and then the paper copy of it when that was handed to her. But she'd already made her choice.

"I believe I'd be of most use in this Afghan position."

"That requires you to learn the local dialect of Pashto. How are your language skills?"

"Outstanding. As you may recall from looking at my records, I took both Spanish and French in school. What they don't mention is that I read and write Latin and Greek. I studied those for fun using online courses. Greek was harder because of its non-Latin alphabet, but not much so. Then, because the Greek and Russian languages share related alphabets and grammar I learned Russian. But only at the basic level."

"I'm surprised you had time, considering your heavy academic schedule. Including three college-level courses."

"I only need to sleep about five or six hours. So I've got more time each day than most people."

The doctor looked closely at her, seeming to evaluate upward his already high regard for her abilities.

"Very well. I'll put you in for the Afghan position. But give me your second and third choices. My input carries a lot of weight, but the Corps will decide which position it wants you in. Remember, they will have several other people to choose from."

Karen pointed to her second and third choices. The doctor entered them and leaned back in his chair.

"I believe we're done. Anything you'd like to discuss?"

"Somewhat to my regret, no. I enjoy your company."

He stood and she did too. He followed her to the office door and opened it for her. They shook hands a second time.

"*Au revoir*, Karen."

"*Hasta luego*, Mario."

An impish urge took hold in Karen. She dropped his hand, rose two feet in the air, smiled mischievously, and disappeared. A puff of wind fanned his face.

A few minutes later the doctor was still sitting limply in his desk chair staring at the space where Karen had vanished when he heard a loud explosion overhead which shook all of Parris Island, followed by a diminishing roaring sound. It was the exact sound of an aircraft breaking the sound barrier going straight up.

He smiled.

Part 3 - Sniper

That Wednesday afternoon Karen Danburn was welcomed home with tears and hugs and a party. School classmates, some of whom she'd met only briefly, showed up. So did many of her former soccer, basketball, and football team mates. Her older brother Alex and his wife Jessica did too. They stayed for Thanksgiving and Friday but returned to their San Diego home midday Saturday.

Their eight-year-old daughter Sylvia came with them. She and Karen spent several hours together on Thanksgiving and the next day, going to the park, mall, and movies. Karen had always loved children and was contented in their company, her time narrowing down to the intense Now of childhood.

The following week she spent as much time with her parents as she could. Since they had to work she had much of each day for solitary idleness. She spent much of that wandering her old haunts. They seemed alien to her now, as if she was seeing them for the first time.

That weekend they all tried to spend as much time as they could together. However just after lunch Sunday Karen walked into the backyard with her duffel bag and a pull-along suitcase suitable for overhead stowing at an airline. She checked with Tiara to be sure that no one was watching except for her parents. She lifted her hand and waved Goodbye. They waved back.

She dropped her hand, smiled at them one last time, and pulled Pegasus's shield around her, going invisible. She flew upward, leaving a swirl of wind behind her.

Staying below the speed of sound she soared in a great upward arc some 65 miles to the south and a bit east toward the Marine base in the Camp Pendleton area. She passed high over the Prince Industries Bluebird Security installation on the north side of the Marine base. Tiara, Suit, and Pegasus reported being probed by very advanced security, one a primitive form of gravity radar.

That she found very interesting but not surprising. Prince Industries was widely known to be at the forefront of scientific research and engineering development, their best-known products being the superbattery and many kinds of paramagnetic vehicles.

To avoid Bluebird's attention she had to come straight down from a 20-mile height toward Camp Pendleton's Visitor's Barracks. She checked with Tiara to see if anyone could see her land. There being none she landed lightly under trees a block away from the offices containing the Officer of the Day. Inside she offered her papers to the OD, a stern-looking woman of forty-something years.

She was expected. After logging her in the OD had a corporal drive Karen and her luggage the half mile to the barracks.

Monday morning she awoke and dressed as required: armless olive tee shirt with USMC on the front in grey, grey and brown camouflage pants, and grey boots. She met other trainees downstairs just outside the concrete-floored parade assembly lot. A waiting sergeant called out their names and had them fall in on the assembly lot.

When everyone was checked in, the sergeant formed them into ranks by height and marched them to chow. There was plenty of choices of food and drink. They ate all together at several tables reserved for them. Karen found the food good.

The first order of business was an hour of class. This was an overview of the course which would last till three days before Christmas. It included how to defend positions, counters to improvised explosives, convoy operations, patrolling, assaults as part of a fireteam, and use of the digital warfare headset which let all troops keep in communication with each other and view maps of the ground in which they fought. They'd also learn to use several weapons: hand grenades, grenade launchers, light and heavy machine guns.

That done they began a 24-hour physical fitness test. They were tested on running, pull-ups and push-ups, agility tests, rappelling down heights from cliffs and helicopters, climbing rope ladders, water tests including heavy loads, and obstacle courses involving running, climbing, and crawling.

They did this with only two meal breaks where the menu was only combat rations.

At the end it was mid-morning the next day. They were then given an hour-long academic test of basic mental functioning, marched to chow, and released till the next morning when they'd find out whether they'd passed.

Karen was nearly as fresh after the tests as she'd been before them. She'd managed this without help from her super-scientific resources.

Some of the other Marines had noticed that she was consistently at the forefront of every test. This earned her some teasing during chow. It was mostly good-natured. Marines admired toughness in others; their comrades might save their lives some day.

Also, Karen had let her blond hair grow out since she'd had Tiara cut it just before recruit training. The three-inch curly locks could have been professionally styled to flatter her face. Though it hardly needed flattering. Without blemish or makeup, her face would have done any fashion model proud.

The teasing by one of the Marines, however, was not good-natured. It relied heavily on sexual innuendo.

Karen ignored it. It bothered her not at all.

It did bother other Marines, however. One of them, an older man who been a Reservist and recently rejoined the Corps, said, "Knock it off, Russo. She'll have you up on report."

Another, a short stocky woman who was aiming for a battlefield intelligence specialty, said, "Or she'll kick your ass."

"Her?" He looked disbelieving. As well he might. He was easily the biggest of all the Marines there, perhaps 6' 4" and massively muscled (a fact which had literally weighed heavily against him in the endurance tests). A broken nose suggested he'd had more than his share of hand-to-hand action.

"Yes, her," said the woman. "This is Karen Danburn. She was Recruit of the Year."

"Hah! Probably slept with the base commander."

The Reservist shook his head, spoke to the sturdy woman. "Did you see the same videos I saw? Of her in hand-to-hand training?"

"Yes. Phenomenal. She'd kick his sorry ass up one side and down the other."

Karen spoke up. "Knock it off, my friends. You'll just make it more likely he'll challenge me someway I can't refuse to fight and I'll have to hurt him. Then I'll be up on report. I don't want to lose a chance at my specialty."

A short skinny Marine Private spoke up. He was barely the minimum physical size a Marine could be. He resembled a fox, and was one perhaps in more ways than the physical.

"There's a way she can kick his ass and not go up on report. Arm wrestling."

Her "friends" looked at him disdainfully. "No way! He outweighs her two to one and, look at her. She's got some strength in those arms. But not his equal."

Foxy smiled. "I'll bet a hundred on her."

Karen was not having any betting involved. That was a sure way to cause a lot of animosity.

"No betting! I won't do it if there is any betting."

"What do you mean, you'll do it?" said the Reservist. "Are you crazy?"

"No," she said. "I can take him."

There was much argument on all sides. Tired as the Marines were, having been up maybe 36 hours, the prospect of a fight energized them, even one as genteel as this one.

"OK," said Karen. "I'll go along with it as long as we get the training sergeant to oversee it. That will make it legal and friendly, and he can see there's no betting."

Thus some 40 minutes later a crowd of Marines came together at the outdoor picnic area near the chow hall. There were perhaps as many as a hundred of them with more joining them all the time.

Karen and the brute sat down on opposite sides of a round picnic table made of tough plastic. It'd had its umbrella removed to give everyone watching a better view. A number of Marines further from the action removed more umbrellas from the tables and stood on the strong plastic chairs surrounding the tables. A few even stood on the tables themselves further away.

A heavy towel was placed on the table in front of each contestant to protect their elbows. The two clasped a hand with the other, their raised fists between them, as the sergeant gave the simple instructions.

When the contestants had agreed they understood the rules the sergeant said, "Get set... Go!"

Karen's reaction time was better than his. In an instant she had his arm pressed to a 45 degree angle.

There were cheers from some and groans from others.

Russo held his position for a minute or two. Then slowly he pushed her arm toward the upright position.

For minutes their arms stayed upright, quivering slightly toward victory for one or the other and back again. Then slowly Karen's arm began to go down. And down. But at the 45 degree angle it stuck. Then slowly began to inch up toward stalemate. Then reached it.

By now her opponent was showing strain, his supporting hand flat on the table surface quivering. He was sweating heavily and his face was contorted in a grimace. Karen's face showed no strain, nor did any other part of her. She might have been a machine.

In truth she could have won easily long ago. But that would not get her what she wanted.

She let her arm stay upright for long minutes, then let it be pushed down and down. She resisted despite the seeming inevitability of defeat, till finally her arm touched the towel-covered table top. That instant she ceased resistance and slapped her free hand on the table top to indicate surrender.

Russo jumped up and yelled out, "Yeah! Yeah!" He was quickly surrounded by friends. They all jumped up and down. Someone poured a can of beer over his head.

Karen stood, smiling at the sight. She was quickly surrounded by her own partisans.

"Too bad," said the Reservist. The battlefield intel woman said disgustedly, "Idiot. She let him win. Didn't you?"

Karen smiled at her. "I would never say that."

At that the crowd around her parted to let Russo through, holding out a hand to shake.

"Damned good show, Danburn. You are a tough bitch. I'll back up that pretty ass of yours anytime."

She smiled back up at him. "But only in a fight. You're not getting those banana fingers on my ass. Not unless you want them broken."

"By God, I think you'd do it." He turned away smiling. In minutes the crowd was nearly gone. Left with Karen was the Reservist, the intel lady, Foxy, and a couple of others.

"I still think you threw the fight," the woman said.

"Think what you want," said Karen. "Just don't go spreading it around. Right now Russo would be a valuable asset in a firefight. I'd hate to have you spoil that."

"OK. OK. Have it your way. I still think you should have won."

She turned and walked away, taking a couple of Marines with her.

She was left with the Reservist and Foxy.

"Whatever the truth," the older man said. "That was a Helluva good show. See you around, Danburn." He shook her hand and left.

She looked at the little man. He held out a hand. They shook.

"Dr. William Conroy, Corporal. I won't say a word, but I know you could have easily won that fight."

She raised an eyebrow.

"I'm a mathematician, investigating training techniques to see if I can make them better. I watched you while we were going through the PT sessions. At first it was to distract me from the pain; you are quite a pleasant sight. Then I began to calculate the effort you expended--"

"How?"

"From variables such as how fast you moved and the angles your limbs subtended and the approximate weights moved. And a few others. I'll bet you could beat most world records."

"Interesting," she said. "I hope you won't go around broadcasting any of this. It would make me seem like a freak."

"No. I don't think it would do anyone else any good--even my dear wife--to know that a superhuman lives among us.

"I'll see you around, Ms. Danburn."

He walked off. Karen watched him for long moments before turning go to her quarters, the first item on her agenda to take a long, hot shower.

<>

Only three of the 63 in the Combat Training course failed in the fitness tests and left the base, perhaps to train up and retake the course.

The remaining weeks were taken up with short classroom instruction periods and longer field class work. This included marches, live fire of the various weapons, martial arts workouts, scaling or crawling under obstacles, locating and defusing improvised explosive devices, and use of the digital warfare headset.

This last reminded her of a very early version of Tiara. She spent especial effort on mastering the headset. In practice she'd use Tiara instead but she had to be able to convince others she was using the headset and using it well.

The last day of class, with just three days before Christmas, was a half-day. Before chow the 60 Marines were awarded a certificate for the training. Accompanying it was a ribbon for their dress uniforms. They were then let go.

Many took off home or wherever. Some went through the chow line, either to get a last free meal before leaving or (in a few cases) because they'd stay on the base for whatever reason.

Karen ate there for political reasons. She'd meet her former class mates again and again over the years. She wanted to be sure they remembered her and favorably. Russo was there, too, for the "free chow" before heading out and the two of them exchanged good-natured insults. None of his descended to sexual innuendo, however. He seemed to have learned his lesson about that, at least with her.

In the barracks she dressed in civilian clothes, packed, and took a taxi to a location off base where she could be thought to wait for friends to pick her up. When the taxi was out of sight and no one was watching she vanished.

<>

Christmas as usual was a happy flurry of gift buying and giving and getting. Karen and her parents spent most of that time in San Diego. It was the first year her brother and his wife had celebrated the holiday there. Their daughter Sylvia was delirious with joy to have all her favorite adults around her. The rest were not far behind in their emotions.

<>

Karen Danburn came down from space over Quantico, Virginia, a bit past noonday on the 1st of January. To the south seventy-something miles she saw the national capitol at Richmond, Virginia.

There was much greenery all around. From a dozen miles up parts of the vegetation was patched orange and red and brown. Fields had patches of white snow also. It was mid-winter here, a great contrast to sunny California which she had left just a half hour ago.

The Potomac River wound south from Washington, D. C., the old Capitol. The small town of Quantico was on the river's western border. A railroad connecting the new and the old Capitols passed through it. Karen drifted down and for a few minutes followed an Amtrak train. Then she darted ahead and dropped down onto the Amtrak station at the edge of the tiny Quantico civic center. It was just a platform with a long roof over it.

She stood invisible near a roof support. When the train came to a stop about a dozen people exited. She took up station behind the last, gave them a dozen feet distance, checked with Tiara to be sure no one was watching her from behind, and went visible. No one noticed her.

There were three taxis waiting for the passengers. The two other Marines waited for most of the civilians to take them and waited. They and a couple of the civilians glanced at Karen but paid her only a moment's attention. Perhaps because it was so cold, only a few degrees above freezing despite a bright sun-shiny day. A north wind led all of them to put their backs to it.

A few minutes later two other taxis arrived. The Marines again waited for the civilians to take the first taxi. They glanced at her. The older, a grey sergeant with Master Sergeants stripes, said to her, "Get in, Lance Corporal. Back seat, please." He took the front side passenger seat taking with him his only luggage, an overnight bag.

The other Marine had a couple of suitcases. Karen had her duffle and a small overhead-sized pull-along case. The driver stowed them in the trunk and held the door for his passengers. He then got in and turned to the older NCO.

"Base?"

"That's right, Tony."

The cab pulled away from the station, turned once, then again, and entered the highway to the south. The driver meanwhile chatted with the sergeant beside him. They obviously had known each other for some years.

The entrance to the base was a little over a mile away. The driver made a right into it. One of two Marine guards came out of a hut and glanced inside the cab. She knew the two sergeants, addressing the older as Master Sergeant and the other as Staff Sergeant. Karen had to hand over the manila folder containing her travel orders and ID.

The guard examined these carefully, handed them back, and waved them on.

Karen's stop was first and she got out, forestalling the driver. "It's too damned cold, sir. I'll get the luggage." She handed him the fare plus a hefty tip. The cabby grinned and thanked her.

The Headquarters Building was a rambling two-story red-brick building. The area seemed deserted but Karen saw several security cameras looking all about. The glass double doors had a sign taped inside it. In large letters it said "PRESS BUTTON AND SPEAK." There was an arrow on the sign pointing to the left.

"Yes?"

"Lance Corporal Karen Danburn reporting for duty."

"You're expected, Lance Corporal. I'll buzz you in. Take the elevator to the second floor. Turn left there. We're at the end of the hall."

The inside of the building was quite nice, not a surprise considering this was battalion headquarters. All walls of the interior had been painted recently and a hint of the paint's sharp odor still lingered. In the second-floor office there was a reception desk against the left wall behind which the Officer-in-Charge sat. Against the wall opposite were comfortable chairs. On all the walls there were numerous photos of people and places.

The OiC was clad in dress camouflage with a chest full of ribbons. She was, however, fairly young. Reading the ribbons Karen was impressed.

She looked up from a desk computer, stood, and held out a hand for Karen's documents, forestalling a salute. "Lance Corporal. Welcome to Quantico. If your record is any indication you're going to be an outstanding student."

"Thank you, Sir."

"Sit if you'd like, Lance. Or go to the head and sit. I've got to check your paperwork against the computer."

Karen sat and picked up a tattered Leatherneck Gazette. She idly leafed through it but monitored the checks with Tiara. Karen did not like surprises and the rarest ones could be the worst. As expected, however, there were none.

The woman looked up and said, "All in order. Here is your Welcome packet in case you don't have yours with you. This--" Karen had stood up and was looking down at the packet and the print-out lying atop it. "--is your barracks assignment and a map from here to there.

"After you settle in you're free to sample our recreation and other facilities." The woman smiled. "Today they're pretty limited. About the only thing open is the bowling alley. But you do have an entertainment center in your room as part of your study carrel. You can get most cable on it. There's also public wi-fi if you have a tablet or laptop computer."

The woman stood up and held out her hand for a handshake. Karen gave it, then stepped back, braced, and saluted. The woman returned the salute.

"Thank you, sir. I'll try not to disappoint you."

The woman smiled again and sat.

Karen left, feeling good about her reception even though she knew not everyone would be as welcoming.

The barracks were a few blocks away. The building had three above-ground floors and one floor half-sunk in the ground. She wondered a little about that last, given that the Potomac was so close and the military base so low and flat. Still, the base was old and surely they'd long ago come up with ways to deal with water seeping into basements.

For a wonder she had an entire room in the barracks. It was small, with barely enough room for a narrow bunk bed, a desk which would be a study carrel and an entertainment center, a small closet, and enough room for an ergonomic chair and a straight-back chair. She could have no more than three guests without crowding and even then they would be intimate. Still, she was grateful for the privacy.

The bathrooms and showers were at the end of the hall, the stairs at the other end. This did not bother her. If she'd been body-shy recruit training would have cured her of that.

It took no more than a half hour to unpack and square everything away. Then she sat in the ergo chair and brought the study computer up. It had a fast optical line to the internet and a reasonably fast computer. Though no luxury item it was adequate for her purposes, especially since she could duplicate the computer with Tiara.

The large flat screen was also connected to a local cable service. She brought up the online guide to shows and found it had both broadcast and a long list of cable channels.

Though she expected she'd not have a lot of time for watching TV or browsing the internet. She intended to spend most evenings socializing with other trainees and Marines and maybe even with those attending the other schools at the base.

This included students and teachers at the Federal Investigation Bureau and the Drug Enforcement Bureau. Through Tiara she had access to every database on the planet, including foreign and secure ones. None of them were proof against the tech of a super-advanced race. But all those facts and theories in the databases could not compare to the wisdom of people who had "been there and done that" and she intended to make the most of the opportunities.

So thinking, she took her toiletry kit to the bathroom where she freshened up. In her room she decided on USMC exercise clothing, covered it well with a long uniform coat proof against the cold and any rain or snow, and set off for the bowling alley.

She'd expected the place not to be overly full New Year's day, but it was doing lots of business. Plenty of other students had arrived today for the several schools and most of them were at loose ends. She made several acquaintances, did some bowling (carefully holding back to merely average scores), and ate a hamburger and fries.

At 9:00 the bowling alley closed. She good-naturedly refused going with several others who wanted to go to an all-night diner in nearby Quantico. Halfway back to her barracks when no one was watching she vanished. A half hour later she was with her parents, telling them of her impressions of the base so far while the two of them expertly wove a steak dinner for the three of them.

At 11:00 PM East Coast time she dropped down out of the sky and, invisible, entered the barracks and prepared for bed.

<>

The next morning she checked in at the building where the indoor classes would be held during the Scout/Sniper course. Her credentials were checked once again. She was given a test of her use of a compass and map to do land navigation and draw simple maps. Then they checked that she'd taken the rigorous semi-annual physical fitness test recently. She had so she was released till 1:00 pm, when she was to report back after chow.

There were not quite fifty fellow students in the classroom assigned to the Scout/Sniper class at that time. She nodded to a few whom she'd met last night, sat in the middle of the room in a chair with a built-in desk surface, and fist-bumped the Marine beside her.

"How much sleep did you get after going to that all-night restaurant?"

The man grinned. "Not enough, of course."

"Tol' ja," she said in a mocking little-girl voice.

He fake-scowled at her. "Nobody likes a smart ass, Danburn."

At that the sergeant at the head of the class looked up from behind a lectern. The room quickly quieted.

"Congratulations, Marines. You have been judged qualified to start on one of the most valuable and difficult courses offered to Marines. Let's hope you live up to that.

"Some of you are used to thinking you're hot shit because you've qualified as Expert Marksmen. Get over it. Everyone here is an Expert. Soon you will all be beyond Expert. You will learn to routinely make kills out to 1000 meters. That's more than 3000 feet. About three fifths of a mile.

"As you gain experience, some of you will learn to consistently make kills at twice that distance. But that will likely take years."

He scanned the students in their seats while taking a sip of water from a plastic bottle.

"Since it's mid-winter here we will take advantage of that to teach you some winter skills. They'll only be simple. There's a regular course in snow and mountain sniper actions. But they'll help you get through this course under these conditions.

"Most of you are not fully geared up for this climate. Use your smart phones or info slates to access the course database. Look at the list of clothing and equipment you will need and buy them at the Base Exchange.

"Reference the four-digit code for this class and all of those purchases will be billed to this class and not to your personal account. Be sure you use this code only for those items. Our computer will double-check to ensure you're not buying beer or porn with that code."

There was subdued laughter at that last remark.

He then went on to give a general overview of the course. Karen and most of the students already knew the contents, but there was always the chance that this info would have recently changed in some important way, so she listened carefully.

It was mid-afternoon when the class was done. The students were let go for the day. However, they were to take from a table by the door a slender booklet which they must master before the next day.

"Hey, Danburn!" said one of her acquaintances from the night before. "We're going out for pizza and beer on the town. You want to come along?"

"Like to," she said to the woman. "But I'm going to rain check. Got some things to do. Ask me next time."

"Aw, Steinberg," a man said. "Can't you tell she's a grind? Probably going to bunk and memorize the manual." The remark was made with a grin. Karen answered in the same humor.

"With you big brains as competition? Don't you know it. Tomorrow guys."

The next day set the pattern for most of the following days of the two-month-long course. The first hour or so was in the classroom. It started with a test of the material covered the previous day, then covered new material.

Then the class was marched to an armory. There each student signed for a weapon and a box of ammunition, then went to a range, received instruction, and fired practice shots. Firing started at 300 meters distance and over several weeks worked up to 1000 meters. It was done in several types of terrain, and standing, kneeling, and prone.

They returned to the armory where they cleaned their weapons and turned them in. In the classroom they did a field sketch and sometimes other exercises.

In the second part of the course scouting was added to the sniper instruction and practice. This included slowly stalking an objective while clad in a ghillie suit: a camouflage suit that resembled foliage.

Karen used her special equipment only to double-check that her activities would allow her to pass all the many tests she was put through. She never used it for any other purpose; her body was more than up to the level required of her. She made records at the very edge of normal human performance.

She could have easily bettered those records. But that would have flagged her as a superhuman to anyone paying attention.

There was one exception to this policy of restraint. She wanted to qualify for the Ranger Scout/Sniper specialty. This would let her operate without the usual spotter partner who accompanied most snipers in every service. These partners backed up the sniper by keeping an eye on the overall area in which the two-man crews worked and kept track of weather and wind for each shot. A life-saver for most snipers, they would have hampered Karen, who would use all her special equipment in the field.

Consequently she used Tiara, Suit, and Pegasus when the competition was held for Best Sneaking (officially Infiltration and Evasion). This was done on the last weekend of the course, and was a three-day 24-hour-a-day series of games. In them she was the only Scout/Sniper no one ever discovered, no matter whether she was approaching a target or escaping after a kill (normally the most dangerous part of a kill mission).

Given a target in the five-mile square course she would take three steps into the course, lie down, begin crawling, and trigger her shield. Then she would loft into the air and spend all the time she'd ordinarily be on the ground slowly drifting toward the target. Returning she would reverse this process.

"God damn it, Danburn!" became a familiar refrain when she would approach the end of a stalk or escape. She would wait until no one was looking near her and drop her shield a few feet away and say "Mission accomplished, Sir."

It got so bad that on the last day the instructors cheated. They ordered spy satellites passing overhead to redirect their visual, infrared, and other sensors down toward the course.

Made aware of this by her own sensors Karen had Suit fake very faint signatures of her final approach. The course runners gained nothing but enough warning not to jump a foot in the air and nearly shit their pants.

<>

Evenings and weekends were busy times for most of the students of the course, though most managed some free time to socialize, see movies, go to an occasional dance or other special event. Karen had more time, she was such a fast learner.

Thus she made the acquaintance of a wide variety of people. And no wonder. She was almost literally shockingly beautiful. And was quickly recognized as supremely capable far beyond those in or even running the course.

This got her an invitation on her fifth weekend to a birthday party for the daughter of the colonel running the base. She'd met the girl's mother at a school play the previous week.

"Dress like the lady you are, Corporal. I want Mindy to see that you can be a top soldier and still be a girl."

Karen laughed and accepted the invitation. For the party she wore a copy made by Suit of a high-fashion gown. This was demure but (to almost every female at the party) obviously at the cutting edge of fashion. She got numerous comments on her outfit by women at the party, not all of them friendly.

A little while after the father-daughter dance the daughter approached Karen and said, "So you're the Good Example."

Karen smiled at the girl and her annoyed expression.

"Jonathan," she said to the tall darkly handsome man in a three-piece suit to whom she'd been talking. "This is Mindy Schmitz, the honoree of this party. Ms. Schmitz, this is Special Agent Jonathan Vincent of the FIB. Jonathan teaches hostage negotiation at the Academy here."

The girl, a pretty blond in a mid-calf blue gown, smiled up at the agent. "My apologies, Mr. Vincent. I should not have interrupted."

The agent reached a hand toward the young woman. She grasped it to shake his hand but he turned it palm down to give it the European kiss: bowing over her hand and giving the back of it an air kiss.

"No apology needed, Ms. Schmitz. I see you two have something important to discuss."

He turned to Karen and said, "Perhaps we'll meet some other time."

Karen smiled at him, he gave her the tiniest of bows, and left.

The encounter had smoothed away most of the girl's annoyance.

"I'm sorry, Corporal. I was taking out my annoyance at my mother on you."

"Let's sit over here," Karen said, pointing at a nearby line of chairs with their backs against the nearest wall.

The girl nodded and walked to sit in one of the chairs. All had rounded plastic backs and bottoms and were several pastel colors.

Seated Karen took a sip of the juice in her plastic cup. "Why were you annoyed?"

"My mother pointed you out to me as a good example of a military person who was also a lady."

"Oh, my. She made a mistake with me. I've been wondering if I should let that handsome agent jump my bones."

"Oh! Really?"

"Actually, just wishing. I'm too cautious for that. I refuse to screw someone I don't deeply care about. Sex is too important to me to chance ruining it with bad memories."

"Hmm."

The girl looked at her thoughtfully.

"Well, sorry. I'll get out of your way." She made to stand up.

Karen put a hand on the girl's nearest wrist.

"Don't go away. Stay and chat a while."

"OK!"

<>

Karen Danburn graduated at the top of the Scout/Sniper outstanding course. She had also qualified as a Ranger. This meant she would be free of a tag-along on her future missions.

She'd received a request from the base commander a few days prior to see him for a few minutes before she left the base. She'd gotten a short time slot from his office's appointment software and showed up there a few minutes before the scheduled time.

The outer office was a moderate-sized room with several desks. She dropped her duffle just inside the door out of the way and placed beside it her pull-along suitcase sized for an aircraft overhead bin. Then she walked across the floor and approached the desk behind which sat the Sergeant Major who oversaw all base affairs under Lt. Colonel Schmitz. This was a sturdy forty-something Latina with pulled-back hair and an olive uniform with an extensive chest of ribbons.

The woman had been watching Karen approach. Karen was in her dress-camouflage uniform and boots with all her ribbons. This was the style approved for travel a dozen years back, with its subliminal message that every Marine traveling was ready in an instant to return to duty and blow whole battalions away. She'd placed her billed "cover" under her arm. Her walk was the easy controlled grace of an athlete in top condition.

"Sergeant Major. Lance Corporal Karen Danburn reporting as per the request of Lt. Colonel Schmitz." A request of course being the same as a command.

"You're expected and on time, Lance Corporal. Knock on the door frame and enter." At the same time one of her hands pressed a key on the keyboard on the computer console in front of her.

"Thank you, Sergeant Major."

Karen did as directed and saw the Base Commander looking up from his desk. He stood. She approached, braced, and saluted. He returned the salute and said, "At ease, Lance Corporal."

He reached across the desk and she stepped forward to shake his hand. He then sat and said, "Sit at ease, Lance."

He regarded her for a moment.

"Congratulations on passing with honors, Lance. I see you qualified as Ranger. A big responsibility for anyone, especially one so young."

"Thank you, sir. I'll do my best to deserve it."

"I trust our few minutes together are not a hardship. I'm sure you're eager to see your family and friends."

"That I am, sir. But my schedule has the usual delays of most travel arrangements. It's no hardship at all."

"Good. The numbers of graduating classes on the base are too many for me to show up at each one. So I try to let the outstanding members of each class know I and the Corps appreciate them."

Karen nodded at that.

"I saw that you'll be assigned to Afghanistan. If you've not done so already, I suggest you study the situation there. It will offer challenges to all of us. And where there are challenges there are opportunities. Keep alert to both."

Karen nodded again. None of the statements had yet required even rote replies.

"Before you go I have a question. It's a bit indelicate of me to ask--"

The colonel had an excellent poker face but Tiara could read the tiniest emotional cues. It helped that she could see underneath people's skins.

"Whatever did you say to my daughter that would affect her so much? She's a changed girl."

"I assume that's a rhetorical question. What we said specifically was of course private." A much more tactful answer than *"You're out of line."*

"But generally we simply spent some time getting to know each other. Mindy is an extraordinary young woman and it was a pleasure to meet her. I suspect that what's going on is that she's been changing all along and you've not noticed because the changes were so gradual. That's what happened to me. One day my older brother was this annoying boy and the next he was all grown up."

A much more tactful answer than *"You've not paid as much attention as you should have to your daughter."*

He regarded her for a moment, then nodded slowly. She could not read his mind, only his emotions, but she guessed his thought was that he'd get no more information from her than that. And possibly that she was right about the gradual changes.

"I imagine you're right, Lance Corporal. Thank you for your insights. Well, I see that our time is up."

He stood and offered his hand once again. "Congratulations again. Enjoy your leave."

Karen smiled and shook his hand. "I'll do my best, sir!"

She stepped back, braced, saluted, received his salute, did an about face, and left the room.

On the way out she nodded at the Master Sergeant as the woman glanced at her and returned her attention to her computer.

Karen retrieved her luggage and left the headquarters. A block away she turned down an alley and disappeared.

A week and a half of leave later Karen arrived at the California State University's School of Mid-Eastern Languages in Hayward, California. This was a day before classes would begin, as her instructions specified.

Coming down from space Karen saw the familiar landmarks of San Francisco below her. There was the Pacific to the west, with a white crescent of an approaching front of clouds far out over the ocean. To the east of San Francisco was the long string-bean shape of the San Francisco Bay running mostly north and south. Further east was the long line of the Bayview hills which paralleled the bay.

Hayward was halfway between the bay and the hills, on fairly flat land. Across the bay was San Mateo, connected to Hayward by a bridge, some six or seven miles long.

From a mile up Karen saw that the Hayward campus was nestled in an area tinted by the brown and green of vegetation. It was a rounded square. A street encircled it and three or four interior streets quartered it. There was an oval sports stadium on the western side and several sports areas for baseball, soccer, tennis and the like. There was a large open parking lot on the eastern side and half dozen much smaller lots throughout.

Most of the buildings were low, one to three stories, but there were a couple of tall ones, one shaped like a round cake, the other like a stack of dominoes.

Invisible she swooped down over the campus. Tiara was displaying a map of the campus superimposed over her vision. From long practice Karen switched back and forth between the two until she found a building with a covered parking lot, the centrally located university library as it turned out. She entered the ground-level part of the parking area and went visible next to a van. She remained nearly invisible because the area was in deep shadow made deeper by the contrast with the bright nearly cloudless day outside.

Then she walked three blocks to a square three-story building with grey sides broken by windows.

She entered the building, part of it leased by the Army to manage all the language students from the several services which sent them there.

The room she was in was like many reception areas. To her left in one corner there was an alcove with a half-dozen chairs backed against a wall in an L arrangement and a low table with magazines scattered atop it. Opposite the alcove, to her right, a desk had been set up in a corner. An Army corporal sat there and looked up disinterestedly as she entered. His gaze lingered on Karen and she smiled at him. He sat a little straighter in his chair but returned to his work.

Opposite the entrance against the wall there was another desk. An Army staff sergeant looked up from it and nodded at Karen. She approached, let her luggage down on the floor, and handed him the now-unzipped leatherette folder with her orders and other papers.

He removed an open manila records packet and set it aside. The next folder was sealed. He unsealed it, glanced at the contents, and spoke to her. He didn't smile but his manner was friendly.

"Welcome to language school, Corporal Danburn. I suspect you'll enjoy it here. You'll dress as a civilian, eat in the cafeteria or off-site, and live in a dorm room, though only with other military. Some of the kids stay up late and are pretty noisy. We like you to have quieter quarters."

He glanced back at her orders and back at her. "I see you have the dual language course for Afghanistan and Pakistan: Dari and Pashto. It's a demanding course, but you must be up to it.

"You'll find the teachers friendly and they'll frequently invite small groups of you into their homes. Try to use as much of the teacher's native language as you're comfortable with, but don't strain at it. That would defeat the purpose of the social situation."

He spoke to the corporal. "Jason, escort Lance Corporal Danburn to her quarters, if you please. She's in dorm 6, room 302."

To her he said, "Welcome, Corporal. See you around." Then he returned to his computer screen.

The corporal stood and came over to Karen. He smiled at her and said, "Follow me. It's not far."

Karen hefted her duffel and pulled her overhead suitcase behind her. NOT FAR was out the back of the building to a small receiving area with a small dock and an opening onto a street. Along one side of the opening was a line of six charging stations for golf-cart-like runabouts with a long rear bed. Three of the carts were gone and three of them were hooked to charging cables.

The corporal punched an access code into the side of the nearest runabout and the cable unhooked itself and coiled unattended into the wall. Karen placed her luggage in the bed and took the passenger seat beside the corporal. He got in and turned to her. They shook hands and he said "Call me Jason." She replied "Karen" as he switched on the runabout.

The vehicle made a quiet whining sound as they sped several blocks. Jason pointed out a few landmarks along the way. Their destination was on the southern side of the campus, a large rectangular area containing perhaps a half dozen four-story-tall dormitories, light yellow with grey accent panels. He passed by them to park in front of one of several three-story tan buildings with a reddish slate-like roof.

She walked alongside him, refusing his help with her luggage. He chatted a bit about the opportunities for fun in the evenings and weekends, not obvious about his readiness to help her have some of that fun but not hiding it either.

Room 302 of Dorm 6 was on the top floor. He led her into the room and handed her the room key from the office.

"Here it is. Quite a step up from barracks, isn't it?"

The room resembled a nice motel room. Painted a warm cream, it hosted a one-person bed, its own bathroom, a desk with an ergonomic chair before it, an entertainment center with a large flat screen, a couch, and a large picture window with Venetian blinds and a view of the campus beyond.

"Yes. I approve."

He smiled and handed her a folder. "Here's the password for the room computer and other latest updates to your getting-acquainted packet. That, you'll find on your desk."

He nodded toward one side of the room. She glanced at it and saw it was a regular desk with pull-out drawers, a large flat screen, an ergonomic chair, and shelves on the wall above the desk.

"You can rent a mini-fridge from Campus Services but there's a cafeteria for all the residence halls. I've heard its chow is OK.

"Well, as the Sarge says, see you around, Corporal." With that he left the room to her.

Karen emptied most of her duffel and suitcase into the closet. Other items went into the bathroom with sink, toilet, and shower, and into her desk. She had only the minimum real items of clothing and toiletries and so on for anyone to see if they cared to inspect her quarters. Everything else was supplied by Suit, who could form virtual matter out of force fields in an instant and real matter in a few minutes by transmuting air into atoms and molecules and weaving them together.

She flopped back-down onto the bed and bounced experimentally. The mattress was firm but not hard.

Getting up she had Suit change to her usual sleeveless blue tee-shirt with a large red T-in-a-heart logo meaning "I love Taylor Swift" on its chest, dark red jeans, and blue tennis shoes. She lounged on the couch and skimmed the getting-acquainted packet. She got the remote from the entertainment center console and checked the channels: local network TV, lots of cable, and Channel 1 was a campus guide. The remote let her click through several campus web pages.

The computer accepted her student password and worked fine but she spent only a minute checking that, then went searching for bed clothes. That was at a small one-story service building centrally located to the residence halls. A cheerful young woman took her order and said the bedding would be included in one packet by Central Services at the day's end along with all the other orders turned in that day.

"If you're not home they'll swipe the door lock with a master card and put the clothing on your bed."

By now it was almost noon. She found the cafeteria and saw it was large and fairly full. She joined one of the two hot-food lines and had the white-coated and -hatted servers dish up a large hamburger lunch.

Along three walls were glass-fronted cold-food fridges. She selected an apple pie and a pint of milk, then a large soft drink at a fountain. At one of the four check-out lines she paid cash, too late remembering that she'd been issued a military-expense credit card.

The dining tables seated up to a dozen each. She saw one near the large picture windows which already had some military people. She approached an empty chair and was noisily invited to sit.

She set about doctoring her open-face hamburger with mustard and mayonnaise and folding it into a sandwich, meanwhile idly eavesdropping. There were too many conversations to make sense of unless she had Tiara gather them into separate audio channels she could swap between. It wasn't worth the bother.

"So, what's your language?" said a skinny black woman across from her. She was well into a salad.

"Joint Dari/Pashto." Karen bit into her burger and raised her eyebrows in enquiry.

The woman's companion, a muscular black man, said, "We're close: intermediate Dari. We're going to be at the new all-service HQ they've set up outside the capitol. We're civil-service. You?"

Karen swallowed, took a sip of her drink. "Marines. I'll be on a protective detail out in the boonies." Just where was not classified but she'd been warned that it was always possible that the college campus areas which military personnel frequented would be bugged.

"Where exactly?"

"I forget. Some long name that went right in one ear out the other."

They dismissed her from their minds and rejoined a conversation to one side of them. Advanced students tended to not have a lot in common with beginners. Ditto civil service versus military.

A beautiful woman, especially one as spectacular as Karen, rarely went long without company. She picked up two admirers quickly, one Navy and one Army. She good-naturedly watched the two make up lies about their military exploits, each more outrageous than the other. Soon half the table was listening in and laughing along with her.

She shrugged off company after she'd put her depleted tray in the garbage conveyer belt.

The rest of the day Karen spent wandering the campus, getting to know the area from on-the-ground first-hand experience. A couple of times she did go to some secluded location and go invisible and upward. From the air she got yet another perspective--or several of them from different heights and locations.

Karen also viewed the eastern hills above Hayward. There were some nice hiking and picnic areas and parks in the lower hills. There was also a large posh country club.

The bay to the west was lovely as the sun sank. Toward sunset clouds gathered out over the ocean beyond the bay and the coastal hills. They were a lovely mix of fiery colors.

Her stomach reminded her as the sun set that it was past dinner time. She flew to San Francisco, some 20 miles as the spaceship flies, had Suit change her outfit to expensive high-fashion leisure wear, and ate at a favorite restaurant just off Pier 9 near Telegraph Hill. There was a lovely view of the bay and the Berkeley Bridge as night fell and the lights came on.

Near 10:00 she returned to her dorm room. Sure enough there was a packet of bed clothing on her bed. She tore it open, had Suit transmute the paper wrapping to air, and dressed her bed with one of the changes of linen. The others she put away in the dresser.

She had Suit banish her leisure outfit to nothingness and nude used the bathroom (which she thought of as the head, to her amusement). Then Suit became pajamas and she fell quickly to sleep to the scent of fresh linen.

The next morning she woke at daybreak, used the bathroom, dressed for jogging, and ran four miles at a moderate speed. She ended the run back at her dorm, showered, and had Suit dress her.

The outfit was navy-colored slacks, light blue armless blouse under a thin navy-colored jacket, and low-heeled black loafers. She had Tiara put her bright hair up in a short pony tail, it having grown out enough to wear that style. Suit placed two modest golden pendants in her ear lobes. It also put a small watch on her wrist held on by a slender black band. All these items were real matter transmuted from air within just a few minutes.

The cafeteria had a nicely varied breakfast menu. She chose a large meal: eggs, ham strips, toast, fruit, orange juice, milk, and a small pot of coffee. She sat at a table with people mostly obviously military, one of a half dozen such tables. They filled perhaps a quarter of the indoor space.

A few of the people she'd met the day before but they sat too far away to do more than exchange waves. So she made the acquaintance of an older Latina Naval officer. The woman's attitude was first a bit stuffy, since Karen was a lowly enlisted person and a knuckle-dragging Marine at that.

Karen used Tiara to do a web search on the woman for enough info for Karen to find a shared interest. This was soccer, almost a religion in Argentina from which the officer's parents had emigrated. They'd had their children play soccer and the woman had become a fan. When she discovered Karen had played the game and helped win the top spots for her high school team her attitude thawed.

<>

The Dari class was in a small classroom because the students were only 17 in number. Their teacher was a slender mid-30s man with Arabic features. His black hair was short and sported a bald patch, his beard and mustache trimly shaved. He was cheery, an emotion Tiara revealed as genuine. He introduced himself then had each student do the same, asking only for their first names.

"Dari is the official language of Afghanistan. It is a version of

Persian, the language of Iran. It is written in an Arabic script. We'll be using an English alphabet version of the Arabic script to make it easier on you. I urge you to try to learn the Arabic way of writing as soon as you can. We offer a short class in that on Saturdays for the first month, but none of you are obligated to come to it."

He went from the general to the more specific, first introducing the consonants of the language. These were represented in the written language, but not the vowels. You inferred those from context.

"For some people this is the hardest part of the written language. For others, not so much."

Most of the consonants were close enough to English to be easy. A few were not. They practiced just the consonants for the first hour, had a fifteen minute break, and spent another hour on them and a few common words and phrases.

The third hour another teacher taught, an older stout Arab woman with a jolly disposition which hid (Karen could tell without Tiara's prompting) some deep sadness.

<>

After lunch that woman taught them Pashto.

"This is the language of the Pashtun people. It also was influenced by Persian. It uses a somewhat different Arabic script. There is less literacy in it than in Dari, so we'll not try to teach you that form. It would be too confusing."

She switched off in the mid-afternoon to a tall thin man of later years with a British accent. He had nearly blond brown hair and features which marked him as a Brit in Tiara's expert opinion. Later in the class he mentioned he'd become a naturalized American citizen more than thirty years ago, proving Tiara right.

By the end of the day everyone could ask a few simple questions and begin to decipher the answers. Karen was the quickest learner, but every student was linguistically talented and spoke more than one language besides English.

Karen was quickest partly because she had Tiara to help her, but she tried to rely on that device as little as possible. She rarely needed to use that crutch.

The rest of the week continued that pattern. On Saturday Karen was one of five who studied the Arabic squiggles used to represent consonants in Dari. She had a perfect memory when she wanted to memorize something and by the end of the day she'd mastered all the script introduced to her. On Sunday she studied the script on her own.

Despite her industry she did find time to socialize. This was nearly as important as the language she was learning. In the military even more than in corporate endeavors you had to work as part of a team. And knowing people who trusted you and vice versa even in the face of danger meant that years in the future when thrown together for some important job you were more quickly up to speed on accomplishing it.

By the end of the second week all 17 students knew each other and the three teachers at least superficially. Karen studied the backgrounds of all the students and teachers through Tiara. This included what caused the sorrow of the female teacher, *Safi* Wazir (whom the students privately called Mama rather than the honorific *Safi*). All her family but she and a very young grand-daughter had been murdered by Muslim extremists in Afghanistan. She'd only survived because she and the child had been half a mile away when the raiders struck.

Karen's very good imagination caused her to almost relive what the extremists had done to the family before and during killing them--including the children. It gave her nightmares. And a hatred of such men almost as deep as Mama's must be.

When the teacher found out (though not through Karen) that the Marine was going to her former country as a sniper she became friendlier than to the other students. Though she showed it very little; it would not do her students or her reputation any good to show favoritism to anyone.

In the third week the teachers began to teach the students some of the history and culture of Afghanistan and the surrounding areas. And on the third Friday of classes the students went to a party held for them at Mama Wazir's house.

This was a rambling one-story house in the nearby upscale neighborhood where many of the teachers and staff lived. It had a dark-brown shingle roof and faux-adobe exterior, the standard style for this neighborhood. It was also similar to the outsides of many rural Afghan homes, though this house was much bigger and more modern.

As Karen and several other students entered the house they saw that the living room was comfortable, large, and decorated with pictures on several walls. Two large red and brown Persian carpets covered much of the polished wooden floor. Several smaller white carpets with black checks insured little of the bare flooring was visible.

The seating was all very low, the long couch perhaps six inches off the floor. Large cushions replaced chairs. Tables were of matching heights, quite low.

Several shallow glass-fronted cabinets contained various curios. These included colorful vases, some beaten copper plates and plaques, and some small colorful wooden boxes.

Mama Wazir greeted each of them by name, Karen last because she was hindmost of the small group.

"I like your dress," the teacher said.

Karen said nothing but bowed her body slightly and her head more. Her outfit was that of an Afghan woman: brown ankle boots, loose green pants, a loose blue dress down past her knees, and a long-sleeved blouse a lighter blue shade. She also wore a large golden shawl which covered her hair and upper shoulders, wound to cover her lower head so that only her eyes showed.

She unwound the shawl. The end thus hung down to her waist. "It's Karen," someone said.

Mama Wazir asked everyone to be seated and showed the way by sitting on the long low red couch. Karen folded herself gracefully at the woman's knees on one of the cushions.

"Where did you get that?" said one of the other five women in language class.

"There's a shopping area in Hayward I heard about from someone who called it Middle-East West. It has restaurants and shops and grocery stores and lots more. I spent more than an hour at one dress shop. They suggested what to buy and how to put it on.

"Is it reasonably authentic, *Safi* Wazir?"

"Yes. There are differences, but every woman has small variations in style. To express her individuality."

Just then two more students arrived. They were let in by a stout man about Mama Wazir's age who came quickly in from the kitchen to answer the door chime. He greeted the two men with smiles.

The two men sat.

"Good," said their hostess. "Now that we're all here, let me tell what I'd like to do."

This was to become familiar with Afghan food. At its most basic it was similar to that of food everywhere. This included bread, meat, and drink. The bread was made from wheat and corn, the meat those of beef, sheep, and goat. The latter was especially popular in the mountains and other more rugged landscapes, goats being very hardy creatures. The most popular drink was water flavored with yogurt and mint, though Western-style drinks such as carbonated beverages were making large inroads in the Middle East.

Cereal dishes were also very popular, especially those of rice, but several other local cereals were also used. Several kinds of fruits were grown in Afghanistan, especially grapes, but other kinds as well, such as pomegranates.

To add variety to the staples Afghans added vinegar, several vegetables such as onions and chili peppers, and many spices.

Mama Wazir turned her head and called a man's name. From the kitchen area came the man they'd seen earlier opening the door for late comers.

"Class, this is my husband, Emal Shah Ahmadzai. Emal, my students."

The man made a slight bow with his body and spoke with a British accent.

"It's my pleasure to meet you. I hope to see more of you in our home. But for now I believe it's time to serve you snacks. I trust all of you have had dinner."

The students all made the abbreviated seated bow required of those meeting someone for the first time. Karen inclined her head as well. His eyes lingered on her face for a moment.

Mama's husband turned his head and nodded toward someone out of sight in the kitchen. From it appeared two teenagers of very young years, a girl and a boy. They were dressed as Mama and her husband were in traditional clothing. They smiled at the language students and walked to the side of the room opposite the long red couch. There they removed a long brown cloth from a waist-high table covering food.

"The *dastarkhan* buffet is an important part of Middle-Eastern custom." The teacher went on to describe the importance of putting out a large and varied menu for guests. Even the poorest people gained status by the excellence of the choices they made from their limited pantry and the presentation of the spread.

The next part of the ritual involved guests who approached the buffet, washed their hands in a bowl held by the young girl, and dried their hands on one of the towels offered by the young man.

Soon everyone had a snack, the male students first, a circumstance for which Mama Wazir apologized but explained that it was a custom about which they needed to know. They retired to the seats on the floor which they had claimed.

The conversation became general, guided by Mama to illustrate customary topics. By the end of the evening Karen and (she judged) the other students felt they had at least a beginning of understanding some of the nuances of the Afghan culture.

<>

The pattern was thus set for the rest of the course: language lessons interspersed with cultural lessons and events, some of them in the area Karen had heard called the Middle-East West. This included watching a dance show in the Hayward Cal State University campus auditorium. It was well attended by CSU Hayward students and faculty, not just the students from the language school.

Karen said Goodbye to Mama Wazir in her office on the campus during the woman's Open Door afternoon time.

She knocked on the door jamb. The woman looked up, smiled, and told her to come in.

Karen was in her dress camouflage traveling uniform. Loose but not very, it was perfectly tailored to her powerful and lovely body. She of course wore all the small assortment of ribbons to which she was entitled.

"I wanted to thank you for all you've done for us, *Safi* Wazir." She spoke in Pashto and the teacher answered her that way.

"It was my very great pleasure, Karen."

Karen looked at the woman through not only her eyes but the sensors of Tiara. The teacher meant it.

"You know where I'm going."

Mama nodded.

"You know what I have to do there."

"Yes."

"I will do it to the very best of my ability."

"There is no need to worry about how I feel. Not all Afghan men are evil. But there are some who are. Killing or capturing them is necessary. Sorely necessary."

"I must go. My schedule is tight. But if I come back this way..."

"I hope you will say Hello to me then."

Karen bowed lower than usual. The teacher responded the same way.

"Go with God, Karen Danburn."

Karen did an about face and left.

Part 4 - Ranger

Karen's orders gave her three days travel time to her next station and ten days leave time. She spent the weekend with her parents. Late Sunday evening she said Goodbye to them, walked into the back yard, and vanished.

Thirty minutes later she was over the Middle East, having passed over night-time Europe to get there. It was late Monday morning.

The Middle East from space was a tapestry of beige, brown, and yellow. Dropping lower down she could see details. The first were the mountains in the northern parts of Afghanistan and Pakistan. There was snow on their tops, forming labyrinths of white. Lower down still she could see oases and strips of green in valleys and other areas.

She'd studied maps of where she would work. It was a long stretch of road running east and west. It connected eastern Afghanistan with western Pakistan via the Khyber Pass.

Rather than go directly there, where she was not expected for 11 more days, she dropped down into the capitol of Afghanistan, Kabul, some 200 kilometers or 125 miles to the west.

Reasoning that she might be asked about her trip to her duty station she alighted at the international airport and floated through the terminal, invisible. The view was unimpressive. It was more like a small regional airport than an international one, but there were lots of travelers. Since the opening up of the country two years ago to foreign investment, especially of the trillions of dollars in mineral possibilities, it had become a magnet for foreigners.

This included the U. S. military, which the government had contracted to provide security and help the country develop its own military. Karen saw many U. S. soldiers in uniform traveling the airport.

She stopped at an automated bank terminal and drew several hundred dollars in local currency from her account in a variety of bills.

She followed some of the soldiers to the outside where they embarked on various buses and taxis. Then she swooped up and turned south toward the downtown area. As she flew she saw a tall mountain range to her right, westward, the higher elevations shrouded in snow. There was a smaller range to her left, eastward.

Kabul was in a mostly flat valley between the two ranges but it had hilly areas. Everywhere there were buildings, some of them which looked as they must have looked during the several thousand years of the country's history. Spotted here and there, randomly to her eyes, were more modern buildings.

There were various more built-up neighborhoods, with shops and restaurants and food stores. They teemed with people, men, women, and some children, crowding each other and the cars and buses which to her seemed randomly mixed with no sidewalk-street distinction. Most were in local dress. A few men were in suits and the women in modern dresses, though each woman wore a head scarf.

She noticed that women were always in groups or attended by men. She understood why when she alighted enshrouded in the blue tent-like burqa, her view filtered through a veil. After an hour of sight-seeing two men approached her. Without a word they grabbed her upper arms and marched her into an alley. There they began to feel her breasts and buttocks.

She tossed the veil up so that it lay atop her head. At the same time she had Suit project an image of someone else's face over hers. It had long tusks which stretched her mouth wide. Her eyes were red pools of light.

One man saw her face, screamed, and ran. The other gasped and turned to run. She grabbed the back of his shirt and pulled. He tore away from her so hard his shirt back split, leaving a strip of it in her hand. He raced desperately away from her.

She laughed until her sides hurt.

Recovering, she became herself dressed in desert camouflage uniform. A long sand-colored scarf covered her hair and her throat, ready to cover her nose and mouth in case of a sandstorm. Resting on her belly was a black submachine gun suspended by straps and on one thigh rode a large black pistol. On her other thigh was a long non-regulation knife. Despite her curves she appeared supremely dangerous. And of course was.

For the next couple of hours she wandered, sightseeing. But her walk was not idle. She was listening to the conversations around her, trying to absorb the nuances of speech. Most of it was in Dari, a bit in Pashto, and the rest in several other regional languages. She was also observing body language, as essential to communication as spoken language.

After a while she turned into an open-fronted restaurant and ordered, in Dari, three meat sandwiches somewhat like Mexican tacos and a large carton of grape juice.

While standing at a long waist-high counter attached to one wall she had lunch with a dozen other customers doing the same. She idly watched the people in the restaurant and passing by. A few looked back curiously, a few more with scowls, but most ignored her. Most of those, she could tell through Tiara, simply accepted her as much part of the background as anyone else.

Done, she still felt a bit hungry, so she ordered a stick of baklava wrapped in some cheap plastic, a bread dessert flavored with cinnamon and nuts and molasses. Tearing open one end she ambled out into the crowd, her fingers protected from the sticky treat by the peeled-back plastic.

Two more hours were enough for her. She disappeared and flew east along the road to the Khyber Pass. Midway there she drifted down to Jalalabad. This was to her a much smaller version of Kabul, however.

For a time she wandered invisible through the winter palace of a former king, then through Nangarhar University. There was little else there which interested her at this time so she soon lofted into the sky once again.

She skipped over the area where she would serve, the western side of the Khyber Pass and the pass itself, a deep cut in the Khyber mountains. She came down in Peshawar, about 40 kilometers or 25 miles inside Pakistan.

Wandering invisible, she found the city very interesting. There were more languages being spoken than in Afghanistan, and there were several colleges and universities. There was an airport and a train station connecting the city to the rest of Pakistan.

Dusk was beginning to bathe the land. She'd done enough for today. She hopped a few hundred miles toward the east and south to New Delhi, India. This was one of the richest countries in the British Empire and the city one of the richest and most modern cities in that country. It was early evening there.

She had no problems finding a room in a four-star hotel. She'd assumed her natural appearance and was dressed in a dark blue business suit with a frilly-collared white satin blouse and low-heeled dark blue dress shoes. She had no luggage but the hotel had no problem with her Platinum credit card.

Tuesday she wandered the area where she would work, the Khyber Pass and the area a few dozen miles west in Afghanistan. Her headquarters would be in an Army base, Post 373. This was small prefabricated town recently set up a couple of miles west of the small village named Baha Tor near the mouth of the pass. The meandering Afghan-Pakistan highway, following a narrow tributary of the Kabul River which created a long green valley, passed to the north of the post then through the pass.

All around the post for a quarter mile the low tough vegetation had been bulldozed bare. It had been surrounded by a twelve-foot high steel mesh fence topped with razor wire. The two bulldozers which had done it still rested inside the fence.

She invisibly scouted the post and got to know by sight some of the hundred or so troops who manned it. Then she scouted Baha Tor closer to the Pass. It was shabby and had little more than a mosque, general store, a small three-story hospital, some other shops, and two gasoline filling stations at each end of the village.

She also scouted the Khyber Pass. This was a narrow, winding valley 50-plus kilometers or 30-plus miles long. The sides of the pass were very close and steep at some points. At others it widened out to one or even two miles wide. The road at some places had hairpin turns. A tributary of the Kabul River passed through the pass, now downsized to a stream which occasionally disappeared underground. At several wider spots the stream reappeared and small villages were strung on both sides of it.

Lunch was a large hamburger platter and a soft drink created from air by Suit. She ate sitting on a boulder atop one of the higher elevations above one of the greenest parts of the pass. Done, Suit transmuted the plate and drink can back to air.

Dinner was in Paris, 3500 miles to the west. It was two and a half time zones earlier than the pass. Then she found a room at a three star hotel with a view of the Eiffel Tower, a lovely sight as night fell and the lights on the tower came on.

<>

So far Karen had been mostly learning the context of where she'd be stationed. She'd spent most of that time in the air from a mile up to a few feet. Wednesday after a buffet breakfast at her French hotel she landed a few miles away from the U. S. military post. She exited Pegasus, who returned to his normal brick-of-soap shape and his usual position a few feet above her and invisible. She began to walk in a tightening spiral around the post.

She felt this to be necessary. These were the areas from which the bandits and haters of foreigners would launch attacks on the post and other nearby areas. And she needed to know more about the area than her eyes and the "gravity radar" of Tiara could tell her. She needed to know the many subtle sounds and scents of the deep brushy areas in which the attackers would hide.

<>

She spent three days at this, taking her time, resting when she needed to. With her enormous physical reserves this was not often.

She stayed visible but wore traditional male dress: a loose long-sleeved shirt, loose pants, a long vest, and a long scarf wound around her head and over her nose and mouth and neck.

From a distance she would appear a male, but since her clothing was much the same color as the mostly head-high vegetation even a person close up would have a hard time even seeing her as long as she stood very still.

Karen ate food from air gathered by Suit and transmuted to copies of her favorite foods. These were identical down to the sub-atomic level as natural food and thus were equally nourishing. At night she slept hidden amidst the brush on what appeared to be leaves but was actually comfortable force fields mimicking a bed. For entertainment when she wanted it she had the resources of all the cable and internet networks in the world, visible whenever she closed her eyes.

<>

Monday morning she visited Jalalabad and flew till she found just what she wanted: a vehicle sales lot. There she had Pegasus study one of the small pickup trucks they used till he could duplicate it. Then she landed halfway between the city and her soon-to-be home.

It was a stretch of east-west highway with no one within miles of it. Along this stretch of highway there was a long line of trees on both sides and she was in shade. To the north the land was green, for the nearby Kabul River stretched far to the east and west. To the south the land was beige and brown and dead.

It took Pegasus a half hour to duplicate one of the battered but mechanically well-kept trucks. The rest of the truck was gaily decorated in the Afghan fashion, with patches of color and writing in Dari and English scripts. The truck bed was dusty and held a few brown leaves, the cab smelled of tobacco and held the remnants of pizza-like food and juice containers.

Satisfied that it met her requirements, Karen had Suit garb her in a male's costume, one stained here and there with what could equally have been oil or spilled drinks but not smelling like either. Then she retrieved her duffel and small suitcase from Pegasus who had been carrying it dissolved but in its memory all this time and placed it in the small luggage space just behind the truck seats.

She got in and merrily began driving east. She turned on the radio. Like everything else in the truck it was functional because it was an exact duplicate of the original down to below the atomic level.

Accompanied by loud wailing Arabic music Karen rolled to meet her soon-to-be companions. Just past mid-morning in mid-April the weather was chilly and cloudy, but the clouds were breaking up and blue was overtaking the grey.

She passed a bus which might have started as a yellow school bus but now was covered with so many rainbow-colored patches and stripes and text that she could not tell what its former color had been. A little boy and girl waved at her out of one window. She tooted her horn.

A couple of white vans passed her going in the opposite direction.

Then she came to a toll gate. A bored man sitting on a high chair in a booth watched as she tossed coins into a toll collection machine.

She was about a half hour from her new duty station. Through Tiara she sent a text message to the captain who commanded it.

REPRTNG EARLY 2 DUTY N ABT 30 MIN DANBURN USMC

It was 35 minutes later when she saw off to the right up ahead Guard Post 373. It was not impressive: several dozen prefabricated metal buildings of several sizes plus a few low blocky concrete buildings. It was surrounded by a low wall of stones. Further out was a twelve-foot high fence made of very tough chain-links. Rolls of razor wire topped the fence.

She slowed her vehicle and soon came to a big sign. In white on olive green it said UNITED STATES ARMY GUARD POST 373.

She turned right onto a two-lane concrete road. It ran a quarter of a mile to a guard shack where two soldiers were on duty. Slowing to a stop she saw they were in full battle gear over their camouflage clothing. This was helmet with embedded communicator, body armor, and web belt from which hung a canteen, pistol, first aid kit, and several smaller pieces of equipment. Each held an M5 carbine across their bellies, trigger fingers near but not in the trigger guard.

She looked up at the closest of the men. He was staring at her. The other was scanning the countryside and the several monitors of infrared and video cameras and motion sensors hidden in the ground outside the chain-link fence. She approved.

"What is your business?" he said in crude but intelligible Dari.

She replied in English: "Lance Corporal Karen Danburn reporting for duty, Corporal...Hathaway. I texted the Captain I was coming in early about a half hour ago."

"I'll phone him."

He raised his voice to speak loudly enough to alert a tiny voice-activated microphone held beside his mouth by a narrow stem.

"Captain, Corporal Danburn is at the gate."

Through Tiara Karen heard: *"I see a truck. That her?"*

"Yes, Sir."

"Check her papers. If they look good have her park the truck by the HQ."

Karen was holding her orders and ID in the hand not on the steering wheel. She had them ready at the vehicle window when the guard asked for them.

He took them and examined them carefully. Meanwhile the other guard switched his gaze from the distance to her. Again she approved privately. For all he knew the papers were a diversion and she'd next lift a hand with a weapon in it.

She nodded at him. His expression did not change but through Tiara she sensed more interest than just duty. She was sure that was because he could see her face, very beautiful despite the lack of makeup. It was a reaction she'd come to expect long ago.

The paper orders and her picture ID badge checked out. The soldier gave them back to her and ordered her to park near the command building. He pointed it out. As she already knew, it was the biggest and most central of them.

She covered the 100 feet or so distance over a continuation of the outside roadway. Looking about she saw what she remembered from her earlier visit: various dirt paths and blocks of bare earth marked out with pegs surrounding existing concrete paths and buildings. Post 373 was still in the early stages of construction.

She entered the large concrete building by way of a heavy metal door set in a steel door frame. Inside, the building was partitioned into a wide front room and several smaller rooms behind it.

Seated at a desk directly in front of her was an Army master sergeant, Albert Taylor. He was First Sergeant of the company and so was responsible for overseeing all the administrative jobs of the company. He was a heavy-set but muscular man with a strong nose and chin and short-cropped grey hair. The man's eyes measured her carefully.

Standing beside the sergeant was a trim soldier with captain's gold bars on each desert camo uniform lapel. He was Matthew Giatelli, the commander of the company of 146 troops. He had an Italian's dark good looks and he was very bright, one of the youngest Army captains ever promoted to that rank since the Global War of the 30s.

For that matter, the sergeant was also very bright. She knew because she had studied both of their personnel files and researched their pasts via Tiara. As she'd done to everyone else in the company.

Karen marched up to the captain, braced, and saluted.

"Lance Corporal Karen Danburn reporting for duty, sir."

He returned her salute and said, "At ease, Corporal. Please have a seat."

He gestured at one of three straight-backed chairs in front of the sergeant's desk. She obeyed and sat in the one nearest the two men, moving with a dancer's grace and sitting relaxed but alertly upright.

The sergeant sat back in his chair and placed his two hands tented together in front of his mouth. The captain remained standing as he spoke.

"We didn't expect you till later in the week."

"Friday," the sergeant added.

"I spent some time with my parents. But they both work during the day. All my friends from school have scattered. So I came early to see if I could do some good."

"Why are you dressed this way? And driving that truck?"

"My job is recon. When I got in I bought some used clothes and a used truck and did some traveling, stopping here and there to soak up the atmosphere and improve my language skills and hear what's going on."

"Traveling? Where specifically, Corporal?"

"I came by here and spent a day memorizing the land for a few miles out. Then I went into the pass as far as the Pakistani border. Then I turned around and came back. On the way there and back I also reconnoitered all the places in the pass where an ambush might take place."

The sergeant stirred in his seat. His captain looked at him and the sergeant spoke.

"Did it occur to you that a woman alone in the Middle East is not safe?"

"I'm very able to ensure I stay safe." Her voice was utterly neutral and non-confrontational. But she saw the small signs that indicated he was angered by her response.

The captain was amused. "Nevertheless, while you are here you will not place yourself in any more jeopardy than can be helped."

"Aye, aye, sir. But respectfully I must remind you that I am an independent command whose job is to 'assist you in whatever way you and I mutually decide is in the Army's best interests.'"

The sergeant did not like that at all. And for the first time the captain was unhappy too.

But they had to accept it. The services had always jealously guarded their autonomy, to the point where in a war sometimes it almost seemed as if they warred against each other. Karen had taken advantage of that and through Tiara changed her original orders to give her complete freedom in what she did here.

Not that she would make waves unless absolutely necessary. Still, she was determined to use her special abilities to the fullest extent that she could as long as that did not reveal what they were.

The captain calmed himself. "We'll have to discuss that matter further. But for now I'd like you to get settled in. I'm assigning you to the company intelligence squad, starting tomorrow. From now on I want to see you in the proper uniform for your duties."

Karen stood. Tiara had just told her that the sergeant had sent a message somewhere via his computer console, and the captain's statement had told her why.

He held out his hand to shake. "Welcome aboard, corporal. Dismissed."

"Thank you, Sir." She shook his hand and stepped back, braced, and saluted. He returned it and retired to his office, a small cubbyhole behind the sergeant.

From another cubbyhole behind the sergeant a short sandy-haired corporal came. He glanced at Karen then looked at the sergeant.

"Dennison, take Corporal Danburn to Barracks 21. She'll be bunked there. On the way go by the supply room and pick up the usual bedding. Have her get settled in. Then go to Lieutenant Wang and let him know his S2 assistant has arrived. Then come back here."

He returned his attention to his computer console, underlining his annoyance with her by ignoring her.

"Thank you, Sergeant. I look forward to working with you in the future." She was mildly amused but kept her face solemn.

He glanced at her and then back at the screen in front of him.

The corporal nodded at her and ushered her out the door, probably trying to get a good look at her ass. If so, he was disappointed. She'd picked Afghan men's clothes which were so loose they hid her sex quite well.

"What did you do to tick off the Sarge, Danburn?"

"I'm a Marine and an independent command. I had to remind him and the captain of that."

"Wow. Try to stay on his good side. He's tough."

"I believe it."

They were now at a building with the sign SUPPLIES mounted over the entrance. He entered the door then held it for her. She followed him.

"Hey, Georges. This is that Marine. We need some bedding."

Corporal Andrew Georges was sitting behind a counter, frowning industriously at a computer screen. Tiara let her know he was watching a set of bikini-clad images of Olympic athletes rather than some military data.

The sturdy pug-nosed soldier tapped a button to hide what he was "studying" and looked up. His surliness vanished when he saw Dennison's companion. Karen's sex was well hidden, but her face wasn't. And despite her attire just enough of her shape showed through her clothing to reveal her sex.

"Yeah, sure. Are you Danburn?"

Karen nodded.

"Welcome to Post 373. Hold a sec, I'll get your bed clothes."

He got up from his chair and disappeared into a back room. Moments later he reappeared with a stack of blankets, sheets, and so on. He hefted it onto the counter top, took up an info slate from his desk, and placed it beside the clothing, atop which he also placed a towel set.

"Sign here," he said, pointing at a slot on the form displayed on the slate.

She did so, saying Thanks.

Karen also said, "Do you know if my sniper rifle arrived? And its ammo?"

"Pretty sure I saw them come in and go to the armory. Let me check."

A quick search of the company's secure database (which Karen monitored via Tiara) revealed that they were here. Karen thanked the corporal and she and her escort left.

Barracks 21 was big enough to house four troops with space left over for a small lounge. The couch in the lounge was occupied by another corporal lying lengthwise in it watching a movie on an info slate. He was listening via ear-buds. Dennison quietly said that was a requirement as he led her to one of the four doors behind the lounge.

"With four people on different work schedules you have to have rules so everyone gets enough sleep. So read the rules posted inside your room sometime soon."

Karen thanked him for his help and walked with him back to the HQ. There she parked her truck in the designated parking lot to one side of the building. She then retrieved her duffel and suitcase. She soon had them unpacked and their contents hung in the narrow open area which acted as a closet. She made the bunk with the bedding she'd left on its foot, then sat on it and looked at her room.

It was as minimal as you could get, the only other furniture a folding chair and a desk just big enough to hold a laptop computer or an info slate. She had neither, having Tiara to do all the necessary functions.

It included a tiny bathroom with a standup shower, barely large enough to wash herself without her elbows bumping the walls. A large sign beside its entrance told her water was metered and warned her not to use more than her daily allowance. If she did the water would be cut off till after midnight.

As she sat there the man who'd been lying on the couch outside in the lounge leaned on the open aluminum framework which held the door to her room.

"Hey. I'm Lopez. You're the sniper?"

"Yeah. I'm Karen."

"Anibal." He pronounced it ah-nee-BOL. "Hope you're good. I always go to sleep wondering if I'll never wake up. Or wake up screaming from being half blown away by a mortar."

"Sleep soundly tonight. I'll be patrolling all night starting about midnight. Smart attackers will wait till they think most of us are asleep."

"I just hope we don't have any dumb attackers. And they don't get you."

"I'm better than you can possibly imagine, Anibal. Now, if you don't mind, I'm going to draw an M5 from Armory and some ammo for tonight, then take a nap before chow. Maybe I'll see you there."

"Count on it."

<>

She did see him at chow, along with Georges and Dennison, both of whom made sure they sat with her.

At the end the meal she was intercepted just outside of the mess building after dropping off her tray and plates, glasses, and utensils at the mess's garbage-intake area. Not that she left more than a smudge of garbage; it was her policy to clean her plate. Her extra-efficient body needed a lot of food.

"Corporal Danburn, I'm Lieutenant Wang. Don't salute. We like to keep the bad guys from knowing the command structure. They probably know already, but it's good to keep up the habit of security."

She knew who he was: head of the intelligence squad to which she'd been assigned. She also knew who were the staff sergeant and two corporals who manned it.

"Yes, sir."

"Come on with me. I'd like to have a short chat."

"Aye, aye, sir."

They walked what amounted to two city blocks to a medium-sized building off to one side of the company HQ. Wang talked as they walked. He moved very easily despite his bulk. This was partly because he had mastered several of the martial arts of which movies and books decreed every Chinese in the world was expert.

"I heard that you got in early, but not before spending a few days doing recon from Kabul up through mid-Pass. True? Gossip?"

"True, sir. I spent three whole days in this area. I especially wanted to see how well your night guards did their job. I'm happy to report they did it well."

"But they didn't detect you."

"I'm a lot better than the irregulars you have around here."

"How do you know that?"

"Because they've been sneaking around out there. I shadowed three different groups. None of whom got anywhere near enough to do any surveillance of the company."

"I also got a somewhat annoyed report from the First that you are an insubordinate bitch who would be doing extra duty if you weren't a fucking jarhead."

"Quite understandable. Nobody likes the fact that each service guards its autonomy too well. Except, of course, for their own service. I regretfully had to remind the Captain and the Sergeant that mine is an independent command."

They arrived at the Intelligence building just then. The lieutenant went inside and held the door for Karen before closing it behind her.

The building held only a staff sergeant. The two corporals who'd be her work mates were off duty or had duty elsewhere.

Karen gave the building a quick visual once over. It was as she'd discovered a few nights ago when she'd dropped down invisible into the midst of the camp and probed everything with her gravity radar. It had several rooms.

The one where she'd work held several desks with straight-backed chairs. Three of the desks had ergonomic chairs, the ones in front of the computer consoles which would be occupied for long stretches of time.

There was a bank of communications and computer equipment along one wall, alight with several green lights and a couple of yellow ones, one of which was blinking. There were also several filing cabinets with padlocks on them.

The sergeant was sitting back in one of the ergo chairs with his feet up on the desk which supported a computer screen. He was idly watching a scrolling list of numbers and images.

He swung his feet off the desk and stood up. He was a medium-height black man with an athletic body.

"Matlock, this is Lance Corporal Danburn. Danburn, this is the real brains of this outfit--"

She said, "Staff Sergeant Tafari Matlock. I know. A pleasure, Sergeant."

Wang chuckled. "I see we've got another brain in our little legion of spies."

"I made up dossiers on everyone in the post before I came. Amazing how much information is public."

The sergeant shook her hand and indicated a couple of chairs near his. Both were ergo chairs.

Karen waited for Wang to sit before sitting herself. The sergeant spoke to him.

"Anyone with that kind of computer savvy is better off on the net than out getting her ass shot off by some ragheads."

"No," said Karen. "I'm better off shooting the asses off the ragheads. Whom I should remind the sergeant are children of God just like the rest of us and entitled to more respectful terms than raghead for the sorry assholes." Her expression was dead pan.

Wang laughed out loud. Matlock suppressed a smile.

"I have to concur. You've read her record."

"Yeah. I just wish our two wizards were as sharp. Well, Wilson is. But Schultz isn't yet up to speed."

"He will be.

"Now, Karen has just told me she was surveilling some insurgents during the last three days before reporting in here."

Matlock examined her curiously.

"I tracked three groups to their base camps. Can I borrow a computer?"

Wang waved at the console in front of Karen. She struck the keyboard to wake it up. Matlock leaned over and typed in a userid and password, holding up a hand to keep her from pressing Enter.

"Those are yours. Memorize them, then go."

She pretended to, though she knew from Tiara what they were. Then she quickly brought up a map of the area and used a forefinger on the touch-sensitive screen to draw a circle around three areas. One was to the east in the mountains just inside the Khyber Pass. One was to the west toward Kabul, the other to the north a dozen miles past the east-west highway.

Wang and Matlock looked at the map. Wang mused and the NCO agreed that the three did not seem to be working together.

Karen interrupted them. "Gentlemen, I need to go take a nap. Unless you can come up with a good reason, at midnight I'm going to spend the night making sure the base is safe. Would you give orders to the gate guards to let me out?"

The sergeant looked at the lieutenant, who nodded. The man then typed a few things on his computer as his boss continued speaking.

"I'd like to see you at 08 hundred. But only if you do not need to get some sleep. I'd like you fully alert for a few hours so I can get you up to speed on things."

"No sweat, Sir. May I be dismissed?"

He waved at her and returned to talking with his sergeant.

<>

Karen did get some sleep, waking just before midnight. She visited the bathroom then used Tiara to be sure no one saw her walk out of her quarters. Instants later she was a mile up inside Pegasus.

Using Tiara's gravity radar she carefully studied the area around the post out to about five miles distance. There were no fanatical

Moslems in the vegetation down below determined to wipe out those cursed foreigners who were determined to bring riches and education and immorality to their country.

That done, she dropped back down to her building. There she used Suit to dress herself in a standard tan and grey camouflage uniform properly sized to her. She added over it a matching harness. It had two horizontal straps, one just under her breasts and one at waist height. Vertical straps over her shoulders connected the two together. She had Suit add two flat ammunition packs which hung from the waist strap on each side of her.

On the front of the waist strap were two large Velcro patches. She pressed the M5 carbine against them. Matching patches on the weapon attached it to her very securely, yet would allow her to jerk the weapon loose.

She also had Suit create a sword stick for her about two feet long. Concealed inside it was what would look very like a straight Samurai sword when drawn. She swung it by its hilt up over one shoulder and down. The stick hit a vertical strap and stuck to the strap as if by invisible Velcro. There was just enough of its handle sticking up behind her ear that she could quickly draw it.

She practiced drawing the sword. It had a front edge of a composite material which would cut steel and a back edge which was blunt.

She left her building and walked to the security "shack" of the base. Contrary to its nickname, it was the size of a house with long sides and a mildly pitched roof, armored. Included in its several rooms was an armory and a control room with video monitors which let the two or more soldiers inside it monitor the base and its surroundings with video and infrared cameras and dozens of motion sensors in and around the base.

She "rang" the doorbell and looked at a video camera positioned above it. In just a few seconds one of the security troops inside the control room recognized her and buzzed her inside.

She pushed the door open when its solenoid-operated lock released it and was inside a reception area. It was empty and dimly lit, it being so late. Just beyond it was a hall, also dimly lit. Inside the hall a uniformed soldier motioned her to join her in the control room off to one side of the hall.

Karen did so, the sturdy blond woman moving aside and letting the door to the room slam shut behind them.

Karen saw the large flat-screen monitors she expected mounted on a wall to her left. Several feet before them was a couple of long tables with several computer monitors and keyboards connected by wireless to hidden computers. Several ergonomic chairs were positioned so that their occupiers could see the monitors and use the computers. Against the wall to her right, the back of the room, were a dozen or so chairs.

Karen turned her attention to the woman of (she knew) 29 years and spoke to her and a tall black private sitting at one of the computer screens.

"Corporal Cynthia Armstrong, I believe. And Private First Class Roland Jones? I'm Lance Corporal Danburn, just reported in today."

The blond woman said, "Yeah. You're that scout/sniper, right? We heard you'd got in."

"Would you check your orders? There should be a note that I'm to go out right about now and do recon."

"Don't need to. I remember it. When will you be back?"

"I'm going to stay out till just before sunup."

The tall black private had glanced at her curiously, then continued scanning the monitors. Without turning his head toward her he said, "What's that on your back, Corporal?"

"It's sort of a high-tech version of a samurai sword. It comes in handy when I want to get up close and personal."

The corporal said, "I thought you snipers stood off a thousand yards."

"If the ground lets us, yeah. But in this kind of terrain a knife is sometimes better than a rifle or carbine. Especially at night."

"OK, Danburn. Go out and do your stuff. Come back safe, OK?"

Karen nodded and left the room and the house. Several minutes later she approached the front gate to the base. It opened slowly outward. When it was wide enough Karen slipped through it and began to jog toward the closest edge of the low brush. When she was shielded from the base sensors by the vegetation she vanished.

<>

Karen flew to the closest of the three insurgent bases, dropped down into its midst, and studied the small group. All of the men were asleep. For weapons they had rifles and other small arms and a kind of short sword or long knife. They certainly were not about to launch an attack on the base. If they did, the alert, able, and well-trained and well-supplied base would wipe them out.

Karen was ready to kill them and anyone else who would kill her mates. But so far there was no hard evidence this group ever would act on that desire. For all she knew they would play soldier for a few days or weeks or months and then go home to plant and harvest and otherwise live out their lives.

This was unlikely. But she thought she'd have plenty of warning if they did decide to act on their desires. Then she would kill them as mercilessly and as mercifully as she could.

The second nearest camp was awake and making preparations for the long march and then long sneak to near the base to set up an attack. This group was larger and seemed better organized than the first group. They also had more and better ammunition. This included heavy machine guns and RPGs: rocket propelled grenades.

Staying a few dozen feet above them, invisible, she drifted along with them for a mile or so. They moved efficiently through the brush, taking paths of least resistance amongst the less dense foliage. The crescent moon to their side and the stars lighted the way to dark-adapted eyes but their speed suggested they'd come this way before.

She was sure they planned to attack the base. She thought over the several options she had and decided on one which was likely to cause the least loss of life among them. One which just might discourage them from ever again thinking of attacking foreigners.

She lifted up to better see the undulating terrain below with her gravity radar. It showed the land and the vegetation on it as if by the light of several full moons.

She found what she was looking for: a small clearing containing sparser grass and almost no bushes. One through which the attackers were bound to pass.

She floated down to a few feet above the earth, exited Pegasus, and turned off her invisibility. She gave Suit a command which garbed her body in a voluminous black burqa which ended not in a squared-off hem but in jagged trailing "feet" visibly not touching the earth. Over her eyes she had Suit ready to place glowing red circles like the eyes of Arabic and Persian genie, or JNN in Arabic script. In each hand she held long swords whose blades glowed faintly red.

She waited. Gravity radar told her the attackers were coming toward her and how fast.

The first of the men who came into the little open area got a dozen or more feet inside it before noticing the still black blot in the air before them. They slowed, then stopped and exclaimed to each other in Pashto.

Karen waited until the laggards bunched up around the leaders of the party. Then she turned on the red "eyes" and spoke through a sort of force field megaphone which turned her Dari into a wailing cry.

THE FOREIGNERS ARE UNDER MY PROTECTION. GO BACK OR YOU WILL ENTER HELL.

There was stunned silence, then whispers, then louder voices. Then they were shouted down by a man in the lead.

"This is a trick! It is a machine! Shoot it!"

He set an example by firing an automatic rifle at the apparition. It had no visible effect. Nor any other kind. Suit absorbed the momentum of each bullet and turned the bullet to air.

Other men began to fire. The only effect was that the luminous swords began to glow more brightly as if made of dying embers being blown back to life. Then as if made of flame. Growing ever brighter.

LEAVE NOW OR ENTER HELL!

By now the demon swords were turning bright blue. And ever brighter.

The leader ran at the demon and struck it with his emptied automatic rifle. It bounced with a clank. The demon's nearest sword did not. It swept through the body of the man and he fell in two pieces to the dirt.

More men ran at the demon. Its swords clove heads and bodies and steel. More men ran away, dropping their weapons, screaming and calling upon Allah. Soon there were only dead men in the clearing.

Karen gave a long shuddering breath. Killing was a horrible act. And this was her first time.

Then she swooped up and followed the fleeing men. Some of them returned to their base. More of them fled further.

She waited at the base for an hour until she was sure the survivors planned nothing more. Then she visited the third camp up in the mountain pass, still feeling a little sick. Happily all those in it were asleep.

She made a last lap around the post, returned to her building, and had Tiara bring sleep to her. She dreamed once of the murder she'd committed but then used Tiara to interrupt any further distressing dreams.

<>

At forty minutes till 08:00 she awoke, the events of the night before only slightly dimmed. She pulled herself out of bed and made a quick toilette in her tiny head. She called a force-field duty camo uniform to her body and headed to the base cafeteria.

Night security guards Corporal Armstrong and Private Jones were there and waved her over to their table. They'd gotten off at 07:00. Shortly they were joined by Georges and Dennison, who were at another table.

The Corporal said, "How did it go last night, Danburn?"

Karen put up a "Wait one" finger while she chewed and swallowed a mouthful of scrambled-eggs-and-bacon and a drink of orange juice.

"At about 03:30 I met a group heading to attack us. They had machine guns and RPGs as well as other stuff. I warned them off and when they attacked me I killed nine of them. That scared the rest off. I followed them and spent an hour making sure they didn't regroup and retry. Then I checked out the other two groups and came home."

Private Jones said, "Other two groups?" at the same time Armstrong said, "You WARNED them off?!"

"Yeah," she said to Armstrong. "I used some special effects to make them think I was one of their demons. But they weren't fooled. At least until I killed a few of them."

She turned to Jones. "Before I reported in I did a couple of days recon and found three groups who were sneaking around in the area. I tracked them to their bases and reported on them to Lieutenant Wang and Sergeant Matlock yesterday."

Georges said, "Damn, Karen. You've been busy!"

Corporal Armstrong said, "I can't believe you tried to warn them off. Usually you just kill as many as you can."

Karen had thought about what she was going to say when people asked her this. Especially the captain commanding the base. Here was a chance to practice her reply on someone of low rank.

"My job is to protect us from attacks. Not to just kill attackers. Prevention is cheaper than protection. If we can make them think a supernatural agency is protecting us, they'll more likely to be discouraged. I mean, they know how to fight bullets. But not demons."

The Corporal made a face. Karen couldn't tell if it was rueful agreement or resignation in the face of foolishness. But the other three looked thoughtful. Dennison even nodded his head slightly as if in some agreement.

<>

Karen entered the intelligence building a minute or two before the hour. Lieutenant Wang and Sergeant Matlock had just arrived. They were standing in front of a large electronic white board and drinking coffee. They were discussing complicated diagrams displayed on the white board.

There were also two corporals sitting at computer consoles with coffee mugs beside their keyboards: Janice Wilson and Abraham Schultz. The woman was slender, black-haired and black-eyed and looked Italian. Her hair was short and chic as well as functional. Schultz was a large blond with a slightly ruddy complexion. He was muscular and his balding hair cut almost invisibly short.

At Karen's entrance everyone looked at her. She was clad in her regular duty outfit of tailored but not tight desert camouflage and wore the short-billed cloth cap designated as the proper "cover." Her shining blond hair peeped out around the cap. To this she had added the harness she'd worn the night before with the same set of weapons, though the M5's stock was collapsed so that it appeared to be a machine pistol.

She flowed into the room like some prowling lioness and came to a halt near the lieutenant but where she could address all of them. Still, yet seeming poised to move, she waited for the lieutenant to speak, who glanced at her weapons but did not question her right to carry them.

"Glad to see you, Corporal Danburn. You look ready to work despite spending a good deal walking around in the dark last night.

Let's get you up to speed."

He introduced her to the two Army corporals. They stood and she shook hands with them.

"I'm glad to meet you, Corporal Wilson, Corporal Schultz. But Sir, before we go much further, I think I should be debriefed first about my actions last night."

"It sounds like you have something significant to report."

"Yes, Sir."

"Very well. We'll take advantage of that and teach you the standard procedure for intel debriefs by actually running you through it. This is something you'll need to do in your role as an intel operator."

He began to walk out of the room.

The sergeant said, "Wilson, Schultz, join us. It can't hurt to review the process. And, everybody, if you need to, get a drink or refresh it."

Wang led the way through a narrow hall. On the way they passed a kitchenette area with a refrigerator and a narrow waist-high table holding a microwave and heated-drink console where you could fashion a mug of coffee, tea, or hot chocolate. There were also paper plates, plastic dinner ware, napkins, and other supplies. Plus a narrow waist-high sink with hot and cold faucets.

The others refreshed their drinks. Karen took a foam coffee cup and made herself a cup of hot chocolate from hot water and a tear-open packet of dry mix. She didn't especially want it but thought it would help build camaraderie.

The debriefing was in a conference room with a table in its middle which would seat a couple of dozen people. Chairs lined the walls and everyone selected one and pulled it up to the table. Wang sat at the head which had an info slate lying in front of him. He waved Karen to a seat to his left. Sergeant Matlock sat at his right side and the two corporals sat beside the sergeant and opposite Karen.

The Lieutenant said, "Every mission has a prebrief before and a debrief after. They can be very simple or very complex."

He was obviously giving a lecture but spoke so informally that it seemed more like a conversation.

He tapped at the info slate to wake it up and give it a command. Opposite him on a wall a large flat screen woke to life. It showed a vertical diagram of oval boxes with brief notations inside them. An arrow led downward from each oval to the oval below. A few arrows also came out the sides of the ovals and looped upward or downward past some ovals to end in other ovals.

"This is a flow chart which acts as a checklist for the debrief. There's a nearly identical checklist for prebriefs. Naturally, since the two cover the same territory, before and after the mission."

He then went through the chart, prompting her at each stage. The first was what her purpose was.

"My job was to find any hostiles, find out what they were doing and going to do, and prevent any attacks."

And what sensors and effectors went on the mission? The first included people and machines, as did the second.

Karen pointed to herself.

"List them."

"My eyes and ears and so on for sensors." And the super-advanced gravity radar of Tiara and Pegasus.

"No night-vision goggles or hearing aids?"

"No. My own built-in sensors were adequate."

The Sergeant said, "We have quite good equipment for that sort of thing in the armory. You might consider checking them out." His tone was so mild it was clearly a rebuke.

"Aye, aye." *I hear and obey*, that meant. But since her command was independent of the Army it meant she was only obligated to *consider* his suggestion.

"And what were your effectors?"

She stated it was her hands and feet and brains, and her clothing and weapons. But did not mention her super-advanced equipment.

Corporal Wilson asked about the sword-stick she carried on her back. Karen drew the sword and showed it briefly, saying that it would cut through steel. Then she slid it back into its sheath without looking at the sheath or sword and without using her fingers to mate the blade with the sheath opening.

Corporal Schultz said, "Aren't you afraid you'll stab yourself in the back doing that?"

"Two reasons. Practice. And weapon design. The opening to the sheath flares. The tip of the blade is a blunt triangle which eases the blade into the opening. And the back of the blade is dull. I actually rest it on my shoulder to help locate the sheath, but that's so brief watchers don't notice."

A map of the base and the surrounding territory flicked onto the screen. It showed the three enemy bases Karen had discovered among other features. Wang explained them to the two corporals.

"Wow," said Schultz. "The Sarge said you'd done some recon before you checked in. This is impressive."

"Thank you, Corporal."

Lieutenant Wang led her through the paths she'd taken, starting at midnight, and added them via dotted lines on the map. He also added time notations at certain points.

"Now we come to my encounter with a group of hostiles."

She described the time and place of that encounter and the approximate numbers and weapons they carried.

Wang said, "Procedure is to double-check all such numbers in several ways. Often we see over and under estimations."

"Some of this can be checked when a squad goes out to where I confronted the hostiles."

Everyone looked at her. Wang told her to explain, in detail.

She did so, including just a bare mention of the "special effects" she used to scare the attackers. She was ready to refuse to further describe or demonstrate the effects equipment, claiming it was experimental and classified.

She thought they might ask about the effects but they ignored her mention of them. Instead they focused on her claim that she fought the attackers with her sword rather than firearms.

Wang plainly disbelieved this. He called a halt and took out his inter-base phone.

"Captain, Wang here. I've got something I need to have checked out immediately if at all possible. Could you send a squad out with satellite-connected vidcams? The location is about nine clicks to the west."

With Tiara Karen snooped on the other side of the conversation. So she knew that a quick-reaction squad would be dispatched within fifteen minutes.

Wang put the phone away and announced that fact.

"I frankly think you are out of your mind, Lance Corporal

Danburn, and spinning a fantasy. But let's act as if you are not and continue the procedure. Describe the 'fight' you had."

"They emptied their weapons at the apparition that I was projecting. Then they tried to attack it. I was able to kill nine of them before they broke and ran. I then followed them as far as their base camp and stuck around to make sure they didn't regroup."

Schultz said, "Why didn't you kill some more of them at their base camp?"

"Partly, frankly, because I was a little sick to my stomach about killing them. It was my first time.

"But there's another reason. The more live insurgents there are who witnessed their fight against a demon the better. They'll spread the story more widely. And maybe we'll face fewer threats. Going up against guns they're prepared to handle. But they don't know how to fight demons."

Schultz said, "They can't exorcise them or use holy water or something?"

Wilson said, her voice thoughtful, "I'll have to check my memory against the literature. But I don't think the locals have that kind of equipment in their mythology."

"And they really believe in demons?"

"Even the educated. Except they're not demons the way we think of them. They're djinn, or jinni. In Arabic script JNN. Supernatural beings, some evil, some good, just like people."

The debriefing continued for a half hour more, then broke up. Everyone but the Sergeant returned to their tasks in the main work room. He spent some time with Karen telling her more about what her duties would be.

This included simple matters such as entering data into the Intel Database, checking for updates to their local version from higher up the chain of command, and doing analyses. She was surprised at how many kinds and how complicated they were, but it helped that there was software which guided analysts through the process.

About an hour later the Lieutenant got a call on his phone. He put it away and called everyone to go into the conference room.

They settled into their former places and Wang said, "We've got the squad in place. They've reconned around the site and it's secure."

He gave a command to the info slate on the table before him. The large wall screen lit up to show the face of a Latino male of middle years in full battle dress including body armor and flak helmet.

"Sergeant Ariaga. *Com'esta*?"

"Pretty good, Sir. We've got an interesting site here."

Wang nodded. There was a camera inside the conference room flat screen, for the sergeant obviously saw him. He moved aside and the view panned over the location of Karen's fight of the night before. Whoever was manning the camera had a pretty steady hand or else it was mounted on a tripod or something similar.

"Here's where the ragheads came into this clearing. They milled around a bit, as you can see from the marks on the ground."

The camera panned down and Karen saw where the attackers had stopped when they'd seen her floating in the air before them.

"They started firing. See all the shell casings on the ground? They practically emptied their magazines to have produced so much glitter. They were firing that way."

He pointed and the camera panned up and sideways to show where Karen had fought the attackers. The ground was littered with bodies, scattered in twisted heaps in some places. The colors were bright in the sunlight of day. The red of still-undried blood and the details of strewn intestines and body parts were especially vivid.

Her stomach lurched and she fought to get it under control.

The lieutenant and sergeant continued studying the scene on the camera but the two corporals turned to look at her. She avoided their gaze by following their example.

"Someone used some kind of anti-personnel weapon on them. Not a machine gun. Maybe a bladed weapon. But it was sharp as Hell and wielded with a lot of force. Take a look at this one."

The camera jumped and then moved several paces closer to the fight scene. Then it steadied and zoomed in on one corpse.

"This one was cut entirely in two at the waist. Look."

On screen could be seen the barrel of a rifle pointing at a dead man, apparently Sergeant Ariaga's weapon.

Karen's stomach lurched again. The insides of the man had spilled out. The camera caught all the details in full color and high resolution.

The camera held the image for a moment, then zoomed back out to see more of the fight scene. It showed the squad sergeant to one side where he'd moved closer.

"There are two more cut open like that. One was sliced crossways at the shoulder. That took a Hell of lot of force. It cut this carbine entirely in two. That's tempered steel, Lieutenant."

Karen kept her eyes on the screen as it zoomed in and down to show the ruined rifle but she could see that the Sergeant across from her was looking at her.

The image held and then zoomed back out and up. The sergeant onscreen pointed down again and the view panned down but did not zoom in.

"The rest of the bodies had their heads cut off. Clean off. All in all nine hostiles, Sir, bit the dust here."

"Good work, Sergeant. Any indications of who or what did this? Do you see tire tracks or boot tracks leading away from the scene?"

"Only those of the ragheads. They went back the way they came, some dropping weapons. In a Hell of a hurry to judge by the boot tracks. They were running as if Satan Himself was chasing them."

"Any more dead hostiles? Further back along their track?"

"Not out to 1000 yards. That's as far as we did a spiral search."

"Do a complete workup of the site. Still and movie shots. Leave it as it is. I'll have another squad come out and do cleanup and physical evidence gathering. When you're done, follow the track for up to three miles for more evidence, then return to the scene to guard it till cleanup gets there."

"Yes, Sir."

The flat screen blinked to black, then to grey and off.

Everyone was looking at Karen. She gazed back, a little nervous under the scrutiny, but her face showed none of it. As perfect in its beauty and composure as that of any PhotoFixed actress, she could have been "grey-eyed Goddess Athena" come to life.

"Hmm," said the Sergeant. "That's quite a weapon you have there, Corporal. Where did you get it?"

"It's a one-off made for me and a few others. By a high-tech client company of my father's."

"What's the name of the company?"

"I signed a non-disclosure agreement. Sorry."

"Hmm."

Lieutenant Wang said, "How much did your father pay for it?"

"He didn't. I did. I have a trust fund."

"It must be pretty generous. That's a very expensive piece of equipment."

"Not that much. I'm one of the beta testers. The results will eventually go into production equipment for the military and other clients."

As she spoke she was analyzing responses via Tiara and coming up with answers with Tiara's help that would be plausible.

"Let's see it again. Lay it on the table."

"Yes, sir. I have to caution no one to handle it. Especially the blade. It's so sharp you can literally cut a hand off and not even feel it at first."

She drew it and carefully laid it on the middle of the table in front of everyone. It gleamed, the hilt molded for her hand a soft shine as if of polished wood, the composite material of the blade a duller gleam of seeming steel.

Corporal Wilson tentatively reached a finger toward it, looking at Karen for permission.

"Touch only, please, Corporal."

The woman slid her finger tip along the hilt, then very carefully along the side of the blade. She drew her hand back.

"It feels like silk."

Everyone was quiet. No one else seemed to want to feel the weapon.

"May I sheathe it again, Sir? I'm very nervous about the blade being out of its home."

Wang nodded his head and Karen smoothly retrieved the sword and slid it home. Everyone else leaned away from it and almost visibly breathed a sigh of relief when she was done.

Schultz said, "How do you clean it?"

"It's self cleaning. Debris slides right off."

The corporal grunted, not quite a laugh.

"Debris. Yeah. Like blood and guts."

The Sergeant said, "And bone. And metal filings. Don't you worry about cutting metal, Corporal? Dulling the blade?"

"No. I was told that it's far harder than steel, the edge at least. It will even cut diamond."

Schultz said, "I'll be very interested when this material starts to go on the market. It just might revolutionize some fields."

Lieutenant Wang said, "Well, that's it for now. Let's get back to work. Corporal Danburn, you and the Sergeant work up a report on the debrief. Tofari will guide you in the format we require. I'd like it by day's end."

<>

The rest of the work day was routine. The two corporals were tasked to teach her some of the duties the two officers told them she'd be involved in. Wang was considerate enough to ask her if she needed to leave early to make up for lost sleep. She did not.

At 1700, the end of the official work day, the Sergeant released her. She retrieved her weapons from the top of a filing cabinet, put them on, and walked out.

She was halfway to the chow hall when she heard a call from behind her.

"Hey, wait up!" It was Corporal Schultz, walking quickly. Behind him came Corporal Wilson, not in quite as much hurry but clearly focusing on Karen.

She waited till they caught up. The three entered the chow lines, separated, but came together when their trays were full, and found a table. They were joined shortly by Georges and Armstrong. Soon the three men were deep in some discussion about an online video game. Wilson rolled her eyes and the two women began to share histories.

They were working on their desserts when a sergeant approached their table. It was Ariaga from the fight investigation detail.

"Hey, you're Corporal Danburn, right?"

"Yes, Sergeant. Lance Corporal Karen Danburn. I recognize you from the video conference we had this morning."

"Well, good job, Danburn. Those ragheads would have given us a bit of trouble last night. They were carrying RPGs and heavy machine guns."

"Nothing you couldn't handle, I'm sure. I checked out your sensor array when I went out last night. I was impressed with what I saw in your guard shack."

"Yeah... Hey, Wilson, could you move a bit and let me sit here?"

"Certainly."

The sergeant's position in front of her separated Karen a little from Wilson, who was right across the table from her, but not so much that the woman could not easily hear. She looked on curiously.

"Thanks, Wilson," the man said to her, then turned back to Karen.

"The thing is, every time we get one of these attacks, and we've been here seven months now and had several, everyone loses sleep and we have to spend more time on security. We need to get this base set up permanent by the time the cold season gets here. It snows and the wind gets in everything. It's hard to do the heavy outside work in those conditions. So we're extra grateful we've somebody who really knows their job to help out."

"Pleased that I can contribute."

"Yeah. They've given us a tough schedule. We need to spend all daylight hours doing heavy construction work, right up to dark. But the sensor guys complain they can't guarantee security near nightfall.

"Tell me, not complaining, but how come you carved up those guys instead of standing out and plinking them? You could have gotten more, and might have got killed working so close up."

She explained her prevention-not-protection theory, and her idea of playing to the insurgents' supernatural fears.

"Well, sounds good. You're a smart cookie, Danburn. I suppose we'll see how it works out.

"Is that the weapon you used?" He pointed at the hilt sticking up over one shoulder.

She nodded.

"Some kind of samurai sword? Can I see it?"

"No, I'd rather not let it out of my hands. Sorry."

"No need to be. No need. I don't feel that way, but some good people I know are very particular about their personal weapons."

He stood up and leaned down to shake her hand. "Good to have you with us, Danburn."

The three men at her table had been listening. Georges asked that was about, and Schultz began to tell him and Armstrong.

Karen and Corporal Wilson got up and took their emptied trays to the garbage area. Outside the building the other woman said, "You want to come to my place and hang out? Or vice versa?"

"Sure. But tomorrow night would be better. I need to turn in early. I got very little sleep in the last two days."

"OK. And call me Janice."

"I'm Karen. See you in the morning."

Part 5 - Agent

Karen went to her quarters and prepared for sleep. But though her eyes were closed she was not drowsing. Via Tiara and Pegasus she was roaming the land and skies outside. Including physical and electronic "vision" of three huge vans which had arrived from battalion headquarters in Jalalabad some 70 kilometers or 45 miles to the west.

The real reason Karen didn't want to socialize that night was that she'd heard that a post-mortem unit in the vans was on its way to examine the bodies of the men she'd killed. After analyzing the cause of death, they'd also stitch them together for burial. And for the sad task of notifying their kin.

But they were forensic specialists as well as mortuary doctors. They would fingerprint the men, collect their DNA, photograph their faces. This data would be stored in the Army's country-intelligence database where it would be compared to previous activities where such data had been collected. This might help them to solve cold cases and see if these men had been questioned about military actions.

Such data could also help to build association charts, to discover and expand how the enemy was organized into larger units. This was especially useful to guard against these larger units attacking the U. S. forces and others.

The clothing and weaponry of the men, and the empty cartridge cases they'd left behind, would also be analyzed.

The first half hour or so told her little new. The crews inside the vans had only been working for a few hours. Tiara could only read what had been entered into the van's database and transmitted elsewhere.

This annoyed Karen. Then she became doubly annoyed. She was acting like a child denied instant gratification.

Restless, she stood and went invisible. Outside she called down Pegasus who, as usual, was hovering invisible somewhere near her. She enfolded herself with his force fields and sent herself a hundred yards upward. From here she could see the entire base and its near surroundings.

She watched for a few minutes but saw no threats or anything else unusual, at least on the outside, even though she used Tiara's visual, infrared, and gravity radar sight. She avoided looking at the buildings with her gravity radar sight, however. It let Karen see inside them. It would tell her nothing she wanted to know, and it would embarrass her to see people at private functions. She'd felt OK about that the first time she surveilled the area, but now she knew a lot of the people.

Then she sent Pegasus a mile high. From here she could see many miles around. She focused briefly on the three enemy camps and the village of Baha Tor at the near entrance to Khyber Pass. Nothing interesting.

She zoomed Tiara's senses in on each of the three enemy camps. The camp of the men she'd attacked was empty and showed signs of hasty exit, with debris lying around. The mountain camp in the Pass had only half a dozen people, two of them viewing the pass with binoculars. The third village had only a dozen men there, chatting, eating, busy with weapons. There were no indications they planned to attack the base or anyone else.

She detected no cell phone activity in any of the three camps. She was a bit surprised, but not much. Cell phones were becoming common in the larger Afghan cities but had barely penetrated the rest of the country. She imagined, however, that it was only a matter of time before they did.

There were about a dozen active phones in Baha Tor. She listened to the conversations for a few minutes but only heard innocuous speech. None of them seemed to have the kind of coded references which would suggest they feared being spied upon. This was unsurprising, since the idea of such spying was not yet common in Afghanistan. That innocence, she thought, would not last much longer.

She lofted Pegasus a few miles higher and watched activity up to the edge of Jalalabad to the west and Peshawar to the east. As usual there were several hundred vehicles traveling the Jalalabad-Peshawar highway.

The sun was setting now, throwing long shadows eastward. These highlighted the huts of the dozens of small villages standing on the greener swath of land to the north of the highway, between it and the meandering Kabul River a few miles to the north. It also highlighted the people outside, their shadows stretching long.

She lowered and swept along the green area from a quarter mile up, idly scanning the scene below, not searching for anything, just looking.

She did notice that in several villages a few people were walking between their village and the river. Curious, she dropped lower. This showed her that they were ferrying water from the river back to the villages. Those villages which did not have wells dug nearby.

A few were wheeling small vehicles like wheelbarrows which carried kegs and jugs of water. Most lugged colorful plastic jugs suspended from handles. Some were children.

Her eyes were drawn to two of these, straggling far behind the others. They were apparently nine or ten, and small enough that they carried small jugs by their handles in one hand and shared a large jug between them.

On impulse, a vague memory of a fairy tale nudging her, she dropped down in front of them about a hundred feet, taking on the appearance of an old woman clad all in flowing black, similar to but less anonymous than the all-covering burqa. From one hand she held the handle of another plastic bucket, once bright blue but faded and scratched now. It was made of a force field but as she hobbled she had Suit transmute air to water inside it. The jug filled up halfway and stopped. This was enough for her purpose.

As the children neared her, moving slowly but not as slowly as the old woman, she pretended to stumble. Trying to catch herself, she dropped the bucket. She gave a distressed cry as the water poured out, darkening the sparsely grassed earth.

She knelt and hauled the bucket upright. Looking inside, she moaned. Only an inch or so of water covered the bottom.

She sat down beside it, hunched over, her head in her hands.

The children passed her by. Looking up through the image of straggly grey hair, translucent to her but opaque to them, she could see them looking at her. They stopped, set down their jugs, and whispered between them.

Decision made, they took up their burdens and returned to her. Beside her, they set them down again and spoke to her.

She looked up and them and smiled, her teeth whole but yellowed.

"Hello. How are you?"

They said the Pashto equivalent of "OK." Then the little girl, who might be a year older than the boy, said, "Did you lose your water?"

"Oh, it's nothing. I can get more."

The two children looked at each other. The girl said, "We can give you one of ours." She pointed at one of the smaller buckets.

"Oh, that's so kind of you. I am very tired. But are you sure?"

The little boy said, "Yes. Here."

He lifted one of the smaller buckets and poured out half its contents. Then the girl poured half of her small bucket into it, so that both small buckets still had some water.

"Bye," said the little girl. The two children picked up their burdens and began to walk away.

"Wait. Let me walk with you."

They stopped to let her catch up with them. In the half mile to their home she asked them questions about themselves. Did they go to school? Did they like it? What else did they do? Play games?

At first they were reluctant to talk, but that quickly passed.

At one of the small square mud huts near the highway they stopped.

"Well, here we are."

The door opened and a young woman stood in the doorway.

"Vahida, Shabaz, who is this?"

The two children turned to Karen, stricken. They had not been courteous enough to ask her name.

Karen said, "I am Setarah. You must be their mother."

"Yes. I am Sharbat." The woman paused. "Would you like to share our meal?"

"Only if I may contribute."

The woman looked at Karen's hands and saw only the water bucket.

"Yes, of course. We'd be happy to share. Come in. I'll get my husband."

Inside she hurried to another doorway, an open one, and called her husband to come meet their guest. He told her he'd be right there. A few minutes later he was, wiping his hands on a soiled once-red rag, now darkened by oil and dirt.

He studied Karen carefully, then smiled. "Welcome to our home. I am Arksalakan Azizi."

"I am Setarah. It is a pleasure and honor to join you, Honorable Azizi."

"Please pardon me for a few moments. Please sit." He gestured.

The room was a small version of language teacher "Mama" Wazir's: carpeted (but covering a packed earth floor rather than wood), a very low couch covered in red cloth, flat cushions for seats, several low tables, and walls hung with small tapestries.

Karen set her bucket just inside the doorway and walked to lower herself to a cushion near the couch. The man took the larger bucket from his children and they followed him to a high stool. He stepped up on it and emptied the bucket into a metal bin above the kitchen level. The children handed their smaller buckets up to him to add their contents.

Down from the stool, he washed his hands in the small nearby metal sink with soap and small rations of water.

Meanwhile Sharbat, after a quick smile at Karen, abandoned her to quickly finish a few preparations for a meal. Then she arranged various dishes on the low table in front of the couch. Her husband came to finish this process, as did the children.

Finally everyone sat down, the man and woman on the red couch, the children on cushions on each end of the table and so to the left and right of their parents, and Karen on the opposite side of the table facing the parents.

As they ate Karen asked the two parents about themselves. The woman worked in their small garden and helped neighbors do the same, trading various vegetables and spices. She also made up small packets of dried vegetables and spices for sale in the small general stores in the nearest two villages. The man did simple fixes to automobiles, though he was having trouble with his own compact pickup truck. It involved the catalytic-converter carburetors pioneered by India in automobiles.

Noticing a small bookshelf containing mostly paperback books Karen commented on them. At that the mother shyly admitted to knowing how to read, a skill looked down upon in women. She and her husband had also taught her children to read. She also taught other children in the neighborhood, those whose parents wanted that.

Arksalakan said, a bit defiantly, "Knowledge and hard work is the key to a better life."

Old-woman Karen agreed and offered up a few lines from the

Quran to support the idea. She had memorized the text while studying Dari and Pashto. This impressed the two adults and from then on they addressed her with the honorific *Safi*.

The typical Afghan feast, as opposed to the regular meal, was of several courses. The two adults as a courtesy had set up a modest feast for their guest, though it surely strained their limited resources. When everyone's plates had been emptied, the mother declared that they'd have dessert as a final course.

Karen held up a hand to deter her from standing.

"You remember that I agreed to eat with you only if I could contribute. And so I have. I have doubled everything in your pantry. And filled up your water tank. I have also cleaned the water and strengthened the tank and its supports."

All were looking at her in amazement, the adult's gazes containing hints of fear and embarrassment. They surely thought she was either insane or, a worse possibility, telling the truth. For who could do what she said unless she was one of the jinn--creatures not known to be universally benign?

The little boy was wondering but the girl was skeptical.

"You don't look like a jineri."

Karen smiled. "What does a jinn look like? Do they perhaps wear green robes because they love green plants? And headscarves of blue because they love the sky?"

She had Suit slowly change her force field near-burqa from black to a satiny green. And her head-and-neck scarf to a sky blue.

This brought a gasp from the girl and a delighted laugh from the boy. The two adults sat back in fear.

"Do not be afraid," Karen said. "I was impressed and delighted that you had taught your children respect and compassion for the elderly. I decided that all of you should be rewarded."

She gazed at the adults while letting Suit change her face and hair slowly to youthful appearance, though an Arabic one not her own. Her eyes had long lashes and were slightly slanted and a pure violet color.

"I have also doubled every item in your wardrobes. And your truck is now as good as new, but it looks no different. For you must not tell anyone of your good luck."

She turned her now ethereally beautiful face to look at the faces of the children.

"You know why that is, don't you? People would think you silly, or be jealous of you and want to hurt you?"

The children both nodded their heads vigorously. For who could doubt the wisdom of jinni? Especially when one was sitting in front of you? And looking you in the face?

"So, now, if you will, dear Azizi *Jan*, bring the dessert. We will finish the meal, and then I must go."

Sharbat rose and hurried to the pantry. The boy said, "Where are you going?"

"Very far away as you know distance. To one of my homes which sits by a vast ocean."

The girl said, "Will we see you again?"

"No. I have important business and will not come this way again."

The mother returned to the table carrying five saucers on a tray. She had selected small fudge squares spiced with cinnamon and containing pistachio and almond nuts. The children each got two squares, the woman four, and the man five. Karen was given five also.

As they slowly savored the dessert the father said, "What do you think of the new direction of events here? In our country?"

"I have not studied them. This is only a stop on my way between two far lands. So I can only offer generalities, not specifics."

She looked at the children as well as the adults and gathered her thoughts. She had been asked to offer genuine wisdom and was not confident in her ability to do so. She tried to temper her remarks with caution, for coming from a supernatural creature her words would have great weight.

"Like all change, it has good and bad aspects. You can expect more riches. And education is good. But people will struggle to get more for themselves than for others, and sometimes this can lead to violence, not merely the jostling and deal-making of the marketplace. I suggest each of you study and think about this, and be cautious. Take the good and avoid the bad."

The woman spoke, a bit timidly. But Karen could tell that the hesitance was not because of her husband. As she spoke he looked on, interested in what she said.

"What do you think of those who say an education is wasted on a woman?"

Karen laughed. "I think an education is wasted on them!"

Arksalakan smiled. Then sobered.

"I thought jinni were myth. Did there use to be more of you in days gone past?"

"Yes. But we were saddened by how humans acted, so full of violence and ignorance and glorying in their ignorance. They ignored our teachings about the natural world, clouds and rivers and the moon and stars and other matters. So we left for a faraway world."

"But you're here now," said the girl.

"But only in passing. Your world for us is like a step on a stairway."

Arksalakan glanced at his children, but said, "We have heard that one of you guards the foreigners near the Pass."

"I have too. I knew her long ago. She is much concerned with justice. She must have stopped here long enough to become angry with the ones who oppose new ways, who oppose peace and plenty and favor keeping a few in power over the many."

She could not keep up her make-believe much longer. Best she leave quickly.

She stood and they did too.

"I must go now. Go with God."

They all bowed, the children as well as the adults. They walked with her to the door and stood watching as she passed outside.

Twilight had shrouded the land in near-dark and left only a brightness in the western sky. She turned to them, lifted a hand, and vanished in a swirl of wind.

<>

Karen made a quick aerial tour of the area near the base. Seeing no threats she came down from the sky, entered her tent still invisible. No one was in the common room, as gravity radar had shown. She dropped her invisibility and went into her room and dressed for sleep.

Lying on her bed she closed her eyes and tapped into the communication network of the vans. Much of the forensic work had been done and she pored through it. It told her little she did not already know. Except the IDs of several of the dead men. She traced out their association diagram. Most of them had been involved in criminal actions before, or suspected of it. Tomorrow she would learn more from her co-workers in the company's S2 section.

She dozed off quickly, memories of her recent visit and meal coming to her now and again. They helped balance her memories of what she'd done the night before.

She had no nightmares that night.

The next day was a Saturday. Only necessary work was done those days and Karen had the day off. She had chow with her growing crowd of acquaintances. Since often THEY had friends, they had gravitated to one of the four very big round tables in one of the corners of the L-shaped dining area.

Janice Wilson said, as they were nearly done eating, "What are your plans for today?"

"I haven't really decided. Do you have something in mind?"

"Let's go into Baha Tor."

"Sure. Now?"

"The mornings are best. The days are already getting hot."

Janice pulled out her info slate and opened up a page.

"Oh, shoot. There's only one more opening."

Karen looked a question and her friend answered.

The number of Post 373 personnel allowed in the village at any one time was limited to keep the villagers from feeling overwhelmed by the military. Each half-day only those who signed up first could go, at least officially, and you could get punishment details if you were caught.

Abraham Schultz leaned over. "Check it again. I think the list is only for Army."

Janice tapped her slate's face and brightened. "You're right. Thanks, Abe. Coming with us?"

"No, thanks, Jan. I'm in the tournament."

Janice almost visibly controlled her tendency to roll her eyes. She thought online games were childish.

The Army people were encouraged but not required to go in "modest native dress" and to speak Pashto as much as possible so as to minimize culture clash. So the two women retired to their tents to dress. They went first to Janice's, who had a dozen different pieces of clothing to mix and match.

Ostensibly this was because Karen wanted the woman to show her examples of proper Afghan female dress, but actually to give Pegasus time to zip into her room and add a few items to her closet. Most of her dress items were created by Suit or Pegasus out of air or force fields and banished when not needed.

An everyday nice outfit for public wear usually included loose pants, a dress over that to just below the knees, a long-sleeved blouse tucked into the pants, a very long vest-like over-garment opened or buttoned, and a scarf which covered most of the hair and was long enough to wrap around the throat and possibly one's face below the eyes.

Janice explained that the colors could be very varied and bright, enough to clash to Western eyes. She chose a middle course, subdued but varied colors. This was forest green pants, blue skirt almost navy dark, gold blouse, a beige vest, a dark gold scarf, and black slip-on flat-heeled shoes. To that she added designer shades, her one concession to Western fashion.

"Very nice," said Karen when Janice pirouetted before her. "I think I'll go for something dull the first time I visit."

Janice also selected a large black bag. Into it she stowed a pistol into an interior holster with a couple of magazines. Town visitors were supposed to carry weapons but do so discreetly.

As Janice was showing off her clothing items Karen had been giving Pegasus instructions. So when she and the other woman arrived in her tent she had two items of each pieces of clothing in her closet. She chose all shades of white and gold for the village visit.

"Not bad," said Janice. "Actually quite lovely. Not up to the Afghan standard. They like a lot of colors. I think it's because they've been influenced so much by India.

"Nice holster-belt combo," she added.

Karen'd had Pegasus add a wide dull-gold belt to her ensemble with a matching pistol holster on one hip and two two-clip cartridge pouches on the other. The pure white over-vest hung open only a few inches and was loose enough that you would have to look carefully to see that Karen was armed.

The only other color in her costume was the glossy brown of faux-wood in the sword scabbard she slung over one shoulder. Her sword straps and sheathe were both of white matching her long vest.

By this time the base bus to the village had already left, but Karen had wanted to drive her truck so was not inconvenienced. She shortly caught up to the slow-moving bus and tagged along behind it. At the village she followed it to a parking area near the center of the village. This was a long gravel lot on one side of the two-lane highway. Two or three dozen Indian mini-SUVs and mini-pickup trucks were in the lot.

Beyond the lot was a winding stream bed for an offshoot of the Kabul River which provided much of the water for the area. It was only a dozen feet wide and shallow but enough to nurture a long line of oaks and some kind of wispy conifer trees.

A few sheds stood on each side of the parking lot. On the other side of the highway were most of the buildings which made up the village, most two stories tall, a few three stories. They were of beige brick and (rarely) of wood. They were strung out along the highway for about a mile. Behind them stood a few more houses, some with dusty gardens behind them.

Karen and Janice got out of Karen's truck and she beeped it locked. They joined the other nearly couple of dozen military personnel and crossed the highway, having to wait for a passing long cargo truck and a gaily-painted passenger bus piled high with furniture atop it, several passengers standing amid the furniture and holding onto it.

The long two-story building was a sort of indoor bazaar with a long line of large windows fronting the highway. At each window was a table with chairs. Many tables had people eating, mostly men but with a few women. Opposite the windows was an equally long line of small food-service shops, mostly Afghan but a couple of Western fast-food places.

Breaking the line of the food places were two wide passageways running far toward the back. On each side of the passageways were small shops with open doorways.

Karen and Janice spent the morning there, sightseeing and shopping. They bought trinkets and a few joke or fun items for their friends back at the base and at home. They also bought a few female items of clothing. One or two were for fun, but most were to keep up their status as reputable women in the eyes of the Afghan community.

The U. S. Army in general and their base commander in particular were looking ahead to remaining in Afghanistan for many years to come. Being respected by the general public was an important part of that aim. It would not be easy, but the U. S. military had two prongs in their attempt. One was to bend to local public opinion in some ways. However, it would also seek to bend that local opinion. Especially toward more modern and gentler ways.

They locked their purchases in Karen's truck. Janice wondered aloud if they would be safe there. The truck appeared as if a bit of work with a crowbar would open it up.

Karen smiled at her new friend.

"It just looks that way. I had it reinforced. It's bullet-proof. Including the glass and the tires and the underside. Rifle fire at point blank range can't do more than scar it. They'd have to bring up heavier weaponry to open it up."

Janice raised an eyebrow. "That must have really cost."

"I've got a REALLY generous trust fund."

They walked back across the street, avoiding the daily traffic to and from the Pass. This included cars and small trucks and busses and large haulers of several kinds. Some of them looked new. Most looked ancient. The older vehicles often were gaily or garishly painted.

"Let's take a look at the hospital," Janice suggested. "They're working hard to fix it up in time for winter. I want to see how far they've gotten since I came here last."

She was silent for a minute, glancing at Karen a few times as they went down the sidewalk. Karen waited; the woman clearly had something she wanted to talk about.

"If you're so rich, why don't you just enjoy it?"

"Be a typical trust fund kid?"

Karen had been asked this before. Thinking about how to answer it had led her to think more deeply about why she didn't lead a leisurely life.

"Two reasons. One is ethical. I've been gifted in so many ways--not just with money--that it almost seems as if I should share my good luck.

"Another is selfish. I'd get bored with just loafing all the time.

Don't get me wrong. I can loaf with the best of them. But I need something to occupy my mind. Something worth doing, not just playing bridge or chess or being a tennis pro."

"But why the military? And why not become an officer?"

"Maybe I will some day. As for why the military: I'm really good at fighting, really really good. I'm almost afraid at what I'd become if I didn't have a good cause to channel me."

Janice laughed. "That's ridiculous! I've known you only a few hours but I already know you better than to think you'd ever become a psychopath. More likely you'd become an athlete. Maybe go for the Olympics."

Karen grinned. "Yeah. The go-psycho idea is kind of pushing it. Though I still half-believe it."

She sobered. "But athletics is out." She glanced at Janice, measuring how much she could trust her. Not just emotionally, but her judgment.

"I'd ruin sports for people. By the time I was fifteen I could bench-press the world record--for men. Run twice as fast as the world record. I'd be hated by so many people."

"I researched you after you were assigned to S2. You did very well in all sorts of sports in high school. But not super-well. You were holding back?"

"Yes. It was frustrating sometimes. But playing with friends, and for my school-- THAT was good."

Janice nodded her head. "And the military is like that for you, isn't it? I feel it too, sometimes, though at other times I'm impatient to get out and get on with my real life."

"And what would that be?"

The woman pointed at the building before them. It was three stories and was obviously either being built or re-built.

"I've always been fascinated with buildings. It started with my doll-houses. Then I got interested in a big old building in the neighborhood. It was in bad shape, but instead of tearing it down completely they renovated it; it was a historical house.

"I used to sneak inside at night and see how they were doing it. I almost got hurt falling through a floor once, but that didn't stop me. I just learned more so I would know how to stay out of the danger spots."

She glanced at Karen, her gamin face mischievous. Karen had a flashback at how she would have looked as a kid.

"I did tell tales at school about meeting ghosts inside the house. I even dared some kids to come meet the ghosts. But that backfired."

She laughed.

"The police caught us and we ended up in jail for a few hours!"

Karen laughed.

<>

They spent nearly an hour walking around and through the building, but only parts of the building. Parts were dangerous but, even more, they had to avoid workmen to keep from getting yelled at.

Next they visited the modest mosque. They couldn't enter it, being non-Moslems and foreigners. Janice pointed out interesting architectural details. One was how the outside front had been intricately decorated by insetting local blue stones into the façade. Another was how the inside prayer space was covered by a sky-blue dome representing the heavens (its outside surface visible from the street).

"See those spires?"

Karen noticed that at each edge of the building there was a tall foot-wide spire with a conical top. She nodded.

"They're symbolic on something this small. But in large mosques they are minarets. Someone climbs to the top of one or more and calls the faithful to prayer."

By then it was time for lunch, after which the morning group would have to give way for a second "shift" of soldiers released from the base. The two periods overlapped, so about three dozen soldiers at one time chowed down at the local food markets. There was a good deal of chatting amongst them. Karen was included, already known to everyone by reputation if nothing else.

<>

Done, Karen said to Janice, "I'm going to visit Landi Kotal in Pakistan. You want me to drop you off back at the base? Or do you want to stick around here and return with the second shift?"

"No. I've been wanting to see it again."

"It's pretty damned dangerous. For everyone, but women

especially. I can't take someone--"

"--someone who can't take care of herself?" She sounded angry.

Karen gauged the woman. She was fit and seemed trained. If she were a Marine, trained and toughened to violence, Karen would have no hesitation taking her. But Karen didn't know how good the Army trained its people.

On the other hand, Karen should be able to protect Janice if they were attacked. And the woman deserved a chance to prove herself.

"Are you prepared to fight if we're attacked?"

"Yes."

"OK. But you're going to need something a little heavier than a pistol and two magazines. Let's get outside of town and I'll fix you up."

They got into Karen's truck and drove a couple of miles closer to the Khyber Pass entrance. There she parked in the shadow of a long line of trees planted alongside the highway a long time ago, perhaps as windbreaks.

They got out and Karen joined her friend on the passenger side. She moved the shopping bags to the front seats, tilted the passenger seat forward, and opened the top of a metal box. It took up the width of the truck and displayed three foam-packed shelves. Nestled in cutouts in the foam were weapons.

"Holy shit," Janice said. "No wonder you wanted your truck armored. That's an entire arsenal."

"It is protected by more than the armor. If someone didn't open this box just right they'd get a nasty surprise."

There were pistols and submachine guns and carbines and two kinds of sniper rifle.

Karen laid a hand on one of the latter.

"Special built. I'll normally leave the Marine's version in the armory and take one of these. This is anti-matériel. It will shoot through an engine block. Or a wall and people on the other side. That--" She pointed. "--has range and an electronic sight that lets me take out targets several miles away. That means people atop mountains or skyscrapers. If I'm lucky I can even take out aircraft."

Janice looked at the array in awe.

"How much did this cost you?"

Karen shrugged. "A good chunk of a million. I told you my trust fund was generous."

Actually the weapons box and most of the weapons were virtual creations with the weight, balance, and functionality of physical ones. They had cost her nothing.

One weapon was physical, however. She'd had Pegasus create it during the two-mile drive. She took it out and handed it to Janice. Then she reached in again and took out a harness and a magazine of cartridges and two flat tan ammunition pouches each stocked with four more magazines.

Janice was examining the compact black submachine gun, her body turned away from Karen so that the weapon never pointed at her friend. Karen also observed that she nestled the butt into her right hand but kept her trigger finger well outside the trigger guard.

"I think that is just what you need," Karen said, nodding at the weapon. "It fires a heavy .223 caliber bullet at near supersonic speeds. I'd think your armory has loads for it."

She had Janice put the weapon onto the passenger seat and take off her vest. She helped arrange the straps and the pouches so that the weapon hung below Janice's left armpit and the pouches at her sides. Then she slid the weapon into the clamshell holster and locked it in place, muzzle pointing down and slightly to the back.

She handed the vest to Janice and the woman put it back on. She twitched the vest nearly closed the way it normally would be worn. Her weapon thus became visible only if she let the vest swing open.

The woman, being right handed, would swing the left side of her vest aside and grab the butt across her chest with her right hand. Then she'd use the heel of her hand to push down on the butt to free it from the holster so she could grasp the weapon and draw it. The clamshell was secure enough that Janice could run while wearing it, though she'd have to hold the holstered weapon with her left hand to keep it from swinging awkwardly.

Janice shrugged her shoulders and adjusted the straps slightly. Satisfied, she turned half away from Karen and drew the weapon as she'd been instructed. Karen watched her weapon handling closely, ready to correct her friend if necessary.

Janice did not need help. She carefully removed the magazine and worked the action to ensure no cartridge remained inside the weapon.

She then practiced replacing the magazine and chambering a round. All while still facing half away from Karen. She repeated the unloading and loading process several times, till it became easy for her. A lot of practice would be needed to make this automatic, but this was enough for her to be minimally proficient.

Meanwhile Karen had sent Pegasus up a half mile and had been using Pegasus's gravity radar to surveil the area around them out to the distance to the Pass: eight kilometers or about five miles.

"Let's get you a little firing practice. I know a good spot for that."

They got back into the truck and drove a couple of miles eastward. Then they drove down a dusty, bumpy side track another couple of miles, climbing upward inside a valley carved into a hillside.

A hundred yards further the valley ended, the hillside thus making a backdrop for their impromptu firing range.

They got out and emptied the contents of four of the brown shopping bags into other bags. They carried the empties to the end of the valley where it began its tilt upward and merge into the rest of the hillside. In the bottom of each sack they scooped sand a couple of inches deep to keep them upright against the slight breeze, making four targets several feet apart.

Back at the truck Karen gave Janice a brief tour of her weapon. In particular, it had a thumb safety and a selector for single, triple, and nine shots automatic. The safety and selector had levers on both sides of the weapon, so it could be fired either right- or left-handed.

"Why don't you fire a few shots aimed single shot?"

Janice slid the skeletal shoulder stock out of its recess and locked it into place. Then she aimed carefully two handed, her support hand under the round flashlight attached near the front of the barrel. She squeezed off a shot. Her gun made a sound as of someone spitting and one of the shopping-bag targets quivered.

"Wow!" said Janice. "I wondered why you didn't caution me to put something in my ears. Even as close as I am I barely heard a sound."

Karen said, "Let me show you another feature."

This was a switch on the side of the flashlight. When thrown one way it was a flashlight, the other way converted it to a laser targeter which shone a red dot on the target.

From single fire Janice worked up to nine shot fully automatic.

After she emptied the twenty-round magazine she called a halt.

"I've had enough. You want to shoot?"

Karen grinned. "Prepare to be amazed. Look at me, not the targets."

Janice did so. Then Karen's pistol was in her hand and had fired, a short quiet buzz.

Janice blinked. She had only seen a blur of movement that put a pistol into her friend's hand. And Karen had fired with her pistol at waist height, standing relaxed and not crouching. A notoriously inaccurate "gunfighter" technique, derided by all pistol experts.

Yet when Janice looked down range, she saw the one remaining tattered target totally gone.

"You must have hit it with at least one bullet. What kind of bullets are those?"

"They're the size of needles. Specially designed not to tumble and spread much. Each magazine holds a hundred."

Janice frowned. "You must be pretty good at adjusting for wind. There's not much, but I definitely had to adjust for it for my heavier bullets."

Actually Karen had cheated. She'd merged with Tiara and had its super-advanced computer calculate windage and other factors and guide her to adjust her aim. Though perhaps cheat was the wrong word; she and Tiara were now so tightly bound that it was questionable that they could be separated even analytically. She'd become a cyborg.

<>

The land was mostly flat for several miles to the east. Then the Safed Koh Mountains ahead of them came closer till the foothills reared up directly ahead. Closer they came to the mouth of the Pass. To one side of the highway was a large sign with white on green writing. In English it declared that this was the entrance to the Khyber Pass, followed by smaller text giving historical information.

The hills reared up on both sides of them as they drove further east. The highway began to twist. Later it split into two, one side higher than the other.

Shortly they approached the border between Afghanistan and Pakistan. The way opened up a bit and small dirt huts appeared on each side of them, the beginning of the strip village Tor Kham. They passed a gasoline station with a large red and blue Dr. Upper soft-drink sign on its side.

A grey stone barrier gateway loomed up, high enough to pass tall trucks or busses but narrow enough only for two lanes of traffic. The bridging top spelled out TOR KHAM PAKISTAN in English and Arabic script.

Just beyond was a toll booth manned by a tall skinny Khyber Rifle soldier of the Khyber Agency clad in a brown uniform. He only glanced at the two women as they drove through, Karen dropping the required coins into the hopper.

"Interesting," she said, "that Afghanistan doesn't have a toll booth here."

"I'd guess they will eventually. But they're not as sophisticated as Pakistan. That's partly behind the new Afghan administration's invitation to foreigners to invest in commerce. Jealousy."

They passed through the village, viewing the one- and two-story buildings on both sides with little interest. The dirt bricks used were of a beige color and the only color came from signs advertising drinks and food. The last substantial building was near the end of the village, another gasoline station.

From there the hillsides closed in again and the highway twisted and turned some more. They passed through five tunnels. Finally the way opened and Landi Kotal valley spread out before and below them.

It was about two miles wide, roughly oval, with a fair amount of greenery from the recent spring rains. The long flattened "base" of the oval was to their right. To their left was the elongated north-pointing "top" of the oval. Karen knew from the map Tiara laid over her vision that another smaller village nestled there.

A half mile further and to their right was a military base, the Michni Post of the Khyber Agency, with a good view of the valley below. She turned into the entrance and parked in a concrete lot along with a couple dozen other cars and trucks. There were also two long tour buses taking up four parking spots.

They got out and walked toward a one-story red-brick reception building. It was guarded by a soldier standing at parade rest under the porch to the building so that he could see whoever came through the gate. Several video cameras were placed about the area, however, so

Karen was not sure if he was useful or merely a visible symbol of authority.

The two women nodded at him as they passed into the reception area. It was filled with perhaps three dozen people, tourists for the most part. Most seemed to belong to one of the tour buses, judging by the way they clustered together and chatted.

They approached a reception desk behind which a young Pakistani woman sat, dressed in dark-blue Western clothes except for a lighter-blue headscarf.

"Hello," Karen said in Pashto. "We are here for the tour."

The woman looked at her without expression and spoke in British-accented English.

"Please go in the next room and place weapons and any other metal objects on the conveyer belt. Weapons will be collected and you can pick them up on the way out of the base."

Karen and Janice passed into the next room which was set up similar to aircraft security procedures. Their weapons were placed in a locker and a claim check given to them so that they could redeem them later. Their keys, coins, and other metal objects were returned to them.

They joined the tour group when it formed up a little while later. Following directions of one of the soldiers who were on duty as security checkers they climbed long outside stairs up to a plateau which held the main administrative building to the base. It was built of grey brick and roofed with red-brick slates. The path and the building were surrounded by a green lawn kept that way by sprinklers.

The reception area inside resembled a small hotel lobby or business office reception. Another couple dozen people were already there. Karen guessed they belonged to one of the tour buses; they were mostly well-dressed Europeans and a few natives of India. The two touring groups merged.

Another young woman dressed similarly to the receptionist downhill greeted them with a smile. She spoke to them in English.

"Now that we're all here we can get started. Please follow me."

They filed into a hall behind the woman and shortly were ushered into a large long room. One side of the room had floor to ceiling windows showing the sprawl of Landi Kotal in the valley below. The other side contained a four-tier set of padded seats. The tourists were directed to find seats, which they did.

A large video screen came alight on each side of the wide picture window. Each showed a map of the Khyber Pass, the mountains surrounding it, and the flatter areas to the east and west of the mountains. A rough oval surrounded the pass, extending a dozen miles on all sides.

The young woman spoke over a microphone. "This is called informally the Five Tribes Area for the major tribes in this area. The valley of Landi Kotal is near the center of the area."

The scene zoomed in to show the valley in greater detail.

"More than 30,000 people live here. We are happy to announce the opening recently of a water pipeline from the higher mountains in the north which should alleviate a chronic shortage of water."

The map showed a red arrow pointing to a blue-coded feature which snaked southward into the valley.

"The low rainfall in this area does have a positive benefit. It lets solar power work effectively all year round. This abundance of power and now water makes this area a magnet for industry. An additional attraction is our highly respected technical school, which you can see on the map and outside the window."

The woman paused to let the audience, nearly fifty people, examine the map and try to find the school in the area below them. Janice pointed it out to Karen, who nodded as she found it via Tiara and her own eyes.

"Let me direct you also to the location of our Civil Hospital. It is just off the main Peshawar-Jalalabad highway through the pass. It has recently been expanded and upgraded to a top-tier institution."

She paused again to let her audience peer at the sights.

"As you travel through this area may I suggest you visit the shrine to the great Pakistani poet Amir Hamza Shinwari, who was born here and lived here much of his life.

"And your visit would not be complete if you did not also visit the great Landi Kotal Bazaar, which your tour guides will help you navigate.

"Now let us proceed to the museum area. After that you are in for a great treat. The Khyber Rifle soldiers will perform traditional dances and a military drill."

The two women waited for everyone else to stand and file out. Janice spoke up.

"Did you get how much PR our guide laid on us? Our estimate is that Pakistan has been galvanized by how much effort their backward Afghan neighbors are making to catch up to them."

Karen nodded. She had gotten pretty much the same estimate through Tiara as she'd listened.

The "museum area" was not large or well stocked. It was a long hall twice as wide as normal halls. On one side behind glass were artifacts from homes and several dummies dressed in traditional clothing and uniforms. On the opposite wall were old photographs. There were also portraits of military men and a fine display of weapons leaning heavily toward antique swords, knives, and firearms.

The doorway to the outside let them into a large rectangular park area. It was actually inside a three-story tall building which was the Khyber Agency fort. It surrounded the park on all sides and was the size and length of a football playing field.

"The fort," said Janice, "has fallen three times to enemy attacks, the first when it was British built and manned. Every time it was built up greater and tougher than before."

They stopped to chuckle at a tall leafy banyan tree. It was "bound" to the earth by three thick chains. Beside it was a large plaque in three languages. The English read "**I AM UNDER ARREST** ONE EVENING BRITISH OFFRS AFTER DRINKING HEAVILY THOUGHT I WAS DESERTING MY POST THEY ORDERED MESS SERGEANT TO ARREST ME"

Further along they lined up behind the others at a parade ground and took seats before a large sign which read THE GUARDIANS OF KHYBER PASS. Underneath it read NOV 1878.

On the parade ground facing them was a military band in brown uniforms. The first row had drums suspended from harnesses, the second row carried fifes. They waited until the tour group was seated and still. Then at a command they began to play and march, executing marches and counter marches, the two rows passing before and behind and passing between each other.

It was quite a stirring display and executed very precisely. There was enthusiastic applause afterward.

In the midst of the acclaim a lieutenant sat down beside Janice. She smiled and greeted him, then introduced him to Karen.

"Karen, this is Lieutenant Jamison Atal Momand. He is the third in command of the Khyber Rifle post. Lieutenant, this is Lance Corporal Karen Danburn, our latest addition to Post 373."

"An honor and a pleasure, Corporal. We must talk later. But I'll leave you to finish watching the show."

He shook her hand and stood to walk away.

The next show was of some three dozen men in traditional blue and white clothing with white caps on their heads. They performed a sort of whirling dervish dance which caused the skirts of the clothing to fan out into great bell shapes above their white pants. A sort of wild music leaning heavily to flutes accompanied them. They were also greeted with great applause.

The final show was of men in brown daily clothing with green trim on the bottoms of the skirts. They marched and counter-marched more raggedly but with great enthusiasm. They carried curved swords which they brandished. At the end the men paired off and executed "duels" with occasional clashing of swords and much circling around each other.

After that the audience stood and applauded and cheered the three groups, each of which came forward to receive the appreciation and to bow before running off. There were three encores before Lieutenant Momand came forward with a sergeant who formed up the men and march them further off the field.

Janice hung back and let the tour group exit the area as the Lieutenant walked to join them.

"Dear Corporal," he said to her with a smile. "I am so pleased you awaited me."

"My pleasure, Lieutenant. May we please address each other informally. We are off duty and I'm showing Karen this remarkable city you Pakistanis have created."

"Indeed, Janice. Lance Corporal, will you likewise grant me informal speech?"

"Happily," she said, trying to imitate the slightly flowery style the other two had adopted. "I'm afraid I don't speak Urdu and can only get by in Pashto and Dari.

"Please call me Karen."

"It's remarkable that you speak three languages. So few of your countrymen have more than one."

Janice may have bristled at that implied put down of Americans but she didn't show it. She said, "Oh, but Karen is fluent in French and Spanish as well."

"Only school-girl dialects, I'm afraid," said Karen.

This was not quite true. With the aid of Tiara she could read every written language on the planet and understand most spoken ones. Speaking them herself, however, was possible only if they were similar in pronunciation and grammar to the languages which she already knew. Some languages were impossible for her, such as the African click languages which might have as many as 48 tongue-click consonants.

"Come walk with me," he said. "We can sit in the mess room and have refreshments while we get better acquainted."

They entered the fort by a door other than the one the tour group had entered and exited the parade ground. The halls were wide enough that the three could walk abreast and make small talk. The Lieutenant made an effort to include Karen in the conversation, positioning her between him and Janice.

In the mess, the small officer's mess, Karen noted, they were served by a soldier in casual-dress uniform covered by a white apron. They all had tea but the two women refused snacks, saying they planned to eat in the Bazaar and didn't want to ruin their appetites.

"The Bazaar," said the Lieutenant, "is a fascinating place even for those of us who have been here a while. As long as the two of you stay together, remain alert, and leave by nightfall, you should be safe.

"But then, any party with the Lance Corporal in it should be safe," he said to Janice, then transferred his gaze to Karen. "Your reputation precedes you."

"Except that no one would recognize me out of uniform," she replied. "And even in uniform my face would be unfamiliar."

"Ah, but you would be wearing your sword. Wouldn't you? Or did you leave it at your base?"

"No, it's with me. Or more correctly in the weapons lockers at the reception center."

"Oh, we can't have that for honored guests. May I send a couple of my men to get your weapons? Yours as well, Janice."

She looked uncertain but Karen was not. No one would steal them; the Lieutenant would be sending two trusted men, for she guessed he had more reasons than diplomacy for his suggestion. What they were she did not know, but through Tiara (and her own increasingly-able reading of the many tiny cues people gave out) she was sure his reasons were strong ones.

"It's OK with me. You?" she said to her friend.

Janice shrugged, willing to rely on Karen's judgment.

The Lieutenant spoke in Pashto on his cell phone, then clipped it back to his belt and spoke to Karen.

"You may not be recognizable with any ordinary weapon. But a woman carrying a sword-- Everyone has heard the tales of the jineri who killed nine men with a sword. There are those who argue she is merely human rather than supernatural. But in either case she is a personage to be wary of."

The man then enquired as to their families' health, asked how Karen was adjusting to her new quarters and routines, and made other small talk.

After about fifteen minutes of this he frowned.

"My men should be here by now. Please wait a moment."

He made another cell phone call, then put away his phone and said, "There was a delay at the reception center. The tour people are leaving and the personnel there mistakenly gave them priority. Your weapons are now on the way."

This was a lie. Pegasus had accompanied the men to the reception area and back. His real presence was the size of a brick and invisible, so he'd been able to stay close. The men had quickly gotten the weapons and then photographed them back in the fort. They had also X-rayed the sword, getting back no image of its interior structure. It was impervious to any kind of forces except for esoteric ones not known to Earthly science.

A few minutes later two soldiers bore into their Lieutenant's presence the women's weapons. They laid them down on the mess table in front of the two women. One of them began to apologize to their boss but he cut them short with a gesture and told them to return to their other duties.

He watched as the women stood, divested their vests, and donned and adjusted the straps and holsters holding their weapons. He was especially interested in Karen's futuristic needle submachine pistol with its long thin barrel and extra-sweptback stock.

"I've never seen one of those."

Karen said, "It's an experimental model. Shoots spin-stabilized needles in clusters of three, nine, and nineteen. Not very accurate beyond ten meters but I can cut a person in two close up."

The women sat down and took up their tea cups.

"And that is the famous Samurai sword, no doubt."

"Not really."

Karen weighed the benefits of remaining mysterious and giving a rational explanation and decided on the second option.

"Its blade is straight and much thinner, being made of a super-hard composite plastic."

"May I see it?"

"Only from a distance I'm afraid. It's so sharp you can literally cut off an arm and not know it until the pain starts."

"Of course."

She stood. In a motion so fast it was a blur the weapon was in her hand. A blink at the wrong instant and the sword would have seemed to magically appear.

Karen turned the blade this way and that so the officer could get a better view.

"Impressive. The blade looks like metal. But it is not, you say. Are we going to see more products made of this remarkable material?"

"I'm sure we will but it might be many years from now. It's very expensive to make. I could only afford it by signing a contract to give a detailed report on its pros and cons."

She holstered the sword, more slowly but still remarkable for its ease, and sat back down.

"Well, it has been pleasant," he said. "But I have duties to get back to. And I'm sure you're eager to see the city. Do take the advice our little tour guide gave you. Landi Kotal may be old and shabby in places, but it has worthy sights to see."

They all stood. The Lieutenant stood and escorted them out of the fort down the stairs into the reception area. He waved to them and left. They did the same, accompanied by a smile from "our little tour guide" who was seated at the reception desk.

Back in Karen's truck, her sword removed but all their other weapons in place, Janice spoke as her friend started the truck.

"Did you really buy that story our dear friend gave us about the delay getting our weapons to us?"

"No. I'd bet they took photos of them. Maybe tried to X-ray my sword."

"'Tried'?"

"The case and the sword are too dense to show any detail."

"Hmm. I have to echo the LT. It's a remarkable weapon."

Their informal tour was as interesting to the two women as it had been advertised. Janice was impressed by the architectural elements of the hospital. Karen enjoyed the end of the water pipeline where the icy waters from the north plunged into a reservoir in a great frothing splash. She guessed that the splashy show was not incidental, that it helped to aerate the water.

The shrine to poet Amir Hamza Shinwari was also impressive. Outside it looked more like a jail, with thick walls and bars on the windows, the windows on the second floor only. Janice explained.

"Fanatics who disapproved of the poet have twice tried to destroy or at least deface it. Each time the authorities have made that tougher."

Inside they saw a second deterrent to defacement: an armed guard who watched those inside as suspiciously as any bank guard. He stared at the two women but when they approached him asking if they should leave their weapons with him he said he'd "been notified" that they would be coming and turned away to watch others.

Inside there were book shelves of poems and artworks from all over Pakistan and from many eras. There were also photos of various personages and where they had been born and lived. In a separate room there were little dioramas of them and their homes. In still another room was a small theater with a continuously running video on poetical and other art subjects.

"I wouldn't have thought poets and artists were so important," Karen said as they left the building.

"Literacy in Pakistan arrived later than in Western nations. So poems which could be memorized and spread by word of mouth were correspondingly more important. Even now with high literacy rates they're still important. Poor Afghanistan with worse literacy is even more dependent."

"This is why so many schools emphasize memorizing the Qu'ran. I was told that in language school but forgot it."

That was true. She didn't add that she'd also memorized the Islamic bible. It was easy with Tiara helping, but Karen had always had a phenomenal memory about subjects she wanted to remember.

This still didn't help her understand what she memorized. That was especially true about the Qu'ran and highly advanced text books. In fact, it had hurt her understanding when quite young until she recognized that downside of perfect memory.

<>

They were walking back to Karen's truck when she spoke to Janice in a low voice, "Do not speak. Do not show emotion."

Janice slanted her eyes to follow her friend's gaze. Three men were standing perhaps fifty feet off to one side. They were heavily armed with knives and pistols and rifles. All had long black scraggly beards.

They began to walk toward the women. Karen stopped and waited, facing them. Janice ranged herself alongside her.

The men swaggered to a halt only a few feet away. The middle of the three sneered at them. He said in badly accented English, "Two whores pretending to be men. We should teach you a lesson."

The three men were smiling in malicious anticipation. Slowly their smiles wilted.

Karen was watching all around her with Tiara's gravity radar. She saw Janice glance at her, then back at the men, then back at her for several longer moments. Karen kept most of her attention on the men in front of her. Her eyes did not blink, or so it seemed the blinks came so far apart. This was her usual response to threat: total, totally cold, fierce attention poised on a knife edge.

"But," said the center man, executing a peculiar jerk of his chin upward, "we won't bother. We would be smeared with your dirt."

He turned abruptly and marched decisively away. His cronies followed him with dirty looks shot back at the women.

Janice relaxed. Karen did not. She continued to stand, gaze locked on the men while they walked a hundred feet to a truck of their own, got in, and drove away. She kept watching till it rounded a distant corner and disappeared.

She had Pegasus loft half a mile and keep them under observation until they had gone several miles down the road east toward Peshawar.

Janice had been speaking to her for a full minute until Karen turned her attention back to her friend. She re-played her memory back fast forward.

She considered one comment her friend had said: "It actually looked like your eyes were glowing." They had been via a command to Suit, but Janice could not have seen it: Karen had directed that the illusion be visible only to the men.

"It must have been an odd reflection from the sun that made it look that way."

They walked on to her truck and got in it. As Karen started its engine Janice said, "Well, that look I saw on your face wasn't an illusion. I've never seen anyone look so blood-thirsty, without moving a muscle. You positively projected deadly menace. But your face was frozen and you didn't shift your weight forward ready to jump on them."

Karen put the truck in gear and headed toward the Bazaar.

"Funny. I suppose you're right. But I've never seen myself when I've been threatened by something. I just go totally focused on meeting the threat with the minimum effort and maximum effect."

"You weren't going to kill those guys? I had the feeling that any instant you'd go from relaxed to slicing their heads off. I've seen how fast you can move."

"Your friend the LT must been right. People will make the connection between the sword and those loonies I put down a few days ago.

"But they were safe from that. To the Pakistanis we're Afghan mercenaries on Pakistani soil. Our good friends the Khyber Rifles would hate having us kill good Pakistanis. I'd have just beat up on them a little bit, taken their weapons from them. They'd be so humiliated by that they probably wouldn't even mention it to anyone."

"You are one scary bitch," said Janice.

It was not an insult. Janice might look like a cheerleader dressing up when she went to work wearing a uniform. But she was not; she was a soldier through and through.

<>

Sunset was gilding the Bazaar when they arrived there. Karen parked in one of the parking lots near the Bazaar which was on each side of a long double-wide street barred to vehicles. The Bazaar paralleled the nearby Peshawar-Jalalabad highway which threaded the Pass.

Out of the truck they adjusted their vests to cover their weapons but Karen made no attempt to hide the fact that she carried a sword on her back.

They entered the western end. The sun was at their backs casting their shadows ahead of them. With two- to four-story buildings on each side of them it was a bit like walking within a canyon.

It was also like an outside shopping mall. Some of the merchandise was fairly modern. Some looked as if it could have been created a thousand years before. The shops were large and small.

The crowd was heavy even this close to meal time. The people included men and women, the latter always in a group or accompanied by a man. Clothing was mostly traditional, some shabby and some expensive. There were also some Western style clothing in the mix, but all the women wore scarves as did Karen and Janice. Most of the men wore little round caps, usually white.

Almost all the clothing was brightly colored, but some women wore all black. Karen with her pure white and white-gold stood out. But the sword made her even more conspicuous. The two soldiers walked in their own little lane of people anxious not to crowd them.

They bought nothing on the nearly mile-long walk to the Bazaar's eastern end, but they made notes between themselves of treats and trinkets to buy on the way back and of places where they might like to eat.

The sun had just hidden its face when they doubled back but the sky was still bright. Now they began to collect and fill shopping bags. Nor were they the only ones.

They were near their beginning when they detoured into a restaurant. There were tables of various sizes in the middle of the room and a buffet near the far wall. But like a lot of Middle-Eastern eating places it had deep waist-high shelves on the three walls nearest the entrance. Plenty of people were standing there eating. Many of those were of families, the smaller children being handed food down to them, but there were singles and triples there too.

They chose to eat standing also, despite being somewhat tired. (At least Janice was; it would take a lot more to tire out Karen's genetically enhanced body.) They ordered by pushing buttons on an ordering console which might have been found in the most modern Western establishments. Soon a waitress delivered the food and waited to be paid, the usual custom in much of the Middle East. They both paid in cash and tipped generously.

Janice liked her food spiced and Karen even more highly spiced. Karen's friend raised her eyebrows and smiled at some of the condiments Karen chose.

People-watching was one of the pleasures of the meal. And they were watched too. Especially the tall athletic woman in blazing white and white gold with a sword upon her back. She might indeed be one of the mighty female jinni, a jineri.

Karen caught a little boy and girl at a table nearby staring at her round eyed. She smiled at them and winked.

They ducked their heads and then looked back up, absorbed in wonder until their parents scolded them for rudeness.

The two women took their time and savored their food and drink. Tired from a day on the go they ate big meals, though Karen's portions were almost thrice the size of Janice's. She was a big woman while her friend was petite.

<>

Night had fully fallen when they left the restaurant and headed toward Karen's truck. The warmth of the day was long gone and chill filled the dry air. They stowed their purchases and drove away.

Traffic was light on the westbound part of the Khyber Pass highway on which they drove. The oncoming Pakistan-bound traffic was heavier. There were only a few cars behind them and a heavy truck before them when they entered the higher, narrower, and twistier section. The road would remain that way most of the way toward the Tor Kham border between Pakistan and Afghanistan.

That strip city showed only a few lights, though there were a few street lights at the border and a few open establishments on each side. Most of the cars behind them and the truck ahead of them peeled off at the border. Though another truck, this one lighter, pulled in ahead of them as they left the city.

Karen had been having suspicions about a car behind her. She'd had Pegasus swoop down close enough to see inside the vehicle. It held the three Pakistanis she'd confronted earlier and one other man.

She'd kept quiet to see if the men would quit their pursuit, if that what it was. They didn't, so she began to reverse-plan how they'd ambush Janice and herself. The likeliest included the truck that was now ahead of them.

When the lights of Tor Kham had vanished behind them she spoke to Janice.

"Don't panic. But I believe we are going to be ambushed soon. Just remember that this vehicle is proof against attacks. Whatever happens, stay inside it with the doors locked."

Her friend sat up, any sleepiness banished. Her voice was calm.

"What makes you say that? Never mind. What do you plan to do?"

"I'm going to let them stop us. Then I'm going to get out and teach them not to attack Americans."

"That doesn't sound smart. Stay inside and we'll call the base. They can have an emergency response team here in fifteen minutes. Maybe faster."

"No. The loonies might just surrender without a fight. They'd probably just get a rap on the knuckles for an attempted robbery. And anyway they might not surrender. Some of our guys might get hurt."

"And you might get hurt. This is a stupid plan."

"Nevertheless. It's what I'm going to do."

Janice clamped her mouth shut. Karen had a manner that was implacable. Nothing short of death was going to stop her. A friend's arguments were not.

Janice drew her weapon, checked it, and shifted her ammunition packs for easier access.

Nearly five minutes later the ambush happened. This part of the highway between Tor Kham and Baha Tor was barren of any possible witnesses. Now there were only one car behind them and one truck ahead. The truck began to slow. It drifted to the center of the two-lane highway and beyond and back again as if the driver was dozing.

Finally it slewed sideways and stopped so that it blocked the road, facing to the side and a bit back toward them.

Karen smoothly slowed her truck. So did the car behind them. Then when she stopped so did they. And slewed sideways to block the women's retreat.

The directions of the car's and the truck's head lights were in opposite directions. Slightly eddying early-evening fog caught some of the light before and behind the two women. The fog-scattered light and the opposed headlights lit the area around Karen's truck brightly.

Karen turned off her ignition and headlights. She reached up and behind her to flick the interior light control to Always Off.

Janice peered before and behind them. Men were getting out of the car and truck which had them blocked. A passing big hauler coming from Jalalabad whooshed by them on the separate Peshawar-bound highway.

Karen ignored Janice's gaze when that woman turned it upon her. Her killing calm was on her. She was fully alert and full of an icy fierceness. Her brain moved at higher speed. Time seemed to slow.

Behind them the men split into two on each side of her truck. They approached to two dozen or so feet away and stopped. They held rifles and machine guns slung and pointing slightly downward but toward Karen's truck.

Four men came from the other truck and stopped in a line the same distance away, weapons similarly slung.

In good English a man in the line before them called out to them to get out, and to leave their weapons in the truck.

Karen got out, taking her sword with her on her back. She slammed the driver's side door behind her. It locked.

"What do you want?" she said loudly in English.

The man may have smiled. The light behind him kept her from seeing it if so.

"We're going to have some fun. Then we're going to kill you."

That declaration--caught on the cell phone clipped to her belt--was Karen's cue.

Her pistol was in her hand too fast to even blur. It just seemed to jump there. She was already moving, fast, fast, toward the side of the road away from her truck. Drawing them away from Janice.

Her pistol buzzed four times. Storms of needles took out all four headlights. The scene plunged into darkness. And she went invisible and upward at the same time.

Tiara's and Pegasus's gravity radar lit the scene below her clearly. She paused fifty feet up and surveyed the scene.

The two groups of men rushed in the direction she had gone, firing toward where she had vanished. The explosions and flares of muzzle light shattered the night for a good minute.

Hidden in the noise was the sound of a truck door slamming closed. Janice had not stayed in Karen's truck.

Panic flashed through Karen. Stupid! Stupid! Stupid! To think that Janice would stay safe while a companion was in danger. Soldiers did not do that.

Janice crouched by the bonnet of the truck, leaned on it to steady her aim, and aimed her machine pistol toward the men, illuminated by their own fire. She fired twice, three-shot bursts. The sound was lost in the enemy's barrage. The bullets were not. Two of the men dropped.

Karen's cold fierce will returned to her. She swooped down and further from her truck in the direction of Baha Tor and the base. She fired two bursts, at an angle so that her aim was off to the side of her truck. The needles would not find her friend.

They made their quiet buzzing sound, spin-stabilized needles nevertheless spreading and beginning to pin-wheel from a hundred's feet distance.

Her muzzle flash was dim. Yet bright enough so that it and the sound of her shots pointed out her direction.

The men began another barrage in her direction. But Karen was already fifty feet in the air. Suit made even the heaviest gunfire irrelevant, but the height gave her a better view of the battleground.

Janice was still behind the truck. She'd also made inroads on the enemy during their second barrage. Another man was on the ground.

Three Janice. Two Karen. That left three.

One of them yelled "Spread out! Spread--" A buzz cut him short.

Both remaining men obeyed, then crouched in the sandy dirt behind a small bush. Their weapons traversed the darkness, their eyes strained to see the enemy.

Time to end this. Karen swooped and took the head off one man with her sword.

Then she darted to a position a few feet in front of the last man. Her aspect was that of a black shroud floating in the air, two red eyes near the top of it.

The last man screamed and fired at the same time. Bullets flew toward the apparition and vanished into nothing when they encountered its force-field shield. He kept firing, holding the automatic rifle's trigger down. Until it ran out of bullets.

He crouched, staring, hardly daring to breathe.

The jinn waited long moments. Then from it came an eerie voice.

FOREIGNERS ARE UNDER MY PROTECTION. RUN BACK TO TOR KHAM AND TELL EVERYONE THERE SO.

The man paused, his face screwed up in terror. Then he carefully and quietly placed his weapon on the ground, stood carefully, turned and began to walk east. In moments his steps accelerated and he raced away.

Karen bobbed up fifty feet and tracked his process into the distance for a full minute.

Karen shouted, "It's over! They're all gone. Good job! Get back in the truck!"

Janice paused, then did as ordered. She must have remembered how well Karen did in the dark.

A dark that was lightened occasionally by trucks on the other highway whooshing by on their way to Pakistan. So far there were no signs of approaching headlights coming from Pakistan.

From above Karen continued to watch him run toward Pakistan. For a time he paralleled the road, then made his way onto it. Then off it as a cargo hauler approached from the direction of Pakistan and passed him. He was staggering now as he continued trying to run.

The big truck slowed and stopped behind the assailants' car. The driver stared at the scene illuminated by his headlights.

Karen dropped down beside the cab, whipped her sword clean of blood and flesh, sheathed it. She rapped on the truck door.

The driver jerked, stared at her. His sudden fear ebbed as he took in her harmless appearance, visible in the back-deflection of the light from the car in front of him. Her big beautiful eyes in a face of unsurpassed beauty looked calmly at him. If a woman was not afraid, why should he be?

"There has been a fight," she said to him in Pashto. "It is over." Then she repeated it in Dari and poorly accented Urdu.

He answered in Pashto: "What happened?"

"Some men tried to kill Americans. They failed. The Americans--we--fought back."

"Oh." He considered her. Reserved judgment. Looked all around as if to see through the darkness on all sides of him. Relaxed.

He tensed again as an armored olive long-body SUV from the American base rushed up on the opposite road and screeched to a halt, followed by another. Troops spilled out of them, clad in helmets and body armor, long-barreled weapons at the ready, their heads turning in search arcs as they looked through the night-sight glasses mounted on their helmets. They spread out in pairs.

Karen put her hands up to channel her voice toward the troops. She shouted, "It's all over! Ease down! It's all over!"

No one eased down immediately. The nearest pair oriented on her voice and the cab of the heavy hauler.

"I'm coming into the light! My hands are up! My hands are up!"

She advanced into the side-scatter of the truck's headlights, not into the direct light. That would light her up too much and damage their enhanced night vision. She stood there, hands up. One pair approached her.

One of the two men recognized her, spoke into a microphone mounted on his helmet. "It's the Marine. It looks like she's been up to her old tricks. I see at least two ragheads down."

Soon the situation was understood by the two fire teams from the base. Their commander, backed up by radio communication from the base, established a perimeter around the battle site and illuminated it with flood lights.

More vehicles arrived from the base. The long-hauler got out of his cab and leaned against it, smoking and looking upon the scene as if it were a welcome diversion from a boring run.

Janice joined Karen as she spoke to their boss, Lieutenant Wang. Sergeant Matlock prowled about, taking photographs of the scene.

A big forensics van came from the base, driving on the westbound Jalalabad highway since all traffic was blocked coming toward the base. The experts weren't going to pass up a fresh battle scene.

More lights were set up all about the scene. Traffic from Jalalabad slowed and bunched up as their passengers gawked at the scene. More troops showed up to direct that traffic onward.

More troops on the road to Jalalabad pushed the attackers' vehicles off the road once they'd been photographed a dozen ways. Karen moved her truck off the side of the road. Then the newest set of troops began to direct the long-hauler onward toward Jalalabad. A while later first one, then a few more vehicles approached from Tor Kham and were also directed on their way to Jalalabad.

Two hours after the events Karen and Janice were allowed to finish their trip and get to bed.

Part 6 - Phantom

On Monday just before 10:00, the time for the regular weekly meeting of the base's department heads, Sergeant Matlock told Karen and Janice they were to attend it with him and Lieutenant Wang. They did so.

The first order of business was discussion of the ambush and their response to it. The two women were asked to give a brief description of the action.

"You were either very lucky or very good," Captain Giatelli said to them when they were done. They said nothing.

"In any case, you both did a good job. You are dismissed back to your duties. And, don't let it bother you if there is some blowback about this."

He nodded and they stood and left.

Outside Karen said to Janice, "What did he mean about 'blowback'"?

"All the men were Pakis. We're Afghans, to the Pakis way of thinking, or worse: mercenaries in the hire of Afghans. The two countries aren't enemies, but they don't like each other."

Karen knew that. Pakistanis considered Afghans inferior, Afghans resented their richer and more modern cousins.

<>

"Blowback" did happen. Pakistan issued a statement damning the killing of seven of its citizens, though without any suggestion that the country would pursue legal action or even diplomatic sanctions. Old Middle-East hands at the base told her not to worry. The bluster was to satisfy those in Pakistan who were most anti-Afghan and anti-foreigner.

The Afghan government and the U. S. State Department issued a statement pointing out that the attackers had been on Afghan soil at the time and several had criminal records. Other pundits in the U. S. also pointed out that it had been seven men bandits versus two (women) military personnel. There was much derision from various sources about how "piss-poor" warriors the men must have been to ambush someone and even then to "get their asses kicked."

Even in Pakistan there were defenders. Those who considered themselves true heirs of the Pathan warrior tradition derided the bandits. Some even held up the two foreigners as the true heirs to the tradition (conveniently leaving out that the foreigners were women).

Karen kept a low profile for the next several weeks, doing mostly office work and only occasionally going out on patrol. Not that this was needed except to keep up her status as a ranger scout/sniper. She had Pegasus float at a mile height during that time and continuously scan the area around the post out to several miles.

Only once did she need to confront roaming would-be attackers of the base. She did so in her persona as a jinn and the attackers fled without even firing a shot.

She and Janice did have to attend a workshop on "Diplomatic and Force Responses To Enemy Attack." Sergeant Matlock told her that this was mostly bull-shit which was to satisfy the anti-military sentiment back in the States. It was a pro-forma slap on the wrist.

The only negative response Karen cared about was a minor annoyance. Her exploits had gone viral on the InterWeb and she was kidded about it at the base.

One example was when she was asked to autograph printouts of a blogsite article headlined as ***Beautiful Badass Beats Bandit Butts***. The article included a brief bio of her high-school exploits, Marine training history, and her high scores leading up to selection as Recruit of the Year.

It mostly had lots of photos. Most were from her high-school sports years with various action shots such as in soccer. There she had spiked a winning shot from an exuberant upside-down flip. But the largest number was from a social web site from when she and some of her friends had visited Venice Beach. She was shown clad in a tiny wet bikini with her nipples obviously at attention from the breeze off the Pacific.

That lead her to be labeled "Corporal Nippelicious" by some of the more juvenile personnel on the post and to a few fights. Though none involved her. Instead she had some defenders who objected to the label. Karen herself merely shrugged off such comments with a faint smile.

The most annoying response to the attack came about a month later--if it was a response. She received an email and a printed copy of orders to report to Marine Corps Jalalabad Headquarters for "assignment modification."

<>

She drove there, spiffed up in her best Marine Corps travel dress uniform. Arriving at the sprawling base on the outskirts of the city she was allowed to drive her pickup inside after a gate guard inspected her printed orders and double-checked them online.

The directions to the Marine Corps Jalalabad HQ building were clear and included a printed map to back them up. Three right-angled zigzags and one left-angled later she parked in a nearly full lot and marched to the large glass double doors giving entry to a two-story building of khaki-drab wood sidings and shallow-pitched dark-green roof.

A guard at a waist-high desk directed her down a hall and up stairs to another hall. Halfway down it she came to an open pair of double-doors and entered. Lieutenant Victor Minetti's small office was just off to her right.

She knocked on the open doorway and he bade her enter. They perused each other.

She saw a slender young man who looked both starved and wirily tough. His uniform was perfectly tailored and seemed starched though she knew that was not a practice but a choice of a fabric which never wrinkled. His hair was nearly irregulation but emphasized his Italian good looks. Despite his youth his sideburns had a tinge of grey.

She gave him a whip-lash correct salute, though it was not strictly required by the book.

"Lance Corporal Karen Danburn reporting as ordered, sir!"

He returned her salute from his seat and said, "At ease, Lance Corporal. Really at ease, slouchily at ease if it would make you feel better. You are not here because of a reprimand or anything even near it."

She sat in one of the two padded chairs in front of his desk and crossed one leg over the other. She did not lean back or relax, however. He sat forward and placed his arms on his desk.

"In fact, you are here because you've been doing such an outstanding job." He looked into her face. It displayed not the tiniest trace of emotion. She could have been a perfectly mimetic robot.

He studied it for a moment, then sat back in his chair, placing his hands over his flat belly.

"I've been monitoring your performance closely since your extraordinary orders came through here. They give you practically unlimited freedom. I don't know whose hand you had to grease or whose dick or pussy you had to slurp. But I was not about to give you perfectly free rein."

Karen smiled frostily. "Neither. My sterling reputation got me that freedom. And I just now remembered. Two weeks after I arrived at Post 373 there was an inspection of stores. Funny how the sergeant who did it looked just like you. Except for a mustache."

He grinned. "Yeah, that was me. Playing junior spy. It made my day."

She was tempted to smile back. But it was too early to let her guard down.

He stood up suddenly. She stood too.

"Come on. Let's go to lunch early, avoid the rush. We can talk while eating."

He set a fast but not hurried pace. He just seemed to a have a fast metabolism. He spoke not at all on the four-block walk.

Base Cafeteria #4 was big. It had a hot line, a cold line, and four long buffet tables under clear sanitary hoods. They separated then came together past the two pay stations. He led the way to a square table near a window where there were two other Marines.

At least, she thought they were. Their clothing was non-regulation though reasonably neat, in the Afghan style. But they had the same air of competence and confidence of every other Marine she'd ever known.

He set down his tray, then himself, and indicated the position to one side. It put her at right angles to him and to a tall black man opposite him. Opposite her was a small woman who seemed 18 at first glance and ageless at a second.

"How nice to find you here!" said the Lieutenant. Karen was sure it was no coincidence but said nothing as he introduced them.

The black man, John Hendrickson, was impressively muscled and appeared stupid. She was sure he was not. Ariel McCarthy was beautiful in the pale-skinned curly-haired manner of many redheads, with the same flawless complexion Karen had, so perfect it seemed PhotoFixed.

Karen wondered if she were a Galactic transplant like herself.

The Lieutenant set to with a hearty appetite. Karen copied him.

Everyone's plates were piled high, even that of Ariel McCarthy who weighed the least of them. Apparently all four had fast metabolisms. None talked, though all eyed each other with veiled curiosity.

They finished nearly together and sat drinking dessert drinks or eating dessert.

"John and Ariel work for me. They are--"

"WITH you," said John with a faint smile. Ariel quirked an eyebrow and nodded slightly, an even fainter smile on her face.

"They're civilian contractors. You, on the other hand, will work under my orders. Very general orders, I should add. I prefer to get good people, trust them, and let them surprise me with their success. I've almost never been disappointed."

He shifted position and took another sip of his highly creamed and sugared coffee.

"The Marines have been poor relatives of the other services for centuries. Only recently have we gotten decent funding and equipment and uniforms at first hand. So early on we developed the tradition of 'Improvise, Adapt and Overcome.'

"You know this, I'm sure. But what you don't know yet is that some of us take it to higher levels than officially recognized. I'm one of those.

"One of my responsibilities is the safety of the highway from here to Pakistan's border. Since you've done so well in the area around Post 373 and up to that border, I'm expanding your responsibilities to include patrolling that highway. When we get back to my office I'll give you official orders to that effect. They'll go into effect immediately."

John said, "What he can't say officially is that he expects you to expand those duties as you choose. If, for instance, you want to patrol the Pakistan side of the border--which is illegal--you may do so. But if you get caught..."

Ariel gave another of her wintry smiles. Karen took that as agreement.

"Then I'll be punished in whatever way keeps the higher ups from punishing him. Sort of thought that."

"That," said the Lieutenant, "is a base lie. I am shocked and hurt you would think me so two-faced. Let's go, Karen, before they say something mean and REALLY hurt my feelings."

He stood, beaming genially, while the other three shook hands and expressed pleasure to be working together. Then he and she left.

Outside the cafeteria he said, "Did you bring your famed sword with you?"

"Yes."

"I'd like to see it."

"Certainly, Sir. But I let no one handle it except me. It's unbelievably dangerous. And kind of personal."

"Fine. Ariel has the same philosophy."

Karen directed him to her truck. While they talked and he chatted about inconsequentials, she pondered Ariel. Her handshake had imparted absolutely no information to Suit's super-advanced probes. It was as if she was not even there. Yet her touch had been warm and strong.

At the truck Minetti said, "I'd like to see a demo of your sword. Why don't we drive to one of the training fields?"

"Certainly."

The field he directed her to had a number of obstacles on an obstacle course and several sandy circular areas where various training was done.

They got out at the otherwise empty small parking lot, she donned the sword harness and sheathe, and they approached an area with various piles of lumber and stone.

"If you will, please draw as you would in an emergency."

The sword appeared magically in one hand.

He blinked.

"Amazing. They'd have no hint you were about to fight."

He peered at the blade. She backed off a foot or so and turned the sword so that he could see it from different angles.

"It's amazingly thin. Must come from the fact that it's a composite material stronger than steel. At least if what I hear is true.

"Would you demonstrate on some material? Like that bush?"

Karen took several long strides in a smooth motion almost like skating. The top then the middle part of the bush began toppling to the ground, severed by two invisibly swift strokes.

Karen went further, to a jumble of wooden lumber and stones. She picked up a 2x4, threw it up, and sliced into three separate pieces before it struck ground. Then she threw a fist-sized stone in the air and sliced it into two pieces.

He had followed her at a cautious distance. When she turned toward him he hurriedly backed up a couple of steps, then peered at the blade again. She held it level a yard away from him, again turning it in several directions.

"It shows no stain of any kind, even dust. Remarkable.

"OK, Karen. Put it away. My curiosity is satisfied."

In the truck on the way back to his office he spoke about something that Karen had thought about.

"I'm not satisfied that the Pakistanis who ambushed you and Corporal Wilson did so out of spite or to rob you. Or just that. It strikes me that an example of such extraordinary material could give Pakistan's materials industry quite a boost."

"Yes," she said slowly, voicing a thought she'd had the day after the ambush. "Janice and I visited the Khyber Pass fort earlier that day and joined a tour there. A lieutenant there was very friendly. He had his men bring our weapons to us from the tour guide reception area where they'd been locked up. As a courtesy, he said, to fellow warriors. It took them long enough to photo them and try to take X-rays of the sword."

"Try?"

"The sword and its sheathe block X-rays."

In his office he handed a blue folder to her which was sealed shut with red tape. She'd noticed it before but said nothing.

"Check these and see if they're clear."

The orders were in stilted officialese but simple and clear.

"They're clear. I understand them and will obey."

"Good. They are in force as of your acknowledgement. Now, good day, Lance Corporal. It was a pleasure to meet you."

"Likewise, sir."

She took two steps back and saluted. At his return salute, she did an about face and walked out.

<>

Back at Post 373 Lieutenant Wang accepted her new duties philosophically.

"Not surprised you've been given more responsibilities. You seem to excel at everything you do. We'll just have to get used to not seeing you around so much."

Her two co-workers, Janice and "Abe" Schultz were less happy, he because she'd taken work off his shoulders and Janice because Karen had become a friend.

"But those are the breaks," the woman said. "I've only been in the service a few years but already I know friends come and go. We'll miss you."

"Hey. It's not like I'm not going to be here at all. I'm still based here."

<>

That was true enough. But her new responsibilities took a good deal of time even though she had the almost unimaginable powers of a super-advanced civilization behind her.

One of those was Pegasus. In him she could fly the entire 80 kilometers from Jalalabad to the Pakistan border at Tor Kham and the 50 kilometers on to Peshawar in about five minutes at just below the speed of sound. From two miles up his gravity radar could scan the land below out to almost thirty miles on each side. That was a huge area for a half dozen men to hide in before hijacking a truck. Still, Peg could see objects as small as a beetle and analyze it an infinitesimal instant.

Thinking about matters, however, she decided bad guys would likely just loiter in one of the small villages on that stretch of highway and intercept a target traveling a known schedule, a schedule easy to find with a little bribery or eavesdropping. Or they could follow it from where it picked up a cargo.

A better tool was Tiara. She was already monitoring all the communications of the entire planet for items of information which Karen could use, such as any text message or phone call mentioning Karen or her parents. This was many megabytes of information every second. But this was trivial for Tiara. And she understood all written and spoken languages.

Karen simply added another item for her to look out for: messages about hijacking cargos on the Jalalabad-Peshawar highway. Afghans and especially Pakistanis had recently become mad about cell phones. Even the most starveling poor person HAD to have a phone. But so few were available as yet that some people actually carried dummy phones.

Of course, encrypting private conversations had become a fad long before cell phones were introduced in the more backward countries. But again this was no problem for Tiara. To that super-advanced computer all messages might as well have been made in the clear.

Another big help was her S2 section. Lieutenant Wang had Janice and Abe analyze hijackings in the two countries for the last dozen years. They came up with several facts which Karen would find useful.

Thus armed Karen spent almost a month before she had a chance to thwart bad guys. But she almost missed it because it was an ambush committed on the spur of the moment. Not planned ahead of time.

A truck carrying electronics from Peshawar to a Jalalabad store which sold TVs, video players, cameras, phones, and such broke down in the longest empty stretch of highway between Tor Kham and Jalalabad. The driver phoned Jalalabad for a mechanic. By chance the dispatcher was being visited by her boyfriend in her office. He heard it and passed it on to some friends of his who were not too far from the truck.

<>

"Wake up, Karen."

Karen had been taking a mid-morning nap after being out all night patrolling the area around the Post. She aroused quickly at Tiara's voice in her head.

She blinked her eyes clear of sleep and yawned. In seconds she was alert. She answered Tiara simply by coming fully alert.

At that Tiara filled her in on the situation, not in words but in a short series of videos interspersed with still images and maps. Her own private and silent virtual slide show.

She got up and visited her bathroom to relieve herself fully and to splash water on her face, even as she was absorbing the last of her briefing.

She scanned the area in front of her barracks. No one was nearby except a couple of troops walking to some assignment, chatting as they went. Karen went invisible, stepped outside the door, closed it behind her, and flew upward fast enough to leave a small dust-devil behind her which no one noticed.

Shortly Pegasus joined her with her pickup truck inside him. Karen flew up beside her truck and, mid-air, opened its driver-side door and settled into her seat.

In minutes Karen was over the broken-down truck. The two men driving it were sitting and lying on the grass under one of the many windbreak trees planted long ago on this stretch of highway. One was smoking.

She landed her truck a quarter mile closer to Jalalabad and got out, invisible inside Pegasus's force field. Invisible herself, she lofted to float fifty feet above the two drivers. And waited.

It was perhaps a dozen minutes later that she saw two trucks driving very fast from Jalalabad to the west. This was the bandits, rushing to get there before the repair truck.

Though there was really no hurry. They could not know it, but the repair truck (the earliest one of four which would be available) would not arrive soon. It was jump-starting a customer.

The two trucks braked to a quick stop near the drivers. Five men jumped out of them and leveled rifles at the drivers.

Those two men wisely raised their hands high in the air. The one lying on his side carefully, slowly, sat up.

Karen was dropping down even as the bandits jumped out of their trucks. She interposed her invisible self between them and the drivers and expanded part of Suit to each side so that it would transmute into air any bullets fired.

The only clue to her presence was a quick waft of air that none of the men noticed.

As she was doing this she was also calling Pegasus to her. This left her now-unshielded truck visible to anyone who looked that way. But no one did.

The bandits shouted instructions in Pashto to the drivers, who rolled onto their bellies and put their hands behind their backs. One of the bandits approached them and tied their wrists and ankles together with plastic slip-ties.

Then everyone busily began transferring electronics goods into their trucks, looking back and forth along the highway to see if any traffic was approaching.

None was. One of the men stopped and frowned as he saw Karen's truck. He said something to another bandit. That man took up a gun and began to walk toward her truck, but he was in no hurry. Probably, she thought, just as happy to let the others do all the lifting and carrying.

When he was a few feet away from her truck she abandoned the drivers, flew up then down behind him, and struck him in the back of his head with her Suit-armored hand. She used just enough force to knock him out. She caught his body as he collapsed and laid him gently onto the ground. She caught up his rifle and had Suit dissolve it into air.

Still invisible she flew back to the robbery in progress. She thought briefly about how to capture the men and deliver a suitable lesson in the futility of disobeying her.

She had Suit change the color of her traditional women's clothing, pants under knee-length dress, long-sleeved blouse, and long over-vest, to bright blood red. She had him materialize her sword in its scabbard and straps in place over her clothing. When she went visible the hilt would be seen sticking up over one shoulder. Around her waist was a gun belt with a holstered long-barreled needle machine pistol. Her hair was covered by a scarf which wound around her throat and obscured her nose and mouth.

Costumed for what she hoped her desired effect she floated down into the place she wanted--in the middle of the highway looking toward the thieves, opposite to where the drivers lay face down. Away from any bullets fired by the bandits.

She blinked into visibility and shouted in Pashto: "Freeze! Put down your weapons!"

All heads jerked around toward her. Their bodies jerked in shock. One began to turn toward her, then another.

She pointed an imperious hand toward the two. "Freeze, I said! Or die!"

One obeyed. The other did not.

Her free hand blurred and was holding her submachine gun aimed toward the turning men. She waited a fraction of a second to see if the threat worked. It seemed longer because her metabolism had speeded up and so time had seemed to slow down.

The threat failed.

Her gun buzzed. A dozen high-velocity needles lashed out toward his face. His head turned into exploding hamburger and blood.

At that the third man shouted in rage and began to level his rifle at her. His head exploded too.

The bodies slid bonelessly in seeming slow motion to the highway or the grass upon which the men stood.

The two other bandits did as they were told: froze then very slowly laid their weapons on the grass or ground under their feet.

Karen relaxed a bit. Time seemed to speed up. But the men were still moving slowly. At least one of them had crapped his pants.

Karen herded them away from the broken-down truck onto the grass a dozen feet further along the highway from the two truck drivers. She ordered them to take the same position: on their bellies, hands behind their backs, ankles together. She went among them, gun back in her holster, and tied their wrists and ankles with plastic wrap-ties materialized out of thin air.

Then with an almost infinitely sharp virtual knife she cut the drivers' bonds. As she did so she let her clothing revert from red to their usual colors.

They rolled over and sat up. They rubbed their wrists, then their ankles. They stood up.

"Who are you?" said the older of the two men. His hair was grey. The younger resembled him. A son? Or nephew?

Tiara identified them after an instant's dart into the internet.

"I'm Lance Corporal Karen Danburn, sir, U. S. Army Post 373. I've been assigned to keep the highway to Jalalabad safe."

He grinned, but there was only savagery in the baring of teeth. He looked at the bandits then turned toward them. He'd made only a couple of determined steps toward them when she said, "Stop! Come back here!"

He did so. "Why?"

"The U. S. Army does not murder or mistreat prisoners."

The son protested, "We would have lost everything! They deserve to burn in Hell."

The father was eyeing the sword upon her back. He said, "I think that's where she came from, Son. This is that jineri we've been hearing about. Don't you see her sword?"

"That's just superstition." His voice and face was sullen.

"Yet here she stands."

The man bowed deeply to her. "We thank you. We are in your debt."

She bowed back, not sure of the etiquette but thinking a jinn would be given some slack.

"You can repay any debt by dealing justly with all men, women, and children. Now please excuse me. I have phone calls to make."

<>

Soon she was joined by Lieutenant Wang and Sergeant Matlock from Post 373 with a couple of armed troopers in the back seat of their post vehicle. Shortly thereafter a U. S. Army helicopter landed. Out of it came Lieutenant Victor Minetti and, interestingly, Ariel McCarthy. The woman drifted off to lazily inspect the scene while the Lieutenant came up to her.

She did not salute, since she was under arms and guarding prisoners. But she nodded. Then she introduced the two drivers.

"Good job, Lance Corporal. I see you had to kill only two. What the Hell did that job?" He nodded at the two corpses. Blood had spilled out to outline their bodies.

"My weapon, Sir. A submachine pistol custom-made for me. Ah, there's one more bad guy. He's out cold, near my truck." She nodded to the side toward where her truck was parked.

At that the elfin "contractor" turned and began to walk toward Karen's truck. She could have sworn the woman was out of earshot from her and the Lieutenant.

The Afghan police from Jalalabad arrived next, then finally the repair truck and mechanic ordered over an hour ago.

It took over three hours before Karen was let go and could go back to the post. She barely made it into the mess hall before they closed for the day. Then she was deluged by questions and a few congratulations and had to work late with Janice and Abraham writing up her report in the correct format.

Nor was that the end of matters. In the end she wrote or

contributed to three separate lengthy reports.

<>

In the following weeks there were two more would-be hijackings in Afghanistan of Jalalabad-bound trucks carrying valuable cargo. She learned of those via phone taps and foiled them both.

On the first she again tried to fool the bandits into attacking her by accosting them without her submachine pistol drawn. The story of her fast-draw speed was well-known by now and the men obeyed her commands to freeze and lay down their weapons.

Or maybe it was the rumor that she was a female jinn. The phone text and voice messages about her intercepted by Tiara made it clear that her garments, blood-red for the few minutes she'd confronted the bandits, had been interpreted as a lust for blood. She came to be called The Red Jineri and was linked to the Blood Jinn of middle-eastern legend.

The second set of bandits simply broke off a planned attack when she deliberately drove by one of three cars they were using to rendezvous for the attempt. She made no indication she saw those in the car but the mere sight of her was enough to derail their attempt.

The Afghan state police, still relatively new at policing an entire country, decided it was THEIR job to patrol the highway between Tor Kham and Jalalabad. They began to do so and Lieutenant Minetti relieved her of her highway duties.

The bandits then shifted their attentions to Pakistan. After a few initial successes Pakistan's Khyber Rifles were assigned to highway patrol duties. Pakistan was not about to be upstaged by the "backward" Afghans.

A final result of her good job at the post was that the Lieutenant also arranged to have a two-man Marine Corps scout/sniper team assigned to Post 373 to take over her protective duties. Karen was reassigned to his team at Jalalabad full time. Many were sorry to see her go, as evidenced by the big going-away party given for her at the post.

Or, maybe, she thought ruefully, a lot of people would grasp any excuse for a party.

<>

The morning after she settled into her new quarters she arrived at her new offices and was greeted outside the square beige block of a building by John Hendrickson. He was dressed in Army fatigues but had no rank insignia.

"Hello, again, Lance Corporal," he said as he stood up from a pink-grey decorative boulder outside the door. He shook her hand. "Come with me."

He led her into a small foyer not unlike a bank auto teller security enclosure. Video cameras looked down at her from two angles.

Karen reflexively traced the electrical paths back to the security room in a picosecond-fast Tiara probe.

He placed a palm against a flat plate on the inside door. A lock clicked and he pushed the door open. Karen followed him in.

It took only a few minutes to get her photo taken and placed on a badge with two diagonal red stripes underlaying the photo and her name. Her hand prints were also taken and entered into the door-lock database so she could enter the building unaccompanied.

Down a short hall was a medium-sized conference room off to one side. Hendricks waved at the people inside but turned into a coffee room a little further along. He gestured at the hot water machine and other paraphernalia. He made a cup of coffee from a loose wicker basket of concentrate packets and she made one of hot chocolate from the same basket.

Back in the conference room they took a seat on one side of the deep brown oval table.

"Am I late?" she said to the Lieutenant.

"Nope. We're not terribly punctual around here. Let me introduce you to everybody. You know John and Ariel, of course."

In all there were thirteen people around the table. They were a motley bunch, of several ages and ethnicities. Some wore uniforms--all but one with no insignia--and some wore civilian clothes. These ranged from a formal suit (black, white shirt, blue tie) to one person who looked like a homeless person from back in the States. His haircut matched: long and greasy.

The one person whose uniform bore insignia was a tall, curvaceous, beautiful blond with long hair and a well-fitting uniform.

"And this is Sergeant First Class Jane Alexander. She keeps the department routine running and makes it look easy--at least until near the end of the year. She is going up two whole rungs and not because she screws anybody. She's going back to school to get her Master's degree. Then this damn shebang will go to Hell."

Alexander smiled slightly. "Probably true! Welcome to the madhouse, Lance Corporal."

"OK, let's start off with an Afghan Security Forces assessment, Jalalabad District. Kuznitsov." This was the homeless person.

After the third report Karen guessed that all the next reports would focus mostly upon corrupt people and criminals, both Afghans and Americans. Nor was she wrong. She also knew from Tiara that everyone here was a spy except the sergeant, the lieutenant, and herself.

Strangely, Ariel was the oldest, at least fifty, though she looked barely twenty. But Karen suspected she was even older. There was no record of a birth certificate and her history just sort of misted into existence.

Was she an alien, as Karen was? Karen decided to be very careful around the woman.

At the end of the three-hour conference, broken by a fifteen minute break where most everyone refreshed their drinks, the subject turned to Karen. And her sword.

The Lieutenant said, "We've all read a précis of your exploits, Karen." They'd much earlier gone to first-name or nickname basis. "Why did you use a sword to terminate those first nine insurgents?"

"I'm very good at finding and killing bad guys. I'd guess all of us here are or could be.

"But we could kill and kill bad guys until we fell asleep on our feet. And the next day there would be almost as many to kill.

"What I wanted to do, with the help of a few special effects and the sword, was convince all the bad guys that they faced a supernatural threat. Many of them don't fear death. They believe that they are virtuous and will go to Paradise. But a supernatural death--who could say they would not go to Hell? Forever."

"Well, it worked," said Kuznitsov. "They call you The Red Jineri. You're supposed to be one of the jinni who drink blood."

"Which is why," Hendrickson said, "you choose to wear all red now when you go hunting."

She nodded. "My job is--was--to keep the Post 373 area safe. I judged psychological warfare a better option. At preventing attacks instead of fighting off attacks."

Minetti said, "It still is. But you, and we, have a wider territory to protect.

"Now, a further question. Where'd you get this sword? It seems to have remarkable properties. The gossip going around is that it's an experimental composite harder than steel."

Damn! She'd been too specific about the sword in trying to cover up the source of its capabilities. Which was an almost infinitely hard and sharp force field covering a real composite material.

"I can't say. I signed a non-disclosure agreement. I got it in exchange for using it and reporting on how well it worked out."

He looked at her for several long moments. She tried not to feel the need to squirm in her seat. Tiara and Suit helped her not at all to quell her discomfort.

"Very well. All of us here have our favorite weapons. I won't try to hinder you at that, or any of you." He looked around the table. Someone muttered, "Better not."

He smiled, turned back to her.

"Managing this group of mavericks is giving me grey hairs."

"MORE grey hairs," someone else muttered.

The Lieutenant turned serious. "I am concerned about one aspect of this. There are plenty of countries who would love to steal your weapon and reverse-engineer it. Something like that would be valuable in lots of ways. The Chinese Empire, for instance, has been trying for years to create the high-temperature high-pressure jet engine motors to run their advanced fighter aircraft. They might send a team after you not even you can handle."

Fierce joy rose in her at the challenge. "Let them try."

"Yes," said McCarthy, surprising Karen. The woman rarely talked, using as few words as possible when she had to.

"They will receive a suitable lesson in humility," the seemingly fragile woman said. A tiny smile curved her lovely lips.

Karen and she exchanged a look. The other woman resumed staring at the far wall as if she were seeing something beyond it.

Perhaps she was.

"OK," their boss said. "We're done. John."

The big black man rose and made a faint come-with-me nod of his head to Karen. She stood, nodded at the rest of the room, and left.

The next half hour Hendrickson led her to her office and briefed her on how to access the large fast desk computer and detailed the usual daily routine.

"Not that there's much routine around here. Most of us are off on some task or other. Most of the people you'll deal with are our in-house staff and specialists."

At that he led her around to greet the half-dozen clerical and other administrative staff, all in U. S. Army uniforms. Then he led her back to a large room sealed off from everything else with heavy armor, top and bottom as well as on all sides. Her hand print AND a retina scan let her into the room. And out of it.

"Every time you enter or exit the fact is recorded. We have the highest security on the base. It's matched only by similar rooms at the other province bases and base HQ. I now remind you that your clearance is Top Secret Army of Afghanistan. Disclosure of any secrets in that compartment are punishable by heavy prison sentences or death."

She nodded.

"You must acknowledge verbally."

"I understand disclosure of official secrets is punishable by heavy sentences. Or death."

"Good. Now mingle and get to know your routine. For the rest of the week you'll work as an intel specialist, mostly in here. Next week the Boss will probably give you some operational assignment."

He stepped back to shake hands with her. "Welcome to the Mad House, Lance Corporal. I'm sure you'll fit right in."

He walked out and Karen turned to "mingle."

<>

Several of the intel people beckoned her to join them at lunch time. A few of the other staff joined in. Soon they were all at Mess Hall #4 seated at two pulled-together tables loudly chatting and eating. No one talked shop.

<>

That night she went to bed early. A little while later she

disappeared. High in the sky she watched the Earth below, mostly dark with a spider web of golden light from Jalalabad directly below her. Peshawar to the east and Kabul to the west were similar spider webs. Faint lines of light between them and beyond shone like fairy gold. All around below were tiny speckles of light. Almost at the western horizon a crescent of orange and red light marked the edge of Earth's shadow.

Events from the last few days paraded randomly before her. Her mind kept coming back to the problem of her sword.

Teams of criminals might try to possess it. Knowing her to be very dangerous, they might try over-kill against her. Maybe a high-explosive fragmentation grenade fired from a great distance which would not harm the sword but would shred her flesh--and that of anyone around her. They might even prefer many casualties and the panic and confusion which would hide them while they picked up the sword.

Or they might try to subdue and kidnap her to torture the source of the sword from her. Perhaps wreaking casualties in the process also.

Suppose she gave them a more tempting target: the company back in the States which had given her the sword. Thieves would have to learn of it accidentally while spying, preferably not on the ground but by cyber-spying. China especially was known to have several thousand specialists in that practice.

And what company would that be...?

Back in bed she puzzled over that as she fell asleep.

<>

That week Karen spent her days becoming skilled at her intel duties and better acquainted with her co-workers. Most of those were the intel staff, a few of the admin staff, and none of the operatives.

She became mildly friendly with Sergeant First Class Jane Alexander. They had dinner together three times. More often they got together for lunch with several other women, among them Ariel McCarthy.

On one Wednesday the lunch was just off-base, at a popular eating spot which included ethnic Afghan foods prepared and presented in a Western-pretentious way.

The first women out of the discreetly armored Army VIP SUV

were Karen and Ariel, one on each side. As the others piled out they stood looking in opposite directions at the parking lot and the surroundings. Then they trailed the other women to the front door.

On the way they sped up just enough to pass on each side of the rest of the group. They entered the double doors, one through each door, and faded to the right and left as the other women entered.

Jane Alexander glanced at the two with a faint smile upon her face. She spoke to the maitre d' about their reservation and the group was led to a long table near one corner of the large dining room. Karen and Ariel took seats on opposite sides of the table.

Everyone accepted menus and studied them. They were presented with iced water in glasses by waiters in dress traditional except for being all in white and black. Afghan women and even men normally chose clothing in a rainbow of colors.

Chatter lessened while everyone chose food, though it didn't completely die down. Several of the women discussed dishes they could cross-sample with others.

When their orders were complete and the group was alone the Sergeant spoke up.

"Ladies. Has anyone else noticed that we have our very own security detail?"

Everyone except the Sergeant and Karen and Ariel looked around at the room.

"You're looking in the wrong place," Jane said. She nodded at the middle of the table where Karen and Ariel sat on their opposite sides.

In a moment first one and then the rest followed her gaze and noticed the two women in "their security detail." Karen smiled back. Ariel continued watching "her" side of the dining room.

Jane laughed. "Our two sisters are probably two of the deadliest women in the country. Maybe in the world. Or maybe I should say people. I don't know of any men I would bet on against Ariel and Karen."

Karen put on a fake-modest look and gazed down at her plate and the snowy white cloth napkin folded atop it.

"Oh, you are talking about little old me?"

Several of the women laughed. For she was an Amazon among women, and even among many men. She was as tall as most men, broad in shoulder and hips made seem broader by a narrow waist. Her smooth muscles were obvious though they were shrouded in loose grey-and-brown-and-sand desert camouflage fatigues. And few who'd seen her graceful flowing stride could fail to think of a lioness.

All eyes turned to Ariel. She seemed even tinier across from Karen. But to the discerning--and all these women were once they paid attention--she was just as impressive.

Ariel gazed back at them. A faint wry look replaced the abstract gaze she usually wore. One eyebrow even quirked infinitesimally.

"Jane," she said. "Your foolishness sometimes tempts me to turn my 'deadly wiles' upon you."

The First Sergeant ignored her.

Valentina, an intel staffer with slender Italian-Argentine good looks and long dark hair, inspected the two women with professional interest. Every one of the women had at least rudimentary combat training.

"I don't see any weapons. Someone could blow us away from across the room."

"Oh, they have them. You just can't see them."

Karen of course had an array of weapons available (though in nascent virtual form inside Suit's memory), up to and including a long laser staff which could blow holes in aircraft at the very edge of the atmosphere.

She gazed at Ariel. She had no doubt the woman had hidden weapons too, but couldn't guess where unless hers were hidden the same way Karen's were. Ariel gazed blandly back.

For a moment Karen toyed with using Suit's graviton radar to probe under the woman's clothes. But she was stopped by two considerations.

If Ariel also had galactic-level protection, dueling body suits might destroy each other, their wearers, and possibly half the planet. But the real block was emotional. Ariel was a colleague, might become a companion, maybe a friend. It would be like stripping the woman bare, terribly unfair and terribly wrong.

Karen gave up, aided by the arrival of the first items of food, crisp breads and dips and savory sauces for the bread. She selected a mini-loaf, broke it in two, and dipped a broken end into a sauce dish.

The table became quieter and the talk turned to who was dating whom or wanted to or had someone back home. There was absolutely no shop talk. When the higher ups worried that even the base cafeterias and snack rooms were bugged no one wanted to chance an off-base eatery was not bugged.

Karen had reflexively swept the restaurant for bugs even before she entered it, made note of all which Tiara detected (which was all of them), and silently generated an anonymous report. This she sent into the database back in the secure room in which she spent most of her time. By next week each one would be traced to their sources and those sources would be bugged in their turn.

She had a good time at the lunch and the remaining lunches of that week and the weeks to come.

<>

At night Karen was also busy, usually lying in her bed pretending to sleep or read or watch entertainment on the flat-screen TV in her "berth"--her small apartment room in Marine Corps barracks.

The first order of business was a method of creating a composite material similar to the one she had falsely described. It had to be one which could be invented by a smart high school or college student with a genius mind. Constructed by very early 21st Century technology. Expensive but not too expensive.

She could choose any one of such inventions created over several thousand years in the Human Interstellar Confederation. There were a good number of them. She reviewed each via Tiara's copy of the Galactic Encyclopedia and finally chose one. It had one feature she liked. It was easy to tailor its color. She lay awake for over an hour, eyes closed, savoring the ruby reds, spring greens, and all the other colors projected onto her brain's visual area.

<>

The next night she solved one of the "company" problems: finding a real company to submit the material-construction patent to the U. S. Patent Office.

Her first thought was to fake a three-man startup who had invented the process and then submitted it. She rejected the idea because she could not create an actual physical company with real employees, one of whom would be a young genius engineer stand-in for herself. They could not be visited by interested industries wanting to exploit the process.

Then she decided to use herself as the genius inventor.

She researched companies which would submit a request to the patent office and get a patent for "her" invention, and other companies which would take the patent and find investors to finance its exploitation. Finally she found a company that had a good track record of doing both.

This was a part of Prince Enterprises. Which was a conglomerate controlled by a genius financier, a late-twenties woman who'd inherited her dead parents millions and several companies. Starting at eighteen she'd turned the companies from million-dollar organizations to multi-million and billion-dollar ones.

So Karen submitted a patent proposal to Prince IP Services, the intellectual properties company. She back-dated it by a year and faked it being stalled during that time by a glitch in a node in the web internet mail servers.

Over the next several days she monitored its progress through Prince IP. In a surprisingly short time, two weeks later, the patent was submitted and its exploitation triggered by the expectation that it would be granted. But that matched the reputation of Prince Enterprises and its boss. They moved lightning fast compared to other conglomerates on the planet.

By then Karen was involved in a field task.

<>

That Monday's briefing the third female operative in Minetti's Mad House ran a finger over the info slate on the conference-room table. Everyone at the table could see a pointer on their matching screens slide to touch a small circle in a large spider web of similar circles. The pointer turned gold.

Helen Storm Cloud tapped her finger and the circle expanded to a light grey oval. Inside it was a name and several numbers and lines of text.

The woman looked up and scanned her audience. She was a sturdy forty-something American of mixed Comanche and Apache blood. Her people came from a high-plains nation which spread over North Texas, South Kansas, and parts of several other mid-western states. The

Nation had been created in the late 1700s and stayed independent despite the burgeoning population of the U. S. in later years. Singly they were fierce and canny warriors. In groups they were professional soldiers expert in guerilla and small-force battles. Some of them were reputed to be Mystic Warriors, superhumans.

Not unlike Ariel and she herself, Karen mused.

"Tariq Fazlullah is the head of the Mehsud Jihad. He got the job partly because he's able and ruthless, quite willing to torture and kill women and children. Whose souls, he says, go directly to Paradise because they become martyrs. Partly it's because of his kinship to these, these, and these influential tribal heads."

At her finger taps three other circles bloomed into grey ovals, smaller ones filled only with a name. With the kinship lines linking them they formed a triangle around the large oval labeled Fazlullah. From them they fanned out and connected to many of the remaining small circles to form a spider web.

"The Jihad has been growing weaker for the last few years. This coincided with the previous Mullah growing weaker as he grew older. Then suddenly he died by assassination. Of course some dastardly American did it.

"That story was fine for almost a year. During that time the Jihad has grown more active. Lots of assassinations, suicide bombs, and so on, over a 100% increase.

"Then it began to be whispered that Fazlullah had killed the old Mullah. Or had it done. Now all of sudden he's being eyed with suspicion. So, interestingly, it's now been discovered who committed the deed. None other than the Red Jineri."

Karen straightened from a slouch and grinned. "Damn! Now I'm killing people in my sleep. Heavily guarded people!

"Did he die by knife, by any chance?"

"No. Shot in the face several times with a silenced pistol. Of course, that clinches it for them. Everybody knows by now of the bandits you killed that way."

"Ah, Karen," said Kuznitzov. "Why did you aim at the smaller targets? Not their chests?"

"My pistol fires needles. Useless against body armor, almost useless against heavy clothing. And at close distances it's not chancy.

For me."

"At any rate," Helen Storm Cloud said, "the upshot is that Fazlullah says his people will kill you as revenge. And once he even said HE is going to kill you."

The Lieutenant said, "Thanks, Helen. Good job.

"Now--" He faced Karen. "--we have a problem I'm not sure how to handle. I don't really believe they can kill you. But in a firefight-- Or a frag grenade or rocket attack, a lot of bystanders can get hurt."

"Offense," she said, "is the best defense, they say. Suppose I do my own jihad on good old Fazlullah?"

He stared over her head, eyes unfocussed. "...if you had good intel..."

Helen said, "I can provide that. I've been inside his compound a dozen times, all times days and nights. No one pays any attention to an ugly old woman, especially if she scurries about anxiously catering to their every whim. I can even escort her in, suitably disguised."

Everyone watched the Lieutenant as he thought--except Ariel, who watched whatever the Hell she watched beyond the far wall when she wasn't giving a report.

He'd been leaning back in his chair. Suddenly he sat upright. "Fine, we'll do it. As long as you two are volunteering. I'm not about to order something this risky without giving you a choice."

He gazed at the two women for a moment. Satisfied they were satisfied, he said, "I think we should meet at 2:00 to plan this out."

The First Sergeant nodded her head at this and made a few notes on her info slate, likely shifting appointments around for him. He then gave two more people instructions to show up at that meeting. Then he called for the next order of business.

<>

The meeting began with a briefing on the geography where the Jihad was active, an eastern Afghanistan province called Waziristan just south of the province in which the Khyber Pass existed. It was mountainous with several large valleys irrigated by snow and rain runoff. Next and longer was a description of the major players in Waziristan, especially those who were in or worked with the Jihad.

Karen said she had no definite plan on how to get to Fazlullah and said no more. The meeting ended and she began working her very definite plan, one she did not want anyone to know about. For she was going to use Galactic technology to further it.

First she began to plant fake emails and phone calls in the Afghan digital text and phone net. Typical was a hurried message from one minor Waziri official left in the voice-message box of another minor Waziri official.

"You won't believe this! The Red Jineri is on her way to assassinate the Mullah! Call me back." Tiara's imitation of the voice was perfect. It resulted in the second official calling back at a time when Tiara had the first man's phone giving off a busy signal.

After several such failed back-and-forth exchanges each man was convinced they'd had a real conversation. Both began calling other officials, friends, and family members. Multiplied by a hundred such exchanges created by Tiara, and it was not long before Mullah Fazlullah and his cronies were convinced they'd soon be under attack.

Karen also had Tiara start a second gossip campaign, this time among the enemies of the Mullah who'd begun the speculation that he'd killed his father. And a third campaign in Pakistan among those who spied on Afghanistan, especially those interested in Waziristan. The Pakis had long believed that the Afghan province should have been ceded to them by the British who planned the partitioning of the two countries from each other and India.

Karen also had Tiara set up blocks of all messages about her or her supernatural alter ego to the several spy nets operating in the area. These included the Chinese Empire, Russian Federation, and the United Kingdom and its client state India. She left intact the messages to other Middle-Eastern countries. She wanted no modern countries having oversight of her exploits in Waziristan, but was happy to have the oversight of those countries who shared the jinn myths.

Karen oversaw Tiara's actions but only two or three times micromanaged them. The robot was not an artificial intelligence, a conscious being. But thousands of years of robotic science had created robots who understood humans well enough to mimic humans perfectly. And could generate and carry out orders as if they were human.

EXCEPT they did it a trillion times as fast.

<>

That night Karen seemed to be entertaining herself or napping in her room. Instead she was spending her waking time doing an unrelated cyber campaign.

This one was to spoof all those who wanted the secret "miracle material process" from her and her sword. This involved the spy nets of the Chinese, Russians, the Brits and Britannic Indians, and various minor players in the global power-play games. Each was fooled into thinking they had cracked the secrecy surrounding Prince IP Services patent and exploitation handling of her request to Prince.

In reality they had not. Even Tiara had not been able to do that with the core part of Prince Enterprises cybernet, though the rest of the Prince net was open to her. Tiara had reported this to Karen with the suggestion that Anna Prince was herself a Galactic.

Though maybe not human. There were twelve other local galactic confederations or empires in the Galactic arm in which the Confederation resided which were as advanced as the Confed. Many of them overlapped, but had never been remotely close to war. Most of their ecosystems were too different for anyone in them to want something from another ecosystem. And those few who were compatible with human ecosystems were peaceful people.

Karen tabled this oddity for a better time to consider it. By the next morning she was ready to travel to Waziristan.

<>

Karen had an early breakfast in her room of a meal generated out of the air by Suit. She made her toilette, straightened up her room, and left.

She exited in her truck from the base's south gate, crossed the east-west highway leading to the Khyber Pass and to Kabul, and entered the southern highway.

As she sped south Tiara sent a fake phone call to several interested Waziris.

"I just saw the Red Jineri drive south toward you! Pass it on."

The land was gently rolling. The highway paralleled on her right a thin southern tributary of the Kabul River which ran east and west through Jalalabad. Thin as the tributary was, it gave enough water to irrigate a succession of small farm plots. And a large square of bright green grass which was a setting for a beautiful mosque of white and blue with the usual four towers from which muezzin made the calls to prayers. A row of rose bushes added a red accent to the greenery.

A little further was a small college campus containing a dozen plain beige buildings with boxy shapes. Housed in one of the buildings, she knew, was a secret research facility.

For a time she passed a series of small farms amid low trees and with checkerboards of green crops livened by irrigation. Then the green swelled enough to support a small village.

To the southwest of the village was a huge solar-power farm made up of many black power collectors slanted to best catch the sun. From it power lines lofted onto the first steel pole of a line of poles leading into the village. Another set of lines came east toward her. They met a line near the highway which ran north and south beside the highway.

The green belt of trees and crop plots continued south more than a dozen miles before diminishing to nothing. By that time a line of mountains to the south was beginning to grow larger to her eyes.

Tiara had been monitoring all messages referring to Karen or to "The Red Jineri" and delivering a summary to Karen of the more important ones. Now the robot alerted her of an impending ambush. It would happen in about a half hour, deep in the mountains.

The alert included views of the mountains from an American spy satellite and maps of the highway she would take through them. A red X showed where the attack was planned. This was a hill overlooking a hairpin turn. Inside the loop was a roadside rest stop.

When the highway lifted into the mountains and began to switch back upon itself, another alert arrived. This one included several photos of five men arriving at the hill. One carried a rocket-propelled-grenade launcher. The other four carried long rifles. Other photos showed them settling in to look down at the loop and the rest stop.

The mountain sides were a boring brown with no features. The highway wound back and forth. A driver could easily become careless or even sleepy. Time seemed to crawl.

After almost half an hour of climbing Karen neared the ambush site. She went invisible, opened the driver-side door, slid out from behind the driving wheel, and lofted into the air. The truck continued on. Pegasus had been around it since she drove off in the truck. Now he extended arms of force to keep the truck moving as if driven. He also placed an image of her behind the steering wheel.

She curved up and then down to float two feet above the earth behind the men. From there she could see over their shoulders and down-slope. Minutes later her truck appeared around a curve, slowed, and braked to a stop in the small parking area beside three umbrella-covered round picnic tables.

The RPG shooter adjusted his aim minutely and waited for Karen to exit the truck. And waited. And waited.

The leader impatiently commanded him to shoot. He did.

The rocket whooshed and sped downward trailing thin grey smoke, showing that it was an older model without smokeless propellant. It struck the side of the truck and exploded with a bang. Tiny fragments of the grenade flew in every direction.

A bright red globe of light swelled around the truck, eclipsing it. It grew brighter and larger and brighter still. The men squinted against tears and shaded their eyes or turned their heads aside.

The globe disappeared as if a bubble had burst.

The truck was revealed. Completely unharmed.

The men stared. The leader cursed.

Karen dropped her invisibility, said conversationally, "You thought to harm a jinn? Fools."

Head jerked around. Eyes stared. At a figure in bright blood red clothing. A sword hilt projecting above one shoulder. Hanging in the air.

The leader screamed and began panic firing on full automatic at the jinn. Who was not affected in the least.

The RPG shooter screamed and ran blindly away, over the lip of the hill where it dropped sharply down. He screamed more as hillside rocks scored his flesh and small tough bushes growing on the hillside slashed him.

The rest of the men also began firing at the jinn. Also to no avail.

The drum roll of shots ceased.

The sword hilt was in the jinn's hand. She darted forward. A head rolled. Another. A third as the man turned to run. A fourth, along with two parts of an arm and of a rifle raised to block a blow, fell to the earth.

Karen looked down at the red slaughter before her. She shook her head. Drew a deep breath to quell her nausea. Bent and fumbled in the leader's pocket, face grimacing, and unbent with a ring of keys dangling from her hand.

She floated quickly down the hillside to the foot where the RPG shooter lay on his back, the launcher beside him.

She watched him regain his breath and thoughts. He opened his eyes, started at the sight of her floating in the air nearby. When she did nothing he cautiously sat up, drawing a harsh breath as he disturbed the abrasions and cuts in his clothing and flesh. He stared at palms and fingers bloodied as he'd clutched at the hillside and bushes.

He looked back up when she spoke.

"Tell everyone what happens when you try to harm a jinn. Do you understand?"

He was dumb, stared at her, but nodded his head.

"Remember. Here. Go home."

She plunked the set of keys into an injured palm and disappeared. When he could see beyond the pain in his hand the truck had also disappeared.

<>

Back in her truck and floating invisible in the air fifty feet above the man she watched him. He limped alongside the road to the place where the ambush leader had parked his truck. He got inside, started the truck, and drove cautiously onto the highway.

For the next hour Karen shadowed the man, ready to intervene via Pegasus to ensure he didn't accidentally or otherwise kill himself.

Near the peak of a pass through which the highway ran they encountered snow on the ground. Karen darted up a couple of miles for a few minutes and saw a long line of white going far to the east and west.

The highway straightened and its slope lessened as it eased down into the Parachinar Valley. She saw a city, Parachinar, at the bottom. She also saw several small rivers flowing down into the valley, which accounted for the abundant greenery. Tiara informed her that all told the valley supported over 100,000 people, about two-thirds in the city itself.

Karen shadowed the failed ambusher until he reached the home of a friend. She stayed over the house until he'd been fixed up enough to use a cell phone and report what had happened.

She then raced the news south, passing over Khost in a larger adjacent valley. The city held at least twice that of Parachinar and the valley was even larger, perhaps ten times as large.

She flew on toward the city of Miran Shah where Mullah Fazlullah lived. The highway and the land under her rose into another arm of the huge area of mountain ranges which blanketed northern Afghanistan and Pakistan and extended further northward into neighboring countries.

<>

At the topmost peak of the mountains she slowed her 200-mile-an-hour pace and drifted down to land atop it. She got out of her truck and stood looking down into the valley. She let Suit sink below her skin so that she was naked.

She could feel the full impact of her surroundings. The air was below freezing, desert dry, and the wind was strong. Beneath her bare feet was rock and around them up to her ankles was snow. Yet even now she was protected from the full impact.

Suit would not let the worst of the cold sink below her skin. And in any case her body was that of humans whose bodies and minds had been improved. For several thousand years, VERY cautiously, their genes had been winnowed of their worst weaknesses.

She sent Suit deeper inside her but after a few millimeters it refused. Its programming was adamant; she could not override the protection which was its main purpose.

Karen took deep breaths as she thought, feeling more of her environment, though even inside her lungs Suit continued to protect her. At least she felt the cold enough to begin shivering.

Down in that valley were men who were determined to make Waziristan an independent country, or at least Northern Waziristan. They were willing to use any means, including torture and murder of women and children who they called "involuntary martyrs." They felt that "Western Satanism" threatened their old ways, with a few men on top using religion as a flail to keep down everyone else.

She did not object to killing them. But would that really work? Was it even just? Sure, the worst of them deserved justice. But some of them might be more moderate, or more kind, perhaps trapped by the cruel straitjacket of the fanatics around them.

A larger concern also bothered her. Was her whole plan of being a Marine really the best for the world and herself? It HAD given her more of the companionship she'd found in high school sports. She HAD achieved something: more protection of those who needed it. But surely she could do so much more.

She sighed, exhaling a white breath which disappeared almost instantly. Her physical pain was increasing, but she could bear much more. However, it had achieved her purpose: to break a little bit of her nearly obsessive drive toward the goals she set for herself, and let her see more of the wider picture. She let Suit snap back to its preferred limits.

Did she imagine it of the emotionless robot? A psychic sigh of relief?

<>

Karen came down into the valley housing Miran Shah a hundred feet above the road from Khost, slowing from flying 200 miles an hour to about 30 driving on the highway. She felt this gave her a better feel for the land than swooping down into town from miles above. The road paralleled a stream on her left coming down from the mountains behind her. Off to the stream side on the road was scattered greenery, mostly bushes with the occasional low tree. On both sides was the usual rocky land barely covered here and there with soil.

It was this bare land which shaped much of the Afghan character, she thought. Plus the extremes of weather. Two weeks before Thanksgiving the bright day was in the 80s, the valley protected by the mountains around it, while in Kabul not very far behind her it was in the 50s and was already edging deeper into winter. But soon even this protected area would find the days and nights harsh.

Karen matched Tiara's maps and spy satellite images with the reality. The valley ran pretty much north and south and was a couple of miles wide and several miles long. Till it met another valley, this one narrower and running east and west for great distances. That second valley contained the Tochi river, filled from the west by numerous small streams of melted mountain snow and running far to the east into Pakistan.

She passed over a couple of bridges which crossed over tiny

streams coming down from her right to join the slightly larger stream to her left. Just beyond the second she entered Miran Shah, marked by three low blocky houses on her left of mud bricks covered by mud plaster. Behind the houses were pastures watered by the stream. A line of low trees marked that water course.

The pastures closest to the buildings housed rows of vegetables. She saw a couple of figures bent over tending the produce.

Then to her right began a line of several dozen houses. Further toward the west was yet another mountain stream which supplied those houses with water before joining the Tochi.

She lifted up to about 300 feet to get a better overview. More and more houses showed up. Some of them with two stories. But all of the same sand-colored material.

She thought Afghans love of color must come from the lack of it in the stuff of which they built their homes. The village-like clusters of houses were certainly boring to her sight.

Now on her left she saw an airstrip which ran further to the south. It was about a mile long. Near its end was a cross-strip running to the east for a half-mile. A propeller-driven light plane was advancing north toward her just after lift off. It zoomed past her, climbing at a shallow angle. She thought it might be a crop duster.

On the cross strip was a two-engine plane. Facing her, it was waiting to advance to the north-south strip and turn right to follow the light plane. Tiara flashed Karen identification of the type: very new, powered by superbatteries and the very new paramagnetic jet engines rather than aviation gasoline.

The increasing use of such engines was a major reason for Afghanistan's new economic policies. It made oil-production countries less important and oil-poor countries like Afghanistan more important.

The modest downtown area was nearing. Karen stopped to soak in the overall shape of the city and identify important land marks.

These included several schools, one a religious madrasa school with an attached mosque, three more mosques, one of them quite big, a small Hindu temple, a small government graduate school with a recent aggressive expansion program, a four-story hospital, a three-story administrative center for North Waziristan with an attached police station, and a long, wide plaza in the downtown area through which the

Khost-Miran Shah highway ran.

She glided down to the plaza, slowed to an amble two dozen feet up, just enough to clear even the tallest vehicles, and rubbernecked.

On both sides were buildings two to four stories high. They were of wood and brick rather than the pervasive mud bricks and mud plaster. They were often garishly painted.

The shops and offices featured a wide variety of products, including many Western items. One of the largest stores sold smart phones, info slates, and computers of many sizes, including a few very expensive ones.

Tiara revealed to her that it had a 24-hour, 7-day-a-week guard rotation and an expensive and very advanced security system. Conservatives in the area highly disapproved of anything that brought Western ideas into Afghanistan, and there had been a suicide-bomb attack a year ago. It had been inept and did little more than kill its carrier.

Karen chuckled at a final piece of information Tiara delivered to her. One of the stores biggest investors and customers was Mullah Fazlullah, who publicly disapproved of such technology.

She continued south to the outskirts of Miran Shah. A large high-walled compound where the mullah lived sat on one side of the road where it neared the Tochi river coming from the west. Inside it was the main building, three stories tall and two or three dozen rooms. Scattered around it were several smaller building, one of which housed a garage.

Karen lowered to a dozen feet inside the compound and circled the big house, noting the guards posted in small blockhouses atop the four corners of the wall. Several men and women were on the ground inside the compound walking to and from the main house and the several smaller ones.

Then she zoomed up and back over the city to the northern side of the city. She landed her truck on the road at a spot where no one could see her suddenly appear, then drove into the city.

The police station was housed in an annex to the side of the town hall. She drove into the parking lot, parked, got out, and entered the tall double doors in the front of the station.

She approached the desk of the combined receptionist and guard, an older policeman in a brown police uniform.

In Dari she said, "Hello. I'm Lance Corporal Karen Danburn. I'd like to see the police chief, or make an appointment to see him."

The sergeant eyed her with careful eyes. He said, "Just a moment, please." He lifted an old-fashioned black handset and spoke into it a moment. He put it down and said, "The Commander can see you now." He then went on to tell her how to get to that man's office.

A long hall and a short cross hall later she came on the office of the Commander. A young sergeant receptionist stood up to receive her and escort her into the large office behind his desk.

The colonel behind the ornate desk at the other side of the room rose to greet his guest. He was very skinny and dressed in a brown police uniform with shoulder tabs indicating his rank and a cross belt that merged with a waist belt on his right side. There was where he'd clip a pistol holster, but none was evident. However, the leather was worn there, so it was not unusual for him to go about armed.

"Honorable Commander," she said in Dari, using the honorific term of respect: *Safi*. She gave a miniscule bow with a deeper head tilt.

He said in British-accented English, "Lance Corporal Danburn. I've been expecting you. Your Leftenant Minelli was kind enough to notify me by email and phone about your arrival. Please, be seated."

"Yes, sir," she said in English after she'd taken his invitation to sit. "Thank you for receiving me so promptly. Your office has many responsibilities. I'm sure you are very busy."

"Never too busy to help our American friends. What can I do for you?"

"My lieutenant doubtless told you that I've been assigned the task of re-investigating the death of the former Mullah Fazlullah. I'd like access to your records of that case."

"I instantly put in a request for those records after I'd received the Leftenant's message. I'm afraid it may take a while. Bureaucracy, you know."

"Quite all right. I have photocopies of them. But seeing the original sources can sometimes give insights not in the formal reports."

"Very true. Of course, the originals are all in Arabic script. I'm afraid you'd have to have a translator help you with that."

"I read Arabic script in Persian, Dari, Urdu, and several other languages. Including Pashto."

The Commander gazed deep into her eyes. His face, which seemed to have long ago had all fat sucked from it, tightened.

"You are a remarkably learned young woman."

"I am indeed, *Safi*. In ways far beyond martial specialties. I can, for instance, literally see when someone is lying to me. Those forensic skills are one of the reasons I was assigned to this task.

"I hasten to say that I have no suspicion you are doing that. To my eyes you are utterly candid." If somewhat evasive.

"I am happy to hear that. Be assured that I will do everything in my power to help you in your task. I will, ah, 'light a fire' under those functionaries responsible for approving your access to the records you desire."

"We could ask for nothing more. Now, I'm sure you have more important duties than to talk to someone as lowly as I."

"Never fear you are wasting my time, Corporal. But I do have tasks I must return to." He rose and held out his hand. She rose, shook his hand, and left the office.

Via Tiara she listened in on his phone conversations as she left the building, got in her truck, and drove to the hospital. They were to two people, one in the records department where he did indeed "light a fire." But the second was to the new Mullah, warning him of her arrival. He cautioned the man that she was far more formidable than her reputation. She was not only a warrior to be feared but an intellect to be feared even more.

Karen sat in the large parking lot beside the regional hospital for Northern Waziristan. She mulled over the Commander's comments. She could not guess his motives. Was he a partisan of the Mullah's movement? Or was he simply a politician trying to balance between the conflicting demands of his office and those of local influential men?

She could not decide. Nor did it matter. She would simply go invisible and sneak into the records room of the police station tonight. A quick glimpse of the material and Tiara would have a photographic copy of its contents.

The hospital was huge, four stories tall with several wings. It served not only Miran Shah but the several dozen small villages sited on the many streams and lesser rivers fed by the runoff of mountains in Waziristan and in eastern Afghanistan.

She had similar success with the hospital administrator as with the police captain: outwardly helpful but secretly not very. Ditto the funeral home where the old Mullah had been laid out for burial.

Later she had a long, sumptuous meal at the most popular restaurant in Miran Shah. Many of the more prosperous residents of the city covertly observed her. "WAS she the Red Jineri?" was the biggest topic of the quiet conversations all around her. In her smart uniform with only a pistol at her side she didn't LOOK like a supernatural being. But the stories about her were too numerous to be mere gossip.

Tiara created and launched several tiny spybots to eavesdrop and report on those conversations. But she only gave Karen a summary of them. None had any information useful in Karen's investigation.

Afterwards Karen disappeared. Later on that night she visited the various record rooms and copied the contents of the several reports on the Mullah's death. She also visited the old man's grave. It was in a plot devoted to the city's most prosperous citizens.

So it was that near midnight a number of people within sight of the grave yard saw a bright white light all about it. None had the courage to sneak near and see what was happening. But the next morning visitors saw the grave nearly hidden by a mound of flowers, all as fresh as if just picked and from all over the world. Some of those flowers were very strange to Afghan eyes.

<>

The next several days Karen drove to various locations and spoke to witnesses to the crime scene where the old Mullah had been found dead within his compound. She also asked a good many questions about the various people who knew the Mullah and who were his friends or enemies. She got only a little information from each but slowly gained a large tapestry of information.

Or so it seemed to the various interested parties who followed her efforts. This she found out from Tiara's spying on people with invisible spybots and through their telephone conversations and text messages.

The most important information was from those who had plotted his death. They were of a rival faction of the Jihad who lived in South Waziristan. They wanted the south to contain the capitol of the nation state of Waziristan when it won its independence from Afghanistan.

Karen traveled to that mini-country and spent some time in Wana, the largest city, and asked many more questions. Again she gained little information from anyone, though the leaders of the southern branch of the Jihad assumed that she knew everything and would soon expose them.

Thus they set up an ambush to kill her when she drove back to Miran Shah. It failed as miserably as the previous ambush set up by the new Mullah. This time she left no survivors. The first the schemers found out about it was when the attackers failed to report. Investigators found each of the nine men crumpled on a hillside. Each one's head had been neatly sliced from their bodies.

Karen made no mention of any attack. She simply appeared in Miran Shah near dark one evening and pressed the buzzer below the video camera mounted to one side of the gate to the Mullah's compound.

She was quickly answered in Pashto and given permission to come inside. Her truck, however, must be left parked in the visitor's parking lot to one side of the gate. She must also leave all guns in the truck. Thus it was that Karen was ushered into the presence of the Mullah with only the sword on her back.

The Mullah sat on a large chair on a slightly raised dais at the back of a large room. It was sumptuously decorated with carpets on the floor and hung from the walls. Also hung were various brazen plates and antique swords and lances and rifles. Only the Mullah sat. His was the only chair in the room.

Karen approached him and bowed minutely to him, inclining her head a bit more. In Pashto she spoke.

"Greetings, O great Mullah. I have come to report my findings to you about the death of your father."

He was a middle-aged Pashtun of ordinary appearance. His clothing was traditional except for a sober combination of dark colors. There were white streaks in his long beard and grey in his side burns.

"Why should I care about your fabrications? We all know you Americans are responsible for my father's death."

"It must surely seem that way, but I know exactly who killed him and how and who ordered it. Of course, if you do not wish to know this, I can leave you and only report to my superiors."

"No, go ahead. Perhaps your lies will be entertaining."

She took ten minutes to lay out all the facts she'd uncovered. They were many and in great detail. Especially exact was her account of who had ordered and participated in the murder and when they had met.

"How can you know all this? It sounds like fiction to me."

Karen shrugged. "I am expert in discovering information people want kept secret. That's why I was sent here rather than another."

The Mullah looked up at a tall old man standing near and a little behind his chair.

"You've recorded all this?"

The man only nodded.

"Very well, Corporal. You are dismissed. I hope this means you will leave Waziristan and never pollute our land again."

"I have another matter to bring up. This 'revolutionary' jihad must be called off. The next atrocity it commits, wherever it is committed, will bring me back here. And my punishment will be severe. I hold you personally responsible. You will be the first to suffer, then all those below you, then all those below them. I will utterly destroy this compound and wipe the very memory of it from this Earth.

"NOW I'm done."

She turned and strode away.

The Mullah let her get halfway across the room to the door before he yelled.

"Get her! Beat her down and throw her to the floor before me!"

The American broke into an incredibly fast sprint which brought her to the heavy double doors before anyone could intercept her. There she met almost a dozen men who swarmed to meet her.

The sword came off her back still in its sheath. That weapon jabbed, swung, and struck down two in an instant. Her feet in their boots were deadly weapons, as was her free fist. She bent, bobbed, and wove a way through them, wielding what seemed like a dozen weapons. Men fell all about her like hay before a harvester.

Then she was through the double door and it slammed shut behind her. All attempts to open the doors failed; somehow she had jammed the locks.

"After her! Bring her back to me! Alive!"

Men ran to other exits and disappeared through them.

Outside the first of them to arrive there saw her swarm up a compound wall, her fingers and toes seeming to find cracks in the wall where there were none. Then she was over the wall and into the night.

Men were dispatched through the compound gate to keep her from her truck. Others vanished into the night after her. Others delayed to make more arrangements to find her. In all more than a hundred sought the fleeing soldier.

Such a one told his story the next morning, first to the Mullah and then in more detail and honesty to a friend.

"Roshan and Izat came with me..."

"I wish I'd been there!"

"Then the same thing would have happened to you. Do you want to hear this or not?!"

At a nod he continued.

"We were prepared, not like those fools who immediately rushed into the darkness. We know the land, unlike that...whatever she is. We had weapons, we took flashlights and extra batteries, and Izat got an electric cattle prod from the barn. The Mullah wanted her alive.

"We kept hearing other searchers calling to each other. We heard shots, some fully automatic. Then less so as we all spread out.

"It happened maybe an hour later. The light began to fail...."

"Wasn't there a new moon?"

"Yes. And starlight. The sky was clear and our eyes had adjusted to the dark. I mean the sky slowly turned black. No moon. No stars. We had only used our flashlights a little. Now we turned on all three.

"Then the flashlights began to dim, too. We put in new batteries. They were no help.

"I said STOP! And everyone did. I tell you, I was almost shitting my pants. Bullets don't scare me. Even that sword didn't-- Much. But this was unnatural. I'd heard she was a jinn. I didn't believe it.

"Till then."

He was silent. His friend poured more hot tea into his cup and waited.

"Then we saw it. Two red coals. Like eyes. They came nearer. We began firing at it-- Whatever IT was. Then the eyes went out. And so did I.

"The next thing I knew it was morning. I was lying flat on my back. And I was cold. I'd slept all night, laying just like that. My muscles had all cramped.

"I sat up. Then I noticed it. All my clothes from the waist down were gone. Even my boots."

"You were naked?!"

"Not from the waist up. From the waist down."

"God!"

"Our guns--"

"Our? Roshan and Izat were there, too?"

"Right beside me. They were the same way. Half naked. Our guns and ammunition were gone. As if they had never been."

He sat, brooding. His friend said nothing. Nor did he, for a long time. Then he spoke once more.

"I wonder what else she did to me while I slept."

<>

Dread ruled the compound. Men huddled and spoke little. They ate little. The Mullah sat on his chair and brooded. No one spoke to him unless he spoke to them. He said little to anyone. Women and children hid.

The silence was broken at mid-morning.

A tremendous crash jerked everyone alert. Those in the throne room froze, listening for more sounds.

Minutes passed. The Mullah finally dispatched someone to find out what had happened. In a short time the man raced back inside, the heavy doors to the room slamming shut behind him.

"Master! The front gate! It's gone! Exploded, turned to dust! And she's coming! She's coming!"

All in the room, only a few where nearly a hundred had gathered the night before, readied guns, nervously, aware that guns had not done anyone any good when used against the jineri.

The two heavy double doors suddenly crashed open, flung completely off their hinges, flying into the room. But before they injured anyone they turned to brown sand or rust then faded away as if turned to air.

Behind it marched the jineri. Only this time she was not clad as a soldier.

The clothing she wore was bright red, so bright it near blinded one. Her boots, her sword, her belts, all red. Her hair was like red incandescent wires, glowing and writhing about her head. The skin of her face and hands was red.

Her eyes were fiery. There were no pupils, nor eyelids. Only two glowing embers filling the eye sockets.

She advanced toward the Mullah but stopped yards away from him. She stood there and stared for the longest time.

The Mullah did not look up at her. He stared at her feet.

"You sought to harm me. For this you are cursed. All your men are cursed, those who chased after me, those who support you still in this compound. Never again will you father children. Your family lines are done.

"So too are the men of the south who conspired against you. Who plotted to kill your father and carried out that plot.

"From now on you will renounce violence, against other men and especially against women and children. Children are beloved of God.

"You may protect yourself from evil men, including foreigners. But with weapons only if they use weapons against you."

Suddenly every weapon in the room, even the antiques on the wall, turned to brown dust which vanished into the air.

"You are too ready to use weapons. I have removed that temptation for a time.

"The old Jihad is done. Revive it if you will, but only if you use peaceful means to gain your ends."

She turned to go but stopped. For a strange phenomenon was happening.

Behind the Mullah a white light the size and height of a man appeared. It grew brighter then dimmed to nothing. Left behind on the dais was the figure of a man standing and facing the jineri. The Mullah twisted around in his chair to see him.

He was clad all in white in the traditional dress of an Aghan man but wearing a floor-length robe over it. Two curved swords were held to his waist by a wide white belt.

Not only his clothing and boots were white. So was his face and beard and hair. All glowed from within.

"Hold, jinn. Justice has not truly been done. Will you hear me?"

The jineri gazed at the face of the man. As did everyone else. Many gasped. For his countenance and voice was that of the old Mullah.

"I will hear you, spirit."

The revenant walked to the edge of the dais to one side of his successor and stepped off it to stand facing the jineri and his son.

"From the other side of death I can see much which is not apparent to mortals. I see your reproach to be just. The means my jihad employed were dishonorable, especially those toward children. But so is your punishment, to cut short the lines of tribe and family. Surely to erase future children from existence is nearly as great an evil as to kill children who already live."

The jineri stood long in thought. No one spoke or moved.

"Your argument has merit. I will take back that curse. But the rest of my judgment remains. Those who continue to use violence will suffer. Do you disagree?"

"I do not."

"Then go to your well-deserved rest."

The glowing spirit bowed low to the jineri. When he straightened he began to fade. But not before he faced his son and spoke once more.

"Beloved son. Goodbye."

The Mullah jerked to his feet and opened his mouth to speak. But the spirit was gone.

Fazlullah looked long on the empty air. His eyes filled with tears.

The red jineri was silent, watching the man. When he sat heavily back into his chair she vanished as well.

Part 7 - Civilian

Three months from the end of Karen's tour in the Marine Corps it was late spring in Afghanistan. Summer was predicted to be hot and dry, hardly a surprise. It always was.

At the 10:00 Thursday briefing as usual only half the seats around the conference table near Lieutenant Minetti's office were filled. Also as usual Karen was peripherally aware of Ariel McCarthy. Who paid her the same compliment. Always they sat across the long oval table from each other.

Ariel never seemed to be bothered by the weather, any more than Karen was. Of course the alien had Suit to control temperatures but she rarely used it. Her body was very good at suffering weather and climate. She wondered idly if Ariel had a Suit. After working with the woman off and on for two years neither of them had opened up to the other. Karen still didn't know if McCarthy was an alien like herself or something stranger.

Afterward as everyone stood up to leave the Lieutenant spoke to Karen.

"Let's go in my office for a minute. I've got a question."

Sitting behind his desk he leaned back, put his boots on the desk, and tented his hands.

"You're so damned hard to read. You're open and friendly but after almost two years I still know only the bare facts about you."

She was mildly curious where this was leading.

"Are you happy in the Corps, Karen? Are you happy here?"

"I'm usually happy, Sir. But not especially so here or in the Corps."

"I'd like a heads-up on what your plans are now that your tour is nearly up. Do you intend to stay in? Ask for an extension of your stay?"

Marines went where they were told and did what they were told--though sometimes in unorthodox ways. *Improvise, Adapt and Overcome* was almost a reflex for Marines. But at the end of a tour they could leave unless in the middle of an emergency.

"I've been thinking about getting out, Victor. I've done about all that's humanly possibly to pacify this area of the Stan. It seems like I should be doing more. Somewhere."

"If you stay in I can promise you as a bonus a promotion to

Sergeant. You have the time in and your evals are through the roof."

"Thanks for telling me. But promotion doesn't mean much to me. I've not kept it a secret that I don't mean to make the Corps a career."

"I had to offer. But there's another consideration. I'm being promoted to Captain. That means I'll be reassigned. I've done everything I can to stay in grade, but my time has come."

Karen laughed. "I think that's the first time I've heard of anyone likening promotion to a tragedy."

He smiled. "It happens more often than you think. I've known master sergeants who mourned being summarily recommended for commissioning as an officer."

He sobered. "What this means is that my replacement may not realize what treasures he has--or she has, excuse me--and not use them properly. That especially includes you. I don't know what you are, but I know you're not human. Or maybe you're what comes after us humans."

Her outsides changed not a bit, but inside she felt shock.

"Interesting. What makes you think that?"

"I have creditable reports of you levitating. And turning your skin and your clothing red, as if you just flicked a switch."

"Have you reported any of this?"

Even as she asked she reflexively ran a search of all the trillions of online documents. She knew the answer.

"No. I know you are not a threat to the human race. I've sent you on missions too many times when you could have satisfied the reqs by just killing someone. Sometimes lots of someones. Instead you try to use non-violent means when that will work. Like that warlord who became the next thing to a pacifist."

"Thank you."

"What are you, Karen?"

She considered what to say. The more he knew the more he could reveal. Maybe accidentally.

She felt so lonely sometimes. Her parents knew about her. And her brother must know something, though he'd never said anything to anyone. But that wasn't enough.

She turned her skin and clothing green. Then had Suit lift her a couple of feet into the air.

"Green is so much prettier than red, don't you think?"

He smiled. "Definitely less threatening."

She settled back into her chair and normal colors.

"I'm human. But from far away. Best I not go into detail."

"Thank you. But that still leaves us the problem. What to do when your enlistment is up."

She sighed. She knew how those master sergeants felt that he'd mentioned. Her situation was not perfect, but was as comfortable as well-worn clothes.

"I'll leave and-- I don't know what the Hell I'll do. I'll just have to figure it out, I suppose."

He rose. "Well, I wish you luck. Now, we've got work to do."

Karen was met at the L. A. International airport by her parents and her brother and his family. She was one of the first passengers off, having bought a first-class ticket. She saw her brother first. He was tall and grinning widely and waving his arms over his head.

She glided toward the small group waiting for her, a tall black-headed Valkyrie in military camouflage dress who moved with tigerish grace. The few people ahead of her and nearby instinctively flowed away from her, most without even noticing what they were doing.

Little ten-year-old Sylvia broke away from the family group and dashed laughing to greet her aunt. Karen dropped her small carryon suitcase, bent and caught her up, herself laughing.

"Nana, you're home! You're home! Are you going to stay this time? Daddy said you are!"

Karen kissed the girl's nearest cheek. "Yes. I'm going to be here a long time." Then she was surrounded by her parents, her brother, and his wife. All were laughing and talking over each other except for Jessica, who was still a bit shy around the strange woman "little Karen" had become since she left for the Marine Corps.

Another eager former passenger lightly bumped Karen on their way to a similar family meeting, trailing behind a "Sorry!"

Karen laughed again. "Come on! We're in the way!"

She lifted Sylvia onto one hip and snugged her to herself with one arm. Then she took off walking, pulling her carryon behind her on its wheels with her other hand. At the stairway down she took the branch opposite the way to the checked-luggage carrousel.

Outside the terminal at the traffic lanes she stopped to let her father lead the way across the traffic and to the spot in the garage where he'd left their car.

Karen was seated in the back seat with Sylvia on her lap, her brother on one side, her sister-in-law on the other.

As they pulled out of the garage Karen said to Jessica, "I hear you got promoted to District Sales manager. How is that working out?"

The slender dark-haired, dark-eyed woman smiled. "I love it. Lots more responsibility but I think I'm making a difference."

"I'll say!" Bulky redheaded Alexander beamed across Karen at his wife. "Sales have increased six percent in the first six months."

Her mother spoke from the front seat, half-turned toward her husband so she could look into the back. "Did you have a good trip, dear?"

"Very good. I splurged and bought first-class seats all the way from Kabul. Then I over-nighted in Dubai and New York at very nice hotels to help get my biological clock back on U. S. time."

Alex nodded, "I understand. Those new hypersonic flights can get you here in one long hop. But then your day'd still be upside down."

All the way home her father said little. He knew (as did his wife) that Karen had flown by Pegasus from Kabul to Denver and boarded a flight there to keep up the fiction that she'd made a three-day trip. It still bothered him and his wife to keep Karen's extraterrestrial origin secret from their son, but they felt it was necessary.

At home she was surprised to find waiting both her maternal grandparents (as she thought them) and several aunts and uncles and cousins. They'd prepared a feast which spilled over into the back yard. There was much noise, made all the more tumultuous by the several children and dogs who'd been brought along.

The party went on from the mid-afternoon to early evening, when people began to leave. Finally there was only her parents and her brother and his family.

They all relaxed in the living room, her parents and Jessica with wine and little Sylvia and Karen drinking tea. Alex was drinking coffee to prepare him to drive them to a hotel. He didn't want to drive back to

San Diego at that time of night and feeling tired.

"Why are you feeling tired, Alex?" said Karen, grinning. "Getting old?"

Jessica said, "It's this big corporate merger he's working on. He's the lead attorney for his company."

Her brother nodded. "Most of the hardest parts are done and I can slack off a bit now. That's why I could take off today and tomorrow. But I still have to go in Saturday for a half day."

Karen said, "Why don't I come down Saturday morning and we can do something? Maybe go to the Zoo or Sea World?"

Sylvia practically began jumping up and down though she remained seated on the couch. "Sea World! Sea World!"

Karen looked at Jessica, who shrugged and smiled back.

"Sea World it is," Karen said. "I'll double-check my memory later tonight. But I think it opens at 10:00. And there's a Pet's Rule show at 11:00 I love. So let's say I get to your place at 10:00--" she looked at Jessica for approval-- "and leave by 10:15. That still gets us there in time to find good seats."

Jessica nodded, and the deal was made.

The next day, Friday, her parents left for work as usual and Karen spent the day flying around Riverview and L. A. in general, landing occasionally and walking around. Twice she stopped to eat.

It felt strange to be here to stay. Especially since she had no plans for her future. Much of her still felt as if she were in Afghanistan.

That evening her parents took her out to eat, then they sat up for another hour just talking. She mentioned her feeling of dislocation.

"You'll just have to give it time," her mother said. "I feel that way a little bit every time I come back from a long business trip."

"I suppose."

After breakfast with her parents in the morning she walked into the back yard, routinely checked for any surveillance via Tiara, folded Pegasus around her, and went invisible and up. She swooped by a car-rental place so that Pegasus could memorize a moderately expensive car with a glossy blue finish.

It took her an hour and a half to slowly fly the 130 miles to San

Diego at a hundred feet up, enjoying the bright morning, small openings in Peg's force field letting through enough air to bring to her all the scents and sensations of the cool Southern California morning. The view was quite lovely on the last half of the trip. It was over the coastal highway and the blue ocean to her right was sending white foam ashore every few minutes as it had for millions of years.

A few minutes before landing near her brother's home Karen let Pegasus form a virtual copy around her of the auto she was pretending to rent. At a secluded area of the suburban neighborhood she landed and went visible. Starting the engine, she drove a half mile into the suburb and parked on the street.

Sylvia must have been peering out her home's living room window. She was out the door and halfway to Karen before the alien could get more than a dozen feet up the front sidewalk.

"Karen, you came!"

Karen put an arm around the girl's shoulders and they turned to walk toward the house.

"Hell could bar the way and I'd still be here." She found some humor in the fact that this was true for any Earthly and many un-Earthly versions of Hell.

Jessica was waiting in the doorway, smiling. She was already dressed for the park in dark-blue knee-high shorts, light blue long-sleeved blouse, and fashionable dark-blue walking shoes. Her daughter's outfit echoed hers, except the shoes were much-scuffed. Sylvia was a little athlete and very active.

Karen wore a similar outfit but with an olive green color palette. Her long curly blond hair cascaded around her shoulders and off her bosom.

"Would you like something?" the woman asked. "Coffee? Water?"

"No. I'm good. What about you, Sylly?"

The girl was dashing toward the car with a small purse on a strap over one shoulder.

"Guess that's our answer," Karen said.

Jessica leaned back inside the house and came up with a pale blue straw hat and a big open-mouthed cloth purse of a matching color, then locked the door. As the two of them walked down the sidewalk she said, "Naturally she's been checking the view every minute or two, wondering when you'd get here!"

"And you? Did you really want to spend the day this way?"

"Yes. I learned long ago to take as little of my job home as I could."

"You've been in this new position six months now. Are you all settled in?"

By this time they'd reached the car and entered it. They secured their seat belts and each checked to be sure Sylvia had too. Satisfied she had, they shared a smile as they faced forward again.

"Pretty much. For a month now I've had my weekends gloriously free of work. What about you? How are you adjusting to being a civilian?"

"It's going to take a while."

"What are your plans? Go to college? Something else?"

Sea World was only fifteen minutes or so away, on the western side of San Diego in the midst of several small bays and coves. The street they took to it passed by Mission Beach and they could see surfers out in the Pacific. Further out were sail boats and power boats.

The parking lot at Sea World was already fairly full but Karen steered to the area closest to the entrance, all the while almost subconsciously monitoring the parking lot from a surveillance satellite that kept track of events around Camp Pendleton and the areas as far south as San Diego and as far north as Orange County. She pulled into a spot seconds after it had been vacated.

"That was lucky," Jessica said.

Karen smiled and said nothing. Nothing could be said, for Sylvia was piling out and running toward the entrance, yelling at someone.

"I hope you don't mind," Jessica said. "I was going to tell you earlier. But she invited two of her friends to go with us."

"Mind? I'm grateful. They can run each other ragged instead of us. Or does Sylvia have a tendency to vanish with her friends?"

"She does. But her friend Mei-feng is very responsible."

"'Beautiful Wind,'" Karen mused.

"Oh. You've heard it before?"

"Yes." She could hardly admit that through Tiara she could now speak most of even the most obscure languages on Earth.

Two women were with Sylvia's two friends. One was Chinese and small, the other black and tall and stately.

Jessica widened her strides for a few steps to close with the two women. "Lydia. Uzochi. I want you to meet my sister-in-law, Karen."

The two mothers turned interested (and cautious) eyes on the strange woman. Karen decided she needed to reassure them that she was not a blood-thirsty savage. She smiled and stepped forward to shake their hands.

"Thank God! Two more people to help keep us from being run off our feet!"

That helped a bit. So too, Karen knew, the fact that she was so beautiful. Few people could shake off the conditioning of the movies that heroes and heroines were almost universally gorgeous.

It also helped that Karen did an almost reflexive data search of the web, limiting it to San Diego and the mother's and daughter's names and a few other conditions. Before they'd found seats for the show she knew that Lydia was a data analyst. Uzochi was a police captain specializing in robbery. This would give her some common grounds when a good time came to drop relevant facts into the conversation.

For the first twenty-five minutes there was little time for that. The *Pets Rule!* show featured dogs, cats, birds and pigs doing all sorts of acrobatic and humorous tricks. The many children watching, and not a few adults, were very noisy in their appreciation.

They had a little over an hour before the next show. This was their cue to eat. There was plenty of variety. The kids chose hot dogs and pizza, Jessica and Lydia generous salads loaded with croutons and miscellaneous protein, and Uzochi and Karen big Mexican combo dishes with lots of hot sauce.

The black teased Lydia and Jessica about watching their diets. A shared glance with the woman and Karen made a mild joke along those lines too. Then the black woman and Karen competed on how much hot sauce they could eat. When Karen saw the other woman begin to approach her limit she gave up before Uzochi did.

Meanwhile they kept a sharp eye on the three girls. Jessica was the one to call it time to go to the next show "so they could get the best tickets." At that the girls raced each other to clean their plates and lead the slow-poke adults to the show.

Blue Horizons featured several dolphins doing tricks while trained birds flew overhead. Afterward children were allowed to feed the dolphins treats under close supervision of park officials dressed in wet suits. There was much hilarity as one dolphin tried to hog those treats, only to be shouldered aside by the other dolphins. Finally she snuck a final treat and rapidly swam away to eat it in private. Lydia told the other women that this was actually part of the show.

There was plenty to see before the final show, exhibits and dioramas and huge transparent-sided pools where all sorts of sea life could be observed.

The *One Ocean* show was so popular even coming early forced the girls and the women to sit apart, though not so far apart that the kids could not be kept track of. It featured several killer whales, among the smallest of the whales but still several times larger than the dolphins. These were fed afterward but only with poles carrying the goodies. None of the poles were damaged so feeding by hand was probably safe, but the animals though well-trained could make a mistake and they were too big to take chances with.

After that it would have been a let down to spend more time in the park. They all adjourned to the Fashion Valley Mall four miles inland because it was the closest. This was a great success, none of them leaving without something that the girls insisted were *absolutely* necessary to their continued happiness.

In the parking lot it took more than a half hour for the girls to say Goodbyes to the others. That was fine with the three mothers, who took a similar time. Karen hid her impatience; she'd always preferred efficiency. But she supposed now that she was a civilian she must learn to take a more leisurely approach to life.

By now Alex was home from his half-day at work. Sylvia took more than an hour to tell him all about the Sea World visit and show him photos taken on her cell phone. Then everyone retired to their rooms to clean up and dress for an evening out at a favorite Italian-Argentine restaurant run by one of Jessica's large Argentine family.

Afterward the four sat in the living room of her brother and his wife, the two of them with a nightcap, Sylvia and Karen drinking a fruit drink.

When the girl began visibly wilting her parents told her it was time to go to bed.

"Can Karen take me up?"

Karen could and the alien and the girl went upstairs, where Sylvia brushed her teeth and otherwise made herself ready for bed. As Karen folded her bed clothes around her, Sylvia said, "Can I ask you a question?"

"Sure." Karen pulled Sylvia's desk chair over by the bed and settled into the chair, legs crossed, so that she and her niece could easily chat.

But Sylvia looked down at her coverlet, her hands twisting a corner of it nervously. Finally she looked up.

"You killed people over there, didn't you?"

For an adult and a stranger to ask this would have been an intolerable invasion. But Sylvia was neither. And this was very important to her. Karen could only tell her the truth.

"Yes. Several of them." She tried to be calm and direct. But it hurt her throat to say it out loud.

"Are you sorry?"

"No. Not even a little bit. Maybe I should be. But every one was trying to kill someone else, sometimes very horribly."

The girl stared down at light sheet, thinking. Then she looked up.

"Why were they trying to do that? Was something--wrong with them?"

"It's the way many of them were brought up. To see everyone outside their tribe as an enemy."

"But I've read about what's happening over there. Sometimes they kill little kids and mothers."

"I can't explain it all. Ask your parents. Or school teachers. Or read. But one part of it is that men are taught from birth that only boys are important, and woman and kids aren't. They might be very fair to other men in their tribe. But only to them."

Sylvia thought about that for a while, frowning down more at the sheet. Then she nodded.

"So you were like police. A protector."

"Yes. That's the way I think."

The girl looked up at her aunt. "What are you going to do now? Become a policeman?"

"Well, that's a possibility. Or maybe an FIB special agent. Or something else. I'll have to think about it."

"OK. Give me a kiss." She sat upright in her bed and lifted her arms to Karen. Karen stood and hugged her back, then pulled the sheet up over Sylvia's waist as she snuggled into the bed.

Karen was at the point of tears as she made her way to the stairs. She paused a moment to blink her eyes clear before taking the first step down.

<>

She was still thinking about the "something else" three weeks later when news came to her which made a big change in her life.

During that time she'd roamed the planet, landing in odd places and spending time there, sometimes just a few minutes or hours, sometimes as long as two days. This included a deep tropical jungle, the top of one of the tallest mountains in the world, and places full of people. The places were small towns and megacities. Being able to speak any language at all and assume any appearance and clothe herself in any costume made it easy.

Twice she intervened in crimes. Both times she had the luxury of not having to kill people to make a point.

Then one morning she received a phone call while she was in Buenos Aires, Argentina, the "Tango Capitol of The World." She'd become enchanted with the dance while watching a Broadway show which featured it. She'd taken a week of lessons from various Argentine teachers, several hours every day, and finally become good enough at the dance to go to the "milongas" where social tango dancing was done.

The very first morning after her first milonga, which lasted from 11:00 at night till 4:00 in the morning, she slept late. Her chiming cell phone woke her.

"Hello. Karen here."

"Ms. Danburn. Am I calling at a bad time?"

"No, not at all." This was true enough. She was able to come fully awake quickly when she wanted to.

"This is Albert Wang in Prince Enterprises' Patents and Licenses Services organization. Your advanced-compound patent has been granted and we would like to discuss where you wanted to go with it. There are several very interesting directions you could take. Could we set up an appointment to discuss them?"

As he spoke she was using Tiara to shuffle through much information, including some of his biographical information and historical data on past rights deals with which Prince had been involved. So far most of it was encouraging; Prince was known to work well with others. For instance, it could have established its own factories to turn out vehicles using the paramagnetic effect. Yet it had sought partners in already-established companies rather than take business away from the companies.

Even more impressive, Anna Prince had early established the principle of introducing revolutionary technical advances in a measured way to ensure they did not cause radically rapid economic impact.

It seemed counter intuitive. Short term profit sacrificed for long-term gain was not the usual practice in the business world.

"Certainly," she said, her mind running in its highest gear, her body fully awake. "What is a good time for you?"

"Any time from tomorrow on. It's more important to select a good time for you; our schedules are flexible."

She set a time: 10:00 Monday morning four days hence. She wanted to go to a few more milongas while she was here. She'd much enjoyed the dances she'd had last night. Tango in social settings was much simpler than the spectacular dances done by professionals in shows who'd danced almost from birth. Yet it'd had an almost hypnotically Zen-like effect on her when she danced it herself with a good partner, as if what was happening in the moment was all there was. Was it a fluke of last night alone? Or could she experience it again?

<>

Ten in the morning in New York was noon in Buenos Aires. So she slept till two hours before that, checked out, and was arcing into the sky minutes later through a grey rainy overcast. The skies above the clouds were clear and sunny and very beautiful. She idly enjoyed the view while she climbed into the blackness above the atmosphere.

Most of her attention was cast deep into the electronic pathways of the world, studying Prince Enterprises and its P&L Services. She avoided Prince's deepest data reservoirs. She'd been reminded once again that it was impervious even to the advanced infotech of Tiara. This made her wonder once again if Anna Prince (or someone close to her) was from the Human Interstellar Confederation.

Nearing New York from above she turned her attention to her dress and hair and makeup. What emerged from an alley near Prince Enterprises Technology headquarters in New York's financial district was a smartly dressed young woman. Her blond hair was up in a sleek braided bun, her pale pink lips showed only a suggestion of makeup, and her clothing was a dark blue business suit with knee-length skirt and a light blue blouse. Her shoes were dark blue with a modest heel.

Albert Wang was a bit of a surprise in person. He was tall, had something of a body-builder's physique, and was very handsome. This was unlike many Chinese she had known, who were shorter and more slender. He was dressed very conservatively, a dark suit and vest, white shirt and blue-and-red striped tie, and shiny oxford shoes. Yet a single purple streak down one side of his neat haircut proclaimed that he could surprise you.

They shook hands and he ushered her into a corner office with a window south over the upper bay and another west over the Hudson River, both very busy with water traffic. That alone told her what she already knew from her data snooping: he was an upper-level legal bureaucrat.

He sat behind his polished antique desk with a minimum of ornaments and paper work. On it was a single blue folder fat with documents. She sank into one of the two client chairs of deep brown leather. It was very comfortable, almost too much so. It could lull one into too much ease.

"I hope you had a good weekend, Karen. May I call you that?"

"Of course, Albert." She smiled at him, a bare showing of teeth less a friendly gesture than a reminder that she could bite.

He was momentarily taken aback, though he hid it well. Perhaps he had fallen into the common trap of underestimating very beautiful women.

"Now. You have several options. One is--"

"I'll take the option of signing my patent to Prince Enterprises to completely handle all rights and licensing. I will trust you to completely represent me in all dealings, and dole out profits on a monthly basis.

"Lest you think me naïve, I assure you I have studied all the various options and the contract you most likely have in that folder before us."

He had been sitting forward in his chair, alertly looking into her eyes, all business but sympathetic. He sat back in his chair, his hands dropping to lie on the chair's armrests.

Slowly he began to nod, perhaps not consciously aware that he was doing so.

"I'm beginning to remember the briefing on you. I see I should have paid more attention to it."

"Yes. You should have noticed that for three years now I've worked in intelligence. So I'm used to researching deeply and quickly into very complex situations."

She leaned forward and reached toward the folder. He put his hand on it.

"Albert, I'm ready to sign your full-option forms."

"I only want to see you sign them when you come back with a competent legal representative. Not to protect you. To protect us. We don't want there to be any chance that you'll someday claim that we persuaded you to sign something against your interests."

Of course. She'd been so certain from her research into Prince Enterprise's P&L Services that she was going to be treated fairly, that she'd missed the other side's viewpoint. That she might cheat THEM.

She smiled. "Fair enough. I'll ask my brother to recommend someone here to represent me. He's a very good attorney in corporate contracts. I'm sure he'll know someone, or knows someone who knows someone. So, if we're done--"

"We're not. Though we can move ahead faster than I'd anticipated. I need to brief you on what is likely to happen with this particular patent. At least at a cursory level. In the folder are more details."

"I--"

"Please."

So for more than a half hour he briefed her. She listened attentively, asking the occasional question. This was more to assure him she was making an effort and succeeding at understanding than because she needed the answer. For through Tiara she was comparing what he said to what was the opinion of experts on developing and profiting from technological breakthroughs.

One thing was clear. She was going to be a very wealthy woman fairly quickly and to the tune of several million dollars as the years went by. The advanced-compound material could be made into many kinds of tough and durable machine parts and machines. This went all the way from ultra-light-weight everyday machines, some as simple as camping gear, to very complex high-performance jet engines which had to be tough and resist very high temperatures.

That night she phoned her brother and got a referral to an intellectual-property rights attorney in New York. The next morning she phoned the attorney's office, where she was quickly bucked up the chain of authority when she explained the situation.

So a few days later she was accompanied back to Prince Enterprises by two attorneys, a sturdy forty-something woman with grey hair and a Brooklyn accent and a slender twenty-something darkly handsome Italian who said little but saw much. After introductions, as if to mirror the enemy, Albert Wang called in a younger woman to attend him.

There followed almost two hours of what seemed to Karen quibbling over minor points. Then Karen stood up at a momentary lull.

"Excellent. So it seems as if we're substantially in agreement. I need a bathroom break and another cup of your excellent coffee. Then we can wrap this up."

Wang and his opposite looked at each other and seemed to telepathically agree. The idiot client had put her foot down and called an end to legal arm wrestling. She seemed to have no more patience for it and they might as well wind matters up and go on to clients who would allow more substantial billable hours.

Soon Karen was signing various documents presented to her by the two younger attorneys in turn. Then everyone shook hands all around, wished each other well and harmonious future relations, and departed.

Out on the street Karen spoke to her two attorneys.

"Hester, Ilario, good job up there. It was pleasure to watch you work. But I'm sure this will be the last time I have to call upon Armbruster and Associates. From now on I'll deal directly with Wang if I have to deal with someone."

The young man smiled as he held her hand for a moment after the handshake.

"Every once in a while I'd look at you and wonder, 'This is an ex-Marine?'"

"FORMER Marine."

"Yes. Well, at the end there I saw it."

The woman said, "I have an idea that this is not the last time you'll want representation, perhaps on very different matters. Remember that our firm handles many legal areas. Think of us first when those matters come up."

"Thank you. I will."

Hester gave Karen a quick impersonal we're-women hug and turned with her assistant toward the yellow cab first in line in front of the building.

Karen walked away, turned into an alley, and disappeared.

<>

For the next few weeks Karen wandered the world, visiting her family periodically. She established apartments in New York, Paris, Mumbai in Britannic India, and Buenos Aires in Argentina. All those places had activities which she enjoyed. The apartments were modest but nice and close to those activities.

It was in New York where she became involved in crime fighting beyond the occasional street crime in the various cities she frequented. An especially vicious drug gang had moved in. The third time Karen read a news story about them she decided to do something about them.

Floating high above the city that afternoon she had Tiara do a search for all reports of incidents of any kind related to the "Alpha" gang's activities. Then, as the world turned toward night and darkness spread across the city below her, she studied the problem of fighting this kind of crime and this gang in particular.

There were attack points all along the pipeline through which the drugs passed. The beginning was in several places, Afghanistan among them. It had to be grown, harvested, bundled, and sent out in some way, by air or sea usually.

The shipments were obvious points of attack. Karen was most interested in those going to New York. But only to the gang she'd decided to destroy. As long as gangs did not kill civilians, especially kids and women, or sell to kids, she did not care about them. Their customers might kill themselves with heroin and cocaine and such but they were grownups able to decide for themselves how to live and die. Besides, the regular police could handle the "peaceful" gangs.

Karen did a preliminary survey of the ways "product" could enter the city by air, water, or ground. New York was one of the major ports of the world. She found that even for the super-advanced computer that was Tiara, and now part of her, this was too much data to select out just that avenue which was relevant to the Alpha gang. Still, she felt the survey was useful; it let her understand the overall transportation turf.

Next, product was collected at the gang's distribution site and processed and packaged in several ways. This site and the people in it, especially the big boss of it all, was what she wanted destroyed.

But it was not easily found. She decided that she needed to find the customers first and work backward to their suppliers and from them to the distribution site.

So who were the customers? Among them celebrities and rich people were the most prominent. So she became one of them.

<>

"Isn't it exquisite?"

Karen turned toward the woman who'd come to stand beside her in the art gallery where she was sipping wine and wandering. It was Hester Springfield, a woman she'd twice chatted with briefly over the last three months and waved at across a room a few more times.

Slender but large-busted, fortyish, well-preserved, long auburn hair with large grey-green eyes, she walked and talked with great assurance. The dress she wore was a knee-length confection of what looked like metal diamond shapes strung point-to-point from neck to knees. Discreet patches of skin shown between links but the overall look was modest.

Karen turned back toward the painting. It was some three feet square in a narrow gold frame. It was made up of blots and swirls of blue and gold paint in no order she could see. It reminded her of a sunny summer day, an image she appreciated now that autumn had brought the first chill rainy day to wash New York. Though she was protected by Suit and her own tough skin she still felt a psychic chill.

"Yes," she said, though she really felt only mild pleasure. Nice but ordinary was her appraisal, if anyone had cared to know.

"I wish I could afford it," said Hester. "It marks a turning point in his development."

"For your museum?" Hester was a respected art critic and part owner and curator of *le petit Musée d'Art moderne*, a small establishment a few blocks south of the American Museum of Natural History on the west side of Manhattan's Central Park.

"Yes. But it's certain to be snapped up by some wealthy person and seen by only a few people. If that. It might just be warehoused until it commands a higher price."

A flash washed over the scene, not bright, the low-medium light used by professional photographers at events like these where they'd be ejected if they interfered too much with people's pleasure.

Hester turned and smiled, putting an arm around Karen's waist and drawing her close. In front of them was a photographer of whom Karen had been peripherally aware, as she was of everyone near her.

"Simon! How nice to see you! Getting plenty of useful shots?"

Simon Morton was a photographer for The New York Courier, Karen recalled from previous encounters, a small newspaper and newszine that covered Manhattan's entertainment beat. Two photos of her had already been featured in the magazine, not surprising considering her perfect face and figure and the tastefully fashionable clothing she'd been wearing.

The bearded older man with a halo of dark hair lowered his camera and smiled back.

"How could I not, with two such lovely ladies as subjects? Are you considering buying the Moretti?"

Hester's smile turned teasing.

"That's for me to know and you to find out. You're staying for the auction?"

"Of course. Could I get a shot of you two framing the painting?"

Hester looked at Karen, who nodded. Under Morton's direction they stood closer to the painting, far enough apart so that it could be seen but enough to get both their figures in the frame. He had them turn toward each other a bit so they seemed to be just turning their heads toward him in welcoming surprise. It took a few shots to get their smiles and stances just right.

As he left Hester thanked Karen for cooperating. "With any luck the photo will prompt a few more people into the museum. If it appears at all."

"I'd not be surprised." Karen was fairly sure it would be, for through Tiara she'd seen him mark the last photo as TBP: To Be Published. He'd used this code on the two previous photos of her which had ended up in his newszine.

"Later, Hester," Karen said. "If you're attending the auction."

"Absolutely. Come sit with me if you don't find some hunk who preempts that position."

It was a little over an hour later when the people attending the showing were called to one of the hotel's mid-sized conference rooms. Chairs had been set up facing a two-foot high dais with a podium on one side and a painting display stand on the opposite side. There was already a painting on the stand's rack. Above the dais a large video screen showed an expanded image of the stand and the painting.

A silver haired auctioneer in a dark suit was at the podium. He waited until the room was full and seated, except for a few scurrying last-second arrivals. He called the meeting to order and began the auction.

Those who wanted to bid had picked up table-tennis-like paddles from a table by the door. Each was white with a large black number on it.

Hester glanced at Karen's paddle as Karen took a seat beside her. They smiled at each other but turned their attention to the auctioneer.

The first few items were physically smaller and went quickly for small prices, though at one point a fierce three-way bidding war drove the price to a surprisingly large amount.

The Moretti was the next to last item to be displayed.

"The bidding starts at $100,000 and only comparable amounts will be accepted."

The bidding went up quickly to $300,000. It slowed then but went up in $50,000 increments to $900,000. There it stalled.

Seconds before it was pronounced Sold Karen lifted her paddle.

"One million."

There was rustle of clothing and a storm of whispers as everyone turned to see who had made the bid. Hester beside Karen inhaled and held her breath.

"We have one million. One million. One million going once. One million going--"

"One million ten." It was a beefy but distinguished-looking older man who'd made the $900,000 bid.

"One million twenty," Karen said.

"One million forty."

"One sixty."

There was silence. The man was looking at her angrily, then turned sharply toward the auctioneer.

"One seventy."

"Two million. And I can keep going." As she could. She'd received three ever-larger payments from Prince Enterprises since signing the agreement with them. With her trust fund and those payments she could play with almost six million dollars.

And she neither needed nor wanted a penny of it for anything important.

"I call challenge. Can this individual pay?" The rival bidder sounded angry.

Karen held up her credit card. It was Osmium, a dull silver labeled only with a silver number little brighter than the rest of the card. A young woman in a black outfit hurried from beside the dais, took it from her, and ran it through a small flat credit card reader. Moments later she lifted her head and nodded at the auctioneer.

"The challenge is passed," the man said. "Are there other bids? No? Two million once. Two million twice. SOLD to the woman in row two."

The last painting sold for $850,000. Karen had made the largest buy of that night.

Everyone stood up, some to go forward to pay for their purchases, most to leave. Hester said to Karen. "I hope you enjoy your painting, dear. Maybe someday you'll let me stop by and appreciate it."

Karen grabbed her arm as Hester turned away. "Come with me."

She looked around. As she'd known he would be, Simon Morton was jockeying around the edge of the crowd trying to get shots of her. She lifted a hand and gave him a Come to Me gesture.

He paused an instant only. Then he was in motion. By the time Karen and Hester had arrived at the side of the room where three young people in black clothing were processing sales he was not far behind.

The largest sales were processed first, perhaps to lessen the chances of escape by remorseful buyers. Karen turned over her credit card and was quickly given a receipt.

"Take this to Security and they will arrange transport of your purchase to your residence or place of business. Thank you for your participation."

Karen moved to a nearby area free of traffic and turned to her two companions.

"Simon, I'm about to transfer ownership of my painting to Hester. Would you like to take pictures? Or a video? I assume that monstrous machine can do that."

"Absolutely."

Hester had already begun to intuit Karen's intention but had not been certain. Her face now brightened with sudden happiness.

"You really mean it?"

"Absolutely. Now let's do this right. Simon."

"Let's go some place-- I know just where. Come." He turned and walked quickly away.

WHERE was a smaller conference room. At its far end was a low dais backed by a red velvet curtain. He positioned them near it facing each other but at a slight angle open to him and his camera. He also consulted with them on what they were going to say. It was brief.

Two floodlights from a large equipment bag shown on the two from off to each side. The floods were not bright but they did add contrast and some shadowing of the scene.

"OK. Rolling."

"Hester, I've enjoyed *le petit Musée d'Art moderne* ever since I moved to New York. Please accept this painting for display in the Museum. I'm sure many people will enjoy it, perhaps long after I'm gone."

She handed the white folded envelope to the woman. Hester accepted it and held out her off hand. Karen accepted it with her off hand as if to shake it.

"Karen, I accept in the name of all our staff at *le petit Musée* and all its many visitors. We thank you deeply."

They shook hands and hugged.

"Cut. That's a take, ladies."

"Good," said Karen. "I wasn't going to do another anyway. If you'd screwed up, too bad."

"Me?!" he said with mock annoyance, then grinned and rushed away.

"Damn," said Karen. "I was going to ask him if he wanted to shoot a formal ceremony where I hand over the real painting."

"Don't worry. I have his number. You really want to do that?"

"Sure. I sure as Hell don't want your painting to be shown in a museum no one goes to. The ceremony should make the Courier. And maybe a few other newszines."

"Especially if you wear something like you're wearing tonight."

Karen looked down at her dress. It was long, simple, pale green, shimmering, hugging her body as if sprayed on. With her long gleaming golden hair and large blue eyes she looked like Aphrodite come to Earth to slum among mortals.

<>

The weekend after Thanksgiving at a wine-tasting event Karen made her first firm contact with a drug user. Her nose, enhanced by Tiara, had several times before scented cocaine in the air at various events. However, Karen had been unable to find the users and initiate contact.

She'd spent the previous weekend with her family in California, then midweek flown here. The weather was especially foul tonight, a recent cold front dumping snow on New York. This did not stop the premiere of a show near the end of the Summer-Fall play season. Someone was trying to get the jump on the Winter-Spring season which would begin in January.

Karen was in a red off-the-shoulder gown which descended just past her knees and matching red high-heeled sandals. It showed a discreet swell of her breasts but was body hugging. She'd checked the scarlet jacket she'd worn in the play at the entrance to this back room which had been tricked out for the modest after-play reception.

"I can't believe how well they carried off a musical version of 'The Glass Menagerie,'" said one of the two women in the small group with which Karen was standing.

"I can't believe they carried it off at all," said the other. "I wasn't impressed. What did you think--your name is Karen?"

"Don't ask me. I'm just a knuckle-dragging former Marine."

Everyone laughed. One of the women said, "Oh, please pardon me. I see someone we absolutely *must* talk to." She and her friend hurried off toward a new arrival at the party.

This left Karen with the bank president who looked like a stereotypical romantic movie star, all boyish face and athletic build in a fitted tuxedo. At least he had the greying side burns one might expect of such an exalted personage.

"What did you think of the play?" she said.

"Bored me to tears. If I hadn't had to show up to keep tabs on an investment opportunity I'd have stayed home with a glass and a classic movie. But it seems to be a success so I'm thinking of making my escape. Join me?"

"Tempting. But I think I'll wander a bit. I was thinking I might contact someone who might put me in the market for something--sophisticated. I'm still too new in town to know my way around." "Sophisticated" was the latest in-word for designer drugs. Which cocaine was not, but marked her as someone "adventurous"--a drug user.

He gave her a considering look, said, "I can help in that regard. But back at my place."

"Interesting. I think I'll take a rain check. Maybe I can manage something a bit more expedient here. I do appreciate the offer. A very tempting one." She gave him a sweet smile which she hoped was a bit wicked as well.

He shrugged and turned away from her.

Now she'd made contact she needed to monitor his movements. She could do so electronically by using Tiara to put tracers on all his electronic communications. She did so now by electronically snagging his identity from the cell phone in his pocket, then widening the search for information on him from that.

Tracers might not work as well as they did in Afghanistan where cell phones and info slates and such were still new. In developed countries people with illicit activities in mind avoided communicating electronically. They knew well how easily such devices could be bugged even if protected by cryptography.

She had Suit create a flying spy device the size of a dust mote and directed it to follow the man and attach itself to his forehead. It would be dislodged the next time he washed his face but would stay nearby till it could re-attach itself, recording and transmitting video and audio whenever Tiara told it to. She told it to disintegrate after a year. Otherwise it would be around for centuries.

She wandered a bit more, greeting and sometimes chatting with various acquaintances. By now she was part of the celebrity scene and smiled and posed once for the usual roving photographer.

<>

Three months passed and the number of drug users she had discovered surpassed a hundred. Only a third used cocaine and she identified several sets of drug peddlers. None of them were connected to the Alphas.

Then in two week's time she snagged three Alpha peddlers. She and Tiara went to high alert, dogging the men every hour of every day. Finally they pinpointed the Alpha headquarters.

<>

Karen floated a thousand feet above Huntersville. This was a neighborhood of maybe 100,000 people on the northwest edge of Long Island's Queens borough, one of the five boroughs which made up New York City.

Spring was here with mostly sunny days. Frigid winds from the north alternated with warm zephyrs from the south. Dirty snow was melting everywhere.

To the west, on her left, she could see the shining Triborough Bridge and the older rusty-looking Hell Gate Bridge curving away to the west and north to connect with Manhattan and the Bronx. Auto traffic was heavy on the Triborough in the mid-afternoon. People below her were out in force despite the knifelike breezes, hunched over and hurrying to work and to shop.

There were plenty of places to shop, and many different kinds of shops. Huntersville was a city as varied as the nations making up the League of Nations, with people from the Netherlands, Germany, Ireland, Italy, Greece, the Middle East, the Far East, and South America.

The alien drifted down to a section of that last group, one known as Little Venezuela. Like most of the rest of Huntersville it was a mix of new houses, old renovated houses, and old run-down houses. The one she was interested in was a three-story former warehouse. It was square and took up one-half of a long rectangular block, next to a deserted-looking apartment building. Its dark brick, cracked and crusted with decades-old dust, gave it a menacing look. Between the two buildings was a parking lot containing several very new cars and trucks.

Karen floated mid-height to the building and focused all Tiara's multi-spectral senses on the edifice, including gravity radar set to penetrate matter. She began to slowly circle the building.

Immediately a three-dimensional map of the insides bloomed in her imagination. As Tiara continued to pick out and trace details, the steel structural skeleton came into focus. So did all the plumbing and wiring and furniture.

Last to appear were the images of the people, who first had been visible only as amorphous blobs. These were translucent, organs and skeletons and everything else. Their clothing and items in their pockets and on belts firmed up. This included weapons, mostly guns, for many of the several dozen people there.

Disturbingly, almost two dozen of them were women and children. She hadn't planned on that. But at least most of them were in the apartment building. It looked derelict from the outside but inside had been much renovated into a modestly comfortable living space.

She had tracked the Alphas to their central lair. Now she could explore their business and them, including the higher-ups who likely lived in more luxurious living quarters.

<>

It took two weeks of snooping to find and decide on a contact person within the NYPD. She considered but discarded someone in the Drug Enforcement Bureau and the Federal Investigation Bureau. They were involved in narcotics trafficking, but the NYPD was fiercely protective of its territory and large and influential enough to do so successfully.

Also, this particular gang had a particular enemy within the NYPD, a detective named Daniel Norton. He had lost a confidential informant to the Alphas in an especially gruesome way. So he'd worked hard to become the lead detective on the Alpha detail within the Narcotics division of the Organized Crime Control bureau. And he was an able man.

Karen created two tiny spybots and had them fly through the 5th Precinct building in south Manhattan, just south of Canal St. in the middle of Chinatown. Norton's desk was one of many in cubicles on the highest, fourth, floor of a nondescript grey building right next to a Chinese medical-supplies house. The desk was in a privileged position in the corner of the building, right next to the coffee and snack room. It was three desks down from the small conference room which was the permanent home of the Alpha detail records and action board.

She settled one spybot atop the computer screen on his desk, allowing her to view his face. She placed the other spybot in the Alpha conference room above the large flat-screen at the end of the room. Then she spent a few days watching him and the people who came into his office and the conference room.

Satisfied she knew the players and enough about them to work with them she called Norton two hours before lunch in the middle of the week.

"Detective Norton."

"I have some information on the Alphas."

"Indeed. Tell me."

"I'll only do it face to face."

"Happy to oblige, Ms--?"

"But only in a public restaurant. What about the Hau-Chr-Gwo-le right across from the entrance from your building."

"No, that won't work. Come into the Precinct Buil--"

"I know where their headquarters building is. And how many there are. And their names."

"Miss, I don't appreciate prank calls."

"The leader's name is Herbert Hernandez."

There was silence. Norton's face showed his uncertainty. He obviously knew the name. As Karen had been sure he did.

"Cordon off the building," she said. A nearly impossible task on the crowded streets. "Bring backup. Wear a wire. Or carry a recorder openly. I'll be waiting. I'm hungry. Bye."

Norton paused only for a second. Then he was up, calling all the other six members of his team to join him in the conference room. He stopped only long enough to quickly get a cup of coffee from the snack room.

When all were seated around the small oval conference table he told them of the call. "It's probably a prank call. But I don't want to take the chance."

"So. Backup?" said the second lead, Mary O'Connell, a wiry older woman with grey hair and a gentle face that masked a most ungentle temperament.

"Not with me. But I want you and Serena to go into the restaurant and find a spot where you can see everything. Go now. Be careful. This just might be the Alphas setting us up. If she knew me she may know all of us."

Serena was a beautiful Italian in her twenties. She bared her perfect teeth in what was less a smile than hunger for a fight. Every Alpha-detail member had a grudge of one sort or another against the Alphas.

Karen let the two women get across the narrow four-lane street, cars parked all along both sides, a couple of them blue-and-white NYPD patrol cars. Then she phoned the older woman's cell.

"Mary, look for a twenty-something redhead wearing all red. In the corner. My back will be facing the entrance."

"Shit! How did you get--?" But Karen had hung up.

The two women entered warily, their hands close to the opening of their jackets. Karen "saw" them via Tiara's sensors. They looked around the room, spotted Karen but pretended only to be gazing about. A Chinese greeter, a young woman in long blue silk traditional dress, approached them.

Mary pointed at a round table in the corner of the room, the last in a row along the picture windows to the outside. The two followed the greeter, trying to keep Karen in sight without betraying it, not easy to do. Karen was lingering over her meal, nearly done.

"Would the honorable lady need something else?" said the manager of the restaurant, a stout older woman in a beautiful green dress. She spoke in Cantonese, Karen already having addressed her several times in perfectly idiomatic but middle-formal speech.

"Please have your excellent tea refreshed, honorable proprietor. And have one of the wait staff bring a menu. I will be having a guest."

The woman brought the new tea pot herself, trailed by a waitress in gold carrying a menu and an extra teacup and saucer for the cup for a guest.

By now Mary had phoned Daniel Norton and told him what to expect at the restaurant, emphasizing that the informant knew her phone number and had been watching her and Serena cross the street. He came directly to the table, his gaze on her but wary of his surroundings. He was a sturdy Irishman with short blond hair and a slightly ruddy face, his natural color, not symptoms of drink or other excess. He stood a moment beside her looking down at her. She turned her head and looked back up.

"Well, you certainly don't look like an Alpha assassin."

"No, Mr. Norton. If I'd wanted you dead I would have waited for you at your home. And probably killed all your family before killing you. If I were Alpha."

He continued to stand, looking at her for long moments. He saw long straight auburn hair and a beautiful pale face resembling that of a fox, hair and face the result of flesh-sculpting nanocytes guided by Tiara. She wore a dark red business suit and matching low heels over a pink blouse. She wore no earrings or other jewelry.

He sat, took the menu from the waitress but looked at her not at it. He said to the young woman, "I'll order in a few minutes. Thank you."

When the waitress was out of earshot he said, "Who are you?"

"Call me Red. I'm a concerned citizen with extraordinary resources."

"You are after the Alphas? Why?"

"I have a hobby of eliminating the worst of humans, and then only when there is no human agency to deal with them."

"The world is full of human monsters who deserve your attentions. Why have you not dealt with them? Why now? Why the Alphas?"

"Be satisfied with your faith's 'God works in mysterious ways.' Now, order, please. We have much to cover."

She gave him an overview of what she knew, some of which the detail knew and much of which they did not. They did not know Hernandez was the leader of the gang, though they had connected him with the Alphas.

Her delivery was matter of fact and with much the business-like style she'd used in Afghanistan to give briefings. As she spoke Karen saw him become more convinced of her truthfulness. Finally she removed a small computer data chip from an inner jacket pocket and handed it to him.

"A much fuller report is on this. I'll be watching and I expect results in three months. After that I'll take matters into my own hands. Unless they plan another of their 'lessons' to their competitors. Then I'll intervene."

"We do not approve of vigilantes. We'll catch you if you do anything illegal and prosecute you to the fullest extent of the law."

"The gang members will simply die of a heart attack in the middle of the night. Your medical examiners will confirm that cause of death."

"You're delusional. This--" He hefted the chip in his hand. "--is garbage. Or empty."

The Lady in Red smiled. "Perhaps the DEB will disagree. Or the FIB."

Norton's mouth tightened. "I should arrest you. You've already told me enough inside information about the Alphas to prove you're one of them."

"A proof that will convince the District Attorney's office? I'd be out of jail within an hour. And you'd have lost a valuable intel source."

She wiped her mouth on her napkin, placed enough money to pay for her meal on the table along with a hefty tip, and stood up.

"You can contact me if you want at red@redlady.com. Be well, Detective Norton."

She walked to the hallway from which the restrooms were entered. Out of sight of everyone she vanished.

<>

The "anonymous tips" supplied by the Red Lady led the Alpha detail to develop enough solid evidence to get arrest warrants. A SWAT team operating in the deadest hour of night arrested the Alpha gang in their warehouse and residence in Huntersville.

Strangely, everyone in the buildings was so soundly asleep that not a single person, including almost two dozen women and children, woke. They had to be transported in ambulances and prison transport vans to a hospital. Miraculously they all woke with no symptoms to explain their near-comatose state.

Part 8 - Vigilante

Karen loved New York. But she loved Los Angeles more. It was home.

She kept her apartment in Manhattan. As she did in the several other cities she visited often enough to want to stay overnight or a few days. They were all small, quietly luxurious, not terribly expensive, and within easy walking distance of interesting shops and clubs.

She wanted the same in L. A., but a little larger and more luxurious, something with two extra bedrooms so she could put up her brother and his wife and daughter for a weekend.

"Where were you thinking for your home?" said her mother. Thanksgiving was just past and she and Karen were cleaning up after the several days past. Karen was amusing the two of them by using Suit to loft dishes and such into the air and float them to her mother. She was also vaporizing waste and vacuuming the floor and the furnishings which needed it. Her mother was standing by the pantry and retrieving and putting away the flying dishes and etc. Her father was sitting in a far corner of the kitchen and adjoining dining room area, one already cleaned, watching, feet up on another chair and drinking coffee.

"Beverly Hills. Close to the shopping. I can treat Jessica and Sylvia when they come visiting."

"Better go to the Beverly Center if you want to splurge, dear. Prices are so much higher in the Hills. Jessica and Alex are pretty well off, but they can't match you when it comes to spending."

This was true. Her income was into the millions per year and accelerating. She had two whole money management firms investing and watching the investments. They also watched each other, and at least once a year she had to listen to their complaints about the incompetence of the other. Which was as she wanted it.

"And the Center is only a couple of miles from Rodeo Drive," her father said.

"Good point. I'll just do a One Big Buy shopping spree at Rodeo Drive with them."

"My little girl is learning diplomacy," her father said fake-proudly. Behind her back she gave him the finger and he chuckled.

Her mother ignored the byplay. She knew what was going on, but as long as Karen didn't make the gesture where she could see it she could avoid reprimanding Karen.

The One Big Buy shopping technique was one her parents had used on her when she was a kid, because she always wanted to buy a dozen things when they were out shopping. It used to annoy her but she now knew the wisdom of learning to prioritize purchases.

"Do you want to do it tomorrow?" her mother said. "I have one stop in Beverly Hills in the morning but I can take the rest of the day off."

"Suppose I drop by here at--9:00?"

"That should work."

Her mother's celebrity client was especially picky about a couple of matters but polite about it. That might have had something to do with Karen, lounging in a chair at a far end of the man's business office and reading from her slate.

He was a famous movie director and married but still appreciated beautiful women. But more importantly he directed action-adventure movies and knew she was a decorated Marine combat soldier. She had seen real action, and he didn't want to seem like a prick in front of her.

At the end of the session he apologized to the two of them for being difficult as he was seeing them to the door.

Her mother laughed. She was dressed in only modestly fashionable but expensive clothing, was fresh, toned, and discreetly but attractively made up.

"That wasn't difficult. That was CAREFUL. I wish everyone was as attentive to their accounts as you are."

"Thank you. You're very gracious. And you, Karen, it was an honor to meet you."

"Thank you, sir. I feel the same."

In her mother's car Karen said, "Nice schmoozing there, Accountant to the Stars. Is he always like this?"

"A bit worse. But I was sincere when I said what I did at the last. A lot of time they are less concerned about the money and more about their personal lives."

"So you're a bit of a shrink, too."

"More often than I want to be, but it's part of the job. Now, let's look for an apartment for you."

Karen already had her info slate in her hands and had copied the dozen more interesting apartments from Tiara to it. This way she could give the slate to her mother and give her a preview of the places in which she was interested.

They looked at three buildings, walked through some demo apartments and once looked at an actual available apartment. They also walked through the properties, investigating the various amenities such as pools and fitness centers and clubhouses.

It was well past noon, so they broke for lunch. Her mother drove them to a favorite of hers called Bar Bouchon near one edge of the Rodeo Drive shopping area. The bistro was beginning to empty out, so they were able to get a table without reservations, which were necessary during the peak times. They even had a nice window view.

"Madeleine! How good to see you again! How is school?"

Her mother spoke French to the young woman who approached them with water glasses. She wore black pants under a white shirt and apron. Atop the shirt was a black vest and a black bow tie.

"Very well, my dear. And this must be your daughter about which you've told me so much."

Karen replied in Parisian French. "Yes. A pleasure to meet you. And if I'm not mistaken you are from the Fourteenth District."

"Oh, dear, it still shows!"

"Only to me. I have a fondness for accents and have studied them. But let's see those menus and get ordering out of the way so you and my mother can chat a bit. If that wouldn't get you in trouble."

"Not now, with so many leaving. Mid-day we have many who are in a hurry to get in and get out."

Her mother ordered the quiche of the day which came with a mixed greens salad and a red wine vinaigrette. Karen ordered salmon with a farmer's market vegetable salad flavored with red quinoa. They both had wine. Taking Madeleine's advice it was a chardonnay white wine for her mother and a Pinot Noir, a light red wine, for Karen.

"Normally," said the waitress to Karen, "I'd recommend a white with fish. But this salmon has a Dill sauce and I think you'll find the red brings out the herbal flavor."

With the orders in and wine drinks at hand the young blond felt free to sit and loosen her tie and vest. It turned out she was a film student at UCLA just a few miles north of Beverly Hills and in her last year of a Master's degree. She had to create a short film along with a dozen other students rather than write a thesis.

Several minutes later she buttoned up her vest and tie and walked quickly away. She returned in minutes with the dishes and a servitor who refilled the wine glasses and departed, while the young woman sat down again and chatted, getting up twice to take care of requests from the two women.

When her customers were near done she went for the check machine. Karen took it from her, quickly scanned the items on it, and ran her Osmium card through its card reader, adding a generous 30% tip.

"You're looking for an apartment? Which ones are you considering?"

Karen handed over her info slate and pointed out those they'd seen and the five more slated for the afternoon. Madeleine then gave them a rundown on all of them, information garnered from her several years being a waiter at Bar Bouchon. Karen made notes on each. She didn't necessarily believe the young woman, but she seemed intelligent and well-meaning, so Karen would take her advice under consideration.

At the third of the five apartments they'd seen in the afternoon Karen knew she'd found the one for her. All the info supplied by Tiara and Madeleine matched with her needs. But beyond that it simply felt right.

"This is it, Mother."

"Are you sure? We have two more to go today and another ten tomorrow."

"Yes. You know I have a computer in my head. All the information matches, including the stuff the owners wouldn't want us to know about. Madeleine gave it thumbs up. But most of all it just feels right."

Her mother looked up at the façades of the two buildings on the two sides of the long green park where they stood. The buildings were four stories tall, painted a pleasant yellow, and connected by hallways at one end to form a U. Palms and smaller trees ran through the center of the park, and the outsides of the complex also had trees and greenery. There was a swimming pool and hot pool atop each wing.

The rooms Karen was considering, Karen now pointed out, had a wide balcony with an awning and looked down on the park. It was easy enough for her to step invisible onto her balcony and fall into the sky with no witnesses.

"Very well," her mother said, "Let's sign for the apartment while it's still available."

<>

Sylvia was ecstatic that her aunt was finally in California to stay, but it was two more weeks before Karen and her mother finished buying and arranging furniture for the apartment.

Then on a weekend Alexander and his family came up on a Saturday morning and stayed overnight. They ate lunch in Beverly Hills, shopped at the Beverly Center, and had dinner in Santa Monica at the far end of the pier at a large Mexican restaurant. Then they spent a couple of hours in the pier's park, where Karen alone of all the adults was willing to ride the neon-lit Ferris wheel--twice.

It was a tired little girl who was finally put to bed in "her" bedroom at 10:00 that night. Then the adults sat on the balcony watching the night deepen over the Beverly Hills shopping area a half-mile to the north.

The conversation was wide-ranging. At one point Jessica said, "Have you decided on what you are going to do?"

Alex said, grinning, "Spend her ill-gotten gains, I suppose." He was a bit baffled by his sister's financial success but proud of it.

The others smiled at his semi-joke but directed their gaze at Karen.

She was silent for long moments but no one seemed in a rush to know the answer. She'd given the question a lot of thought and how to present it without going into her special advantages.

She spoke slowly. "Something to do with law enforcement, I know that much."

"You could join the police," Alex said. "But I suppose that would be a let down. In Afghanistan you were pretty much on your own. Just given an assignment and it was up to you how you did that."

Everyone there knew roughly what she'd done overseas.

"What about the FIB?" said Jessica.

"You have to have a college degree for that. College is three years at the minimum and it's too structured and slow for me. I can take in what amounts to four months of study in a week."

Alex did not doubt her. He had always known his little sister was very bright. "And then," he said, "you'd still have to take orders and follow regulations and all that."

"I'm thinking of starting a security firm, specializing in information gathering and protection."

Alex was a bit alarmed. "If by information gathering you mean on organized crime-- You might attract the attention of some very dangerous people."

"I'd love that." A shark might have grinned the way she did now. "I'M very dangerous people."

Alex and Jessica looked at each other, unsettled. Her parents were not. They knew the truth. Entire armies were less dangerous than their daughter.

"Oh, I don't underestimate the problems. But I've already come up with several ways to anticipate and guard against them. This includes threats against you three and Mom and Dad."

"How--?"

"I've been inventing other things than that advanced-compound process. Some of them are software based, such as very advanced cryptography, which is useful both to protect and hack into protected infobases. Some are physical, what I call nanomachines."

"Nanomachines," said Alex. "I know that's a real growth market. But I didn't know there were much commercial success with them so far. If you're not just blowing smoke or fooling yourself, you could patent that stuff and get rich."

He grinned. "I mean richer."

"No. This stuff is too dangerous. I'm going to keep it to myself as proprietary technology used to get the job done."

Jessica had been following this but without the alarm Alex had shown. She had a very considering look. Karen wondered suddenly if somehow Jessica had intuited some of Karen's true nature. The woman had been known to make very long intuitive leaps before and have them proven right.

Alex yawned then. "So basically you're going to be a glorified private eye." He stood up.

"Sorry about that," he continued. "But we got up a bit earlier than usual for a Saturday. I think I had better try out your brand new bed. Coming, love?"

Jessica nodded.

Karen's father spoke as the two left, quietly but not so quietly as to sound as if he were hiding anything. "What are some of those protections?"

She answered in the same conversational tone.

"For the last two years or so all of you have had a sort of guardian angel. It does nothing but look out for danger. It reports it to me and I can direct its actions from a distance. Such as have it call 999 or other things like use force fields to give you first aid. Meanwhile I could be flying there to help. You know no place on Earth is farther away than a half hour for me."

"If you're on the Moon?" her father said. "Or Mars?"

"Peg can jump to a quarter of the speed of light in a fraction of a second. Mars is fifteen minutes away at its farthest."

<>

Karen rented a floor of a small nearby office building, the top one plus the rooftop garden. She had the much neglected garden renovated and several umbrella-covered picnic tables installed. These plus the several potted trees made it easier for her to conveniently take Pegasus up unnoticed. It could also be used to interview clients and to take breaks.

The top floor had a communal center area for conferences and planning sessions when she finally managed to hire help. The four corner offices were for executives, though two of them for now were used as a work room and a kitchenette.

A large back room she had made into a computer room. Karen had ten barebones computer systems installed in two facing racks, put data storage systems into them which could hold enormous amounts of information, and connected them to a satellite link on the roof. She connected everything to a surge-protected power supply with a huge superbattery backup and started it up. Controlled by Tiara it came up flawlessly.

She was satisfied she had a setup which would work for several years of expansion and act as cover for her use of Tiara's supercomputer. She had a short video made which went on MyVids.com and issued a challenge. She would pay a million dollars to the first hacker who could penetrate her system and retrieve a message containing a large prime number.

That sort of challenge attracted a lot of competitors. After three months she declared the contest closed because no one had succeeded. She issued several prizes for best efforts ranging from a half-million dollars to $100,000.

She also made note of who all the hackers were in case she wanted to hire from that pool. Or put them in jail. Many were anonymous, or tried to be. Unsuccessfully. No one could hide from Tiara.

With her Advanced Security Group established as a player in the information-protection arena she sent out a message to several large companies. It said they had one or more holes in their computer systems which could be penetrated. But ASG could close the holes.

She got responses from several companies. First one then more hired her. She was in business.

By Easter Karen was well settled in Los Angeles. She still visited the far corners of the globe for fun but less so than when she'd first mustered out of the Corps.

When someone entered the door to the ASG offices she turned from the table in the middle of the main room. She was looking down at a number of papers and brochures scattered atop it and was drinking a cup of coffee.

The man was a forty-something Latino in a brown business suit with a white shirt and gold tie. He was strongly built but only reached to her chin. He held out a hand. They shook.

"Ms. Danburn, I'm Sergeant Mendes from the LAPD. Could I have a few minutes?"

"Absolutely. I need to freshen my coffee. Like to have a cup for yourself?"

"Don't mind if I do."

On the way to the kitchenette a short distance away she said, "I see you have a Corps tie tack. Were you in?"

He'd retired a Master Sergeant after twenty years in the military police, he told her as they got coffee and seasoned it, then walked to two easy chairs near the central table and cater corner from each other. With retirement pay and his LAPD salary life was comfortable.

"Sweet," said Karen. "I imagine you did your homework before coming here and you know about my service."

"That's why I'm here, that and your business. I know you are focusing on commercial espionage and security. But you did counter-terrorism assessment in the Corps. I thought you might like to revisit that field."

He took a business card from an inner jacket pocket and handed it to her. It read **SGT Sergio Mendes**. Underneath his name was **Counter Terrorism and Special Operations Bureau** and two phone numbers.

"Recently we've gotten hints that an act of terrorism is being planned somewhere in the metro area. But none of our hints have led anywhere. I wonder if you could surveil the public channels and come up with something."

Karen took another sip of coffee and said, "I'd imagine the Department has a pretty hefty digital services section."

"The Information Technology Bureau is pretty damned good. But it's always busy and has to prioritize and 'hints' are pretty far down the list. I thought maybe I could hire you to help out."

"Sure. But our fees are a bit hefty."

"I have a budget which could probably stretch. And authority to hire 'confidential informants.' You'd be one."

"Sure. I'll give you a 'promotional services' discount just for old time's sake. We both being Marines."

She grinned. "This might just be why you're wearing a Corps tie-tack today."

He laughed and lifted his cup in salute.

<>

Later that day she spent several hours studying the copies of the reports on the data chip he'd given her. The confidential informants were really confidential, at least on her copies. Each was listed as CI followed by a number.

Most reports were transcriptions of verbal reports. Some were text messages. There was also a page the contents of which was simply the words OUT FOR TRANSLATION and the notation that the speech was in Chinese or another Oriental language.

She phoned Mendes at this office, guessing he'd be working late. He was.

"I see some of your 'hints' were in Chinese. Do you have a file of them you could email me?"

"Yes. But what good would they do you? I can't afford to pay you to hire a translator."

"No need. I have a machine translator that will do the job of both text and verbal speech. The results are crude but usually good enough for government work."

He laughed. "Which I am. What's the email address you want me to send it to?"

It was ten minutes before the mail program on her info slate pinged. She snatched the message via Tiara as it came in. She used a slate at work to hide the fact that she had Tiara but only used it when someone was around to observe her.

She quickly saw why the translation service might not have delivered results yet. The voices were in several dialects of Chinese, mostly Mandarin but also of the Wu, Hakka, and Yue dialects. The dialects were not very intelligible by speakers of the other three dialects.

They were no problem for her, however. She decrypted the encrypted emails, which most of them were, and translated everything and transcribed it to text. It took her only about an hour. The hundred or so intercepts were fairly short, mostly about ordinary matters such as picking up grocery items.

But the content of several was obvious. The speakers had apparently thought the fact that they were encrypted and in Chinese enough to be safe. Likely meaning, she noted in her report, that they were amateurs rather than agents of the Chinese Empire.

Each of the intercepts had a position code. She plotted them on a map. Most of the messages had been sent from a part of the L. A. metroplex she thought of as Chinaworld, an expanse several miles east of Chinatown which was easily a hundred times Chinatown's size.

The locations were all near each other. She focused on them and discovered they had all been made in or near several Chinese restaurants. They were all on the miles-long east-west Valley Boulevard in the cities of Alhambra and Rosemead.

The Sergeant put the information before his superiors. They set up a task force with him as the head and investigated the leads Karen had given them. Within two weeks they had developed enough detail to set up several raids.

Secretly Karen monitored their activities and those of the terrorists to backstop the LAPD to make sure the task force did their job in time to neutralize the threats. Then she floated above the SWAT teams who were sent to arrest everyone to ensure they were safe. The teams were well-prepared and highly skilled professionals, however, and she did not have to swoop to the rescue.

<>

By the time Fall brought the usual cooler seasonal Los Angeles weather to the city Karen had expanded her company by hiring three computer professionals full-time, two men and one woman. All were experts in information security, honest, and individualists who could work without supervision.

She decided to branch out from information security to physical security. She would offer body guarding, building and site guarding, and bounty hunting. In each area she had to undergo training and certification. This took several months.

When she became eligible to work in those fields she added those capabilities to her web site and sent out notices through several channels. As expected she had no enquiries for a time. Then she had an enquiry for a short-term body guard and set up an appointment to see the interested party.

At 10:00 that day she was sitting on the couch in the square in the center of the front room which she had designed to be the communal waiting area and conference room. She was pretending to read an info slate while actually using Tiara to research something half a planet away.

Someone came in the front door. She stood up to greet him. She saw a tall man who looked like a stereotypical action hero. He was a famous movie actor who often played one.

Scott Cooper was dressed in worn jeans, scuffed tan work boots, and a short-sleeved blue-and-white checked shirt. His hair was black and a bit long and a recent shave had not completely cleared his jaw of beard shadow. He had the requisite strong jaw on a face both boyish and seemingly tough. Of course he had wide shoulders and big biceps.

He glanced at her and then around the office.

"Ms. Danburn? Could we speak privately?"

"You expected a corner office or a conference room? I like unconventional decor."

He glanced at a young woman in a far corner working in a low-walled cubicle on a large laptop atop a desk. She was blond, pretty, and dressed all in black.

"That's Jill. She's totally engaged in her work and would ignore a troll or an elf. Much less you."

He grinned. It had the charm to be expected but Karen judged it to be natural.

"I made the appointment as J. A. Edgar. My real name--"

"I know who you are, Mr. Cooper. Would you like coffee or some such?"

"Coffee would be nice."

She turned and they walked toward the kitchenette. This took them right by Jill's office but the woman ignored her and the actor. There were security cameras all around the building and inside it. Some were very well hidden. Some weren't and so would act as alerts if someone blinded them. Jill had already seen Cooper on her computer screen, reflexively researched him, then forgotten about him. And she'd assumed Karen had done the same and didn't need to brief her.

Karen and the actor idly discussed the early-morning 4.8 earthquake and its effect on traffic (negligible) and daily routine (also negligible) while they poured and seasoned their coffee. Then she retired to one of the easy chairs near the couch and waved him to the end of the couch nearest her.

"I need a body guard for a few days. Someone mentioned you and I became curious. So here I am."

"I presume you read my bio on our site. So you know my qualifications."

"Yes. And I must be honest, one of them is that you don't look like a body guard."

"An obvious body guard, which I can supply, has the advantage that they look like what they are. It's much better to scare off confrontations than deal with them."

"Well--" He studied his coffee cup. "I'll be honest, it wouldn't help my image to be seen with a protector. It's not a matter of ego--" Flash of teeth and charm. "Though I do have that--but commercial realism."

She nodded. "It would also help your image to be seen with a beautiful woman. How would I act? Fawning is not something I do very well."

"Could you act bored? But not really be? I'll be honest, there is only a remote possibility of a real threat. Recently I've picked up a stalker. There's a court order for her to stay a hundred feet away from me. But people violate court orders all the time."

"Bored is good. It gives me an excuse to be looking all about as if for SOMETHING to relieve the boredom. That way I can better inspect the crowd, gauge sight lines--"

He sat up from a slouch. "Sight lines? She's just a silly woman--"

"Who could hire someone to shoot you from a distance. If she's really nutty. Besides, I guard you from all possibilities, including the unexpected and remote."

He relaxed, took another sip of coffee, and set the cup on the corner table between the couch and her chair.

They discussed terms and times. At one point he said, "Don't you want to write any of this down?"

"I have perfect memory when I want it to be. I'll enter all this into a standard form and email it to you for your approval."

When they were done he said, "One other matter. I need you to dress appropriately for each event. I'll be happy to pay for designer and one-of-a-kind outfits--"

"I'm fairly wealthy and can easily afford all that. Including some very high-end jewelry. The only thing I require from you is contact info for your dresser or manager so I can coordinate with your outfit and the events."

He removed a card from his wallet and handed it to her.

"If you've money why do you work?"

"I'm good at it and enjoy it. Why do you work?"

A moment's thought, then he nodded agreement. He hesitated.

"If I'm out of line... Please excuse me...."

She waved a hand to indicate he should go on.

Still he hesitated. Karen waited patiently.

"You've killed people.... Did you enjoy that?"

It wasn't idle curiosity. Nor morbid. It was an important matter for some reason.

"No. What I enjoyed was doing something well, which usually meant protecting others. When I could carry out my duties using other means I avoided killing. But when it could not be avoided, I did it as quickly and efficiently and painlessly as possible. It never gave me nightmares, as it did some. I never enjoyed it, either, as did others. I just--did it."

She thought for a few moments.

"One action they never show in movies such as yours is that in the military we always have an after-action review. Part of that was asking if the task could have been done better, or in other ways, and the pluses and minuses of how we went about it. I always looked for a more peaceful solution. And sometimes I was able to use it the next time."

She watched him as he digested her answer. Finally he stirred.

"I ask because in most of the roles I play I have to kill people. It bothers me a bit. I wonder about the message the movies send. I wonder about people who do kill people. What makes them act the way they do? Are they pleased, sorry... Unaffected?"

She thought a bit.

"When we're in a fight we have no expression, unlike in the movies. We're totally engaged in the moment and not shouting or baring our teeth or doing anything else dramatic. But afterward... Here's a bit you might use.

"After one incident was over and we could allow ourselves emotion, one man who was with me looked down at the bodies on the ground. And he shook his head just a bit, and tightened his lips just a bit, and I just knew what he was thinking. 'What a FUCKING waste.'"

The part about the man who was with her was false. It had been her reaction, not that of a figment. Everything else was true.

She waited for him to absorb her words.

"Thank you."

<>

The night of his movie premiere Karen arrived at his home in a rented limousine with built-in security features and a driver who was also a security person expert in avoiding danger. The driver did not know that she was part of the security team, only that he was.

The driver, a tall black man in a chauffeur's outfit, walked up to the door of Cooper's ranch house on the southern San Fernando hillside a few miles outside the loop around Los Angeles. It was one of a half-dozen estates strung along the hillside, at the edge of the first sharp up-tilt of the land toward the south. Some of the estates had horses which could be ridden along a shared riding path that wound east and west for several miles.

Satisfied there were no lurking stalkers from his discreet surveillance of the surrounding area he rang the door bell. When Cooper opened it he said, "Your ride, sir."

"Thank you."

Cooper shut the door behind him and walked just behind the chauffeur to the car. The man held the door open to the back seat, receiving a smile from the movie star, then went around the car to get in and drive away.

"You look nice," Cooper said as he secured his seat belt.

Karen did indeed. Her hair curled to her bosom past one shoulder, gleaming golden. She seemed to be wearing nearly invisible makeup. Her body was sheathed in a tight sky blue dress with a discreet décolleté which only revealed the top swell of her bosom. From her neck a pendant held suspended a single large diamond. From her earlobes hung matching smaller diamonds.

Her face, as always, was almost shocking in its perfection.

"So do you, dear," Karen said, following the loose script she and he had perfected over several exchanges of emails.

"Tuxedos are so boring. But once I suggested livening it up a bit to my manager and she almost tore my head off. I sometimes wonder which of us is the boss." His smile was as charming as ever.

<>

The trip to the Burbank Media Center, the heir to Old Hollywood, took barely a half hour despite the busy Friday night traffic on the freeways. They chatted about inconsequential matters on the way.

Pegasus in his natural form, an invisible rounded brick, paced the limo fifty feet above it. Karen was linked to his sensors as well as those of Tiara and Suit and so was very early aware of the fuss around the part of the Media Center rented for the occasion. Even using just her own senses, however, it was easy to spot. Roving searchlight beams visible from several miles away lit the night skies.

Closer traffic was being directed by police. The limousine displayed a blazon on one turned-down sunshade which got them diverted into the street leading up to the drive to the rented theatre.

The driver followed two more limos up to the drop-off point. While waiting in line he turned in his seat and reached his arm toward Cooper. In his hand was a card.

"When you get ready to leave, sir, call this number. We'll have someone standing by who can be here in fifteen minutes.

"Now, when we stop before the welcoming personnel wait till I come around and open your door. Please wait for it. I'll be scanning for threats, so I won't open the door if I see one."

"I understand. Thank you for an uneventful drive."

"My pleasure, sir, madam."

Photoflash units, already active when the car door was opened, intensified their activity when the star exited the door. He smiled and waved to the photographers but quickly turned and helped Karen from the limo. The activity intensified even more as she put a blue high-heeled shoe and long shapely leg out the door and rose into view, Cooper's strong arm giving her a bit of aid.

Black-clad event security kept everyone away from them as they walked on the red carpet to and through the two wide-open glass doors to the theatre. Inside they were greeted by event helpers and escorted to another red carpet, this one running left and right along the back wall. There they were met by the first of a gauntlet of media personnel, a very tall black woman in a long gold dress holding a microphone with a TV news logo on its front.

"Scott, you're looking dashing tonight! And who is your radiant friend here?"

"Melissa," he said. "You're looking radiant yourself. This is Karen Danburn."

"Karen... May I call you that?"

Karen flashed a smile at the woman. "If I can call you Melissa!"

"Are you looking forward to the show tonight?"

"Why, of course, I am. I know Scotty has been working so hard on this latest film. He's hardly had time for me." She gave an exaggerated pout.

The woman laughed. "Who are you wearing tonight?"

"He's one of my favorite designers. He's a local genius who refused to leave L. A. for New York or elsewhere. He's Yoshida Tanaka."

"I'm sure you'll enjoy the show tonight." The woman was turning away from them even as she spoke to the next star approaching her.

Cooper followed Karen to the next reporter in the gauntlet. They spoke to over a dozen such before they were ushered into the theatre proper and thence into seats in the front row. Along the way he waved and sometimes spoke to others in the theatre. Twice he stopped and reached down to a seat abutting the aisle to shake a hand.

Karen did not have to pay attention to anyone and so was free to scan the arena which presented itself to her sight as they walked. At the front row, however, she had to shake hands or receive air kisses from the several people with whom they'd share the row. This included the director and two producers of the film and several others.

Once seated, however, she put on a bored face and resisted Cooper's efforts to include her in the conversations. She spent the time scanning the surroundings, both with her own senses and those of Tiara.

When the lights dimmed she leaned over to whisper in the actor's ear. As arranged, she pleaded a need to use the bathroom. He mimed concern and waved her away. As she left she heard him pass along her excuse to others.

She spent a few minutes in the restroom till loudspeakers announced that the doors into the theatre were about to be closed. Then she hurried to slip back inside and find a back seat where she could monitor internal happenings and watch the movie. She liked it, once she was able to come to terms with the inaccuracies of finding and fighting a group of terrorists.

As the lights came up she waited for Cooper to exit the theatre, which he did after a half hour in company of his former co-workers.

"Did you get to see the movie?"

"I did. I'm sorry I couldn't get to you. The ushers would only allow me to sit in a back seat." This was not true, but the story they'd agreed upon beforehand.

Just then several people he knew came up to congratulate him and Karen slipped away. She pretend to amble around in mild boredom, but actually she was tracking Genevieve Astor, Cooper's stalker, as she made her way further into the theater complex.

Finally when Astor was at the right place in her approach Karen moved up to Cooper's side and whispered in his ear. He grinned and made his excuses. The two walked away together, her snugged up against him. This was both for appearance and to guide him out the proper exit.

"Where are we going?"

"To the most likely place to meet Genevieve."

He halted. "The idea was to avoid her."

"That was your idea. My idea is to meet her and dissuade her from future attempts to get near you."

"It's impossible. Others have tried."

"They don't have my resources. Now, are you coming? Or would you rather wait for me to come get you?"

He hesitated, then continued walking along the path they'd been taking. "I'm just coming to make sure you don't do something illegal. I don't want the poor woman hurt."

She said nothing.

The halls they were walking were increasingly bare of people. Most of them were service people hurrying to clean up after the event and put the theatre complex back into order. They turned left, then right. Then at a door she stopped.

"Now, if I've judged this right..." she said to him. He started to speak but she put her fingers to her lips.

A minute passed. Two. Cooper waited without apparent impatience. Then the door opened and a woman slipped through into the hall.

"Hello, Genevieve."

The woman started. Her eyes grew wide.

She was an attractive blond woman in her mid-thirties, dressed like a chef or servitor in white. Apparently a disguise.

"Who are you?" She spoke to Karen but only had eyes for Cooper.

Her eyes were opened wide and she seemed totally focused on him.

Karen shifted into her sight line. The woman moved to step to the side but Karen put a hand on an arm. Genevieve struggled but only for a moment. Suit had injected a flood of nanocytes into her which calmed her and put her into a mildly suggestible state.

"I'm a psychic, dear. I came here to tell you that there is a man for you. But it's not him."

"Yes, he is! I love him!"

"He can't love you back. He doesn't like women."

For a wonder the actor neither said nor did anything.

"But surely--" The woman's eyes focused on Karen for the first time. She took in Karen's beautiful face, tight dress, and womanly curves.

"I'm just an escort hired to keep him company for a few days, maybe spread out over a few weeks, to cover for him. When he told me about you I said I could help. He doesn't believe in psychics though. He only came along to make sure I did nothing illegal."

"But--"

"How else could I know exactly where you would be and be waiting for you? Now hush and listen and let me tell you about the man you will meet.

"He won't be handsome, until you get to know him. He'll be kind, share some of your likes, and fall in love with you. You will learn that he can be trusted, and that he will want to take care of you. And let you take care of him. You DO want to do that for the right kind of man. Don't you?"

Genevieve nodded, her eyes wide.

"You will meet a few men who appear right at first. But then you'll find there are better men out there. So don't fall for the first man who seems right.

"Now, come with us. We're going to take you home."

She put an arm around the stalker and led her back the way she'd come. In a moment Cooper followed.

Karen had put in a call to the security limousine service when she'd judged the time right. Even so the three had to wait nearly five minutes till the limo pulled up. While they waited at the curb Karen engaged Genevieve in conversation, listening to the woman talk about herself. Aside from being mildly insane (something which other nanocytes injected into her would fix) she was an intelligent woman.

The night had become cool. Cooper took off his coat and draped it around Genevieve's shoulders. The woman paid him little attention besides saying Thank you. She was now almost wholly focused on Karen.

It was another half hour before the limousine pulled up outside Genevieve's apartment. Karen told the driver to wait and all three walked up to the front door.

At it Genevieve gave Cooper back his coat. She looked at him fully for the first time that night.

"You poor man. I hope you have a happy life, Scotty."

She turned and went inside.

The actor looked after her for a moment, holding the jacket over one arm. Then he looked at Karen and offered it to her. She shook her head.

He put the coat on and they returned to the limo.

"Scotty? That's twice tonight a woman has tried to give me that nickname. All the years I've avoided it, and the curse strikes again."

Karen laughed again.

"The funny thing is, if I had met her in normal circumstances, I might really have gotten together with her. If she weren't nuts."

"It will take a while, but she'll be better soon."

"What did you do to her?" He glanced toward the driver.

"Something I've used before. It's a trade secret. Don't ask."

He brooded a while, then spoke again.

"Be honest. What did you think of the movie?"

"I enjoyed it. After I got over how screwed up the anti-terrorist actions were. I was impressed, though, how you were able to make the secret agent believably human. Not some killing machine with no more emotions than a lawn mower."

At his home he got out but leaned down to speak to her. "Come in for a little while?"

"Some other time. Are we still on for the rest of the weekend? I think Genie will be fine. But I think I should be around just in case."

"Let's do it." He raised his voice enough to project his voice to the driver. "Thanks for a good job. Have a good night." Then he was gone toward his door.

As the driver pulled away he said over his shoulder, "One of the nicer ones."

She leaned forward to speak. "Do you get a lot of them?"

"Surprisingly, yes. Some ass-holes, of course. But mostly just people in a hurry or worried about the meeting coming up."

<>

Saturday there were two events which Karen attended as Cooper's bodyguard.

One was a private beach party at an estate which had access to a semiprivate beach near Topanga Canyon just north of Santa Monica. The beach area and the residences above the beach had security, but it had plenty of holes for anyone determined to breach it and the talent to do it.

Karen wore a modest green bikini and much of the time a light robe. She and Cooper swam and played games such as beach volleyball (where they were on opposite teams). They also lounged and chatted till the sun neared the horizon.

Then they had a barbecue with steaks and hot dogs and other meats and veggie burgers and veggie dogs. They did this along with other film people from the movie just completed which, with families with kids and other guests, numbered almost a thousand people. It was catered half by the studio and half by Cooper, part of his thanks for their efforts.

Later they showered and dressed at a friend's nearby house and went to several clubs to dance and schmooze with people.

Cooper said at one point, "This is actually business, not play. I used to love this, but nowadays I'd rather skip it. But you've got to keep in the public's eyes and chat up some of the people in the industry."

With that he turned away to smile and wave at someone in the distance, then turned further away to shake hands with someone else.

They returned to his home at 2:00 in the morning. He seemed exhausted when he hugged her in the limo, then turned to exit the vehicle and walk to his front door accompanied by the driver.

<>

Sunday mid-morning she arrived at his house in a secured limo yet again. They had brunch and chatted. The official news story if anyone asked was that they'd spent the night together.

The view north out over the San Fernando Valley from a rooftop garden was spectacular. Morning fog was wisping away to slowly reveal the metro area. The sky was the usual bright sunshiny Los Angeles day, cleared to deepest blue by a pre-dawn cold front two days ago.

"Here Easter is just past and it's still just comfortably warm by mid-afternoon. And it stays pretty much the same all year round. Have you ever been in a deep snowy winter?"

"Twice. In Afghanistan."

He shifted in his seat.

"About that. In this meeting at 2:00. I actually wanted you there because of your military background. I'd like to pick your brain. But you can just stay out of the meeting, being the bored girlfriend while you prowl the country club. I doubt if there's much of a security problem the club doesn't already handle, though."

"No. I'll sit in. I'm perfectly able to shut down any annoying questioning."

"Thanks. Meeting you is giving me all sorts of ideas for my next film. Or the one after. Scheduling isn't worked out yet, but I think it will be the romantic comedy which I do next.

"Now. What's your family like?"

From there the talk moved to his family, and thence to exchanging stories about their early lives.

At noon they changed their sloppy early morning clothing to light summer clothing. He wore a short-sleeved gold cashmere sweater over khakis with brown loafers. She wore an A-line skirt of green patterned with orange leaves and a blue halter top which showed off her smoothly muscled arms and back. Low-heeled tan sandals completed her attire.

The Garden Hills Country Club was only a few miles away. Like Cooper's home it was on the south side of the Valley just before the hills lifted upward. Below it was an upscale suburban landscape

There was much meeting-and-greeting at the large lobby of the club. Karen hung back a bit and looked people over. From there Cooper and his entourage moved into a conference room through a bar where some of them picked up drinks and snacks. One side of the room was all glass doors slid open to let in the spring air and allow people to wander into the pool area and garden beyond.

Cooper sat in the middle of a long oval-shaped conference table, Karen by his side. After some chatting around the table he called the meeting to order.

"First, I'd like everyone to meet my friend Karen. She has some experiences which can give us some story ideas. Karen, I won't throw a bunch of names at you. Instead I want you to know that everyone here is sort of a brain trust for me and my business partner, Judith Epstein." He nodded across the table to a fiftyish grey-haired woman with a vigorous manner and emphatic way of speaking.

"Their experience includes writing, directing, and producing movies." At each profession name one or more people lifted a hand in brief greeting. "We also have a set designer, costumer, location manager, and a computer tech person. And some people I don't know what the Hell they do."

There was low laughter there from all present. Karen smiled as she eyed the people around the table. As each person lifted their hand Tiara did an InterWeb search and collated information about them. After all the years with Tiara the info was no longer like a wall of data. It was instead more like other information which she'd learned, readily accessible if she turned her attention to it but otherwise unnoticed.

After almost an hour of talk about the upcoming romance film there was a short break to refresh drinks and snacks and stop by the bathrooms.

Cooper said as he and everyone else sat down at the table, "Talking to Karen has been giving me ideas for my next action film."

He turned his head toward her. "Would it be too much to ask if you were to talk about your time in the Corps?"

She shook her head and spoke to the others at the table.

"I was a Marine Corps scout/sniper. I served a tour in Afghanistan, most of the time in various intel sections."

"Did you see some action?" asked a curly-headed younger man who she remembered was a computer expert.

"Yes. If you mean did I kill people, Yes."

She paused to let her words sink in, then went on.

"In almost any other context I'd say 'None of your fucking

business'. But this is a subject Scott thought important to explore. And you may too in your next action movie. Or the next.

"I talked with Scott about how I and other Marines feel about killing. I'm not going to repeat that. But it's an important subject for anyone who does what you do. Do you portray your hero as a killing machine with no more emotion than a robot? Or with a lot of depression about it? Or something else?"

She paused to see if they wanted to hear her speak more.

"A scout/sniper is mostly known for the sniper work they do. But it's the scout part that in the long run is more important. We bring back info about the enemy and the terrain and other matters. We are asked to work as a sniper only in certain situations.

"But you make films, so visual stuff is more important to you. So I'll talk about the sniper part of my job.

"In my experience 'making harmless' people and equipment is less important than the effect of a sniper on morale.

"Visualize this. You are a soldier whose company has taken over a village or whatever. You are patrolling streets. One of your comrades falls over dead. And you've heard no shot. Because from a mile or more away a sniper has fired his or her weapon.

"If it's at night--and I did most of my work at night--it's even scarier.

"But day or night the impression of invisible death is the same. So we're called ghosts, or shadows, or nightmares. And they can do almost nothing about us.

"Morale is more important in the long run than military superiority. An army which thinks it will fail, usually will fail. And an army which thinks it's invincible often will win."

"But," said the curly-headed man. "If you have an atom bomb and your enemy is a savage, you're going to win."

Karen smiled. "True. Morale isn't a guarantee. But it's a Hell of a potent force."

She said little more after that. People mulled over what she'd said. Some then ignored it for the rest of the two hours of discussion. Others kept coming back to parts of it.

Karen was not bored. She followed the discussion with fascination at how it meandered and looped back and meandered again in a totally new direction. And how Scott Cooper took part. He said little. He never exerted his authority in an obvious way. But she soon saw that he was the guiding force behind this collection of bright, driven people, none of whom were shy about pushing their views.

She'd never thought actors and actresses were especially dumb. But she'd never given then credit for being smart either. Scott was very smart.

Slowly there took shape plans for two different action heroes, one a loner, one a team player. The loner would be the hero of a movie. The other would be the core of a TV crime series. Scott would star in the movie. He would be one of the producers of the TV show.

Finally Judith Epstein and Scott seemed to communicate telepathically about something. She spoke.

"Very well. That's it for me. The rest of you can keep on gnawing the bones but I've got a bat mitzvah party to go to."

She finished putting her papers and info slate into a briefcase, stood, sort-of saluted Scott, nodded to Karen, and quickly walked out.

The meeting quickly raveled away. As Scott was saying last Goodbyes to a few people an older man who'd been ID'd as a location manager approached her. He was sturdy, weathered, with bright eyes. Karen knew he had been a career vet in the Marines.

"What was your count, Ms. Danburn?"

She knew what he meant. She eyed him, decided.

"Twenty-one Confirmed, Sergeant."

He didn't seem surprised that she'd guessed the rank at which he'd retired.

"Impressive. Especially for someone supposedly doing mostly intel."

She shrugged.

"See you around, Danburn." He nodded and walked away.

"What was that about?" said Scott as he approached her.

"Just a bit of shop talk. He's a former Marine."

"I'd forgotten that. What was it about?"

"Nothing important. You hungry?"

"For more than one thing."

"Me too."

<>

They had a long dinner at the country club, near picture windows which showed the view down the long gradual slope, to where the San Fernando Valley descended into night and lights came on all along it. Then they retired to his home where they made love twice, first frantically, then later much more slowly.

She spent the night. In the days and weeks to come she spent more of them there.

<>

She was a body guard several times more, mostly for celebrities. Those who knew she dated Cooper were more likely to be first curious then satisfied by her service. Especially when she dealt with a few threats efficiently and quietly. She hired one, then two personal security men to work on a contingency basis.

One of them seemed to have good managerial skills. She hired him full time and let him manage the other guards. He built up a roster of guards who could be hired for shorter and longer terms of service.

This lead naturally to site and building security. Especially since her computer expertise, proven by her information security success, was also useful in designing and installing the security systems in new buildings. She partnered with several construction firms to do the actual installation.

Her information security business grew even more. She added another man, making four employees, then two more.

Thanksgiving came. She and her parents made their second trek to San Diego for that weekend. Scott Cooper came along. He had an easy way about him which made him welcome and quickly eroded any awe others had of being with a movie star.

Christmas was a two part affair. Her brother and his family came up two days before Christmas Eve and stayed two days more. Scott was there for the Christmas morning present opening. Then at noonday Karen and he left on a leased private plane, one of the new hypersonic jets made possible by Prince Enterprises superbatteries and paramagnetic jet engines and paramagnetic ground-effect "wheels." It brought them to Montreal where his family lived, arriving just before the early sunset of midwinter.

Karen was welcomed by his family, which included a younger brother and an older sister. The only thing which took away from the visit was the sister's unsubtle hints that the family would appreciate her marrying her brother and producing nephews and nieces for her to spoil. Karen was unsure if this was meant to encourage or discourage a marriage.

She and Scott spent the day before and after New Year's Eve in New York. Their kiss at midnight at a party was caught on several smartphone cameras and within hours had propagated all over the world.

<>

On the first Wednesday of the New Year Karen and most of her staff were at work. At 10:00 she was sitting on the main-room couch in the socialization square, facing the double doors into the suite, waiting for a client.

The doors opened and two people came in. One was a severely attractive mid-40s tall blond woman in a grey business suit with an A-line dress, modest matching heels, and open-throated lilac blouse with a lacy collar. Her companion was an early-30s man in a more formal dark-blue suit complete with white shirt and blue-and-red striped tie. His hair was dark and conservatively cut and he had Spanish good looks.

Karen rose and greeted the two. "Ms. Johnson, Mr. Benedict, I believe."

They nodded. The woman then the man extended their hands. They shook and Suit confirmed their official identities and Tiara used the DNA information to search the web and discover their true identities. While escorting them to the conference room Karen skimmed their dossiers but didn't go deeply into them. It was easier to pretend ignorance if she was truly ignorant.

The door was shut and everyone seated at the conference table when "Ms. Johnson" said, "Is this room secure?"

"As secure as any site on the planet."

The woman not-quite hid a frown and passed her a business card. "Benedict" did the same. They had at the top **Temple Business Analysis and Support Corporation**, their cover names, a bland title, and a phone number.

"We're actually employees of the Central Intelligence Bureau. We'd like to hire you to do a job for us. But first we'd need you to sign a confidentiality agreement."

"Certainly."

Benedict took a sheaf of papers from his narrow leather briefcase with a fingerprint lock and placed it on the table in front of Karen. She leafed quickly through it then signed it using the pen he'd offered her.

"You DID take note of the criminal penalties for breaking any part of that agreement, didn't you, Ms. Danburn?"

Karen nodded.

"You read the document rather quickly."

"I can quote it back to you word for word, if you want."

Benedict looked at his partner.

"It's possible. Remember her high school tests? Her scores were off the scale. When she graduated with honors she'd finished three difficult college-level courses. And most revealing of all, at 17 she invented a materials process which is revolutionizing modern manufacturing and made her a multimillionaire."

The woman examined Karen as if she were a bomb which might go off any second.

"Maybe this cure is worse than the disease."

Benedict shrugged.

Johnson took a deep breath and let her breath out.

"We've recently discovered not one but three viruses which have been loose in this country, and presumably elsewhere, for at least a year. We don't know where they came from and we're unsure how to defend against them. We'd like to consult with you."

"I'll need two weeks at your closest cyberwar facility. I'll get the answers to both of your questions in that time. It will cost you five million dollars, one million up front."

Johnson stood up, looked down at her partner. "She's delusional. Or scamming us. We're wasting our time."

"No, we're not."

She considered a moment, then sat down.

"We don't have that kind of money."

"Yes, you do," said Karen, smiling. "I'll even consult your clandestine budget and find it for you."

"Oh, fuck. I believe she actually could."

"I wouldn't be surprised. But you read the threat assessment. She's the lesser of two evils. And anyway she's proven she's a patriot a dozen times over by laying her life on the line to protect this country."

Karen was leaning back, watching the two of them. They were silent a moment, looking at each other, seeming to commune silently. Or possibly going over much the same thinking.

They turned to her.

"Very well. I'll convey your demands and get back to you."

"It will take you three days, with possibly some wrangling over the weekend, to get a decision. I'll be at your Burbank cyberwar facility Monday morning at 8:00 ready to work."

Johnson stared at Karen.

"Oh, come now, Ms. Johnson. Anyone who could do this job would also know the geography of the threat area."

Benedict looked at his colleague. "Chances are she already pretty much knows the answer to the questions we're concerned about. That's why she knows how much to charge and how long it will take to pin down the details."

That was perceptive, though he was wrong. Karen COULD have known if she cared to. In fact, she vaguely knew of dozens of such as-yet-undiscovered viruses. But until they became a threat SHE considered important, she went about her daily life as usual and let Tiara keep track of them.

<>

As she'd promised, Karen drove to Burbank Monday morning to the two-miles-wide and several-miles-long industrial center on the south side of the city which extended into Glendale to the southeast. The cyberwar facility took up a city block and had a high fence around it, one of several such facilities for various companies. Dozens of smaller companies inhabited other buildings in the industrial center.

She parked in the large open-air parking lot next to the chain-link fence and presented herself to the guard shack. A Visitor's badge awaited her. She signed for it and took the sidewalk the guard pointed out to her to the main entrance of the somewhat shabby-looking three-story building.

Inside she was met by a young man in a khaki-colored suit minus a tie. He welcomed her with a handshake and had her leave her briefcase, purse, and aluminum equipment case with a second security guard. It would be inspected and conveyed to her later.

Again, nothing she had not expected. The cyberwar facility had several physical layers of protection, starting with a tie-in to all the video cameras positioned throughout the industrial complex.

They took an elevator up to the third floor and along a long beige-carpeted hall to an open area. She was met by agent Benedict, who waved her escort away, and took her into a corner executive office to meet the division head, John McLemore. He issued a welcome and a few platitudes and politely dismissed them.

"Oodles of excitement so far," she said. Benedict grinned. Without Johnson around he was less restrained, less business-like. In fact, he seemed to be mildly excited about her visit. But then he seemed to be bit of a fan of someone who, it turned out when he introduced her around to several people in the several nearby offices, was something of a celebrity in the cyberwar community.

At about 9:00 Karen's belongings arrived on the third floor, vetted as containing nothing dangerous. Benedict gave them to her and led her to the office which would be hers for the next two weeks.

"As you requested, there's a data port which will give you access to the web and to parts of our site which are relevant to your task. And, as you see, the other assets you requested."

This included a desk and a chair which could recline completely. It had a lower-leg support which would tilt up when she tilted the back down.

"Looks good. Let me get set up."

Karen set her belongings on the desk and herself into the chair. She moved the purse and briefcase to one side of the desk out of the way. Before her was the equipment box. Out of it came a pair of light data gloves such as those used by video gamers. There was also a set of wrap-around goggles with a mirror-fronted surface, likewise used by gamers. Last was a rounded black slab the size of a hardback book.

She donned the gloves and punched the infrared communication On button on one wrist. She also punched a similar button on the goggles and plugged a cord from the slab into the wall's data socket. The gloves and the goggles now talked with the slab and through it to the web and the parts of the cyberwar facility allowed her.

She put on the goggles and relaxed back in her chair so that she was almost horizontal.

"You may recognize an augmented reality system like the ones gamers use. I bought an advanced developmental version and have added to its capabilities. I can see you and everything else, but also a representation of the web."

"Interesting. So how are you fixed for lunch?"

"Whenever you're ready, or whoever is going to your cafeteria or out, stick your head in the door."

"OK. Though if you're deep into something, tell us. We'll go away. We wouldn't want to interfere. But if you go out alone for lunch, tell whoever's in the outside office. We wouldn't want to trigger a security alert."

"No problem. Later."

He paused, looked at her enigmatic visage, and left.

Now Karen had to do something tricky. Normally she simply set the parameters for a search and Tiara delivered it, sometimes instantly, never more than an hour. But if she did that two possibilities might happen.

Someone would say "Ohmigod aliens are among us!" Or much more likely, "She's part of the conspiracy, maybe even built the viruses herself."

So she would have to mimic someone merely human though a very extraordinary one doing a search. She did this by letting Tiara set up the images before her, then guide her through them.

First came a command screen. Prompting by Tiara she activated it by focusing her eyes on an icon and triggering a particular brain-wave sequence, a standard gamer practice. It was like pushing a button with a finger. Her eyes now acted like a computer mouse.

Then, her hands lying at her sides, she began typing on the virtual keyboard which appeared on the screen before her eyes. The data gloves had force feedback so that her fingers inside them felt much as if she were typing on a keyboard. She used it to sign on to the custom-built supercomputer inside the slab.

Another command and the web beyond the supercomputer showed as balls connected by lines. The image was in 3D and the balls and lines had different colors which told her something about them.

She fisted her hands as if she was grasping the steering yoke of an airplane. Slight movements of her hands seemed to push or pull on the yoke and turn and tilt it. She began to "fly" in the virtual space shown in front of her.

She approached a ball and it swelled into a box, semitransparent. It was a file in a computer somewhere out on the Web. She "parked" herself and now her hands had arms which she could use to reach out. She grasped the box with one hand and poked a red button on it to open it.

It was a column of numbers arranged in rows. She flicked it with a virtual finger to send the rows of numbers scrolling upward. She quit scrolling and looked at a row. Nothing interesting. She flicked a finger and the box shrank back into a ball.

The next ball/box showed paragraphs of text. Still nothing. Another showed a video. Sound came out of the tiny speakers in the goggles near her ears.

So far she'd only been browsing the InterWeb the same way gamers did.

One large unconnected ball off to one side was the cyberwar computer to which she was allowed access. She dove into it. More balls connected by lines.

One was placed for her to "see" right away. She opened it and it was a report on the viruses. She began to study the contents. It was jargon-dense and the writers did not seem to know how to write paragraphs shorter than half a page. Nor was it especially well-organized.

Karen sighed and focused her excellent mind on its task.

At a quarter till noon Benedict rapped on the door jamb. Karen surfaced back to the real world and looked up at him.

"Feel like lunch?"

She sat up, removed her interface visor, stripped off her gloves, and stood up.

"Just finished wading through one of the worst thickets of jargon I've ever come across. I could definitely use a break."

As they entered the hall outside her office he said, "The cafeteria's not bad. Or there's a burger place a block over from the main gate."

"I could go for a burger. And to stretch my legs."

Outside the building they joined a stream of workers headed for the main gate. The morning, which had started out with a chill grey overcast, had turned into a more typical warm bright California day.

<>

After a leisurely lunch and reports now absorbed, Karen began to surf the three-dimensional color-coded representation of the InterWeb and its many side roads into company databases. Slow at first to navigate, after a while her pace picked up. By the end of the workday she was "flying" through it so fast the computer administrators had to expand her allotment of bandwidth and processing power.

By the end of the first week Karen told Benedict she'd become moderately familiar with the three viruses and had some guesses about where they were from and how to protect against them. She'd need the remaining week to pin down all the details.

The next week she again mimicked doing searches which Tiara had done within the first hour of her first day. By now she was following search paths so fast that others commented upon her progress with awe. Her bandwidth and processing power had to be upped twice more.

<>

At 10:00 on the second Friday of Karen's job for the CIB she presented her results at a meeting in one of the conference rooms on the third floor of the Cyberwar main building. Present was the director John McLemore, Ms. Johnson, Benedict, and a dozen other people.

At the foot of the long oval table McLemore stood up. This was the signal for the various people to cease chatting and attend to business.

"I believe we're all here. Ms. Danburn has told me, as I'm sure you all know, that she's ready to deliver her results. Ms. Danburn."

Karen stood up as he sat down. Today she was in full formal costume, suit dress and jacket of blue, light blue blouse, and modest heels matching her suit. She wore no jewelry. Her gleaming blond hair spilling down one side of her head and covering her breast was more than enough decoration.

"Thank you, Mr. McLemore. Here is the situation." She pressed a pen-sized remote control. Behind her position at the head of the table a large flat-screen on the wall lit. She moved to one side so everyone could see the screen.

A map showed the Chinese Federation. Two large red Xs marked two cities, one on the east coast and one far in the interior.

"The coastal city is Guang-Zhou. The cyberwar facility's location is directly across the strait from Taiwan. This is not a coincidence. Taiwan has long been part of the Chinese Empire but it's a separate province despite its small size. It's one of the powerhouses of the Empire's economy, especially in science, industrial research, and information technology. It's thus politically powerful."

She paused and surveyed the audience, then turned her gaze on McLemore.

"Too powerful according to some of the advisors to Empress. This facility does as much spying on Taiwan as on the rest of the world. I've created a separate partition of the project database to which only you have access. It includes much info relevant to this topic. I believe it should have a separate Top Secret Taiwan classification or some such."

She looked back at the room as a whole.

"I should warn all of you that this information is likely soon to be classified separate from the Top Secret Virus3 classification to which all of you are allowed. I only mention it, and must mention it, because you need to know this to understand the Guang-Zhou virus. That data is now in another partition of the project database called GZ Data. Director McLemore will decide which of you have access to it."

Lawrence Coulter, whom Karen secretly called Colonel Custer for his looks and dogmatic attitude, spoke angrily.

"You take altogether too much on yourself, Ms. Danburn. Who authorized you to create these separate partitions?"

"No one. It was necessary so I gave myself the authority to do so."

"Director McLemore, this woman should be charged with criminal offenses."

Benedict spoke to Coulter. "Sir, I believe if you re-examine Ms. Danburn's contract, to which you have access and surely have read, you'll find clauses which support her right to do so. Perhaps we could put your suggestion on the back burner so we could continue this briefing? Rather than have her carted off to some make-shift jail in the facility?"

Coulter made an impatient waving-off gesture.

McLemore made a gesture to Karen to continue.

"The other two viruses came from this location." A click of the remote showed again the large-scale map of the Chinese Empire. Two more clicks centered the map on the second large red X a bit east of the center of the country and began a slow zoom in. A large reservoir came into view then slid off to the side as the map focused on the banks of a river which fed the reservoir. The X disappeared to reveal the outlines of a city.

"Detailed info is in the partition I labeled YS. This stands for this small city called Yun-Syan. Here is the building where the cyberwar facility is. It has an innocuous label, that of a large industrial company.

"The two viruses are distantly related. I believe the earlier one was accidentally released or released as a test version. As with the Guang-Zhou virus, I've placed in the database schematics of its structure and details of its functions for you to study.

"Also you'll find details on how to protect against the viruses, though you might want to see if you can come up with that on your own. As a learning experience. Or to double-check my work.

"I'll now take questions." She sat down in the chair at the table's head. As a last action she returned the display to show the overall Chinese Empire map.

Coulter was frowning over his information slate. Karen guessed he was accessing her contract, though she didn't care enough to have Tiara probe his device. Director McLemore was turning over something in his head and frowning slightly at the map. Benedict was motionless, calmly waiting to see what would happen next. Most of the rest were poring over various details in the project database, except for one man whom she guessed was trying to set up a mid-day assignation with his mistress or (less likely) wife.

The Director spoke first.

"What actions would you suggest we take to protect ourselves against these viruses and further similar ones?"

"I can suggest nothing. But I'll lay out some alternatives.

"The first is physical action. The Guang-Zhou facility could be attacked by a SEAL team from the sea. The Yun-Syan site could be attacked by loading someone on a Condor long-range drone with an added life support module and weapons cache and dropping them from 100,000 feet or so within a 100 mile radius of it."

Coulter said, "There are obvious drawbacks to such actions."

"I totally agree, Doctor."

An analyst named Billy, always ready to a jab a friendly needle in someone, said, "Could you be that someone, Karen?"

She smiled at the joker. "I'd charge ten million dollars, half up front. And only if I had complete final say on all planning."

Coulter snorted. The director looked at Karen with considering eyes.

"Another possibility would be to modify the viruses and return them to their sender. It would be a great joke.

"You can also issue updates to the anti-virus suites to find and neutralize the viruses.

"Another action is to monitor the two sites for other further deployment of viruses and try to counter them.

"A further possibility along those lines is to tag every virus deployed so that you could track and neutralize it."

"How would you do that?" said Benedict.

"I'd penetrate each site and modify their equipment. But that's not in my current contract. I'd charge two million for each site, half up front."

Coulter said, "I think that would be wasted money. Our people can do that also."

Benedict said, "Except if we accidentally tip off the Chinese they could backtrack and attack us. I'd only trust Ms. Danburn to do that. The money would be well spent."

Director McLemore said, "Excellent work, Ms. Danburn. Thank you for helping us out on this. Now, if everyone will excuse me, I have another meeting."

As everyone filed out of the conference room Ms. Johnson spoke to Karen. "I concur with the Director, Ms. Danburn. I had my doubts about you but you've shown they were unfounded. Would you consider working with us again?"

"I'd be happy to. But I warn you my fees are likely to be higher." She said this with a smile but she was speaking the truth. She already had Tiara guarding the country from destructive viruses and did not feel like repeating the charade she'd just pulled off. She had other matters on which she wanted to use her time.

Part 9 - Hero

In mid-summer Karen read a news story in the Los Angeles Chronicle which both chilled her and heated her rage to almost the explosion point. And it would have resulted in an explosion if she'd only known where to aim it.

A young woman had been found in South Beach who had been mutilated by having her nipples sliced off. More would have happened if her three attackers had not been interrupted by a routine police patrol. One criminal had fired upon the two policemen until his two companions had screeched to a halt in a mini-pickup truck in the street behind him. He'd abandoned the alley and jumped into the back of truck and was gone.

The two police had raced down the alley toward the back street but stopped to help the woman. Helicopters and other police cars had quickly been dispatched but had no success in the search.

The young woman was now in the large new South Beach hospital under a police guard. She had refused to talk to anyone about her experience or who might have attacked her.

The method of attack had been similar to one eight months ago, a story which Karen had missed. Then the woman had been mutilated the same way, likely to punish her both physically and psychologically since (the reporter suggested) women's breasts were so central to a woman's self image. But she'd also had her tongue cut out, possibly after she was dead--

Karen had to stop reading for several minutes at the suggestion that the victim had still been alive when that mutilation had occurred.

Lastly the earlier woman had been stabbed in the gut many times to finish her off. Such a death likely would have been slow, further evidence of the viciousness of the crime.

Karen had known of equally horrible acts committed in Afghanistan. She'd developed a thick emotional skin to help her cope with the atrocities, especially those where children and women were killed by bombs or gunfire. That skin had worn thin in the years since.

She went on indefinite leave from her business that day. The Red Jineri from Afghanistan had decided to set up her bloody shop in Southern California.

<>

High above Earth Karen floated in Pegasus. The planet lay blue and beautiful and peaceful below, decorated by the snowy white dots and swirls of clouds. A tall storm front swept in a huge crescent across the center of the country, also snow white from above even though below it the skies were grey and black and rained chill water onto the surface. Spider web flickers of white light revealed to her eyes several lightning storms within the front.

She noticed the sights only subliminally, using the seeming serenity to help give her some of that quality. Most of her mind was using Tiara to search for information which would help her find the criminals she sought.

The two attacks suggested retaliation by a gang for some indiscretions the women had committed or were thought to have committed. Such were the conclusions in stories by reporters and confidential reports by police. The gang was unknown except for fragmentary reports from various sources. They'd been given the name Scorpions by one reporter and the name had stuck.

That there was only one gang was a supposition. It was always possible a second gang had copied the scary means of the first murderer for the same reason: to use fear to silence possible talk by women owned by the gang.

The gang or gangs were believed to be prostitution rings, or ones with prostitution as one of their sources of income. The clothing of the two attacked women suggested they were prostitutes. So did the locations of the crimes.

South Beach ran east and west along the southern edge of the Los Angeles metroplex just before it merged into the Orange County metroplex to the east and south along the curve of the beach toward the south.

The city was mixed geographically, with some very upscale residences shading down toward several shabby but not quite slum areas. The beach front had several high end hotels and apartment buildings strewn along it. At the south end of the downtown business district was a small land-locked island with a very expensive entertainment and hotel complex. An international film festival was held there each summer. There was also a yacht regatta each year which touched there as part of a very long promenade along the Southern California coast.

Karen turned to researching prostitution, first generally and then specific to South Beach. Almost an hour of online research and she was ready to search in person. She loosed her grip on the local space-time fabric and fell toward Earth.

<>

Invisible Karen slowed to orient her vision with the map populated by Tiara with Xs for the streetwalking hotspots identified by police arrest reports. The largest strip was three blocks of an east-west street parallel to Ocean Boulevard: Fourth Street. The Boulevard was one of the main centers of nightlife in South Beach, with a number of upscale shops and restaurants. Fourth Street was ten blocks north and could be described as "midscale" with such businesses as used-clothing stores, family and fast-food restaurants, and several convenience grocery stores.

Young people strolled on Fourth Street, some as couples, some singly, a few in clots of four to seven. About a third were white, another third Latin-American, a quarter some kind of Asian, and the rest black and other ethnicities.

Older people also walked there, including some families going to or from the several sit-down restaurants or the midscale film complex. There was also busy auto traffic.

The red-light area of Fourth was a bit to the east amid a somewhat downscale area. Flying over it Karen saw a couple dozen women dressed in short tight skirts, high heels, and blouses displaying the upward curve of pushed-up breasts. They walked a block one way then reversed, a continual circuit. They were about equally spaced from each other, none crowding the others. Occasionally two or three would chat briefly before continuing their circuits.

Flying lower she saw that their hair was often teased up higher and their faces heavily made up into supposedly sexy features.

Several times as she watched cars slowed and stopped and one of the women would approach it, bending down to chat. A minute or two and they would get into the car.

Karen followed several cars. Sometimes they found a spot several miles away in one of the several strip lots along the Boulevard where there was an ocean view, but it was sex not sights which were on their minds. Sometimes they parked in alleys or in motel parking lots. Half the time those near a motel got out of the car and went into rooms in the motels.

Three times after the sex the drivers of the cars pushed the prostitute out of the car and drove off, leaving the "girl" cursing but unhurt. The prostitutes phoned someone and shortly afterward were picked up by their pimp.

Fearing for the woman's safety the first time Karen flew very near but the woman received no more than a mild slap and some yelling. The second time the only punishment the pimp gave was to say the lost fee would come out of the woman's cut of the evening.

Things quieted down a bit after 2:00 in the morning. Of course it was a weekday; Karen guessed quitting time would be an hour or two later during the weekends.

Three nights of this and Karen had made little progress. Trailing the pimps home had found none of them joining more than a couple of other men with similar "jobs." Certainly none were an organized gang.

She decided to take more direct action.

<>

Sunday at 2:30 at night Karen saw the most-upscale pimp collect the night's earnings and walk toward his car a few blocks away.

A gleaming white very-expensive car pulled up beside his car before he could get into it. A hand under his jacket, the handsome black man looked down at the woman at the driver's wheel. He leaned further and surveyed the rest of the car. It was empty except for her.

She was something to look at. A redhead with long curly hair, a lovely foxy face, and a curvaceous body in a tight green evening dress. An emerald necklace graced her half-revealed bosom and emerald pendants her ears.

"Jerome. I've heard good things about you."

"Have you?"

"I've heard you have a big cock and awesome staying power."

A grin revealed very white teeth. "You heard right."

"Climb in. Let's talk."

Jerome glanced fake-casually around, then walked around her car and got into it. The door slammed behind him with the solid quiet Thunk! of the most expensive door seal.

"You seem to be quite the man-about-town, Jerome."

"Oh, I know my way around."

"What's a nice motel nearby?"

He directed her to one, not five minutes away. On the way they chatted about daily events, for all the world like old friends. At the motel he went inside the office and came out a few minutes later with a grin and a key. They parked and went up one flight of stairs, she ahead of him. On the way he got a very good look at her bottom. It did not disappoint him.

He opened the motel-room door with the key and went inside ahead of her, turning on the lights. He heard the door behind him click closed and turned.

She was no longer smiling. She stood straight. Her dress had somehow turned to a tight-fitting red jump suit, her high heels had turned to low-heeled red boots.

"What is this?"

"We're going to talk. I mean you are going to talk."

He pulled a pistol from under his jacket and pointed it at her. She was uncowed. Perhaps for good reason. Gossamer veils flowed and streamed around her, almost forming a globe but never for long. A wind from nowhere ruffled her long curly red locks.

"Go ahead and shoot. No one can hear the shots. Or hear you scream."

Panicked he fired at her as rapidly as he could pull the trigger. The bullets disappeared; the shots were muffled. She was unharmed, almost bored.

The last shot fired, Jerome tried to fire more. The gun's hammer rose and fell, rose and fell, producing only dry clicking sounds.

He dropped it and pulled a knife from a pocket. It snicked open and he ran at her, stabbing with the knife. The veils swirled around the knife and it disappeared. His rush was stopped a foot from her. The veils looked like gossamer but felt more like invisible molasses. He was caught, arms out, clutching at nothing.

She put hands under his armpits and threw him at the bed as if he were no more than a kitten. He bounced, rolled, fell half off the bed.

She walked toward the easy chair beside the bed, sat, the veils disappearing. She crossed one booted foot over her knee. He noticed that the sole of the boot was spotless.

"Eight months ago a woman was stabbed to death, her tongue cut out, her breasts mutilated. A few days ago another woman almost died the same way. I am here to avenge them both."

"What are you?"

"To the men who did those acts, a demon. And to you, if you do not tell me all you know."

"They will kill me if I talk."

She lifted her hands palms up. Flame danced on and above them. He could feel furnace heat on his face. Sweat broke out on it and on the rest of his body.

The flames ceased.

"Not if they can't find you. You are healthy, young, can find a job. You can start over some place far away."

"I have a wife and child."

"A pimp? One who sells women? Forces them to be raped? Over and over again, year after year? I don't believe you."

"It's true. Look! Look!" He fumbled in his pants, pulled out a wallet, opened it, held it out to her.

A red nearly invisible veil licked out and caught the wallet, pulled it to her. She looked at the photo beside his driver's license. It showed a black woman and a young boy smiling at the picture taker.

"We'll be here an hour. No one will know what we talked about. If anyone ever finds out about that hour, they'll think we fucked, not talked. When you leave--if I let you leave--you can go on with your life as before.

"Now tell me everything you know about the Scorpions."

At first doubtfully, then more easily, he talked.

He didn't know much. They weren't very visible even to the rest of the underworld. He thought they liked the name given them but called themselves Demons. He knew a few nicknames, el Diablo, el Segundo Diablo, and so on. He'd heard the common given names Juan, Pedro, and a few others but not any family names.

All of that was annoyingly generic. When he began to talk about their common places to do business the information was more helpful. These were a few high-end hotels.

"That's all you know?"

That seemed to be so. He strained and came up with the thought that they'd only been active in South Beach for three years, but that was clearly a guess.

He'd been truthful, she was sure from her reading of the dozen subtle body clues of which he was likely not even aware.

"Very well. I'll take you back to your car now."

She stood up and suddenly she was back in her tight green dress and emerald jewelry and high heels. She let him lead the way and closed the motel-room door firmly behind her.

They did not speak on the way to his car nor afterward. Still fearing a last minute change of heart he quickly got into his car and drove away.

A fearful glance into his rear-view mirror did not show her white car. It was if it had vanished off the face of the Earth.

The hunt for the Scorpions seemed to narrow down to prostitutes who worked out of upscale hotels. Consequently The Red Lady showed up the next Friday night at one of the major hotels in South Beach, the Tropicale. It was located on the mile-wide semicircular artificial island across from the most upscale part of the city. The hotel was right next to the South Beach Arena and Convention Center and so did great business almost every day of the year.

Karen was dressed much as she had been when she met with Jerome the previous week, though she'd toned down the green dress. It was not as tight and went just below her knees. She also topped the outfit with a forest green jacket.

She dined at the hotel's restaurant. It opened onto the Safari Bar and Night Club, which was already beginning to fill as the dinner hour began to wind down and the restaurant became an overflow area for the bar.

She was positioned near the border between the two establishments and so had a good view of those arriving. This included half a dozen women who she quickly recognized as being likely prostitutes. They looked no different from the many other young women out for an evening, but stood out mostly because they were not part of a pair or larger group of women banded together for companionship and safety.

She had Suit create a tiny nearly invisible spybot for each and pilot it to land on each woman's skin. There it was absorbed into their bloodstream and would remain for several months before self-destructing by dissolving. The spybots also used sensors to sample the women's DNA and to read items in their purses which could identify them. Most had driver's licenses or credit cards. For the women without them she used other means to identify them. Soon she had very detailed dossiers on each.

At 9:00 she paid her bill, adding a very generous tip to her waiter. As she did so she said, "I'd like to stay here for a while. Can you transfer my bar tab for the rest of the evening to my room? I'm here for a week for a convention."

The young man, a student at the South Beach College a dozen miles to the northeast, quite handsome in an Italian way, smiled at her.

"Of course. But you could have done that earlier, Madame."

"But then I wouldn't have had a chance to tip you. I always like to reward good service. This way I can tip directly, rather than have the hotel give you a standard tip."

"I appreciate that, Madame. Have a good day--or night, as it were." He walked away with a jaunty step.

It was not just for kindness that Karen had done this. She now had an ally on the days when he worked if she needed it.

For the next two hours she watched the crowd. She kept ordering drinks at regular intervals to keep the management from pushing her to leave. She also politely fended off a number of approaches from men and one woman. Except for two men who obviously thought she was a working girl. She had to be very forceful with them, threatening (and ready) to get management to eject them from the club.

The manager came over to her table after that, an older man who'd seen it all if one could judge from his expression.

"Madame, I must apologize for some people's rude behavior. You are a guest of the hotel?"

"Yes. Here in southern California for a vacation. Here is my credit card, if you'd like to check to see that I'm a law-abiding citizen, not some citizen of the, ah, demimonde."

He smiled at her. "Demimonde. Ah, quite. No, that won't be necessary."

He walked off, but Karen could tell that he had read her name off the card and would check that she was a guest. Further, he'd run a search on her. Finding, of course, Tiara's prepared identity as a senior executive for a software services company.

During those two hours she noticed all the prostitutes leave with clients. Tracking them through the spybots she could tell that they took the clients to a room in the hotel or one of the half-dozen nearby luxury hotels for sex. Three of them returned but the others apparently were booked for an all-night stay with their escorts.

Perhaps this was why three more women showed up at the night club. Karen tagged each with a spybot and read their dossiers.

So far none of the information she had suggested a connection with the Scorpions. As she continued to track the spybots more information might turn up which would. But that might be days or weeks, if it ever happened. It was time for other measures.

Near midnight Karen selected one of the women, acting from intuition rather than using anything Tiara and the spybots gave her to select the woman. She began to watch the petite woman with lovely long dark gleaming hair, olive skin, and a slender but attractive body encased mostly in white. Whenever the woman's gaze swept Karen's part of the nightclub she would see Karen watching her, looking directly at her eyes.

Finally she came over to Karen's table.

"Hi! Mind if I join you?"

"Please do."

"I'm Sherri."

"Scarlett. Come here often?"

"Ever few weeks. The drinks aren't as expensive as they might be, considering how popular this place is. And the snacks are great. You have to watch your weight here. What about you? I haven't seen you around before."

"I'm here on business for a week. I figured I'd come here the weekend before and get my biological clock in sync."

"Where are you from?"

"Puerto Rico. My company does business with the Argentine space program. The U. S. has a bilateral trade agreement, so we get South American contacts and trade through Argentina without paying some big penalties."

"Interesting. Tell me more."

"Suppose we go to my room? We almost have to yell here to be heard."

"I'd like that."

They chatted about the plane flight "Scarlett" had supposedly made, part of which had been on a direct-flight from Miami on one of the new hypersonic liners.

Inside her room Karen said, "Let's order some drinks on my tab. Whatever you want."

"I might order something very expensive."

"Be my guest. If so, order me the same. I might learn a new favorite drink."

Sherri got an impish look and went to the room's desk where the hotel menu lay in a leather-bound book. She came back to the sitting area of the large room and sat on the white couch which was part of a U made by it and two bookending matching chairs. She lifted the phone on the lamp table beside her end of the couch and ordered a French white wine with an exotic name.

Karen sat on one of the U end chairs and they chatted more while waiting for room service, Scarlett about Puerto Rico and Buenos Aires (which Karen had really visited) and about the student studies Sherri was finishing at South Beach State College. The woman was actually truthful about that.

Karen took a sip of her drink. It was interesting. She might come to like it, so she had Suit memorize it so it could copy the drink when she wanted. Sherri also sipped, eying Scarlett with a measuring eye.

Scarlett set down her glass.

"I'll get to the point. How much do you charge for an hour of your time?"

Sherri nodded, so minutely she was likely unaware that she did so. She believed she'd judged Scarlett was a customer.

"Three hundred for straight sex. More if you want special services. I don't do some things."

Scarlett opened her clutch purse, took out $400 in fifty-dollar bills, and handed them to Sherri. The woman put the money in her purse.

"When you tell your manager how much I paid you, tell him

whatever makes sense to him. Or her. But what I want to do is talk."

Sherri gazed back at her, caution but not fear behind what she intended for a poker face. It would have fooled most people.

"I am an agent for an organization which protects sex workers from extreme abuse. A few days ago a woman was mutilated and came close to being killed in this city. The method suggested a murder eight months ago. Supposedly both were committed by a group called the Scorpions."

The fear was obvious on Sherri's face. "I don't know anything about them."

"Perhaps. I won't try to force anything out of you. You can leave now if you want. But leaving early might give the wrong message to anyone who sees you. Stay for a full hour. Say nothing. Watch TV. Read a book. Or chat about anything at all."

Scarlett was semi-slouched in her chair with one ankle over a knee, seemingly not able to get out of her chair quickly and attack or chase the young woman. Sherri relaxed somewhat.

"What is this organization?"

"I can't tell you much. Just that we're large, well-organized, and have very advanced tools at our disposal. For instance, one of our operatives tonight observed all possible working girls downstairs, identified them through facial recognition and other means, and compiled dossiers. Then he relayed the info to me via microphones implanted under my skin."

"Why did you pick me?"

"Intuition. After doing this for a long time you get better than all the computer intelligence at judging people."

"Are you-- I've heard rumors of an organization that does something like this. They're all over Europe and have started on the East Coast. Is that you?"

"Maybe."

"What are you going to do to the...Scorpions?"

"Don't play innocent. I can read faces very well. I know you've heard the name."

"Just the name! And enough to know you don't mess with them!"

"Calm down. I told you I won't try to force you. Or fool you, for that matter. Quite aside from the morality of such means, they are rarely of much use."

The young woman calmed, took a sip of her drink, eyed Scarlett, took another sip.

"What are you going to do to them?"

"Find them all first. Then eliminate them as a threat in such a way as to give everyone who sells women incentive to treat them well."

"What way?"

"There are several options. Use your imagination. But maybe not just before you go to sleep."

<>

Sherri truly did not know much. Nor did the several other women with whom Karen spoke that week. But each knew something that she was willing to mention. By next Friday much of it fit (sometimes not too well) into a jigsaw puzzle view of the Scorpions. Who Karen privately called the Diablos because that name was a commonly mentioned part of the puzzle.

Karen knew something was bothering the woman she'd picked up on her second Friday night at the Tropicale. But she showed none of her knowledge and matters proceeded as they often did, with the young woman ordering drinks.

The doorbell to the suite chimed.

Karen stood. "That will be room service. I'll get it."

The black-and-white clad waiter who entered the room did indeed carry a tray holding a bottle in an ice bucket and two chilled wine glasses. He moved past her and put the tray on the low glass-topped table in front of her room's couch. Then he turned toward her with a long-barreled pistol in his hand.

"Make a sound and you're dead."

Karen froze.

"Get the door," the man instructed the woman on the couch.

She did so, almost crying as she passed Karen, saying "I'm sorry! I'm sorry! I'm sorry!"

The door opened again and two more men came in the room. Both were big and wore business suits and ties. The young woman made her escape as they entered. Karen was amused to see that she had taken her purse with her.

The man with the gun said, "You've been asking too many questions. Now you're going to get some answers. You'll come with us and make no noise or try to escape. I'll be right behind you and shoot you the instant you try anything."

Karen said nothing. Nor did she show fear. This bothered the gunman.

"Roberto, give her a little obedience training."

One of the men stepped forward and punched Karen in the gut. Or tried to. She stepped backward just enough so that his fist barely brushed her.

He swore. "Stand still!" He took a step forward.

Karen picked him up by his armpits and threw him at the gunman. The two crashed to the floor. The gun flew across the floor.

The third man stepped forward in a crouch with a blackjack in his hand. He moved it in circles and spirals in front of her face, supposedly mesmerizing her with the threat.

"Oh, stop that!" Karen said. "Or I'll take it away from you and stick it up your butt."

He ignored her, his eyes fixed on hers. He inched forward.

Karen was keeping an eye on the two other men who were slowly getting their feet under them. But when the blackjack man made a sudden rush toward her she fended off the 'jack and struck him with a downward blow to one thick neck muscle. He fell as if pole axed and rolled on the carpet from side to side, a hand massaging the painful trapezius muscle, his face screwed up.

The gunman lumbered toward his pistol. Karen glided forward and put a foot on it, standing almost face to face to him.

"If you three clowns make more trouble for me I'll spill your guts all over this carpet."

She swiped a hand behind her over one shoulder and brought it back with a long shining blade in the hand. The two standing and one prone man stared at it with fascination.

She repeated the swiping motion and the blade disappeared.

"I have a business proposition for your boss. I've gone to a great deal of trouble to get his attention. But I don't intend to be treated disrespectfully. So you two--" She pointed at the muscle men. "Get out of here. Your friend and I are going to this meeting alone."

They looked at the gunman. He said, "Go on. Meet us there."

The two men left, though not before Karen had Suit tag them and the other man with a spybot.

Karen picked up the gun, ejected the clip, jacked the weapon so that the chambered cartridge flew out of it. She snatched the cartridge out of the air and fed it to the clip. Then she replaced the clip and handed the reloaded weapon back to the man.

"Can't have you without protection, can we? And words of warning. If you ever again point a gun at me you'll be dead before you can pull the trigger."

"What the Hell are you, Lady?"

"You call yourself a devil? Well, now you've met a real one."

The sweat broke out of him so badly she could smell it without Tiara's heightening her nose's sensitivity.

He spoke not at all as he led her to the underground parking garage. They entered it, entered his car, and he drove them out of the cavern into the street beyond, turning right into a long curve which led into the South Beach Boulevard heading east.

"How far is it?"

"About ten miles."

"Fine. So a half hour in this traffic.

"So tell me about yourself. Your name, your childhood, how you got into this line of work."

He glanced away from the traffic for a moment to look at her. Why did a self-styled demon, who might actually be one, want to chat? About something so--unimportant?

"Go on. Entertain me. Lie if you want."

He spoke slowly at first, hesitating often, occasionally glancing quickly at her to judge her reactions. As she remained attentive, even prompting him with a question or comment, he became more confident, and more engrossed in the story he was drawing out of himself.

It was not especially original. Young boy of Mexican parents growing up in the poorest L. A. Latin barrio, not good at or interested in school, joining a youth gang, conviction of petty crimes, two brief periods in prison.

This took them a half-dozen miles, where they crossed a low

bridge over a tributary of the South Beach Bay. Off to their right was a marina with several hundred sail boats and yachts, some big enough to live on, the whole well-lit in golden light at this time, late evening.

Out of the second prison stay he got a temporary job with Los Diablos. This led to a permanent position. Which revelation caused him to become cautious. His speech slowed and finally stopped.

"It's OK, Antonio. I'll not ask you to betray your companions."

He said nothing. They rode in an odd state of camaraderie for several minutes.

"We're almost there," he said.

The residential neighborhood through which they had been driving dwindled to nothing. Off to the left the land had become marshy, without any buildings, a wildlife sanctuary she could tell from a map Tiara supplied her. Then a road off into the sanctuary came up and Antonio slowed to cross the highway and enter it. To the left now was the marsh. To the right was a quarter-mile-wide stretch of scrub land.

A half mile into the two-lane street a three-story near-mansion loomed ahead. It was well-lit and surrounded by a chain-link fence.

He slowed before a gate into the compound and stopped at a security panel. He pressed a button and a voice asked who it was. Through Tiara Karen could tell they were being inspected by two security cameras on each side of the gate ahead of them.

"It's Antonio. I have the visitor the Don wants to talk to."

The gate ahead of them slowly opened. Antonio drove through into a block-long street through a green lawn which entered a circular turnaround. Beyond it were more lawn and a pink sidewalk leading to the demi-mansion. Two men stood before the entrance, a set of tall double doors.

The car parked just beyond the sidewalk leading up to the front of the house. The two got out. Antonio waved her ahead of him.

The two men looked her over very carefully as Karen neared them. They were big men in suits which concealed pistols, clearly visible to Karen via Tiara's X-ray-like gravity radar. Plus a variety of other property, wallets and coins in their pockets and such.

"Where's Roberto and Enrico?" said one, a blond.

"They're coming behind us," said Antonio.

The men stepped aside. Karen walked up the several low concrete steps and Antonio hurried ahead of her to open one leaf of the double doors.

Inside was a short hall with a tile floor. It opened into an entrance room with rooms off to each side for (she guessed) restrooms and coatrooms. Beyond that was what had been built as a ballroom but was now a sort of throne room. At its far side a low bandstand had been converted into a dais set with a throne. If a large leather-covered easy chair could be called a throne.

An elderly Latino sat there, wearing a grey suit with a white shirt and black bow tie. On his feet were cowboy boots with stainless-steel toes. He was stout and had much grey in his hair. To each side of him stood two of his sons, or so their resemblance to him suggested.

Perhaps two dozen men stood in the room in groups of two to five. They all wore suits or jackets, some leather and some of blue jean material. And every one had one or more guns hidden underneath the jackets.

She was the only woman in the room.

Karen might have been intimidated by all the masculine stares which seemed to strip her of her clothing, if she were an ordinary woman who could be intimidated. Especially as she wore party clothing, a tight green dress under a forest green jacket and wore three-inch-high heels. The kind of outfit most men would take to mean she wanted them to desire her.

Antonio walked a couple of feet ahead of her as they approached. At the foot of the dais, he inclined his upper body slightly as if sketching a bow to a monarch and spoke in Spanish.

"Chief, here is the woman you wanted to see."

"Very good, Antonio. You may go."

"Yes, sir. But there is something you should know."

The boss looked at him, waiting.

"She came voluntarily. And she's very dangerous."

The older son sneered and laughed. "Sir, he's on drugs. Or crazy." Tiara supplied a short biography of him, as she could now do for everyone in the room. The instant Karen had stepped into the room Tiara had begun scanning them through her gravity radar. It had taken her less than a second to complete. Meanwhile Suit had tagged everyone with a spybot.

The younger son, a leaner version of his father, examined Karen with a predator's caution.

"Sir," Antonio said. "I know this sounds as if Ricardo is right. But I'd rather be thought crazy than fail to warn you. I don't think she's human."

Karen had watched all this with interest. Now she took one step forward to stand beside Antonio at the very edge of the dais.

"Antonio is correct, Mr. Zaragoza. My looks are deceiving. I am a special agent with special tools and talents. Some of them make me very dangerous.

"But it's too early to speak of danger. You wanted to talk with me. I am here."

The boss nodded at Antonio and waved him away. The man slipped into the crowd which had been slowly drawing nearer the drama being played before them.

"You will excuse us if we take you at your word. Manuel, search her for weapons."

The older son looked bored. Karen guessed he wanted to roll his eyes but didn't dare to. The younger man walked to the edge of the dais a full dozen feet from Karen and stepped down onto the floor. He walked up to her, eyes very alert as he approached.

By now Karen had slipped her coat off and held it out to one side at arm's length. She also held her empty hand out to the other side.

Manuel first took the jacket from her and examined it, feeling for hidden weapons. As he did so he kept several feet from her. When done he set the jacket on the edge of the dais and approached her.

Karen still had her hands out to the sides. She slowly turned in a complete circle as he approached so that he could observe her back as well as her front.

"Be respectful," she said. "I will hurt you badly if you are not."

His older brother blew out his breath and shook his head, a disgusted look on his face. Manuel said nothing but he was circumspect on patting her down, not lingering on any part of her, begging her pardon for feeling in her hair and running his hands down as much of her inner thighs as the dress would allow.

He backed away from her. "She appears to have no weapons on her, Father."

"Good. Miss, what should we call you?"

"Scarlett is as good a name as any, Sir."

"You have been asking questions about us. Why?"

"My organization has heard about the recent attempt to mutilate and murder a young woman who is likely a prostitute. This echoes a similar incident eight months ago. We are not opposed to prostitution. But we highly disapprove of such actions. We want the guilty ones delivered to us for punishment."

Zaragoza had been growing angry as she spoke.

"I will not go along with such absurd actions."

"Then we will be forced to act against your entire gang. We will not be gentle."

"All I see is a stupid young woman who has no backup and no weapons acting a part."

"Can you really gamble that there is not a private SWAT team waiting outside who will kill everyone here if I say so, or do not phone them within the hour that I am safe?"

He paused in thought, turned to speak to a short man standing just to one side of the dais.

"Alert the security room. See if there is such a force outside."

Karen said, "Really? Do you really think they would not be shielded from your security?

"I suggest an alternative to giving up the guilty to me. Put me, with just the clothing on my back, and knives, in a remote area. Send the guilty men after me after five minutes carrying whatever weapons they want. Whatever happens, you will not be attacked.

"Unless, of course, you commit another atrocity."

The older brother spoke up, a smile on his face. "I like that, Father. It should be fun."

Zaragoza thought for nearly a full minute. Karen stood still, motionless, seemingly (and actually) bored.

"So be it. You will stay here tonight. Tomorrow morning we will take you up on your offer."

Ricardo began to grin widely. His younger brother showed no emotion but Karen could tell he was uneasy.

<>

At 8:00 someone banged on the door to the room Karen had been

given for the night and yelled something incomprehensible about breakfast. She was ready but gave them a few minutes to leave, then exited the room, leaving no sign she had ever been in it. She'd slept floating in the air cradled by Suit in perfect comfort.

She followed the scent of the man down the hall and downstairs to a buffet-style dining room. It amused her that part of the lair of the feared Diablos was set up like a high-class hotel, complete with female and male servitors. She wondered how much those servants knew about their employer.

She ate nothing; Suit had already transmuted air into her preferred breakfast. But she did sample the excellent coffee with Suit's biochemical sensors and, finding no drugs in it or the cream and sugar, took a mug of it to a table and sipped it while waiting for events.

To observers she would have seemed serene and dreaming. Inside she felt vaguely nauseous. She would be executing five men today and, evil as they surely were, she did not like that she had to do it. To keep her mind off the situation she surfed the near-infinite variety of Earth's electronic noösphere.

"Scarlett. It's time."

It was Antonio, seemingly her designated shepherd. He was dressed as he had been the day before, in a suit and tie, but with a lighter blue color palette. He seemed nervous.

Karen took a last sip from her mug, stood up, and followed him.

The "throne room" had a smaller and slightly different mix of men, about a dozen in all. She had Suit tag two new additions with a spybot.

Zaragoza, "El Jefe," looked and dressed much the same, as did his younger son, Manuel. The older was dressed in what looked for all the world as if he were ready for an African safari, complete with khaki roughwear and boots, big floppy-brimmed hat, and an elephant rifle.

Karen stifled her smile and surveyed the four men standing off to one side of the dais. They were dressed in similar outfits and carried an array of weapons: rifles, pistols in holsters, a submachine gun, and each had at least one knife visible or otherwise on their person.

"Scarlett," said the Chief. "Are you ready?"

"Yes, sir, I am."

"Where did you get those clothes? And those swords?"

For the upcoming event she'd selected a grey-and-green

camouflage uniform with a now-thrown-back hood and matching camo gloves. Two long swords were sheathed on her back, brown hilts visible above her shoulders.

"From my car."

He frowned. "You were supposed to be locked in your room."

She smiled and said nothing.

He raised his voice. "Who let her out?"

The men in the room looked at each other. Some actually shuffled their feet in nervousness.

The Chief grew angry. "Tell me now. Or you're dead men."

"Don't blame them, Sir. Locks mean nothing to me. And before you check with your Security room, I know how to avoid videocams."

He visibly reined in his anger. Ricardo let his loose.

"This wasn't in the agreement! She said she'd fight in her dress and just with knives!"

His brother spoke up. He hid it well but Karen could tell he was enjoying his brother's anger.

"She said 'the clothes on her back.' Are you scared because she's wearing pants? Or that the knives are long?"

"Spoken like a lawyer!" Ricardo looked as if he wanted to lunge around his father and strike his brother. Who obviously had no more fear of (Karen judged) a bullying sibling.

Manuel shrugged. Karen knew he had a law degree from UCLA's prestigious law school. With honors. And was slowly converting his father's quasi-legal businesses to fully legal ones and covering the many informational tracks back to their questionable past. In his own way he was more important to the family business than Ricardo.

The patriarch shrugged off the annoyances.

"It's time we got this done with. We have more important business to attend to."

"I'll be going along, sir," Manuel said. "With your permission. I will ensure that all act with the honor expected of our house."

The Chief looked at his younger son for a full minute, ignoring Ricardo's protests. Then he jerked his head in agreement.

"Very well," said the young man. "Miss Scarlett, if you'll accompany me. Antonio, you will drive us."

Trailed by Antonio he and Karen walked out of the room, down a hall, down a stair to a hallway through a suite of underground rooms, and into a garage basement. He ushered her to a big silver SUV and held a rear passenger door open for her.

Karen slipped the sword harness off and grasped the two swords and their sheaths with one hand. With the other hand she closed the door behind her. Setting the swords on the floor ahead of her she donned the seat belt and adjusted the shoulder harness.

The opposite side passenger car door slammed as Manuel joined her, then the driver's door as Antonio entered. He started the machine and drove them into through the garage and then up and out of the building. Moments later he buzzed open the gate to the compound and took them onto the dusty road leading away from the area.

"You don't seem nervous, Miss."

"This is routine for me. I long ago lost count of the men I've killed." This was true enough. Or would be if she could truly forget them. Tiara gave her a perfect memory when she wanted it, and she'd been born with an excellent one.

"But two swords? Against all the firepower arrayed against you?"

She shrugged.

He sighed. "I guessed as much last night. In a way it's a relief. Ricardo was taking the family on a downhill path even before Father dies. But it means I'll have to take over. I've never wanted that responsibility."

"But at least you will have years to prepare. Your father is basically a very healthy man."

Antonio pulled onto the paved highway on which he'd driven Karen and himself to this place. However he turned left to head away from the South Beach part of the metroplex and sped up to match the fast-moving traffic.

Manuel and she settled into thoughtful silence.

It took them a half hour to drive further out of the metroplex. They met the interstate freeway and drove for a few miles north, then at San Juan Capistrano took the highway east toward Lake Elsinore. The land became increasingly hilly with patches of forest and open land, some cultivated, some not.

Manuel said, "It seems a long way to travel just to kill you. We could have done that at home and disposed of your body more easily."

Karen grinned at him. "Having second thoughts?"

"No. Just pondering how you manipulated us into this."

"Your father may be wiser than you. Maybe he knew that I would have killed every one of you."

He didn't believe her. He did believe that she would have killed and maimed many before she went down under overwhelming force.

Finally they pulled off the Lake Elsinore Highway onto a rough country road, paved but not that well kept up. It became a dirt road and then dead ended. Ahead was scrub land with high brown grass and many low bushes. A bit beyond a dense forest loomed, mostly oaks and pine trees.

They got out. Scarlett donned her swords and began to walk into the scrub, pulling the hood up over her head. In moments she disappeared. Literally. Antonio watched open-mouthed as she became a ghost. Manuel betrayed no surprise. Nor felt any.

Ten minutes later the five men who would hunt the silly girl who had challenged them showed up. With them were two dozen of the Chief's enforcers.

Every one got out of their cars, mostly SUVs with a couple of mini-pickup trucks.

"She's in there?" Ricardo asked his brother.

"Yes." Manuel was silent for a moment. Then he hugged his brother and stepped quickly back.

"Go with God, Ricardo."

The rifleman looked surprised, then contemptuous. He turned quickly away and marshaled his four companions. They began to pace into the scrubland, first bunched together then spreading out into a wider and wider line till they were about ten feet apart. They scanned the ground and the low vegetation. One of them pointed at the ground when they were about a hundred feet from the watching men. A short time later another pointed at a bush.

It happened quickly.

From behind a bush a camouflaged figure rose. Two swords flashed. Two men fell, heads rolling off bodies collapsing like puppets with their strings cut. The apparition flowed toward the third, who was only beginning to turn toward her and bring his rifle up. A sword flashed and he fell. The fourth turned fully toward the enemy but his shots went wide. Or seemed to.

Ricardo was the last man. His rifle spoke. Once. Twice. Then he was down.

His shots could not have missed. And the bullets would have stopped a lion, a grizzly, or even an elephant. They had no effect.

He was screaming as he died. The avenger had not given him an instant death.

Manuel forgot his long-steeped anger at his brother and his earlier resignation when he realized his brother would almost certainly die today. He screamed curses and drew his pistol from under his coat. Most of the other men raised their pistols and rifles.

But at that moment a loud whistle behind and above them grew to a scream. Everyone turned and looked up. Coming toward them was a black craft like a jet fighter. In an instant it grew larger and swept over them.

In front of them it slowed abruptly and flipped its nose skyward. They could see a long body and delta wings. In holes in the middle of each wing whirled propeller blades blurred to invisibility.

It flipped onto its back then as quickly rolled upright. Low, almost front-to-face with them, they could see holes in its body in which machine guns must lurk, each one of which could shred an automobile to scrap. Rockets which could destroy tanks and houses and platoons swung beneath the wings.

The machine rotated slowly left and right and left and right and back again, for all the world like an animal eyeing its prey.

A giant's voice spoke. "LOWER YOUR WEAPONS."

All did. Except one. He screamed and began firing a pistol at the monster in the sky.

It did nothing. The bullets disappeared.

He was reduced to clicking the trigger of his empty pistol. He screamed again and threw the weapon at the machine. It disappeared without even raising a clang or clunk when it touched the craft.

"PLACE YOUR WEAPONS ON THE GROUND. THE NEXT ONE WHO ATTACKS ME I WILL DESTROY YOU ALL."

Walking under it toward them from the death ground the killer came, camouflaging hood down again. Her red hair was restless in the wind from the jet's wing propellers. She spoke up.

"Better do what he says. Pilots have itchy trigger fingers."

Manuel turned toward his men. "Do it!" he called. He bent and placed his weapon on the ground. Beside him Antonio slowly drew his weapon and bent also to follow his example.

One by one, then by twos and threes, the rest followed suit.

Nearing Manuel the woman said to him and Antonio, "Pick up your weapons and holster them. Then come with me." She turned her back and walked away, oblivious to any threats. Or safe from them. Manuel remembered that his older brother had fired twice into her at almost point blank range and harmed her not at all.

As the woman approached the aircraft it lowered to about four feet height. The propellers in its wings slowed to a whisper as it slowed to float on its paramagnetic cushion. A curved section on the side of its fuselage pivoted down from its bottom edge. At the end of the section's pivot it was at a 45-degree angle. The inside surface formed a ladder with two hand rails to aid those who climbed the short stair.

Scarlett went up into the plane. The two men followed. Inside they could see the ceiling was high enough for tall people to walk upright. All along much of the interior were seats, a dozen in a row on each side of a central aisle. Each seat had a lot of leg room and was sized for big men.

She sat in one near the door they had just entered and motioned the men to sit beside her. She fastened a lap belt then two crossed shoulder belts. They copied her.

The sound from outside became muffled when the doors closed behind them. As if from a distance they heard the wing propellers speeding up toward a scream. The plane rose beneath them then began to accelerate forward, pressing the passengers back into well-padded form-fitting cushions.

"This is a troop transport. We can carry a strike force and land anywhere to conduct an assault. It's armored against fairly high-velocity projectiles so the pilot's commands to lay down your weapons was more a matter of principle than because he feared damage."

She paused and eyed Manuel. He'd become calmer.

"You should call your father and let him know how you're returning. And warn him not to let anyone shoot at us. These craft have trackback radar and will destroy anything which shoots at them."

Manuel did as he was told. Then called one of the men back at the execution site and relayed his father's orders to bring in the bodies of the five dead men.

It was only a minute later that the plane slowed and maneuvered in what felt like a downward path. This proved to be true when the motion of the plane ceased and the door in which they'd entered unsealed with a hiss and rotated out and down.

All stood up. She motioned them to go first.

The plane had come to rest four feet above the roundabout driveway fronting on the main entrance to the mansion. It was floating on its paramagnetic cushion but the wing propellers still spun, giving off a hissing sound. The stairway had opened facing the front doors.

A dozen men were fanned out on each side of the doors. They were all armed, most with rifles or submachine pistols and all were obviously angry. Manuel ignored them and led the way to and through the doors. The armed men trailed the three of them in.

If Scarlett was concerned about the men at her back she did not show it.

A half dozen more men awaited them in the former ballroom. Manuel's father sat in his chair. He glowered at the woman as she came in behind Manuel and advanced to the edge of the dais. Manuel and Antonio faded off to either side of her, the latter a few feet behind the others.

"It is true?" Zaragoza said to Manuel.

"Yes, father. All five of them are dead."

"She must have cheated somehow."

"She walked into the brush and disappeared. She must have almost immediately gone to ground and hidden.

"Ricardo and his men started out after her five minutes later. As agreed. They were heavily armed-- Well, you know that. You saw them off."

"And then what happened?"

"They were careful. They walked in a line, side by side, close together, trailing her. Then they opened up the line. Maybe five feet, no more than ten, between them.

"She rose out of a pile of leaves. She killed two of them so fast they had not even fallen when she ran to the third and killed him. The next, Alberto, just barely got his gun up and firing before he was dead too. Ricardo also got shots off. Two. I'd have sworn he hit her dead center. But she wasn't hurt. She killed him then."

He dared not say that she done so in a way that made his death slow and agonizing.

"Is this true?" Zaragoza was obviously holding in his anger when he asked the woman that.

"Yes. You have fulfilled our bargain. I will leave you alone. Unless you abuse more of your women. Then I will return and kill all of you."

"Go."

She turned and walked away from the dais. The men, a dozen from outside and the half dozen from the inside, parted before her. Some watched her sullenly, several watched their boss.

She was nearing the exit to the room when Manuel saw with horror his father give a signal.

Every man there except for Manuel and Antonio began firing at the woman, continuous fire to tear her into hamburger.

She turned back. Stood as the weapons fired again and again. Unharmed. The firing became faster. Frantic.

Every weapon but one ran dry. This was one man firing a pistol. Then he ran dry.

The men stood stunned. A couple fumbled to reload their weapons with shaking hands.

"My turn," she said.

A fire seemed to kindle within her body. Red light broke out in spots from head to toe, grew larger, grew orange light within the spots. In seconds she was a pillar of fire in a vaguely human shape.

From behind her two huge curves folded upward, seemingly wings with bright white wing bones and bright golden skin. Each wing curved up and forward like an unfurling flower. At each bone tip was an eye-searing violet barb. The barbs curved further to point like fingers at some of the men in front of the creature.

Dazzling violet pulses flashed from the fingers. Men flared to brief violet cocoons of light. When they faded ashes floated down toward the floor. Of bones or weapons or any other item there was no sign.

Manuel threw an arm over his eyes to shut out the sight. He did not run. Running might catch her attention. And there was no place to go. He expected to die.

Long seconds passed. The light which his arm and closed eyes could not completely block went out. He opened his eyes and slowly let his arm slide downward.

Men knelt, heads down. Some praying, to God or perhaps to her. Or lay on their sides in tight balls. There were perhaps a dozen of them still alive.

Manuel jerked around to look for his father. Only a pile of ash in front of his seat remained. His chair was completely untouched.

"Manuel."

He turned slowly back toward the demon. She was back in her camouflage outfit with two sword hilts projecting above each shoulder.

"You are Chief now. I trust women will be well treated henceforth."

Suddenly his knees were weak.

"You-- You're not going to kill us? Or force us out of business?"

"Good lord, no. Whoring can never be forced out of business. The only thing that can be done is to ensure that whores are treated well."

Suddenly she was gone. Shortly a shriek rose outside and quickly faded into the distance. The demon and its chariot were gone.

<>

In the days following various government agencies communicated with each other, mostly via highly encrypted emails and hand-carried documents. The Witness Protection Agency relieved the South Beach Police Department of its care for the woman who'd been mutilated and nearly killed. The special agent who escorted the woman to the airport was a solidly built redhead in a business suit which did not hide that she had a submachine gun holstered under an arm.

At the South Beach Airport a private jet was waiting. When it took off it was followed by a black aircraft which was heavily armed. A hundred miles out the deadly machine peeled off and disappeared into the distance.

<>

In the air, after an excellent meal, the woman gave the fullest statement she could, of her attackers and what she knew of the organization of which she'd been a part. She was shown photographs of five dead men. Three she identified as her attackers.

The gory images of the dead men bothered her not at all.

The woman underwent breast surgery with which she was very happy. Not only did her nipples regain full function but she was able to negotiate some minor breast enhancements during surgery. Similar negotiations led to changes to the planned surgeries on her face.

She was given a new identity and certificates for the career she sought in gardening and floral businesses. A hefty trust fund allowed her to purchase such a business, a modest building but in a good location.

In the years afterward she sometimes thought that her attempted murder was the best thing that had ever happened to her.

Part 10 - Guardian

The South Beach episode was not the last time Karen meddled in crime-fighting, though usually her contributions were less direct. She sent anonymous tips to various police departments. She also consulted on security with more and more companies who feared they had been or might be targeted by spies, electronic or otherwise. She or her employees continued to capture court-dodgers. And her physical security wing grew to two dozen part- and a dozen full-time guards.

<>

She heard about the atrocity in Nigeria on the second day of February, well into her second year of dating Scott. They'd shared two New Year's Eves and now nearly shared each other's home, with clothing and other items at each place.

It was a Tuesday. He was away on business and she was on her balcony looking out over Beverly Hills. She was having her second cup of coffee while part of her enjoyed the Southern California spring and another part was skimming the InterWeb via Tiara.

Just before dawn a paramilitary force had attacked the small regional airport in the eastern Nigeria city of Gombe, a city of some quarter of a million people. The attack lasted three hours, then had been repulsed. The surviving force drove south and dispersed into the countryside.

It turned out that this had been a diversion. At the same time there had been an attack on a small college on the eastern side of the city run by a Sufi Islamic order. It mostly taught Western-style agricultural and botanical sciences plus some more general studies such as literature.

Several dozen soldiers had surrounded the campus and proceeded to slaughter every man they could find, machine-gunning them in their beds for the most part, though sometimes burning them to death inside buildings and shooting anyone who escaped.

Karen grimaced at that, quelling nausea.

Then they had raped all the women. The older women they also beat to death or nearly so after they raped them. Then they burned them.

Nausea from THAT could not be quelled. Her imagination, always good, had been enhanced by Tiara. Her stomach roiled and burned, the outsides of her arms and legs prickled with a bodily chill.

Then the women had been culled of the less attractive or the unruly, killing them with machine guns or beatings or hacking them with machetes.

Mission accomplished, they set fires to every structure and drove away with several dozen "brides" in several trucks, busses, and vans.

The coffee cup fell from her hand and Karen fell into the sky, instantly enveloped by Pegasus. She screamed at the sky, rage hot inside her.

Pegasus fled upward at twice the speed of sound, rocking all of Los Angeles with a shock wave. Ten miles up she accelerated to hypersonic velocities, crashing air aside so violently that she ionized air. Only a failsafe inside Pegasus kept her from jumping to a quarter of the speed of light. Even in the rarefied stratosphere that would have created an electromagnetic pulse so strong that Western civilization might have been wiped out.

At the top of the atmosphere she arced over eastward toward Africa. THEN she jumped to quarter-light speed.

The terrorists would find out from personal experience what it was like to burn alive.

By the time Karen reached African airspace her rage had cooled to an icy determination. And reason returned to her.

She had little doubt she could find and rescue the survivors of the attack, then wreak vengeance upon the terrorists. Nor would she have a problem seeking out the diversionary force no matter how much they split up and hid.

But that would simply be cutting off an arm of the terrorist movement. The Jihadi al Taher, the Purifying Jihadists, extreme even among Muslim extremists, would continue.

She began to think and plan.

The attacks had ended about eight hours ago. The kidnapping contingent, traveling on highways and roads perhaps 50 miles an hour, could have traveled 400 miles. But not west further into Nigeria.

Most likely it had been to the east. The "Purifiers" were known to headquarter in Cameroon somewhere. The spiritual head of the movement even had a small town on the shores of Lake Chad on the extreme northern edge of Cameroon where the country narrowed to twenty-something miles wide.

The highways and roads toward the kidnappers sheltering country zigzagged quite a bit. But even so the terrorists likely would be arriving at their base camp--right about now: 4:00 in the afternoon.

Africa from space was orange, beige, and brown on its northern half above Nigeria and Cameroon, green on its southern half. Karen looked into the memories of the various spy satellites which looked down at the territory. She found nothing useful. Africa was not very interesting to the powerful nations of the world. She could see only very broad images in the several spectra used by such satellites.

She lowered into the atmosphere to about ten miles height and tapped the Nigerian databases.

It had taken the country's authorities several hours to realize that the airport attack had been diversionary. But it was that attack they considered most worthy of spending resources. Only one helicopter and one light plane with surveillance equipment had flown east.

The helicopter had stopped at the various zigzag points on the eastward highways, usually at small cities or towns. The officer in charge of the search had asked the people there if they'd seen a group of travelers heading east who looked as if they might be the terrorists.

Only at the first was there much information. After that the quarry had split up into more innocuous travelers. Of them the big bus carrying the "brides" was the most conspicuous. The officer had tracked it to Mubi, a city of some 130,000 near the Cameroon border. Just beyond the city it had been abandoned. The women had been transferred to several vans, apparently. But the officer found no one who would admit having seen this.

At that the official search stalled. Poor Cameroon envied and hated the more populous Nigeria, one of the richest of the African countries. None of its citizens would say anything useful to the Nigerians, if they even bothered to talk at all.

But Karen knew where the women had been. It was time to use the super-advanced facilities available to her to hunt her prey directly.

Pegasus grew a small transparent globe with various spiky extrusions and sent it flying over the narrow northern part of Cameroon at about 30 miles height. There it saw in all spectra including gravitons. It began to make a detailed map of the area.

Meanwhile Karen lowered to the location of the abandoned bus and sent several invisible spybots into it. On the floor of the vehicle were bits of litter, mostly plastic wrappers of food. The kidnappers and kidnapped had eaten at least twice.

The spybots also had mechanical noses. These built up personal profiles from DNA from dandruff and other detritus of the human body. Including tears.

That last detail almost broke Karen's tight control of her emotions. She struggled with them for long moments.

Cool again she sent the small horde of spybots flying out of the bus where they spread out high and low to track the vehicles of the kidnappers.

It was easy for the first few miles. Her quarry had entered a narrow two-lane paved road off the main road which headed almost directly east toward Cameroon.

Karen swooped down to fly a hundred feet above the road, her swarm of spybots below and a bit ahead of her. The land around her turned from mostly green to mostly brown. Low hills rose on both sides, only lightly covered with vegetation, some green, most brown.

She passed several clusters of homes. Most of them had round stone walls with conical thatched roofs ending in a spike. These had doors painted green and blue and windows trimmed in the same colors. A few larger buildings were rectangular and made of metal.

Here and there were parked battered mini-pickup trucks and an occasional small tractor used for tilling the meager nearby fields of some low grain or vegetable plants. In each of the primitive demi-villages there were usually a few basic cell phones and an occasional smart cell phone. Tiara monitored them for ongoing or recent calls. None yielded useful information. The kidnappers were not here. Nor had those who lived here cared enough to talk about them.

A few miles further on she passed a small village with a general store in its center. It had one attached gasoline pump. The automated records from recent gasoline and food sales showed purchases which suggested the terrorists had stopped here.

The low hills receded behind her. She passed into Cameroon. There was no sign or other indication of the change from one nation to another.

Shortly the country road dead ended into a four-lane Cameroon highway running north and south. Traffic picked up, a mix of small cars and trucks, with the occasional larger bus or long-range hauler truck.

Karen lifted up to a half-mile height and paused to think.

There were three or four larger cities and several smaller cities within the half-hour drive she thought left to the terrorists. Both would provide places for them to live. But she thought they'd camp sooner and divvy up the young women to be parceled out to their new "husbands."

She lifted up a few miles higher and absorbed the data her spy sphere had observed. Then she banished the force-field construct back to nothingness. Tiara automatically matched the data with all the maps and photos already available and came up with a composite which she superimposed over the view below.

Four places were marked with big red Xs. She swooped down near the closest. Nothing. Up and then down again.

The second X marked a small city of about a thousand people. It sprawled halfway up a small hill and was fed by a major highway which cut through it. One- and two-storey shops lined each side of the highway. The houses on the hill were a bit upscale: larger houses with red-tile roofs and lawns greened by irrigation.

A spiral search around the city revealed the headquarters of a medium-sized farm of several buildings a couple of miles away at the end of a country lane. Flying low over the area Karen saw the head of the household in an interior yard speaking to a man with a long beard and an automatic rifle slung from one shoulder.

She listened to them from a few feet away. With Tiara's aid she understood the Fula language as easily as if she had been born to it. They were discussing the disposition of the people in the man's party into several houses and their feeding afterward. Karen could not tell whether the farm's owner was a sympathizer or had been coerced. Any of his anger or shame was too well hidden.

The conversation done, she rose up a few dozen feet to watch as the women were let out of several vans and herded into several houses, ones Karen's gravity radar showed had been emptied of any inhabitants. No men went into the houses, so Karen decided she needed not intervene to protect the captives from rape or other harm.

Hate burned inside her guts. She wanted to do what she'd originally thought to do: burn each of the terrorists to death in a slow conflagration, not the instant immolation she'd granted the South Beach gangsters. Or rampage through them, a human buzz saw which exploded bodies like watermelons. She wanted them to feel the horror and pain they'd visited upon others, then die.

But several concerns held her back. For one she wanted to protect the girls, as she thought of them, from harm, and seeing such carnage might harm them. Too, she wanted to prevent further terror attacks; mysterious deaths would not do that.

So she waited, suspended invisible in midair, ate a dinner which was brunch on her biological clock, and planned.

The thirty men settled in the courtyard or patio, mostly squatting or on cushions but a few in chairs brought from a house. They cleaned weapons and other gear and congratulated each other on their strike against the infidels.

The sun grew low and the blue sky took on a burnished tinge to the west. As shadows lengthened all around servants from the main house appeared bearing food and drink and eating utensils and low tables. The men set to with good appetite and conviviality.

As the meal began to wind down one of the men suggested they bring a virgin or three out and have some fun with them.

Karen tensed. But the leader shot down the idea. They would get money for the women. And delivering them would enhance their reputation with their leaders. All the rank-and-file agreed. Some men happily suggested to the loser several ways he could satisfy his urges. The use of farm animals was high on the list.

A fight almost broke out but the leader quickly quelled it.

Dinner took enough time for twilight to come upon the patio. Time for Karen's show.

<>

It began with errant gusts of wind too small to notice at first. Within minutes it was casting dust into the men's eyes. It quickly became a circling whirlwind. Drops of water pelted the men.

A brilliant lightning bolt crashed down from the clear sky and the wind quickly ceased. It took long moments before ringing ears could hear and dazzled eyes could see. They revealed a figure standing near one building a dozen feet away.

It was a tall black woman of generous proportions. Completely hairless, including her head. Randomly swirling veils of rainbow light barely clothed her body. Her nipples were huge, her sex blatant.

Patches of her skin shone red, restless patches which randomly expanded and contracted and moved. Within the red patches spots of orange and yellow and blue came and went.

All of the men jumped up. Several leveled weapons at the figure but were shouted down by the leader.

"What do you want?" he said loudly in Fula, then in English.

The figure said nothing but took a few steps closer. Her eyes were burning coals. They probed the crowd.

The leader repeated his question in English, then again in Fula and French.

The figure took two more steps. They took her a yard from the man who'd urged having fun with a girl.

In Fula she said, "You wanted to have fun?"

She lifted a hand. Fire leaped to the man. Engulfed in flames he began to scream, then tried to run. He got only a few steps before collapsing. He rolled on the ground, still screaming.

Rifles opened up, some at point-blank range. The woman noticed the bullets not at all. Not so the burning man. He jerked at each bullet impact then relaxed, dead, still burning. In moments only ashes remained of man and clothing and his rifle and everything else.

"Pity," she said. "He deserved a longer death. He wanders now in Kuzimu. Perhaps he will learn the errors of his life and ascend to Paradise. Most likely not."

One man, then two more ran forward and struck at her with their emptied rifles. The weapons clanked and clanged as they struck the figure for all the world as if it was made of stone or steel.

She shook her head from side to side. "Your urge to destroy will destroy you."

Suddenly the men became towers of flame. Heat thrown off by them struck the faces and bodies of the other men as if a sudden furnace door had opened before them. They shielded their eyes or turned away.

The heat ceased. Looking again toward the creature they saw three heaps of ashes added to the one before her. She gestured and the heaps swirled up in tiny dust devils and blew away.

The leader fell to his knees. He raised shaking hands.

"Spare us, Goddess!"

"Why should I? You have raped, tortured, and killed."

"Only to purify the world!"

"An honorable goal. But you used evil means."

"Teach us!"

"You must teach yourselves. For that you need humility."

The men's boots and clothing and weapons and all else dissolved into air. The hair all over their bodies disappeared.

The goddess rose into the air and turned toward the sheds and small buildings which housed the captives. Alighting in front of the nearest she knocked on the door, then rose in the air again to knock on each of the other doors. At each she called out: "Come out! You are free!"

First hesitantly and then in groups of two or three or more the young women came out. Most were clad in grey robes reaching below their knees, some robes sleeveless and some with short sleeves. On their heads were scarves or head bands, on their feet sandals.

One girl, a little taller than the rest and more robust, spoke in Fula.

"Where are the men?"

The goddess waved behind and to one side.

"The snakes are fangless and skinless now. Forget about them. I'm taking you home."

The women--little more than girls--peered at her and then at the men in the distance. A few grinned, but more as if baring teeth than expressing humor. A few still had hesitant or fearful looks. More were curious or impressed at the sturdy, mysterious, dangerous reality before them.

"Who are you?" said the tall girl.

"I have many names. Call me Oya. Come with me if you want to go home."

The large woman turned and walked away. Though her figure was bulky she moved with easy grace.

Some girls hesitated, looking at each other. The tall girl walked behind with certain steps. First one, then more followed, until all the sixty-some women came in lines and side by side, some holding hands.

The woman walked out of the rough square formed by all the buildings, past the smaller ones and the big one where the owner and his family lived. Most peered at the naked men in the center of the square. Some of them peered back. It was lost on none of the women that the men covered their groins and looked on with fear.

The small band wended their way around a large barn and an open-air garage of farm equipment and vehicles and into a grassy field. Ahead of them a couple of hundred feet away was a mosque.

Or so its general shape was, two stories tall and square with four narrow cone-topped spires at the corners resembling the towers from which calls to prayer were issued. The walls and roofs seemed made of gold. A large flat dome covered much of the top.

As they approached it two tall doors opened outward. Inside could be seen a ballroom or assembly room floored with a checkerboard of black and white tiles.

Some hesitated at the doors, but not long. Inside they stopped and bunched up behind their leader. A few moved to stand on each side of that tall young woman.

The goddess turned to them.

"Go through the doorways in front of you. Place your clothing on the tables on the walls beside the tubs of water. Bathe and dry yourself off with the towels on the benches. Then dress in your clothes again. They will be clean by the time you are finished. Then come through the next doorways."

She vanished.

Again their leader hesitated not all. Nor did her four companions, as they now seemed.

The doorways were doorless and tall with arched tops. Large tubs of white porcelain were placed side by side with several feet of distance between them and a bench of the same material in the spaces between. Each bench was piled with folded white towels.

The water steamed gently. When the women stepped carefully into the liquid it was very warm but not uncomfortably so. The water effervesced very slightly and dirt and stains quickly dissolved. Sore muscles eased.

The tubs were big enough for four women with some distance between. The girls soon fell to chatting about their sudden new circumstances. A few even laughed and splashed each other. Most submerged and scrubbed their hair once the leader had done so.

The leader enjoyed the experience with the others, making the acquaintance of her four acolytes, as they seemed to be, if she did not already know them. But she was the first to rise and step out of the tub. She went to the nearest bench and lifted a towel. It was large, thick, and knubbly. It soaked up water quickly as she scrubbed herself.

Suddenly she stopped and stared at her knee, ran a finger over it then rubbed it with a hand.

"Look!" she said to a nearby friend. "I had a bad scar here. It's gone. And my knee is no longer sore."

That woman looked, then looked at one of her arms, then at a thigh.

"It's the same with me! My scars are gone too."

This set off an orgy of self-discovery. All reported healing of one sort or another. But eventually their discoveries were exhausted and they turned to dressing themselves.

There were discoveries here too. Not only was the clothing they'd placed on the tables dry but it was made of a finer material, a bit thicker yet nonetheless cooler.

Their sandals were also changed. They appeared little different at first glance but had become something closer to moccasins. The material was thinner too. It flexed easily but one girl, the youngest of them all but the best student at the school, discovered an interesting property. When tapped the bottom felt as hard as stone.

"Halima," she said to the tall girl. "I can't test this here, but I think if I struck this with a hammer or a knife it would protect me."

The young woman fingered her dress, then struck herself lightly on her belly with a fist. Then she struck much harder.

"Ow!" She flexed her hand and shook it.

"I think all our clothing is much better at protecting us."

Halima thought a moment.

"Let's see if the Goddess will tell us, Rifkatu." She turned away from the rest of the girls and walked toward the second set of doorways. Her astute companion was scarcely a half step behind her.

The black-and-white checkerboard tile flooring continued into the next room. It contained three long oval tables sitting side by side, each covered by a white table cloth. Chairs were on each side. On one side of the room was a long buffet with bowls of food and pitchers of drink. There were also plates, glasses, and eating ware, all of white porcelain or something similar.

Seeing no Goddess, Halima called on the rest of the young women to eat. She went to the buffet and led by example.

In the following hour the young women became acquainted or better acquainted with each other. There was much discussion of their changed situation, and even some laughter, despite all that had happened to them and to those victims left behind.

When they were essentially done a bright cocoon of white light appeared at one end of the middle of the three tables. Standing within it was the large woman Oya. The light vanished.

"Hello," she said in her strong contralto. "Sit down. Finish eating."

Everyone had jumped up at her appearance. They sat, some more slowly than others. So did the goddess, in a newly appeared seat at the head of the middle three tables, the one furthest from the baths.

This put Halima on her right hand, Rifkatu on her left, and Halima's three other lieutenants at their right and left hands--all positions Halima had ordered.

"I am glad," Oya said, "that all of you seem to be much recovered. You have not perfectly recovered. It will take you time to do so.

"I must tell you a few facts. Then I will take you home.

"You are cured of all your ills and will never get sick again. You will recover from hurts much faster, and think better. You are not changed otherwise.

"Your clothing has been improved. You can give it away or sell it, but its special qualities will only work when you wear it. It will protect you better than before, against heat and cold and wetness. And also against bullets and knives. This includes the parts of you which seem bare, such as your arms or ankles.

"You can also change its size, tighter or looser, shorter or longer. Also its colors and designs.

"Yes, like that, Halima. But please wait to experiment further. I have more to say.

"Beside you on the table you will see a smart phone. It will only work for you. Not for others who try to use it. It will let you access a bank account which has been opened for you. Each of you now has a good deal of money in that account. Use it however you wish, foolishly or wisely, that is up to you."

She was silent for a few minutes while each of the women explored the phone and its uses. They were very ordinary, as was the appearance of the phone. It appeared to be a moderately but not greatly expensive popular brand. But when a few women swapped phones to test her statement that it would only work for its owner the assertion proved true.

"Are there any questions?"

Little Rifkatu was quick to raise a hand.

"What do you want from us?"

"I did not do this to buy your service. I only wish you to live your life as happily as you can contrive."

"Why did you not save all of us at the school?"

"I only learned of your ordeal after it happened."

"Shouldn't a goddess know everything?"

"The greatest god may know everything. Lesser beings, even ones greater than human, do not."

There were other questions, a few naïve or silly. The woman dealt with all of them seriously, though she said she did not wish to answer some. Finally she stood.

"It's time to go home. Come with me."

She walked away from the tables. Through yet another set of the arched doorways they came to an empty room. Behind them the doorways disappeared, leaving a blank wall behind. A few of the girls looked troubled by the disappearance but their concern faded by the sudden appearance at the far end of the otherwise featureless room of tall windows. The women came to stand looking out. The room was wide enough for all of them to see out though they had to stand close together.

Outside and below was the blue ball of the planet, Africa in its center. Most of their continent directly below and to the right, eastward, was dark with land-bound stars showing where cities and towns lay. Far to the left, westward, white clouds swirled over the day-lit Atlantic Ocean.

There were gasps and sighs from many of the girls. A few cringed back from the airless abyss just a few feet in front of them. Then slowly they returned to their places by the window.

"Oya," said Rifkatu, "could we go all around the world before we go home?"

"Yes. It will have to be a quick tour. We should not take you home late. Your families are already very sad because of losing you."

Slowly then more quickly the planet below them rose up toward them. It began to spin so that they traveled further into the night side. Some of the girls pointed out various cities as they passed over them, correcting each other's guesses.

Rifkatu, on the goddess's left hand, said to her, "We are very poor, aren't we?" She meant how few lights showed below.

"Yes, dear, I'm afraid you are. But that will change. It's already changing. You've come far in the last few dozen years."

Faster spun the world below them. Soon they were over the Middle East. The more geographically aware pointed out the names of the cities where lights clustered. Then came India and China. Near Japan the night ended and blue ocean came into view, the mighty Pacific.

The ship they were on, as it must be, rose higher and moved faster.

Then, as North America came near, it lowered again. Much lower. Soon they were only a few miles up and the Los Angeles metroplex came into view.

Miles upon miles of buildings passed below. Automobiles in the millions, they must be, flowed over highways and streets.

Rifkatu murmured to Halima, "It must be about 1:00 in the afternoon below."

"You are correct," said the goddess.

The spaceship rose higher and the world below spun faster. Soon they were over New York City and lowered once again to view the city. Low enough so that someone pointed out the Statue of Liberty.

Higher again they rose. The Atlantic spun below them. Next the ship lowered to fly over London. Many of the young women were knowledgeable about the city, though none had ever visited it. Nigeria had long been owned by England and English was the official language of the country. Most schools used textbooks written in English and geography courses included all of the British Empire.

The ship rose again and began to move directly south.

"Attention, everyone," said the goddess.

"We'll be arriving at Bauchi Park in ten minutes. I have issued calls to all your parents telling them to meet us there. Leave this place when we arrive. I will stay nearby to watch over you till each of you leaves for home, though you will not see me."

There was much excitement at that. A few minutes later a few of the young women came up to her. One of them spoke to her.

"My parents do not have a phone. How will they know to meet us?"

"Do not worry. I have made arrangements for that as well."

The women waited in mounting excitement as they watched France and Spain then the Mediterranean Sea pass below them, then Algeria and Niger before Nigeria began to rush up below them. Then Gombe, alight in the late-evening night.

There were shouts as the park was recognized, a large mostly rectangular expanse of green with a soccer field in one corner. Floodlights all around the field came on as the ship sank downward to land on the green.

At that instant the windows in front of the goddess and the girls disappeared. As did all the rest of ship. There was a slight jolt as everyone dropped an inch or so onto the grass.

They recovered their balance and gazed around. The grass was damp from a shower earlier in the day and the air was humid but the sky was clear. The flood lights shining down on them made the green of the soccer field even brighter.

The young women began to spread out. A few moved slowly toward the edge of the field beyond which the parking lot lay but slowed as the lights of vehicles began to appear in the lot. Car doors slammed and adults ran or walked toward the girls. The two groups quickly merged as girls and parents and their siblings and other relatives found each other. The noise level rose.

Halima and Rifkatu stayed together as they met their families. After greeting their families they looked around. The goddess was nowhere to be seen, but both were sure she was nearby, invisible. Halima spoke loudly to a spot behind her and upward a bit where she imagined Oya floated.

"Thank you! I will never forget you!"

A passing breeze caressed her face and she smiled and turned toward her family.

Shortly the crowd began to diminish. Within fifteen minutes only a handful of girls remained. Only two or three appeared anxious however. The goddess had said she'd wait.

Finally only one girl remained.

"Goddess? Oya?"

The woman appeared in front of her.

"Don't worry. They are coming. They were with friends and had the furthest to come. I'm with you."

She put an arm around the young woman, a solid warm presence. The girl's face relaxed.

True to Oya's word it was only a few more minutes when a new set of headlights appeared in the lot, two sets in fact.

"Go to them, dear."

The girl stood on tiptoe to kiss the woman's cheek then she was running.

<>

For the next several days Karen was busy following the data she'd harvested off the kidnappers phones before she'd destroyed them with all their other possessions. She gained more data from the spybots she'd embedded in the terrorists bodies every time one of them made a call on a borrowed or stolen phone.

Most of the times she did some variation of the actions she'd taken with the first group, masquerading as a goddess from West African mythology. She killed a few more with furnace-hot fire but all of them instantly. Burning that one kidnapper slowly to death was an angry action that afterward had made her sick to her stomach and would give her nightmares for weeks to come.

But for now she slept very little. Until the day before she was to confront the leader of the Jihad al Taler leader. She made sure she got a full night's sleep because she wanted to make sure she handled it with all her faculties about her.

<>

It was early morning when the goddess Oya settled before the largest building of several near the shore of Lake Chad on the narrow northern tip of Cameroon. Only a few miles to either side was the eastern border of Nigeria and the western border of Chad.

It was raining heavily. The yellow buildings were drab in color and the small surface imperfections of their sides seemed magnified.

No one was out in the rain. Penetrating gravitar showed only a half dozen people anywhere in or near the large Jihadist building or the rest of the village. It normally must hold two or three hundred people.

The receiving room of the large building, a two-story near-mansion, held four of those people. One of them was the Ayatollah of the Purifying Jihad, Mohammad Shirazi.

A crash as of a nearby lightning strike shook the building. Moments later a bright cocoon of light appeared before the elaborate chair of the shrunken little man who led the Purifiers. All eyes teared from the brightness and turned away.

When the light disappeared the goddess Oya stood in its place. Rainbow veils swirled restlessly about her ample body, hardly hiding her ample bosom and sex. Her black skin showed restless spots of lava-like fire, red and orange and blue. The spots came and went in seeming randomness.

The woman just stood and looked at the old man. He stared grimly back. The old woman standing beside his chair who might be his wife was fearful. So was the man of middle age who seemed to be some sort of aide. The big young man in a soldierly khaki uniform behind the old man's chair assumed a stolid appearance. He kept his hands well away from the pistol on his belt, however.

"Well," said the Ayatollah in Fula. "Are you just going to stand there and try to frighten us?"

"Would that change your preaching of theft, torture, rape, and murder?"

"You may send me to Kuzimu for all I care. But I will not retreat from righteousness."

"Then learn humility."

Oya gestured and his clothing and all his bodily hair fell to dust.

He screeched and sought to cover his groin. The woman gasped and threw the shawl upon her head over his privates. The guard grabbed his pistol butt but quickly jerked his hand far out to the side.

"Your hair will never grow back. All clothing upon your body will rot to stinking dust. From this time everyone who comes near you will be sickened. When you die you will not rise to Paradise but sink to Kuzimu."

The woman and the tall man near the old man began to retch, the man violently enough to vomit. The soldier further away grimaced and moved a dozen feet further still.

The goddess vanished in another bright light. Moments later thunder crashed and the building shook worse than before.

"How was your trip?" said Scott as he took her lone suitcase from the L. A. Airport luggage carousel.

"Oh, OK," said Karen as Scott extended its pull-along handle and they began walking toward the exit.

In the shaded driveway in front of the terminal a limousine waited. He ushered her into the rear passenger seat and went to the back of the vehicle to place her suitcase in the trunk popped open by the driver. He opened the opposite passenger door and entered. The driver peered into his rear-view mirror to ensure both his passengers were seat-belted in and smoothly entered the outgoing lanes.

"You don't sound too positive."

Karen mustered a smile for him.

"It was a tiring trip. But in the end I got everything done that the customer wanted. It's just the time there is eight hours later. For me it's late evening and I've been going to bed early."

"Well, I hope you're up for dinner before you crash."

Her smile was broader. "I can always eat."

Scott had long ago adjusted to the fact that she ate as much as he did even though he was half again her weight. He simply nodded.

At his home a dinner awaited, cooked by a chef brought in especially for the occasion. Karen smiled little and answered questions about her trip with monosyllables or inconsequentials. Finally Scott addressed the fact.

"Your trip wasn't just business, was it? Or did something happen?"

Karen was silent for long moments. She could not meet his eyes. Then she did.

"Yes. Something happened."

"Are you OK?"

"I am yes. Physically. But I'm sick at heart about something."

"Tell me about it."

"No. I'm sorry. But I can't." She looked away from him.

He looked at her for long moments. Then he stood and walked around the table to hug her.

Or tried to. She shrank away from him and he halted, pity and anger warring upon his face. He turned and returned to his seat.

He took a sip of a drink he tasted not at all.

"I've sometimes wondered if you ever really left government service. You're absent without explanations. Or slight ones. There are things you never talk about.

"I'm guessing you're a CIB agent, doing what you did in Afghanistan. Or something along those lines. But I don't care. I love you. I want to be with you."

Karen took a deep breath and slowly let it out. She gazed at him. Her heart ached and her eyes burned with unshed tears.

He was such a good man. He had to hide behind the distant façade every celebrity must cultivate and every boss must present to those who worked for him. But he did many small acts of kindness, automatically and sometimes anonymously, for he cared about people.

He deserved someone better than her. Someone kinder. Someone who did not kill almost as a reflex and always for a reason. Someone who did not have to hide herself and her actions from him. Someone who could not be utterly cruel. Memories of the screaming burning man she'd killed in Cameroon haunted her sleep.

The words which came husky for her throat were twisted with pain.

"You're right. Not about specifics. And it's gotten to the point where--" She had to swallow. "I can't be with you anymore."

She got up and ran to the door. Outside a black sedan with darkened windows waited. She fled down the steps and a rear passenger door opened. She jumped inside and the car drove away.

Scott was left in his doorway looking after her.

<>

The next day her suitcase and briefcase were delivered to her parent's door. A day later all her possessions at Scott's house.

<>

That night she ate with her parents. Her mother pushed her to talk about what had happened.

"I won't tell you the details. Just say it was a bad one."

"So bad you broke up with Scott."

"Honey, don't push her."

Her mother rounded on her husband but let go her anger.

"She should talk about it."

"Maybe. Probably. But talking doesn't always fix things. Time will."

Her mother twisted her mouth.

"I don't like it." But she said nothing more, just got up and enveloped her daughter in a hug. After a moment Karen's father hugged both of them.

<>

Karen floated a hundred miles above Los Angeles as the world turned toward night. Directly below her the California coast was settling into darkness. The Pacific was a beautiful blue in front of her, to the west. White clouds decorated the expanse. Several patches near her were single clouds like polka dots decorating the sea. Further westward was a long crescent swirl of an approaching weather front. On the farthest curve of the Earth a golden oval in the blue ocean was the reflection of the setting sun.

Maybe she needed a vacation. Yes, that was it. But where on Earth should she go?

No place with very many people. She was weary of all their problems, so many caused by their pettiness, narrow thinking, selfishness, and outright cruelty. A mountain peak? A desert island? A deep forest?

The crescent moon a quarter of the sky above the horizon caught her eye.

She'd only visited the Moon once. Its barrenness had not appealed to her. Now it did.

A thought and Pegasus morphed the space plane he'd formed around her into an interplanetary yacht, twice as long and roomier and more armored against the rigors of super-fast travel.

A deep hum grew louder and higher until it was a soprano shriek that briefly stabbed her ears until silence returned. The powerful engines of the super-advanced spacecraft leaped it to a quarter of the speed of light in an instant. Stars and the Moon shifted from white to bluish white. The Moon rushed toward her.

Five seconds brought her to the satellite. There was another hum which rose to another shriek and Pegasus was floating a hundred miles above the Moon.

Karen gazed on the grey and battered curve of the satellite. She supposed to a scientist the sight was interesting. To her it was boring. It certainly didn't soothe her depression.

What was Venus like? Pegasus found it in the blackness and told her it was almost a quarter of the way around the Sun from Earth. It would take her about a half hour to get there.

Go, she told him. Again there was the hum and the shriek, then silence.

For the next half hour Karen read from the Galactic Encyclopedia inside Tiara. The entry on Venus went on for what would be dozens of pages in a printed book. Many of the terms had links to other entries. Most of those she ignored.

One fact she found very interesting. There were two versions of the Encyclopedia: her private very complete version and a much smaller version suitable for release to Earth's general public.

She puzzled a bit about that. Did her biological parents expect her to come out of the closet someday as an alien? And then to give the public version to the people of Earth?

She quickly shrugged off the questions; she had no way to answer them. She returned to her study of Venus.

Soon the planet loomed up before her, then instantly floated serenely still after the usual sound effects. Coming up from directly behind in the planet's orbit she saw it half lit by the sun. One side was a white pearl, the other side a darkness a bit deeper than the interstellar night beyond with its pinpricks of far-off stars.

She sipped the last of a cup of coffee flavored to her taste, then released the cup. It did not fall in the artificial gravity of the super spaceship. It vanished, transmuted back to air.

The sight was even more boring than the moon, though the pearly glow was lovely. She sent Pegasus plunging into the eternal cloud cover of the planet.

A few miles up she dropped below the grey overcast and Pegasus slowed to hover.

The undersides of the clouds showed some bumps and differences in color, but only in shades of grey. The land below was smoother than that of the moon, its surface protected from meteors by atmosphere. But it was not featureless. There were hills and valleys of brown, grey, and beige.

Find me a volcano.

Pegasus obeyed. The planet whirled beneath her. Though she did not hear it, she knew the spacecraft left shock waves behind as the craft flew at hypersonic speeds, not worrying about bothering anyone with thunderous sound effects. Nor did she hear anything when Pegasus stopped and the thunder caught up to her.

The volcano was everything one might expect, a tall cone among several others, its top and sides split and red-hot lava trickling downward. The liquid pooled on one side and spilled out of the pool to trail snake-like away into the distance.

She had Pegasus hover a dozen feet up near the river of fire. She stood, the comfortable easy chair under her vanishing. A door opened in one side of the spaceship and she floated up and out into the open.

The view around her was unblocked by the edges of the viewing window inside Pegasus, but it was just as perfectly clear. She floated down to stand on the river bank.

Underneath her soles she felt some minor bumps but not the searing heat of the planet's surface.

She looked all around and above her. There Pegasus floated, a featureless finless dart the size of a jet airliner hovering a dozen feet in the air, its grey skin tinted red by the light of the lava flows. The grey clouds above her were also red lit. Karen turned back to the river and began to walk along the bank.

It felt like a walk along any dry riverbed back on Earth. Her weight was about 90 % what it would be back home but she didn't feel any different. The air did feel a bit like molasses to move through but it was only noticeable because she thought about it. The temperature was comfortable inside Suit though she knew it was several hundred degrees hotter, literally hot as Hell.

As she walked she began to notice that on the ground were seemingly random clusters of small cauliflower-like plants which at first looked like stones but on careful examination were bushes with tightly furled leaves.

The ground shook beneath her. She stopped. A spectacular yellow fountain burst from the top of the volcano. She could see boulders and stones and dust lift into the air. A quick question to Tiara returned the answer that any missiles would bounce off her and Pegasus's shields. Seconds later the sound of the explosion reached her. Tiara told her that without her shield it would have burst her ear drums and killed her.

She was as safe here as back home: completely safe. In fact, she could go to the Sun's surface or to the frigid comets which swung around that orb as far out as halfway to the nearest star and feel at home. Anywhere in or near the solar system, she was safe.

Except perhaps near Saturn. She'd learned from the Encyclopedia years ago that around it were many dozens of invisible subspace gateways. Through them space ships could travel many times faster than the speed of light to other interstellar locations. And hundreds of ships did every year.

It was presided over by a computer which had been there for millions of years. The computer had unimaginably powerful weapons which let it keep all the travelers safe. It also kept out of the "subways" travelers who were dangers to other travelers and to the inhabitants of the solar system to which Saturn was home.

Karen lifted into the air and turned toward her space ship.

<>

It took Karen a little over five hours to travel to Saturn. She spent the first hour or so studying the Encyclopedia's information on the planet. The most interesting information was that its upper air was inhabited by an ancient and very wise race. They were flying things shaped somewhat like the sting rays of Earth's oceans but several miles wide. And their bodies were more like balloons than solid bodies.

"Do they know about humans?" Karen asked Tiara. The information wasn't in the parts of the Encyclopedia she'd read.

Her answer was not in words, but a link which pointed to another part of the Encyclopedia. The short answer was Yes, but they were not interested in primitives, which even the super-advanced Confederation humans were to them.

Also interesting was that there were several hotels for aliens buried under the surface of one of Saturn's moons. Some of the ships stopped near Saturn for a while so travelers could spend some time in one of them. They did so for all sorts of reasons, including shopping and relaxation and conferences.

"Is Earth safe from them? From tourist types and hunters of native keepsakes and fauna and so on?"

Yes. The guardian computer would turn back any aliens traveling further than a certain distance from the planet. Besides, the aliens were from advanced civilizations most of whom had no interest in primitive Earth.

"I have to wonder that Earthly astronomers and space probes could miss all the spaceships traveling between portals or the hotels."

The viewers, human or mechanical, would have to be looking at exactly the right place at exactly the right time. Also, some evidence HAD been seen: gravitational ripples in the orbiting ice crystals which made up most of the spectacular rings of Saturn. But their cause was assumed to be made by the tidal effects from the several dozen satellites.

Next she studied the subspace subway system and its invisible immaterial computer manager and guardian. Not nearly as much information on them was in the Encyclopedia, even the full one rather than the abbreviated one suitable for Earthly natives.

She was about to spend the rest of the trip in sleep when Pegasus alerted her.

"We're nearing an asteroid which might interest you."

"Oh?"

In some three thousand years its orbit would intersect with Earth. It was big enough to extinguish all life on the planet. But it was unlikely to.

"Why?"

Earth alone would very likely be far enough advanced technically to protect the planet. But it would also surely be part of the Confed by then, and THEY could give the protection.

"I don't like to take the chance. Can you deflect or destroy it?"

Pegasus's weapons were advanced enough to take out entire stellar armadas of warships. It could certainly handle an asteroid.

Karen could have sworn the spaceship's answer was smug. Though it was silly to think a mere machine had emotions.

"Best to destroy it. Would you show me what it looks like first?"

The image was of a battered grey boulder shaped like a potato. It spun slowly on two axes.

"Do it."

Nothing happened to the image.

"*What happened?"*

The weapon used acted many times faster than the speed of light. The asteroid HAD been destroyed. But it was six light-seconds away, more than a million miles of distance.

Karen waited the six seconds. But the image still did not change.

"Now what?"

"You expected explosions? Flashes of light? It has been turned into gravel and dust which even thousands of years can't weld back together. It will expand and spread too far apart to be a threat."

Damn it. He DID sound smug. Her machines had been developing emotions or something like them in the years she had owned them.

She mentally shrugged and lay back in her easy chair. It morphed into a bed beneath her.

<>

A soft chime woke Karen. She swam up out of sleep. When she was alert enough Pegasus told her they were two light-minutes from the giant planet. Meaning, she drowsily realized, in eight minutes she'd be in the presence of a computer with near-godlike powers.

A shock went through her. It could swat her like a mosquito!

She sat up then stood up in one desperate motion. Her skin felt as if it had been splashed with ice water. Her breath stopped, then restarted with a gasp. Her heart pounded so hard it seemed as if her chest would explode.

She'd forgotten what fear felt like in the years since her eighteenth birthday and receiving the gifts which made her super-powerful and nearly invulnerable.

She collapsed back into Peg's instantly materialized virtual pilot's chair. She forced herself to take a deep breath.

Her heart rate eased toward normal levels and the pressure inside her chest eased. Reason returned to her.

"What will it do when it sees us?"

Pegasus replied that it had been "seeing" them since they passed beyond Jupiter's orbit.

"What will it do when we get close to Saturn?"

He did not know. Nor did Tiara have that information in her databanks. Suit had no opinion either, but then it had less need to think about anything beyond protecting and serving her immediate physical needs.

The only way to find out was to slowly approach Saturn and let whatever happened happen.

Maybe she should turn back.

<>

Return to the swamp of despair she had left behind? She'd rather die.

Surely the immense computer would simply erase her, not kill her slowly.

Hmm.

The eight minutes passed. Then came the sound effects she expected: the low deep hum rising in volume and pitch to a sudden shriek, then silence. The stars ahead of her instantly shed their blue tinge.

Ahead a tiny pearl grew in size. Its famous rings seemed to materialize and tilt into existence as their straight-on approach curved upward above the plane of the solar system.

At first Saturn's size grew quickly. Then it's seeming expansion slowed. Pegasus was slowing, slowing more. Until he stopped.

Saturn now filled half the blackness ahead of her. The Sun, behind

Karen, made it a huge glowing presence. The planet's pearl-like glow was modulated by bands of darker and lighter material. The rings around the planet at first appeared to be two solid circlets separated by a small gap, the inner ring the brighter. Then Pegasus increased the resolution of the image. Karen could see that the two rings were actually several smaller rings. And that a third much dimmer ring spun outside them.

Karen waited for something to happen. Nothing did. Long moments passed.

Her heart rate slowed further till she was calm.

Nothing happened still.

GUARDIAN. The booming word from something so much larger than her filled the insides of Pegasus.

Except that was only her first impression. Her heart, instantly sped up, quickly dropped back to normal as nothing else happened and as she tried to understand what had just been "said" to her.

It was not a sound but more a thought inside her head. Its meaning grew as she tried to remember what had been said.

Someone or something thought of itself as a guardian, of Saturn and the subspace subway station around it and a huge globe of space around that as far as Jupiter's distance. And it also thought of her as a fellow guardian. The guardian of Earth and its people.

Her immediate reaction was to object to the idea. Then it grew from a nonsense idea to a puzzling possibility. Was that why she had been sent to Earth?

She knew parenthood in the Confederation was an almost sacred activity. Immortals could have children only rarely, so they were very precious. More than a thousand years of debate and careful experiment had evolved parenthood to the point where only the most mature and dedicated were allowed to embark upon it. Children were brought up with much love and joy and carefully moderated discipline. Families remained families for centuries and millennia, slowly growing to hundreds and thousands of people with ever-more distant connections.

For any child to be taken out of that kind of family and sent to a primitive planet must have been done only with great reluctance and pain and for a very good reason.

This didn't mean she WAS a guardian. But it meant something.

Maybe she should just accept the idea and see what happened.

Whatever the reason it was not to be a self-pitying drama queen.

She acknowledged the computer: *"Guardian."*

It had waited with infinite patience. Or maybe only a microscopic part of the immense mind had. It answered her now, with thoughts rather than words, though she interpreted them as words.

WHY ARE YOU HERE? HOW CAN I HELP YOU (WITHIN THE CONFINES OF MY DUTIES)?

Hmm.

"I am expanding my understanding of reality. May I tour this area? May I enter the...hospitality hall?"

YOU MAY. YOU WILL NEED A GUIDE.

A silver candle with butterfly wings appeared in the air a meter in front of her. Though that was only the first impression. A few seconds of looking at it showed more details. Which she would have to examine later more closely.

"Thank you."

IF THERE IS NO MORE I WILL LEAVE YOU. CALL TO ME WHENEVER YOU NEED MORE WAYS I CAN HELP YOU (WITHIN THE CONFINES OF MY DUTIES).

"I will. Goodbye."

GOODBYE

Then somehow she knew that a presence was gone.

She looked at the candle. Perhaps it looked back.

But she saw no eyes. The body of the candle did look like creamy wax but there was no detail. The slightly glowing head was just the rounded top end of the cylinder. It was matched by a non-glowing rounded bottom end.

The wings had more detail. Each wing had two oval lobes of lacy material with a rainbow of colors from the blue end of the spectrum. She saw swirls and crescents and patches of color which blended into each other at their edges.

"Hello."

"Hello ugly alien."

"Hey. No insults."

"That was not an insult. It was merely a random esthetic judgment designed to evaluate your emotional responses."

"A machine with an attitude and a nasty mouth."

"Oh! Now that WAS an insult. I am not a machine."

"What are you?"

"An intelligent organism, of course. From a civilization far more advanced than yours. Now, enough pleasantries. What do you want to do?"

"I am curious about the subspace system and its portals. Can you tell me about them? My references are limited."

"I only have a working knowledge. The tunnels lead to other portals far away. You fly your spaceship into them and emerge minutes or hours later in another stellar system."

She asked it more questions and it answered her.

To use a portal you first consulted the Catalog, which seemed to be part of the Guardian computer, about destinations. This seemed to be a limited sort of encyclopedia. As a test, she thought at it and browsed through a half-dozen very different destinations. The information was fairly generic, more a quick identification than any sort of tour guide.

You selected a destination, then consulted the Scheduler and made a reservation for a particular destination and a seconds-long window in a particular portal. You waited a thousand miles or so away from the portal. The time arriving, you flew into it at a set speed. And that was it.

"What does it feel like to travel inside? Can you see out?"

"It just feels as it always does in your preferred environment. And if you have a window you can see out. But there's nothing to see but darkness."

Hmm.

"Can I visit Saturn's inhabitants?"

"Only the top one. The interior species are not welcoming. And the top one is not interested in anyone up here."

Tiara volunteered that she had very complete information about Saturn's species any time Karen wanted to consult it. The information included visuals so she could "travel" in a virtual environment.

"Oh," said Moth (the name Karen had given it). "You have a much smarter you inside You. I should have known. The outside You is so primitive."

Karen ignored the "random esthetic judgment designed to evaluate her emotional responses" and asked if she could visit the hospitality hall.

"Yes. But you have to leave your spaceship in the docking area."

Karen ignored the caveat and asked for directions. At this Moth flipped from a "standing" position to a "flying" position with its head pointing toward the image of Saturn on the spaceship's transparent window in front of Karen. It began to give her and Pegasus instructions.

The spacecraft moved "down" and in toward Saturn. Within minutes Karen saw a tiny grey dot in the starscape. It quickly resolved into a round cratered moon. A dip into Tiara's memory revealed it was Rhea, the second largest moon of Saturn.

Pegasus lowered toward a large whitish splotch with rays splayed out to each side of it. As he got nearer Karen "heard" a rapid back-and-forth conversation between him and something else. From Tiara she learned that he was getting landing instructions from a traffic computer.

Suddenly a round opening appeared in the ground. It was dark inside but Pegasus could "see" with gravitar. He settled into a cradle which Karen could make out when she tapped into his sensor center. There was a barely perceptible impact and her weight went way down.

"You are now enclosed in an atmosphere." Moth said. "We can leave your ship."

Pegasus opened a door in his side and Karen followed Moth through, moving very carefully in the low gravity until the hospitality center gave her an approximation of Earth's gravity. She stopped and looked around.

A dim light illuminated the area around her. On one side was the large bulk of Pegasus, as big as a jet passenger aircraft back on Earth.

Suddenly he shrank to his usually rounded brick state.

"What?!" shrieked Moth.

"Don't get your knickers in a twist, organism. Don't you know anything about force-field machines?"

Moth had darted fifty feet away and flipped back into an "upright" posture. His wings were a bright red.

"Hmmph," the entity said and flipped flat into flight mode. "Come along."

Karen followed him with Pegasus close behind and above her along a wide causeway toward a wall which contained tall arched doorways. Beyond them was a mellow yellow glow.

As she walked she glanced to the left and right. For a long way in each direction dimly lit spaceships rested. Most were a good deal larger than Pegasus had been. In the far distance one truly titanic ship was docked. Her gravitar resolved even more craft further in each direction.

Approaching the nearest doorway she had Suit adopt a fashionable Parisian outfit: black leggings ending in black modestly heeled half-boots, blue pleated A-line skirt, lavender blouse, and dark blue short jacket. She had it braid her hair up into a chignon bun. She had Tiara adjust her makeup to a simple pattern with pale pink lip coloring, but left her eye areas alone. Her long eyelashes were quite decorative enough.

She stopped just beyond the doorway in a hall that surely stretched for a mile or two to left and right. The floor was a smooth golden color, the walls a lighter yellow and the high arched ceiling an even lighter yellow.

What took most of her attention were the aliens passing to and from the many doorways behind her to and from similar doorways in front of her. The mix was as weirdly varied as the aliens she'd seen in the several *Star Battles* movies to which her brother Alex or her friends had coaxed her.

They were of all colors and sizes, from Moth's size to three times her own. They wore motley (to her) clothing or space suits. Some walked, some flew, some slithered, some hopped. Some were slow, some were in a hurry (or simply naturally fast).

Nearest her and on her right maybe ten meters away came a trio of blue catlike centaurs walking on their four legs with their fronts upright. They wore only various straps of all the colors of the rainbow, to which were attached various pouches and small cases. One held in its hands cords from which hung what looked for all the world like shopping bags.

It was a her actually, with perky breasts, each with a small nipple. She looked over at Karen and smiled and said something cheery. Karen made a miniscule nod in her direction but made no other acknowledgement. God knows what mild or martial faux pas she might commit if she did anything else. Even her nod and focused gaze might be an insult, but she didn't feel right making no acknowledgement at all.

The two parties passed each other with no fuss, however, as all the while Tiara was opening her memory banks to Karen about the catlike beings.

Karen was quickly relieved to find that the greetings just exchanged were innocuous. The Blues and humans were the most alike of all the advanced space-going aliens in the Galactic neighborhood of this spiral arm. Millennia had passed with no serious conflicts between the two. Indeed, there had long been a modest amount of beings who had morphed into the other species and lived amongst them.

That last jolted Karen a bit. She knew vaguely from her readings in the Encyclopedia that humans could easily and routinely change their sex and much else, but she'd missed the part where they could change even their species.

She put those thoughts aside as she entered the second doorway. Beyond was a huge indoor mall a hundred feet wide which rose several stories upward and ran perhaps a kilometer before her.

Moth said, "You can open your helmet. The air here is breathable by your kind. It is clear of allergens, toxins, and illnesses which might endanger you."

"No thanks. I'll stay sealed." Suit's "helmet" of course was completely invisible and weightless. There was no advantage to abolishing it.

Moth made a sound which was a good approximation of a human's disdainful sniff. Its translator was REALLY good.

"Suit yourself. But the Boss has run this station for millions of years and never had a problem."

Karen ignored it and for the next several hours window shopped. The wares were often quite strange but occasionally could have been sold on Earth.

Several times they passed eating places. Again most were strange but a few were vaguely familiar. She supposed that beings which shared compatible atmospheres and environments tended to have compatible cultures and cultural artifacts such as shopping and restaurants.

At the far end of the mall they came to the entrance to what Moth said was a hotel. She checked with it and with Tiara. They told her that it was OK to enter the lobby so she did so.

The big room was not that alien as she looked around it. It even had a receptionist's "desk" which was opposite the huge doorway they had entered. Though it was more like a stand-alone shelf than a desk; there were no receptionists on the other side. Instead there was a viewscreen on the wall. As she approached the desk the image behind it shifted from featureless grey to a sight so good that it was if she looked through a window at a sylvan glade. Beyond it was a small pond fed by a stream that meandered through it from a meadow beyond the pond. The sky above the meadow was blue.

"How may I help you?" The voice which came out of the air was a contralto which leaned enough to the bass side so that it could have been spoken by either human gender.

"I'm merely exploring at this time and became curious."

"By all means be welcome and stay here as long as you want. Compatible food and drink and habitation are available."

"Ah, how would I pay for it?"

"You do not pay for any services except for housing. That will cost you a specified amount of electrical current as long as you stay here. Your vehicle is able to provide that."

Karen had forgotten that Pegasus had stayed with her, compact and invisible a few feet over her head. It had been that way for years and she often forgot he was there.

"Thank you." She turned and reentered the mall.

By now she had become a bit tired. Her shoes were comfortable despite their heels but she had walked a lot. She had Pegasus morph to a small floating chair of the kind she'd seen several entities rest in. Then she set off toward a round hole in the mall floor which seemed to be the proper place to change floors, as she saw other "people" floating up or down from floors above or below this one. She had to wait a few minutes for a hole to open up in the flow. Then she had Pegasus go up one floor. There she began to return to the spacecraft docks.

Halfway back, two hours later, prompted by the odors of a nearby restaurant, she realized she was very hungry.

"Moth, is the food there compatible with my metabolism?"

"Likely. But you need to ask that of the restaurant staff."

She looked within the large open doorway and saw tables shaped and sized to humanoid forms, from a selection of several designed for other species. The "staff" was a viewscreen atop the table which showed a 3D image of a tropical seashore.

Assured the food was safe and tasty for her species she ordered what looked from the menu's images to be something like salmon and rice with a mixed salad and iced tea. There were even little packets of sugar. This clued her into Tiara's collaboration with the restaurant preparation staff--a matter transmuter like those of Suit and Pegasus.

When the food arrived Moth asked if she needed its services any longer. She decided she did not. It vanished.

She ate with a good appetite, looking around at her two dozen or so companions. They included three green insect-like creatures seated at a triangular table, a group of a dozen "people" who were vaguely beaver-like, and a large stalk of cauliflower "sitting" all by itself and apparently sucking through a straw something from a large bowl on its table.

At the far edge of the cafe she also saw a tall humanoid male in a black bodysuit which made him look like an action-adventure movie assassin or cat burglar. He had a buzz cut and a handsome face which reminded her of those on statues of Greek heroes in museums.

He was dreamily staring at nothing when she first saw him but when she was nearly finished with her meal he rose and approached her table.

"Excuse me. May I join you?"

She nodded at the chair opposite her. He sat.

"I am Embry blue gene-line Alton-87 cross red Ongy-1134."

"You may call me Karen."

"If I may be intrusive, what is your gene line?"

"I'm sorry. I cannot tell you that." She didn't know what the Hell her gene line was or whether she wanted to tell him if she did.

"I hope I've not given offense."

"No, of course not."

"Ah. I believe I see. You are a Guardian."

A quick query to Tiara yielded the fact that interstellar police severed their ties to their families as part of loyalty to law over kinship or other social ties.

She smiled at him. "The station's guardian thinks so."

He looked impressed. "You have conversation with It?"

She could practically see the capitalization of "It."

She nodded. "May I call you Embry? Why are you traveling?"

That he was human soon became clear. It took little prompting to get him to talk about himself and his concerns: what sounded to her somewhat like that of traveling salesman and entrepreneur businessman. What he sold or bought or traded and for what compensation she did not understand but did not let on.

A few times he pretended polite interest in her, but it took little to get him back onto his favorite topic: himself. It seemed even super-advanced humans were still as self-centered as primitive ones.

Though to be fair, perhaps that quality was native more to sales people and entrepreneurs of any species.

After an hour of this Karen had enough.

"You are a fascinating person, Embry. But I have business to attend to."

She rose. He did too and bowed to her. She returned it but with only a very modest one. A Guardian was much higher on the social ladder (Tiara had told her) than he was.

"Good hunting, Karen."

She walked out of the café. Her gravitar told her that he followed her but turned toward the hotel.

Good hunting? Did he think she was on a job, seeking a criminal?

By now her taste for window shopping had dimmed. She floated on Pegasus slowly enough to see inside shops and their displays but looked into only a few of them. Soon she was back at the dock she had left earlier. She had Pegasus manifest his interplanetary spacecraft, entered it, and left Rhea behind.

The five hours back to Earth left her plenty of time to think and go over her experiences at Saturn.

She kept coming back to her few minutes communicating with the computer which controlled the subspace subway system. To the part where it referred to her as a guardian. It seemed to understand her better than she understood herself. Not surprising, giving its nearly god-like nature.

Was that why she'd been sent to Earth for adoption? To be its guardian? If so, did she want to go along with the plan?

Well, in a way she had already begun to police the planet. She'd started doing that in small ways as a Marine Ranger. Then as a civilian, most recently in Nigeria where she had destroyed the Purity Jihad.

What was a guardian, or Guardian in the sense used in the Human Interstellar Confederation? The Encyclopedia had lots of information on that.

Typically they took up that profession only after a century or two in several other professions. Often this was after working on primitive planets, like Earth or even more primitive ones, in an organization vaguely like the Peace Corps. They experienced violence, something very rare in the Confederation core worlds, and learned that they had a taste for it. That when faced with wolves, so to speak, they became wolfhounds.

Over decades and centuries of life Guardians typically apprenticed at very low levels similar to those of cities and counties and states, then the planetary level, then at the higher levels working as police for entire zones within the Confederation. The very highest were the peripheral agents who roamed the edges of the expanding Confederation in starships the size of small moons, each one a carrier of many smaller more specialized ships.

As a planetary guardian she needed to follow certain loose standards and procedures. She should also learn a lot of the institutional wisdom collected over millennia.

Karen dipped into that last and found that the Encyclopedia organized it into logical chunks and "subchunks" which made it easier to find what she needed in almost any situation. Then she could adapt that advice to her particular situation.

Earth rushed toward her, in instants changing from a tiny blue dot in the black starscape before her to a globe which nearly filled the emptiness before her. Pegasus hummed and shrieked to a halt.

Dawn was creeping over the eastern edge of the United States, beginning to touch America's seaboard. Millions of people below her were coming awake and getting ready for a new day.

She thought of the people whom she knew: Sylvia and her niece's little friends, her sister-in-law and brother, her parents. Scott. The people who worked for her and with whom she'd worked. All the people she'd ever met, many of whom she'd liked and a few she'd loved.

Warmth grew in her breast. Her arms ached to hug them to her. To protect them.

But if she chose to be their guardian she would also be responsible for everyone else. Young and old, evil and wise and ordinary people, their problems simple and problems heartbreakingly complex.

She had enormous power, especially to destroy. But to build, to inspire?

Did she want to do it? COULD she do it?

Time passed as she watched the blue beauty below. Then the thought came.

There was only one way to find out.

Earth's Guardian loosed her hold on spacetime and fell toward home.